In the
Face
of
Death

AN
HISTORICAL
HORROR
NOVEL

Chelsea Quinn
Yarbro

BENBELLA BOOKS
DALLAS, TEXAS

BenBella Books Edition
Copyright ©2001 by Chelsea Quinn Yarbro

BenBella Books
6440 N. Central Expressway
Suite 508
Dallas, TX 75206

Send feedback to feedback@benbellabooks.com
www.benbellabooks.com

Printed in the United States of America

10 9 8 7 6 5 4 3 2 1

Library of Congress Cataloging-in-Publication Data

Yarbro, Chelsea Quinn, 1942–
    In the face of death : an historical horror novel / by Chelsea Quinn Yarbro.
        p. cm.
    ISBN 1-932100-29-6
    1. United States—History—Civil War, 1861–1865—Fiction. 2. Indians of North America—Fiction. I. Title.

PS3575.A715 2004
813'.54—dc22

                                                          2003023151

Cover illustration by Jael
Cover design by Melody Cadungog
Interior designed and composed by John Reinhardt Book Design

Distributed by Independent Publishers Group
To order call (800) 888-4741 • www.ipgbook.com

For
Megan Kincaid,
who knows a thing or two
about "Uncle Billy"

Author's
Introduction

MOST OF THE TIME the first questions that begin one of these historical excursions for me are not readily identified: in this case I can identify at least one factor, which began a long time ago when I was in my high school American History class. We were assigned papers on the Civil War; the topic was ours to determine so long as we could show a connection to the conflict. I wanted to do a paper on how the various Indian nations felt about the Civil War—it struck me that they must have had opinions about it, for certainly the war impacted their lives. Although my teacher did not agree, she let me do the paper for the research experience; and quite an experience it was. What I learned then about digging up material has stood me in good stead ever since.

To answer the question: yes, the Indian nations had opinions, and sometimes deep internal divisions on the subject of the Civil War; many of them were recorded and can be found to this day.

From time to time ever since, I have played around with the idea of using that wedge of American history as a setting for a novel, but I did not have the key to the story until I found a book at a friend's house in Oakland (alas, both the book and the house were victims of the 1991 Oakland Hills firestorm). This was a collection of memoirs of the Civil War in the Confederacy as ordinary non-combatants experienced it. The title of the work was *The War Down Home*, and it had been privately printed for the families of the contributors in 1907 in Alabama. This book provided invaluable information, which I could crossbreed with the work I had already done during my first, speculative forays though the material on record. Eventually the book you are reading now took shape, aided and augmented by the many accounts I subsequently found regarding the decade leading to the Civil War, as well as the better-known records of the events of the war itself. For no event is wholly unheralded, though the signs are always more clearly recognized in retrospect, when focus and perspective are sharpened by experience and hindsight. By beginning a decade ahead of the war, some of the social conditions and changes that shaped the society of the time can be shown in context.

Of course, I had to deal with the novelist's dilemma: you as readers know how the war ends. Taking a major conflict in history—the American Civil War or the Siege of Troy—there is constant temptation to make it seem as if the people participating in the events knew at the time how it was all going to turn out; which they did not, any more than any of us know what will happen tomorrow, or an hour from now, or a minute. Luckily, where the Civil War is concerned, there are a great many contemporary reports on both sides to reveal what the participants actually saw and thought at the time.

My thanks, of course, to Dave Nee; to Lou and Myrna Donato for their help in locating research material; to Alan Anderson and his family for the loan of their book (which I suppose I should have held onto); to my many friends who let me see family material relating to the Civil War and the events around it; to Mike Ward and the wonderful people at Hidden Knowledge who published a book that fit no known (or all too many) categories; to Glenn Yeffeth and BenBella Books for finally bringing it into print; to the World Horror Association, for the Grand Master award; to the Lord Ruthven Assembly for enlivening the academic discussion on vampires; to the booksellers who do so much to keep my vampires where their fans can find them; and to my readers for their tenacity and enthusiasm.

Chelsea Quinn Yarbro
Berkeley, California
September, 2003

I know of no courage greater ...
than the courage to love in the face of death.

William Tecumseh Sherman
to Queen Victoria

Contents

———————◆———————

England

EXCERPTS FROM THE JOURNAL OF MADELAINE DE MONTALIA,
FEBRUARY, 1845 THROUGH AUGUST, 1847.

LONDON, 18 FEBRUARY, 1845

*... Spoke with the American journalist again, and he assures me that it
is possible to arrange to study some of the Indians still living their traditional lives in his country. He does not know to whom I should apply to
make such studies ... He has said that many of them are war-like and do
not trust strangers, Indians or whites. Perhaps they have good cause for
this, if what I have learned so far is true.*

*The journalist is eager to go to Egypt to see the Pyramids and report
on a few of the expeditions there. He has many misconceptions about
Egypt, both as it is now and as it was long ago. I have told him a little of
my experiences at Thebes and warned him that he may well encounter
more corruption in the officials around him than he is used to. He answered that Americans are used to crooks in politics ...*

LONDON, 23 JUNE, 1845

*... and I find I do want to learn more of the Indians in America while
they are still alive to speak for themselves. Saint-Germain has warned*

me how quickly things and peoples may vanish. Surely, if all I have heard is accurate, the lives of these people are changing rapidly and many will soon be altered beyond recall. How can I turn away from this challenge, to study these people now, learn how they live, before they are gone?

How frustrating it is to be here, on the edge of learning and yet have no way to pursue the necessary information. So little has been attempted in assessing the lives of the Indians, or gathering accurate data about the Indians, and so much of what has been done is written with questionable motives, based on premises that are misleading. There is nothing much more I can do until I cross the Atlantic and meet these beleaguered people for myself...

The prospect of hardships does not deter me; how could it? Egypt taught me to endure many inconveniences, which subsequent studies have taught me to prepare for, and if all I have to fear is a lack of scented soap and a newspaper to read, then I am undaunted. I have come through worse than a lack of personal amenities, gaslight and civilized company...

LONDON, 4 NOVEMBER, 1845

...I am going to have to find someone who has met Indians, so that I may learn how best to go on when I am among them...

LONDON, 26 MARCH, 1846

...Geoffrey Prestigne has promised to introduce me to his Canadian second cousin, a fellow who has lived among the Indians for much of his life, and who has recently come to England to take up his inheritance. He cannot imagine how much I want to know about them. I hope he is not so contemptuous of these people as many of the Americans seem to be...

All society here is buzzing about India and the Sikhs, who are trying to reestablish control of their own lands, or so it would seem...

LONDON, 19 SEPTEMBER, 1846

... After the performance of Don Pasquale, *Geoffrey at last presented his second cousin to me: Reverend Daniel Maywood, a widower of thirty-eight years, well-read although not greatly educated, who stigmatized Donizetti's little farce as frivolous ... Geoffrey had already explained my purpose in speaking with him; he did his best to discourage me in this venture, stating that he felt I would not only be disappointed by what I saw, but that I could be in considerable danger. It is his opinion that most of the Indians would not look kindly on a white woman going among them. He was distressed when he learned I do not wish to go as a missionary, for that has been his work throughout his adult life ...*

LONDON, 22 DECEMBER, 1846

... I have spoken with Reverend Maywood again, and I am more certain than ever that the Indians will be a fascinating and rewarding study. I had no idea there was such diversity in their tribes as Maywood describes, which only spurs me to greater efforts, for I begin to see that the task I have set for myself is a larger one than I had first supposed, and more urgent. Yet the more I question him, the more reticent he becomes; this he excuses by saying he does not wish to encourage what he describes as my caprice. He is determined to dissuade me from going to America. I have admitted to some trepidation about such an undertaking, but in truth, it is more the ordeal of a sea voyage that gives me pause than any reluctance to expose myself to the risks of living with Indians ...

LONDON, 5 APRIL, 1847

... At last I have found someone willing to aid me. Captain Augustus Fowler of Savannah, Georgia, who has brought a vast quantity of cotton to the mills of Birmingham and Manchester on his ship Minerva, *has*

been willing to listen to my inquiries without undue animadversions on the folly of my interests. He is like the other men I have met from the southern United States, very gallant and courtly, but fixed in his ways as many from the northern states are not … He informs me that most of the Indians of the eastern coast are being moved off their lands and put in new territories in the western part of the country and that those Indians living on the prairies have been much visited by missionaries. This, in spite of the United States currently being in dispute with Mexico. Such action will surely trap Indians between the warring nations. I recall what Saint-Germain told me of the peoples of South America, and that was more than two centuries ago. So much has been lost already, I fear I may already be too late to learn all I wish …

LONDON, 30 JULY, 1847

… The house is leased out to a family for a period of twenty years. They have signed the papers and my solicitors have settled the whole matter of maintenance and payments with them to our mutual satisfactions. My furniture and other effects will be sent to Monbussy and the care of those tending my estate on the Marne. I will have my usual chests of earth with me and have made arrangements to receive shipments of more every year or so, with provision for them to be delivered to ports of call to be determined at a later time. I have been warned that these cannot be reliably delivered west of the Mississippi, so I have arranged to have a second shipment made, in case one is not received …

I leave from Plymouth aboard the French four-masted bark Duc d'Orleans *bound for Baltimore in the state of Maryland on the 18th of next month, less than three weeks from now, so I have much to arrange in the little time remaining here in London. There are funds to be transferred and certain expenses to be met in my absence, all this before I leave for the United States.*

I have already warned Captain des Ciennes that I do not travel well over water and that I will remain in my cabin for most of the voyage. I have given him to understand that I am going to join my brother in America, to make my traveling alone less suspect than it might be otherwise, and he has been very well-paid to keep his doubts to himself. It would not do to have him inquire too closely about my life here, for he might find my longevity disquieting. I doubt he will do so, for he behaves as if he thinks my protestation of seasickness a polite mendacity to protect myself from unwanted attention: women going so far alone are often the targets of intrusive flirtations or greater affronts. Not that I am unable to take care of myself in such circumstances ...

ON THE ROAD TO PLYMOUTH, 8 AUGUST, 1847

... My preparations are made. Saint-Germain has been informed of where I will be, and how I may be reached, if that is necessary. My funds have been established in a letter of credit from my London bank in the amount of £100,000 that will serve me throughout the United States, or so I am reliably informed. I have purchased such maps as may be had of the known territories of North America. I am beginning to think it would be sensible to go all the way to the Pacific, to see what has become of the Indians there, where the Spanish have ruled for so long. Since I am going to be on that continent in any case, and am free to set my own agenda, I must make the most of my opportunities, which may never come again ...

I wish I enjoyed sailing.

California:
Eight Years Later

SAN FRANCISCO, 18 MAY, 1855

At last! And only four days later than anticipated when we left the mountains. Had I been willing to travel on the river from Sacramento, we would have arrived on the date anticipated... If all goes as I have requested, six cases of my native earth will be in one of the warehouses, waiting for me, which is just as well as I have now got down to less than a single chest of it.

My escorts have brought me to a very proper boarding house on Sacramento Street, and gone on themselves to suitable lodgings. A Missus Imogene Mullinton, a highly respectable widow from Vermont, owns this place and takes only reputable, single women. She has given me a suite of three rooms at the top of the house, her best, and for it I am to pay $75 a month, or any fraction of a month; a very high price for such accommodations, but I have discovered that everything in San Francisco is expensive. The suite will do until I can arrange to rent a house for three or four months. In a week or so I must begin my hunt for one, after I have got my bearings here.

... I have the records of my studies to occupy me, and I welcome the

opportunity to review and organize what I have learned of the Indians I have met these last seven years. There is so much I have to assess. This respite will provide me the opportunity to decide how I may best structure my book on what I have learned on my journey west...

Tomorrow I will have to pay off my escort, which will require a trip to the bank to establish my credit there, and to begin making my acquaintance with the city. Doubtless the excellent Missus Mullinton can direct me to Lucas and Turner; the documents from their Saint Louis offices should be sufficient bona fides to satisfy them.

AT THE CORNER OF JACKSON AND MONTGOMERY, the new Lucas and Turner building was one of the most impressive in the burgeoning city; located near the shore of the bay and the many long wharves that bristled far out into the water, the bank was well situated to sense the thriving financial pulse of San Francisco.

Madelaine, wearing the one good morning dress she had left from her long travels, stepped out of the hackney cab and made her way through the jostling crowds on the wooden sidewalks to the bank itself. As she stepped inside, she felt both relief and regret at being once again back in the world of commerce, progress and good society. Holding her valise firmly, she avoided the tellers' cages and instead approached the nearest of the desks, saying, across the balustraded barrier, "Pardon me, but will you be kind enough to direct me to the senior officer of the bank?"

The man at the desk looked up sharply. "Have you an appointment, ma'am?" he asked, noticing her French accent with faint disapproval, and showing a lack of interest that Madelaine disliked, though she concealed it well enough. He was hardly more than twenty-two or three and sported a dashing moustache at variance with his sober garments.

"No, I am just arrived in San Francisco," she said, and opened her valise, taking out a sheaf of documents, her manner determined; she did not want to deal with so officious an underling as this fellow. "I am Madelaine de Montalia. As you can see from this"—she offered him one of the folded sheets of paper—"I have a considerable sum on deposit with your Saint Louis offices, and I require the attention of your senior officer at his earliest convenience."

The secretary took the letter and read it, his manner turning from indulgent to impressed as he reviewed the figures; he frowned as he read through them a second time, as if he was not convinced of what he saw. Folding the letter with care, he rose and belatedly gave Madelaine a show of respect he had lacked earlier. "Good gracious, Madame de Montalia. It is an unexpected pleasure to welcome you to Lucas and Turner."

"Thank you," said Madelaine with a fine, aristocratic nod she had perfected in her childhood. "Now, will you please show me to the senior officer? You may use those documents to introduce me, if that is necessary."

"Of course, of course," he said, so mellifluously that Madelaine had an urge to box his ears for such obsequiousness. He opened the little gate that separated the desks from the rest of the floor, and stood aside for her as she went through, her head up, the deep green taffeta of her morning dress rustling as she moved. "If you will allow me to go ahead and…" He made a gesture indicating a smoothing of the way.

She sighed. "If that is necessary."

He made an apologetic grimace. "Well, you see, there are very few wealthy young women alone in San Francisco. And you were not expected." Again he gestured to express his concern.

"No doubt," she said, and halted in front of a large door of polished oak. While the secretary rapped, Madelaine examined her brooch watch, thinking she would be fortunate to be out of the bank much before noon.

"Come in," came the crisp order from a sharp, husky voice.

The secretary made a slight bow to Madelaine, then stepped into the office, discreetly closing the door behind him, only to emerge a few minutes later, all smiles and half-bows, to open the door wide for her in order to usher her into the oak-paneled office of the senior officer of the bank.

The man who rose behind the orderly desk surprised Madelaine a little; he was younger than she had expected—no more than his mid-thirties—sharp-featured, wiry and tall, with bright red hair, steel-colored eyes, and a pinched look about his mouth as if he were in constant discomfort. His dark suit was neat as a uniform and he greeted her with fastidious correctness. "William T. Sherman, senior officer of Lucas and Turner in San Francisco, at your service, Madame de Montalia."

She shook his hand at once. "A pleasure, Mister Sherman," she said, liking his decisive manner. "I hope you will be willing to help me establish an account here."

His face did not change but a glint appeared in his eyes. "Certainly."

He signaled to the secretary. "Jenkins, leave us to it. And don't close the door."

Madelaine saw that the secretary was flustered. "But I thought—" he said.

"I will handle the opening of this account. Given the size of this lady's resources, such an account would need my authorization in any case." He came around the end of his desk not only to bring a chair for Madelaine, but to hurry Jenkins out of his office. He carried one of the Queen Anne chairs to a place directly across the desk from his, and held it for Madelaine. "Madame?"

As she sat down, Madelaine smiled up at Sherman. "Thank you," she said, and noticed a quick frown flicker across his face.

Taking his place behind the desk once more, Sherman spread out two of the letters in her packets of documents on the wide expanse of leather-edged blotter. "I see you deposited ninety-five thousand pounds sterling in the Saint Louis office of this bank in 1848. The most recent accounting, from a year ago, shows your balance only slightly reduced." He regarded her with curiosity. "That is a considerable fortune, Madame. And odd that it should be in pounds sterling, not francs."

"I inherited most of it," she said, not quite truthfully, for in the last century she had been able to increase her wealth far beyond what her father had amassed. "And I have lived in London for more than ten years before I came here. Much of my money is in England." She made no mention of the funds she had in France, Italy and Switzerland.

"And you have not squandered it, it would seem. Very prudent. Unusual, you will permit me to say, in a young woman." He looked at her with increasing interest. "What do you want me to do for you? How much were you planning to transfer to this branch? In dollars?"

"I would think that twenty-five thousand would be sufficient," she said. "In dollars."

He coughed once. "Yes; I should think so. More than sufficient. Unless you are determined to cut a dash in society, you will find the sum ample. That's five times my annual salary." He confided this with chuckle and a scowl. "Very well, Madame," he went on more affably. "I will put the transaction in order. And in the meantime, you will be free to draw on funds up to . . . shall we say, five thousand dollars?"

Madelaine nodded. "That would be quite satisfactory, since you are able to contrive to live on it for a year, though prices here are much higher than I anticipated. Still, I should be able to practice good economy."

10

"You certainly have until now, given the state of your account." He cocked his head, a speculative light in his eyes, his long fingers moving restlessly as if searching for a pencil or a cigar. "Unless these funds have only recently passed to your control? In that case I would recommend you seek an able advisor, to guide you in the matters of investment and management..."

"Mister Sherman—" she interrupted, only to be cut off.

"Forgive me. None of my business. But I can't help but wonder how it comes that you want twenty-five thousand now and have spent less than half of that in the last seven years?" He braced his elbows on the desk and leaned forward, his chin propped on his joined hands.

"My studies did not require it," she answered, determined not to be affronted by his directness.

"Ah, you were at school," he said, his expression lightening. He slapped his hands on the blotter and sat back, his questions answered to his satisfaction.

"Something of the sort," she responded, in a manner she thought was almost worthy of Saint-Germain.

SAN FRANCISCO, 23 MAY, 1855

Missus Mullinton has given me the address of an excellent dressmaker and the first of my new clothes should be delivered tomorrow. There are six other ensembles on order, to be delivered in three weeks. Once I have settled in, I will need to order more... I suppose it is worth getting back into corsets for the pleasure of wearing silk again...

There is a private concert tomorrow afternoon that Missus Mullinton wishes to attend and has asked me to accompany her. Now that she knows I have money and some social position, she is determined to make the most of them, convinced I will add to her consequence in the town. I might as well go with her, for if I am going to remain here for three or four months, I will need to enlarge my acquaintances or risk speculation and gossip, which would do me no good at all. So I will hear the concert and indulge in whatever entertainments are thought proper by San Francisco society, and learn what I can of the lands to the south of here. And there may be another advantage in such actions. Perhaps I will find someone who is to my liking, whom I please, who is willing to be very,

very discreet. In a place like this, lapses are not easily forgiven by any-one...

Prices for everything are very high here. Some say it is the wealth of the gold rush, making people careless of money, and others say it is because it is so costly bringing goods overland or sending them by sea, around the Horn...

My chests are at the Jas. Banner Warehouse near where Columbus and Montgomery streets converge. I must make arrangements to retrieve them soon, not only because I am low on my native earth, but because the costs for storing the chests are outrageous. I had rather keep them in the safe at Lucas and Turner for such sums...

THE HOUSE ON JACKSON STREET was a fine, ambitious pile, made of local redwood timber and newly painted a deep green color, unlike many of its paler neighbors, with the trim in yellow, to contrast the white lace curtains in most of the windows. It faced the street squarely with an Italianate portico of Corinthian columns, set back from the roadway and approached by a half-moon drive.

When Missus Mullinton alighted from the rented carriage, she fussed with her bonnet before stepping aside for her guest to join her.

Madelaine de Montalia had donned her new dress, an afternoon frock suitable for early suppers and garden parties, and as such, unexceptionable for this concert. It was a soft shade of lavender, with bared shoulders framed by a double row of ruched silk. The bodice was fitted and came to a point in the front over a skirt of three tiers of ruched silk spread over moderate crinolines. For jewelry, she wore a necklace of pearls and amethysts; her coffee-colored hair was gathered in a knot, with two long locks allowed to escape and fall on her shoulders. An embroidered shawl was draped over her arms and in one hand she held a beaded reticule. As she descended from the carriage, Madelaine silently cursed the enveloping skirts.

A Mexican servant, whose angular features revealed a significant admixture of Indian blood, ushered them into the house, explaining in heavily accented English that the host and hostess were in the ballroom to receive their guests, as he bowed in the direction they should go.

"We are not the first, are we?" asked Missus Mullinton, afraid that she had committed an intolerable gaffe.

"Oh, no. There are others here already," the servant assured the two women with a respectful lowering of his eyes.

"Thank goodness," said Missus Mullinton in an undervoice to Madelaine as they went along the corridor to the rear of the house. "It would not do to have it said we came early."

"Why ever not?" asked Madelaine, who had become more punctual as she grew older.

"My dear Madame," said Missus Mullinton in shock, "for women to arrive while only the host and hostess are present smacks of impropriety, particularly since you are new in town." Her long, plain face took on an expression of shock as she considered this outrage.

"Then it would be better to arrive late?" asked Madelaine, trying to determine what Missus Mullinton sought to achieve.

"Heavens, no, for then it would seem that we did not appreciate the invitation," said Missus Mullinton. "I am very pleased that we have made our arrival so well." She raised her voice as she stepped into the ballroom antechamber. "You may find our entertainments here sadly dull, Madame, after the excitements of London."

"Possibly," said Madelaine. "But as I have not been in London for eight years, I think what you offer here will suit me very well." She smiled at the couple approaching them, he of medium height and bristling grey hair, she a very pretty woman with a deep bosom and fair hair, in a fashionable dull red afternoon dress that did not entirely become her; she was at least a decade her husband's junior.

"Missus Mullinton," said their hostess. "How nice of you to join us." She took Missus Mullinton's hand and kissed the air near her right cheek. "This must be your new guest." She turned to Madelaine. "I am Fanny Kent."

"And I am Madelaine de Montalia," she said, curtsying slightly to her hostess before taking her hand, though they made no other move toward each other.

"And my husband, the Captain," added Fanny, indicating her husband. "My dear, you know Missus Mullinton. And this is Madame de Montalia."

Horace Kent bowed over Madelaine's hand. "Enchanted, Madame," he declared, and then shook Missus Mullinton's hand in a nominally polite way.

The four other couples in the room were presented, and by that time another pair of guests had arrived, and Madelaine gave herself over to the task of learning the names of the people in the room, hoping that she would not confuse any of them as their number steadily increased.

"I have already had the pleasure," said the latest arrival, some twenty minutes later. Sherman bowed slightly to Madelaine.

"Yes," said Madelaine, taking refuge in a familiar face. "I met Mister Sherman on my second day in the city."

"At the bank, I suppose," said the man accompanying him, another foreigner with a Russian accent. He beamed at Madelaine and continued in French, "It is an honor to meet such a distinguished lady traveling so far from home. We are two strangers on these shores, are we not?"

Sherman looked from one to the other. "Madame, let me present Baron deStoeckl. Baron, Madame de Montalia."

"Delighted, Baron," she said, and went on, "and I had thought that everyone in California except the Indians were here as strangers, and far from home."

"Touché, Madame." As the Baron kissed her hand, he said, still in French, "I hope you will excuse my friend's curt manners. There is no changing him."

"And remember," said Sherman in rough-accented French, "he understands what you say." With that, he gave Madelaine a polite nod and passed on to greet General Hitchcock, who had just entered the ballroom.

"He misses the army, or so it seems to my eyes," said the Baron to Madelaine. "If you will excuse me?"

She gestured her consent, and a moment later had her attention claimed by her hostess, who wished her to meet Joseph Folsom. "He is one of the most influential men in the city," Fanny confided. "And you will be glad to know him."

Madelaine allowed herself to be led away; she saw Missus Mullinton deep in conversation with an elderly lady in lavish half-mourning, and thought it best not to interrupt her.

It was almost an hour later, after the string quartet had beguiled them with Mozart and a medley of transcribed themes from the opera *Norma*, that Madelaine once again found herself in Sherman's company. He had just come from the bustle around the punchbowl bearing a single cup when he saw her standing by the window looking out into the fading day. He strolled to her side, and remarked, "The fog comes in that way throughout the summer."

She turned to him, a bit startled, and said, "So Missus Mullinton has warned me, and advised that I carry a wrap no matter how warm the day," and went on, "What do you think of these musicians?"

"More to the point, Madame, what do *you* think of them? Undoubtedly you have more experience of these things than I do." He sipped from his cup and then said before she could answer his first question, "I would fetch you something, but that would cause idle tongues to wag. With my wife away, I cannot risk giving any cause for gossip that would distress her."

"Certainly not," said Madelaine, regarding Sherman with some surprise. "Though on such an occasion as this—"

"You will forgive me, Madame, for saying that you do not know these sniping cats who have nothing better to do with their conversation than blacken the reputations of those around them." He bowed slightly and was about to turn away when he looked down at her. "You may find it difficult to move about in society, single as you are. If you were not so beautiful a young woman, Madame, and so vivacious, there would be little to fear, but—" And with that he was gone.

As Madelaine and Missus Mullinton were taking their leave of the Kents at the end of the concert, Fanny Kent drew Madelaine aside, with signs of apprehension about her. She made herself come to the point at once. "I could not but notice that Mister Sherman spoke to you earlier."

Madelaine knew well enough to laugh. "Yes; some minor matters about when I could sign certain papers at the bank. Mister Sherman wished to know when I would be available to tend to them. I gather they will be ready earlier than I had been told."

Fanny looked reassured, her rosy cheeks flaming with embarrassment. "Oh, Madame, I am so sorry. I have mistaken the…But as you have just come here, and have not yet learned…I was afraid you were wanting to fix your interest…oh, good gracious."

"Dear Missus Kent," Madelaine said pleasantly enough but with grim purpose, "I am aware that Mister Sherman is a married man."

"Yes, he is," said Fanny Kent flatly. "With three hopeful children."

"And I have no intention of making life awkward for him. What a goose I should be to do so foolish a thing. Great Heaven, Missus Kent, he is my banker. I rely on him to look after my financial welfare while I am in San Francisco." She smiled easily. "And because he is, I will have to speak to him upon occasion, and call at his office to take care of transactions that married women leave to their husbands to perform, but which I must tend to for myself. I hope that people understand the reasons are those of business; I have no motives beyond that."

"Of course, of course," said Fanny hastily.

"It would be most inconvenient to have to contend with malicious

15

speculation over such minor but necessary encounters." This time her smile had purpose to it.

Now Fanny let out a long sigh, one hand to her opulent bosom. "It is very sad that Missus Sherman has had to be away from him just now," she said. "The run on the bank has left him exhausted, and his asthma, you know, has been particularly bad. To care for those two children as well—" She put her hand to her cheek. "Not that you have any reason to be concerned. I'm sure the worst is behind him. He managed the crisis of the run quite successfully and now Lucas and Turner is likely to stand as long as the city. It would be a terrible thing if scandal should fix to his name after he has won through so great a trial."

Madelaine blinked as she listened, and realized that Sherman had been right to warn her about gossip.

SAN FRANCISCO, 29 MAY, 1855

My first monograph is complete and I am about to send it off to the publisher in Amsterdam on the steam packet leaving port tomorrow, with another to follow in two weeks. It is my hope that some of what I have written may awaken others to the plight of the Indians, for they are sorely tried, and it is distressing to consider what could become of them as the United States continue their expansion...

I must also look for a house. I need some place where I can lay down my native earth and restore myself through its strength, and I do not want to have to pay Missus Mullinton another $75 for my apartment, pleasant though it is. Some of the other women are starting to question how I live, especially my refusal to dine with them, and I must make an effort to stop their speculations as soon as possible. If I had an establishment of my own, and my own staff, I could deal with these problems more summarily. No doubt Lucas and Turner can assist me in finding what I want...

"THIS IS AN UNEXPECTED SURPRISE," said Sherman, coming out of his office to greet Madelaine shortly before noon two days later. He motioned Jenkins aside and indicated he expected her to follow him. "I have the papers ready for you to sign. They'll go off on the next steamer and the funds will follow quickly. In these days we can handle these transactions in less than two months. But let us discuss your matters less publicly. If you will be kind enough—?"

"Of course. And I thank you for giving me a little time; I am sure you are very busy." As she made her way back to his office, Madelaine realized that many of the customers and about half the staff in the bank were staring, either directly or covertly, at them. She knew it was not just because she had worn her newest walking dress, a fetching mode in grape-colored fine wool; she drew her short jacket more closely around her as she took the chair Sherman offered her, realizing that once again he had left the door half-open.

He settled himself behind his desk. "Now then, Madame, what are we to have the pleasure of doing for you?"

Madelaine squared her shoulders. "I want to rent a house. At least through August, possibly for longer."

Sherman stared at her. "Rent a house?" he repeated as if she had spoken a language he did not adequately understand.

She went on without remarking on his surprise. "Yes. Something not too lavish, but as comfortable and suitable as possible. And I will need to hire a staff for it. Probably no more than three or four will serve me very well."

"You want to rent a house," Sherman said again, as if he had at last divined her meaning. "But why? Is there something not to your liking at Missus Mullinton's?"

"Only the price and the lack of privacy," said Madelaine as politely as she could. "That is not to say anything against Missus Mullinton. She has been all that is courteous and attentive, and her establishment is a fine one, but not for what I am engaged in doing."

"And what might that be?" asked Sherman, disapproval scoring his sharp features.

"I am writing a book," said Madelaine candidly.

Sherman's glower vanished only to be replaced by an indulgent smirk; Madelaine decided she liked the glower better, for it indicated genuine concern, and this showed nothing of the sort. "A book?"

"On my studies here in America," she said with a coolness she did not feel.

"Have you any notion of what must go into writing a book? It is far different than making entries in a diary; it requires discipline and concerted effort." He continued to watch her with a trace of amusement.

Stung, Madelaine said. "Yes. I have already written three volumes on my travels in Egypt."

"When you were an infant," said Sherman. "You told me you have spent your time here at school, and before that—"

"Actually, I said I had been studying," Madelaine corrected him. "You were the one who said I had been at school."

Sherman straightened in his chair. "You were not in the convent!" He declared it with conviction. "You have not the manner of it."

Now Madelaine had managed to regain control over her impulsive tongue, she said, "That is nothing to the point. All that matters is that I find an appropriate house to rent. If you are not willing to help me in this endeavor, you need only tell me, and I will go elsewhere."

This challenge put Sherman on his mettle. "Certainly I will do what I can. As your financial representative, I must question anything that does not appear to be in your best interests." He gave her a severe stare. "If you will let me know your requirements and the price you had in mind to pay, I will have Jenkins begin his inquiries."

"Thank you," said Madelaine, her temper beginning to cool. "I will need a small or medium-size house in a good location, one with room for a proper study. I will need a bedchamber and dressing room, a withdrawing room and a parlor, a dining room, a pantry and a reasonably modern kitchen, with quarters for a staff of two or three." She had established these requirements for herself over eighty years ago; one more thing she added in an off-handed way. "Also, I must be able to reach the foundation with ease."

"The foundation?" Sherman repeated in astonishment. "Why should the foundation concern you?"

Madelaine thought of the trunks of her native earth and felt the pull of it like exhausted muscles yearning for rest. "I have learned that it is wise to know what the footing of a house may be," she answered.

"Most certainly," Sherman agreed, pleasantly surprised that Madelaine should have so practical a turn of mind. "Very well, I will stipulate that in my instructions to Jenkins." He regarded her with the manner of one encountering a familiar object in an unfamiliar setting. "How soon would you like to occupy the house?"

"As soon as possible," said Madelaine. "I want to get my work underway quickly, and I cannot do that until I have a place where I may examine my notes and open all my records for review; at the moment most of them are still in trunks and are of little use to me." She smiled at him, noticing for the first time that he had dark circles under his eyes. "If you will excuse me for mentioning it, you do not appear to have slept well, Mister Sherman."

He shrugged, looking slightly embarrassed. "My son was fussy last night; he is very young and he misses his mother. I wanted to comfort him, and so I..." He made a brusque gesture of dismissal, then relented. "And for the last few days my asthma has been troubling me. It is a childish complaint, one that need not concern you, Madame."

Madelaine regarded him with sympathy. "I know what it is to suffer these conditions, for I, myself, cannot easily tolerate direct sunlight." She hesitated, thinking that she did not want to create gossip about the two of them. Then she offered, "I have some preparations against such continuing illnesses. If you would let me provide you with a vial of—"

"I have nitre paper," Sherman said, cutting her off abruptly. He stared at the blotter on his desk. "But I thank you for your consideration."

"If you change your mind, you have only to let me know," said Madelaine, noticing that Sherman's face was slightly flushed. "Think of it as a gesture of gratitude for finding my house."

He nodded stiffly. "If you will call back on Monday, I will let you know what Jenkins has discovered. What was the price you had in mind, again?"

"Anything reasonable. You know what my circumstances are," said Madelaine as if she had lost interest in the matter. "And you know what is a reasonable amount for a landlord to ask."

Sherman nodded, his expression distant. "And the matter of a staff? You said two or three?"

"If you will recommend someone to help me in hiring them, I would appreciate it." Why was she feeling so awkward? Madelaine wondered. What had happened in the last few minutes that left her with the sensation that she had done something inappropriate? Was it something in her, or was it in Sherman?

"There are employment services in the city," said Sherman, looking directly at her. "I will find out which are the most reliable."

Madelaine was surprised at the intensity of his gaze. "I don't know what to say to you, Mister Sherman, but thank you."

He rose stiffly. "On Monday then, Madame."

She took his hand; it might as well have been made of wood. "On Monday, Mister Sherman."

SAN FRANCISCO, 6 JUNE, 1855

It is still in his eyes. When Mister Sherman and I met at the soirée given by General Hitchcock I saw him watching me; never have I experienced so searching an expression, as if he wanted to fathom me to the depth. It is not like Saint-Germain, who looked at me with knowing; Sherman is questing. This considered inspection had nothing to do with the soirée: the fare was musical, for the General has some talent for the flute, and he, with the accompaniment of Missus Kent at the piano, regaled his guests with a variety of airs by Mozart and Handel, all very light and pleasant. Yet for all his watching me, Sherman hardly spoke to me during the evening. If he seeks to avoid gossip in this way, he will not succeed, for his Russian friend deStoeckl asked me why Sherman was making such a cake of himself, a question I cannot answer...

I have been given the description of three houses Mister Sherman thinks would be suitable to my needs. One is on Shotwell Street, with a simple front and the amount of space I would like, but lacking a second chimney at the back of the house, which causes me some concern. There is a second house, on Franklin, somewhat larger than the first, and quite new, having been built only two years ago, and in the second-most-fashionable part of town. It is all quite modern, and comes with many furnishings included. It would take three servants for maintaining the place, doubtless. The third is on Bush Street, where the hill becomes steeper; it has a small stable behind it, which affords some advantage, but is not as well-situated as the second. I will go to inspect them in the next few days, to make up my mind...

THE ROOMS IN THE HOUSE ON FRANKLIN STREET echoed eerily as Madelaine made her way from the front parlor to the withdrawing room.

"I am sorry that the landlord has not carpeted the place," said Sherman, walking slightly behind her. "I have discussed the matter with him, and he is willing to make an adjustment on the rent charged because of the lack. You will be expected to provide those, as well as the draperies and bed. The rest is as you see," he added, indicating the furniture all swathed in Holland covers.

"Actually, I don't see," said Madelaine, "but I know the furnishings are here." She continued through the withdrawing room to the hall leading through the dining room to the kitchen and pantry beyond. "And the servants' quarters? Where are they? Upstairs?"

"They are in the rear of the house," said Sherman, the roughness in his voice not entirely due to a recent attack of asthma. "A detached cottage with three apartments."

Madelaine paused in the door to the kitchen, thinking that having the servants out of the house at night could be a real advantage. "Are they adequate? Do they have sufficient heat? If the summers are as chilly as you say they are, Mister Sherman, it will be necessary to provide adequate heating for them."

"There are stoves in each of the apartments," said Sherman stiffly. "That will be sufficient to their needs."

"And they dine in the kitchen?" she said, looking into that room.

"Naturally," said Sherman, and veiled a cough.

"What of this location? Is it...acceptable?" she asked.

"It is well enough," answered Sherman, and added as if against his will, "I have only recently moved from Green Street, which crosses Franklin a block from here, to a house on Rincon Hill; our house was three blocks short of being fashionable. To please my wife."

"Who is visiting her family," Madelaine finished for him.

"Yes." He waited until the silence was too laden with unspoken things; he then chose the most trivial of them to break it. "There are so few areas where women may live safely alone in this city, though this comes as close to being that as any of them do. The location is not the most fashionable, but it is not inappropriate for a single woman keeping her own house, conserving her money, and assuring her good reputation in society."

"All of which is important." Madelaine turned to him. "I will need to find a good draper. I will need heavy curtains and draperies for the windows in the front parlor and the withdrawing room, as well as for the bedrooms."

He looked impressed by her resolution. "You have not yet seen the third house, Madame de Montalia."

"Why should I waste your time and my own when this suits my needs so well?" Madelaine asked, coming toward him.

Again he masked a cough, a sign of discomfort in him. "You haven't seen the bedrooms upstairs. They might not suit your purposes, or you

21

could decide that the withdrawing room will not serve you well as your study," he pointed out. "I do not want you to contract for this house and then complain to me later that it is not what you wanted."

Madelaine smiled at him, annoyed that he would not admit she knew her own mind, and decided to enjoy herself at his expense. "Dear me, Mister Sherman, are you always so hesitant?" She could see that he was uneasy with this challenge, and she pressed her advantage, feeling his uncertainty about her as if there were a third person in the house with them. "From what General Hitchcock told me the other afternoon, I thought you were decisive. Captain Buell says the same thing."

Stung, Sherman regarded her through narrowed eyes. "What do you mean, Madame?"

"I mean that you doubt my capacity to choose that which suits me," she answered, coming closer to him again. "This house will do well. The cellar is large enough and secure enough for my purposes, the rooms are pleasant, the location is satisfactory, as you yourself have indicated, and it requires very little attention from me. You tell me the rent is not too high for the house. Since it is all those things, I am willing to take it on a lease through...shall we say September?"

"You will have your book written in that time?" He flung this back at her, his face nearly expressionless.

"The greater part of it, certainly," she answered, unflustered; she enjoyed the awkwardness he felt in response to her confidence.

He shrugged, making it plain that he washed his hands of the affair. "Be it on your head then, Madame." His eyes belied the indifference in his demeanor. "I will arrange for the lease to be drawn up this afternoon; you may sign it at my office this evening, if that is convenient."

"Excellent," she said. "And perhaps you can recommend a firm to move my things to this house at the beginning of next week? We might as well be about this as soon as possible."

He offered her a small salute. "Certainly, Madame."

"When I have established myself here, you must advise me how best to entertain, so I will not offend any of the important hostesses of San Francisco." She meant what she said, and was relieved that for once Sherman seemed convinced of that.

"If my wife were here..." he began, then let his words trail off as he stared at her.

"If your wife were here, we would not be having this conversation, Mister Sherman," said Madelaine, being deliberately provocative, and wondering what it was about him that so intrigued her, beyond his apparent fascination with her.

"No," he said, and looked away toward the vacant window and the view of the street beyond.

SAN FRANCISCO, 10 JUNE, 1855

I am now in my house on Franklin Street, near the intersection with Newcomb Street, and very pleasant it is, too. The draper is making up curtains, draperies and valences for me, and they will be installed by the day after tomorrow, or so he has assured me, which will do much to make the place more comfortable during the day. With my chests of native earth in the basement, and my mattress and shoes relined, the house is already quite pleasant. In a week or so, it should all be in order. I think I will go on very well here.

This part of the city is quite new and was not in place to be burned in the fire of four years ago. Houses are being put up just two blocks away, and occasionally I can hear the hammering, but nothing so loud that it disturbs me. This part of the city attracts newcomers of some means, and there are almost none of the shacks one sees in so many other places. There is a family in the house on my right, four children and a fifth to come. On my left there live two brothers and their sister, who inform me that just ten years ago, the land this whole block is sitting on could have been bought for $16. Now the price for the land alone, not even considering the new buildings on it, would be much higher. There are men charging upward of $1,500 for the rental of a warehouse, rates which are being paid gladly, so great are the profits being realized now.

This afternoon I interviewed over thirty applicants for my three staff positions, and have chosen a housekeeper-cum-maid who has but recently arrived from Sweden, a woman of middle years named Olga Bjornholm. Her English is passable, and her French is adequate. She tells me she came here to be with her sister and her husband, but that they have disappeared; she wants to work until she finds them, which I have said is satisfactory to me. I have found a man-of-all-work, named Christian van der Groot. He is a strapping fellow who tells a tale of a merchant family bankrupted by the incursions of war. He came here to find gold, but realized that he could do better helping to build houses and guard them than he could panning in the mountain rivers, and so here he is. I have yet to find a cook for the household. I am reluctant to ask Mister Sherman for more assistance, for I sense that his attraction is deepening, which causes him distress. It is apparent when he speaks to me that he does it with confusion springing from his increasing attraction.

If only my attraction were not deepening as well. It has been so long since I have let myself be loved knowingly; for the last decade I have taken my pleasure, such as it has been, in the dreams of men who have been interested in me. And it suffices me, that gratification, but it is not nourishment. For that, there must be intimacy without fantasy. And I cannot help but long for more, for knowledge and acceptance, though why I believe I should find either from William T. Sherman, I cannot tell, except for what is in his eyes.

Tomorrow I will have a desk delivered, and I can begin my work in earnest, at last.

OLGA BJORNHOLM'S HAIR WAS MOUSE-COLORED and done up in a coronet of neat braids as she presented Madelaine with her cloak. "For it is getting cold tonight, I think," she said. "Tell the coachman to keep the top up."

"Yes, thank you, Olga," said Madelaine, half-pleased and half-annoyed to be fussed over in this way. She went down the steps to the carriage and waited while the coachman opened the door panel for her and assisted her into his vehicle.

"It's the French theatre, isn't it, Madame?" asked the coachman, knowing the answer already.

"Yes, Enrique; and the theatre will arrange for a carriage for me to come home. You needn't wait," answered Madelaine as she pulled the fur rug across her lap and drew up the hood of her cloak in anticipation of the cool embrace of the fog. She desired as well to conceal all the jewels she wore, for there were brazen gangs of thieves who would not hesitate to attack a lone woman and her coachman if the plucking looked promising enough; the fine necklace of pearls and diamonds at her throat and the pearl-and-diamond drops in her ears were more than sufficient temptation for such street hooligans.

They arrived at the French theatre on Montgomery Street fifteen minutes later, and found themselves in a crush of carriages trying to get into position at the front of the theatre, where the sidewalk was broader and two wide steps were in place for those leaving their carriages. Ushers were at the edge of this boardwalk helping the arriving audience to alight.

"I don't think I can get much closer, Madame, not in another ten minutes, and you would then be late," said Enrique as he looked over the line of vehicles waiting to discharge their fares. "It is less than a block from here."

"It is satisfactory, Enrique," said Madelaine with decision, handing him a small tip. "I will walk the rest of the way; if you will watch me, to be sure I am not—"

"I will watch, Madame," he said, drawing up his carriage to the boardwalk. "Do you need the steps let down?"

"No," she replied, "I can manage well enough. The street is well-lit and I doubt anyone will opportune me with so much activity about." With that, she opened the door panel, set the rug aside, and stepped down from the carriage into the street, swinging the door behind her to close it. She was about to turn when she felt her cloak snag on the door-latch; as she struggled to free it, she stumbled back against the coach.

"Allow me, Madame," said a voice from behind her; William Sherman reached out and freed her cloak, then held out his hand to assist her to the wide, wooden sidewalk. "Good evening, and permit me to say that I am surprised to see you here."

"At the French theatre? Where else should I be?" Madelaine recovered her poise at once. "Thank you for your concern, Mister Sherman. Why should you be surprised."

He looked at his pocket watch. "The curtain will rise in five minutes. You will have to join your company at once."

"Then we will have to hurry," said Madelaine, starting along the boardwalk in the direction of the French theatre. "But there is no one I am joining, Mister Sherman. Or who is joining me. I am a French-woman here for the pleasure of hearing her own language spoken, not to indulge society."

"Surely you do not intend to go to the theatre unescorted?" He gazed at her in dismay. "No, no, Madame, you must not."

"But why?" she asked reasonably. "I have attended the theatre alone in London." As soon as she said it, she realized she had slipped; it was rare for her to make such an error.

"Never tell me you went alone to the theatre as a child," he countered. "Not even French parents are so indulgent."

"Not as a child, no," she allowed, irritated that her tongue should have got her into such a pass with Sherman, of all people.

He stopped walking, and looked down at her, cocking his head; the lamplight made his red hair glow like coals. "As a gentleman, I should never ask a lady this question, but I fear I must."

She returned his look. "What question is that? I have told you the truth, Mister Sherman."

"Of that I have no doubt," he answered, so directly that she was startled. "I can perceive the truth of you as if it grew from you on stalks. No, the question I ought not to ask is, how old are you?" Before she could answer, he added, "Because I have received an accounting of your money in the Saint Louis office of Lucas and Turner, and with it a portrait and a description to verify your identity. It would seem that you have not altered in the last decade. You appeared to be about twenty when you first went there, and you appear to be about twenty now."

Very carefully she said, "If I told you when I was born, you would not believe me."

He studied her eyes and was satisfied. "That, too, is the truth." He again looked at his pocket watch. "We are going to miss the curtain."

"Does this mean you are escorting me?" asked Madelaine.

"Perforce," answered Sherman with a faint smile.

"But what of the gossip you always warn me about? And your wife is still with her parents." Madelaine noticed that the theatre-goers had all but disappeared from the street. She glanced at Sherman. "Are you really set on seeing Racine?"

His face did not change but his voice softened. "No."

"Nor am I," said Madelaine, who had seen *Phedre* more than twenty times in the last sixty years. "Surely there is somewhere we can go that will not cause tongues to wag?"

Most of those going to the theatre were in their places; the few that remained on the street hurried to reach their seats before the curtain went up. They paid no attention to Madelaine and Sherman.

He coughed once. "There are rooms at the casinos, private rooms. Men dine there in private. Sometimes they are used for assignations."

"Would that bother you?" asked Madelaine. "Going to such a place?"

"It should bother you," said Sherman sternly. Then he made up his mind. He took her by the elbow and started to lead her in the direction away from the French theatre. "My carriage is in a livery around the corner on Pine Street," he said.

"I wish you would not hold onto my arm in that manner," she said to him. "It's uncomfortable."

He released her at once, chagrined. "I meant nothing unsuitable, Madame." He put more than two feet between them. "You must understand that I sought only to guard—"

"Oh, for all the Saints in the calendar!" Madelaine burst out, then lowered her voice. "I meant nothing but what I said: I dislike having my arm clutched. But I am glad of your company, Mister Sherman, and your protection. I know these streets can be dangerous."

He paused at the corner of Pine Street. "I will take you home."

"Yes, please," said Madelaine amiably, "take me home; after we have our own private discussion."

This time there was an eagerness in his eyes as he looked down at her. "What did you mean by discussion, since you are clarifying your meaning, Madame?"

"That, in large part, is up to you," said Madelaine, regarding him steadily. "I will not seduce you, or demand what you are unwilling to give; I want no man who is not willing to have me."

He laughed abruptly. "What man would that be? One who is dead or prefers the bodies of men?"

Madelaine answered him seriously. "I do not mean only my body, Mister Sherman. If that is all I sought, it is there for the taking, all around us. I mean one who is willing to see into my soul. And to let me see into his."

Taken aback, Sherman straightened up, and stared down the dark street. "Let me make myself plain to you, Madame, and if what I say is repugnant, then I will deliver you to your front door post haste. No matter what you may stir in me, I cannot, and I will not, compromise my obligations to my family. I am in no position to offer you any advantage, Madame. I am married, and that will not be changed by any desire I may feel for you."

"I don't recall asking you to change, or to hurt your family," said Madelaine as she put her hand through his arm. "I only remember suggesting that we spend the evening together."

"And that I may have you if that is what I wish," he said, as if to give her one more chance to change her mind.

Madelaine's smile was quick. "I am not challenging you, Mister Sherman. I am seeking to spend time with you."

"Whatever that means," said Sherman.

"Whatever that means," Madelaine concurred.

SAN FRANCISCO, 16 JUNE, 1855

... Tonight will be better.

THE SHEETS WERE FINE LINEN, as soft as antique satin, and there were six pillows and a damask comforter flung in glorious disarray about the bed. In the wan spill of moonlight from the window, Sherman was standing, wearing only a loosely belted dressing gown, and smoking a thin cigar as he gazed out into the darkness. "The other evening and now this. What must you think of me?"

"Nothing to your discredit," said Madelaine quietly, hardly moving as she spoke. "I think you do not trust what you want."

"That's kind," he said tightly. "Many another woman would be offended."

Madelaine turned on her side to look at him, regarding him with a serious expression. "If that's not it, what is bothering you?"

He met her eyes. "You are."

"Why do I bother you? Would you rather not be here?" she asked, more puzzled than apprehensive.

"No. There is no place I would rather be," he answered evenly.

"Then why—?" she began, only to be cut off.

"Because it is what I want," he said bluntly, and stubbed out his cigar in the saucer she had set out for that purpose. "A man in my position, with a wife and a good marriage, has other women for necessity and amusement. It isn't that way with you. You are not a convenience or an entertainment. You are not convenient at all. You are what I want. All of you. And I should not. I must not." He started toward the bed, tugging at his sash and flinging it aside as he reached her. He stared down at her as his robe fell open. "Do you know what it means to want you so much, to go beyond reason with wanting you? I want to possess you, and I fear that you will possess me. I am afraid that once I touch you, I will be lost."

"Is that so terrifying a prospect?" she asked, moving to make a place beside her in the bed.

"Yes." In a shrug he dropped his dressing gown to the floor, letting it lie in a velvet puddle.

"Then come and stretch out beside me. We can talk like friends, all through the night." She piled up two of the pillows. "I don't require you take me."

"How do you mean?" he asked sharply.

"If you do not want to touch me at all, you need not." She regarded him kindly. "If you would like to, then you may."

He scowled. "How can you say that you want me, that you have me here, in your house, in your bed, and not care if I—"

She sighed. "I've told you before, William—"

"Don't call me William," he interrupted, seeking a distraction from the confusion that warred within him.

"I won't call you Mister Sherman, not here," she said, slapping one of the pillows with the back of her hand; though it was dark, she could see his face clearly and knew that he was deeply troubled. She strove to lighten the burden of desire that so plagued him, and decided to stay on safe ground. "What does the 'T' in your name stand for?"

"My friends and…and family call me Cump," he said, swallowing hard.

"Cump?" She was baffled.

"My given name is Tecumseh," he said at last. "The Ewings added William when they took me in after my father's death. So that I could be baptized into their Catholic religion." He sat on the edge of the bed and absently reached out to stroke her hair.

Madelaine knew he had just given her a very special gift. "You're named for the chief of the Shawnee."

"Yes," he said with urgency as he reached out and wrapped his long-fingered hands around her upper arms. "How did you know about Tecumseh?"

"I know he had a twin brother, Tenskwatawa, and they were both called The Prophet." It was not a direct answer, but all she was prepared to give now. "Come to bed, Tecumseh. You don't have to do anything you don't want to."

He glowered at her, then looked down at himself, sighed, and swung his legs up and under the covers. He stared up at the ceiling in the darkness. "What should we talk about?" he asked, his manner forbidding.

"Anything you wish, or nothing at all. Either will please me if it is what you want." As much as she wanted to lie next to him, to feel his flesh against hers for the length of her body, she, too, lay on her back and stared at the ceiling, noticing a faint crack in the ornamental plaster-work. She wanted to bridge the rift between them, and sought for something she could give him, as he had offered her his name. "Let us share secrets, as friends do," she suggested impulsively. "If you like, I will tell you how old I am."

"That is a wonderful secret for a lady to share with a friend, and quite an admission for any woman to make." He laughed once, then looked grave. "Very well. On my honor I swear I will never repeat it," he told her somberly.

"You had best not," said Madelaine, and plunged ahead, telling herself that surprise was an advantage with this man. "For I was born November 22nd, 1724, at Montalia, my family estate, in the far south of France."

For several seconds, Sherman was silent. Then he chuckled. "1724, not 1824. That would make you more than a century old, Madame."

"I am," she said, beginning to worry.

He turned toward her, trying hard to keep the incredulity out of his voice. "All right. I deserved that. For the sake of argument, we will say you are ancient, a veritable crone. You are one hundred thirty-one years old, or will be in November." His chuckling continued, rich and easy, the hard lines in his face relaxing so that he, himself, now appeared younger than he was. "And how did you attain this great age without looking older than a girl just out?"

"Because I died August 4th, 1744. I was just out," she replied, trying to keep her voice from trembling, though she could not disguise the chill that seized her, making her quiver.

"August 4th, 1744," he repeated, as if hearing the words again would change them. His chuckle turned to coughing, and he took a minute to bring his breathing under control. He lay back on the pillows, willing himself not to cough. "You don't expect me to believe this, do you?"

"Why not?" she answered, fighting the desolation that swept over her. She was afraid her teeth would chatter. "Tecumseh, you know when I am lying. I am not lying now, am I? This is the truth."

"The truth?" he scoffed. "Well, Madame, you sure look mighty pretty for a corpse." He rolled on his side, propped himself on his elbow and stared at her. "How can you claim to exchange confidences and then tell such bald-faced…" The words straggled; when he spoke again, he was awed. "You are telling the truth, aren't you?"

"Yes," she answered, as if from a great distance.

"But how? …" He touched her face with one long finger; he did his best to comprehend the implications of what she said. "Dear God, Madelaine, how?"

She gave him Saint-Germain's answer. "I drink the Elixir of Life. And I do not die. I cannot die."

"Then tell me something of your youth." His steel-colored eyes grew sharp. "Who was ruling France then?"

"When I came to Paris, Louis XV was King," she answered calmly, though she continued to shiver as much from the strength of her memories as from apprehension about Sherman. "That was in the fall of 1743. I went to my aunt so that she could introduce me into society."

"What sort of fellow was he, Louis XV?" demanded Sherman, making her answer a test. "I warn you, I know something about the man, and will not be fobbed off with vague answers."

"Venal, luxury-loving, indolent, handsome, over-indulged, manipulative. In a word, spoiled." She stared at him, surprised when he took her hands in his. "I escaped the Terror, which is just as well."

"A lovely corpse without a head, that would be difficult," agreed Sherman in ill-concealed excitement.

"A corpse is all I would have been. Those who taste the Elixir of Life are not proof against all death. Madame la Guillotine is as deadly to me as to you. So is fire." She looked directly into his eyes. "In the time I have lived, can you imagine the number of times I have said good-bye?" And how many more times I will, she added silently. She thought of Trowbridge then, his devotion which had cost him his life to save hers, and Falke, going willingly into the furnace of the Egyptian desert in order to be free of her.

"No, Madelaine. Don't despair," he said, with the urgency of one who knew despair well. His arms went around her and he drew her close to him as if to protect her from the weight of grief. "It is unbearable," he murmured, pressing his lips to her hair.

She rested her head on his chest, listening to his heart beat, hearing the pulse quicken. "I am told one learns, in time." Her breath was deep and uneven.

He reached to turn her face up to his, searching out secrets. "What are you, then? I'd better warn you I don't hold any truck with the supernatural. And don't preach religion at me, whatever you do. I get enough of that from the Ewings." He made an impatient gesture at the mention of his in-laws.

"No religion," she promised. "Other than that most religion is against those of us who come to this life." She stretched to kiss him, feeling yearning and resistance in his mouth. "We die, but slip the hold death has on us, and we live—"

"On the Elixir of Life," he said, one hand sliding down her flank. "And how is this mysterious Elixir obtained?"

"It is taken from those who are willing to give it," she answered quietly. "Where there is understanding, and passion, there is also great...joy."

"Joy," he echoed as if the word were terrible even as he pulled her inexorably nearer, kissing her with what he had intended as roughness but what became a tenderness of such intensity that he felt all his senses fill with her. He tried to push her away but his body would not answer the stern command of his will, and as she guided his hands over the treasure of her flesh, he surrendered to her with all the strength of his desire.

"Slowly," she whispered as she flicked her tongue over his nipples, seeing his shock and delight. "It is better if you savor it."

"God and the Devils! I am ready to explode!" He kicked back the sheet to show her, proud and embarrassed at once. "Hurry, Madelaine. I am at the brink."

"Not yet," said Madelaine, bending to kiss him again as she straddled him. "Do not deny yourself the full measure of your passion, for you would also deny me. This is not a race where the glory goes to the swiftest." Then, with exquisite languor, she guided him deep within her.

His breath hissed through his clenched teeth. "I can't..."

"You can," she promised, remaining very still until he opened his eyes. Then she began to move with him, feeling his guard fall away as his ardor became adoration at the instant her lips brushed his throat.

They lay together until the first pre-dawn call of birds warned them of coming day.

"I don't want to leave," Sherman said, kissing the corner of her mouth. "You have enthralled me, Madelaine."

"And I am bound to you, Tecumseh," she said.

With sudden passion, he pulled her close against him, his long fingers tangled in her hair. "What have you done to me?"

32

"Touched you," she answered. "And you me."

As he rose, goose-flesh on his pale skin, he touched the arch of her lip. "We will have to be very careful, very discreet. They know, the women here, that a man has appetites, but they will not look on you with the same understanding."

"Yes," she agreed, "I know," and turned her head to kiss the palm of his hand.

He gathered up his clothes with care and dressed quickly, listening for the sounds in the street. "I don't want anyone to know I've come here," he told her, his manner stern. "For both our sakes."

She had got out of bed and pulled on a heavy silken peignoir. "I am not about to cry it to the world."

He paused in the door, regarding her steadily. "No, you are not," he conceded with a curious mixture of relief and exasperation. "It isn't in you to do that." Then he smiled, and the harshness left his face. He held his arms open to her and she ran into them.

SAN FRANCISCO, 1 JULY, 1855

Yesterday I met Tecumseh's two children, though he tells me he has a third child, Minnie, living with her grandparents, an arrangement which does not entirely please him. The children currently living with him were with him at a puppet show presented near the old Mission; a number of San Francisco society brought their children to this entertainment, and I came with the Kents, at their invitation.

He is clearly fond of both children, but takes the keenest delight in his son Willy, who is still a baby; the boy has hair almost as red as his father's, and is quick and amiable. It is no wonder his father dotes on him...

At last I have sorted out my books and journals. Most of my notes are prepared and ready, and I am about to set to work in earnest...

SHERMAN READ THE FIRST THREE PAGES in growing disbelief. "Indians," he said to her at last, "Indians! What in infernal damnation do you mean with this?"

Madelaine watched him as he began to pace her front parlor, ignoring the raised, cautioning finger Baron deStoeckl offered him. "It is the subject of my studies." She was in a deep green afternoon dress and her hair was neatly dressed, as suited any woman prepared to receive guests, and the filmy light from her curtained windows gave the whole room a soft, pale glow.

"Indians! What is the matter with you? How can you be such a romantic fool?" He was dusty from riding and made no excuse for it as he prowled his way about the room, refusing to look directly at her, for fear he might give himself away. "What do you know about Indians?"

"I have been studying them," said Madelaine, determined not to argue so uselessly.

"Studying! A nice word for it! But what do you know about them?" He put down the pages in triumph.

"Not nearly enough," she answered calmly. "That is why I study them, to end my ignorance."

"But you do not know what they are like; you prove that by what you say now," Sherman persisted. "You are one of the dreamers, thinking you have come upon discarded wisdom or neglected perceptions. You haven't a notion what kind of superstitious, bloody savages they are."

"Some might say the same of me," Madelaine said in an undervoice, then spoke up. "I have already spent time among the Osage, the Kiowa, the Pawnee, the Arapaho, the Cheyenne, the Ute, the Shoshone, and the Miwok, without anything untoward happening to me. I am working from my journals and other records I have made of them to prepare my book."

Sherman stared at her aghast. "Is that what you were doing after you arrived in America? Living with Indians?"

"For the most part, yes," Madelaine said, her face betraying no emotion.

"Don't you realize how dangerous that is?" Sherman insisted, this time looking directly at her. "You think they are all the noble savages Europeans so admire, but I've fought Indian skirmishers, mapping in the South, and I know what they can be. I do not need a pitched battle to show me what cruelty they embody."

"They did me no harm, and I do not think they would ever do me any," said Madelaine. "Once they realized what I wanted to know, and were convinced of my sincerity, they were most cooperative. They permitted me to study them. As I expected they would do, since they are reasonable peoples." It was not quite the truth, and she was aware that

Sherman knew it, but she was not willing to debate the matter with him.

"You were luckier than you had any right to be," said Sherman brusquely, breaking away from the spell of her violet eyes.

"How can you say that?" Madelaine asked, unable to keep from responding to his challenge though she realized that he was deliberately provoking her. "What danger is one European woman to them?"

"I was referring to the danger one European woman is in from them, little as she is willing to acknowledge it," said Sherman dryly. "I have some experience of Indians, remember. I have seen the Seminole, Madame, and know to my cost what implacable enemies they can be. They killed troopers who were doing them no harm whatever. They would ambush a few men and pick them off with arrows and blowguns. Indians are dangerous. And if the European woman is not willing to accept my advice, then be it on her head."

Baron deStoeckl cleared his throat. "Perhaps each of you has made a point? In your own ways," he suggested in French. "I do not mean to increase dissention, but it seems to me that there is good reason to concede points each to the other."

Sherman rounded on him, his brows drawn down, his mouth a thin line. "I do not want any misfortune to befall her."

"And I do not want any greater misfortunes to befall my Indian friends, since they have endured so much already, though they never complain of it," said Madelaine, sensing that Sherman might understand this better than he admitted. "You do know that many of them have been forced to change their way of life since the Europeans arrived here."

"As the Europeans were forced to change their ways of life when they came to this wilderness." Sherman sighed once, his breathing strained. "It was not like visiting another European country, coming to this one. It still isn't, though we have cities and a few of the amenities of life. Not as we do in the East, of course, but this is not the frontier, as it was when I was here eight years ago. Then there were only a dozen streets in the whole of San Francisco." He sat down abruptly, his face draining of color as the severity of his asthma attack increased.

Madelaine recognized the symptoms; she asked Baron deStoeckl to tend to Sherman for the moment so that she could fetch something that would ease his labored breathing.

"Certainly," said Baron deStoeckl.

"No need," wheezed Sherman.

"Because it offends your pride to be helped?" Madelaine suggested, then excused herself and hurried toward the back of her house, calling to Olga to assist her. "I have a number of large stoneware jars in the cellar. Will you bring me the one with the green seal? At once."

"Certainly," said Olga, who was busy with the washtub on the stove. She wiped her hands on her apron and took a lantern, struck a lucifer and lit the wick before descending into the cellar through the door in the rear of the pantry.

Madelaine occupied herself making a toddy of honey and brandy, which she knew Sherman often used when he could not burn nitre paper. As Olga emerged with the stoneware jar tucked in the crook of her arm, Madelaine said, "Break the seal. Use a knife."

"What is the matter?" asked Olga as she blew out the lantern flame and set to work on the seal. "And why do you need this to deal with the situation? What is in this jar?" She would not look directly at Madelaine as she went on.

"Mister Sherman suffers from asthma, and just now it is troubling him," said Madelaine as calmly as she could. "I see no reason why he should continue to suffer unnecessarily. A little of the liquid in that container, mixed with hot water, should offer him some relief."

"But what is it?" asked Olga as she set about opening the jar.

"A very old remedy. I obtained it while traveling in Egypt." She made a gesture of satisfaction as the kettle came to the boil. "Here. Bring me the jar. You have it open, don't you?"

"Yes," said Olga uncertainly as she sniffed at the mouth of the jar. "It has no odor."

"No, it doesn't," Madelaine agreed as she took the jar and tipped some of its contents into the cup she had prepared. "That is very good. If you will cork the jar and put it back in the cellar?"

Olga shrugged and did as she was told.

Madelaine finished making the toddy and hurried toward the front parlor where she could hear Sherman trying not to cough as he labored to breathe. Baron deStoeckl was patting Sherman on the back and frowning at his efforts, when Madelaine moved him aside and held out the cup and saucer to her stricken guest.

"What's this?" Sherman demanded with difficulty.

"The toddy you've mentioned to me. It will make you better directly," she promised him. "Drink it before it grows too cool to help you."

Sherman glowered at her, but took the proffered cup and winced at the heat as he sipped at it. When the contents were half gone, he was noticeably improved, his breathing more regular and less uncomfortable. "Thank you, Madame," he said as soon as he was sitting upright.

"Finish the toddy, Mister Sherman. You are better but not restored yet." Madelaine watched him sternly as he drank the rest and set the cup and saucer aside on the rosewood end table beside his chair. "Very good."

"I am pleased you think so, Madame," said Sherman with a wry smile. "What a stern task mistress."

"I am concerned for your well-being, Mister Sherman. Who else would handle my affairs as well as you have?" This was intended to restore some formality to their conversation, but it did not succeed.

"What other banker would care enough to ignore the impropriety of your studies?" Sherman said with a gesture of capitulation that made the sharp-eyed Baron deStoeckl raise his brows in surprise.

"I doubt you will do that, Mister Sherman. I suspect you will adopt a flanking strategy and try to wear down my resolve through a series of skirmishes, like the Seminole," Madelaine did her best to make this a teasing suggestion, one that was not to be taken seriously by either man.

Sherman grinned. "Yes, a series of skirmishes along your flanks would be most rewarding."

The Baron lifted his hands to show he was helpless against these blatant flirtations. He leaned down and made one last attempt. "My good friend William, I think you are taking advantage of our hostess."

"I would certainly like to," said Sherman incorrigibly. Now that he was feeling markedly better, he was seized with high spirits. "A covert campaign is required."

"God and the archangels!" Baron deStoeckl burst out. "What of your reputations?"

Sherman regarded his friend with an arch look. "What danger are they in? You will not repeat what we say here, will you? I know Madame de Montalia will not, and neither will I, so where is the problem? He will keep our secret." He got up and strode to Madelaine's side, purpose in every line of his lean body. "Don't preach to me about good sense and prudence. Not now. Not here." With that, he caught her up in his arms and bent to kiss her.

Few things flustered Madelaine; this unexpected demonstration unnerved her thoroughly. She felt her face redden, and when she could speak, she said, "What a burden you are putting on your friend. Think, Tecumseh." She glanced at the Baron, about to apologize for the impropriety of it all when Sherman took her by the shoulders and nearly shook her.

"Damnit, woman, I want someone to know." Sherman looked down into her eyes and his sternness vanished. He went on quietly, "I want at least one man I can trust to see what I feel for you, so that I will be able to talk with him about what you mean to me when...this is over."

"When your wife returns," said Madelaine.

"When you leave," said Sherman.

Baron deStoeckl bowed to them both. "You may rely on my discretion," he promised them in French.

———◆———

SAN FRANCISCO, 11 JULY, 1855

Tecumseh has been in one of his black moods these last three days, and nothing I can do seems to cheer him... He has warned me of these bouts of desolation which come upon him from time to time, though he understated the severity of his incidents. Nothing, he claims, can be done to mitigate them. Even his children are unable to lure him from the terrible despair that has overtaken him. He has sent word that he will not dine with me this evening or tomorrow evening or the day after. Had he not warned me of these starts of his, I would be more troubled by him than I am, and I am troubled enough...

My work on my manuscript has gone well, which is very satisfying. I have completed my chapters on the Osage and the Kiowa, and I am well into my chapter on the Pawnee. I have been reviewing my notes on the Cheyenne and the Ute in order to organize the material more suitably. If this progress continues, I will be able to send the entire manuscript to Amsterdam before the end of October, which will please me very much.

I will have to extend my rental here until November at least, so that I may complete my work...

"PRAY DO NOT TAKE HIS MANNER to heart, Madame," said Baron deStoeckl to Madelaine as they danced at the summer ball given by

Captain and Missus Elihu Hazellet; he avoided using Sherman's name in case they were overheard. "He will soon be as filled with enthusiasm as he is now consumed with desolation." He missed a step and began to apologize.

"It's not necessary, Baron," said Madelaine, "neither this nor your intercession for your friend."

"You are more understanding than many another woman would be," said the Baron gallantly.

The musicians, crowded into an alcove, were doing their best to follow the erratic beat of Captain Hazellet, who had seized the baton from their leader and was enjoying himself hugely.

"Come, Baron, it is not as if he were courting me, for that is impossible. I would be more foolish than is permissible if I were to demand all the attentions and courtesies that fashion demands." She noticed Fanny Kent in the arms of General Hitchcock and nodded politely.

"I hope my friend comes to his senses and rejoices in his good fortune," Baron deStoeckl told Madelaine as they swept down the room. "Permit me to tell you, Madame, that I am much impressed with your wisdom."

"Wisdom?" scoffed Madelaine, though she flushed with the compliment. "What would be the use of making demands of him? It would serve only to embarrass us both and I am convinced would not engage his affections in the least."

The musicians came to the end of the waltz; Captain Hazellet reluctantly surrendered the baton to their leader once again.

"Permit me to bring you a glass of wine," said Baron deStoeckl as he led Madelaine off the floor.

"Thank you, Baron, but I do not drink wine," said Madelaine; she could feel Sherman watching her from across the room and it was difficult to resist the urge to return his stare.

"Then tell me what I may bring you," said the Baron, his gallantry unfazed by her courteous refusal.

"Nothing, thank you," said Madelaine, releasing his arm as they reached the chairs around the ballroom.

"Poor Captain Hazellet," said deStoeckl smoothly, covering the awkwardness he sensed in Madelaine. "He is hoping that the government will give him the license to import more Chinese to work on the railroads. He is making a grand show in the hope that it will convince his relatives in the Capitol to provide the license."

Madelaine took her seat "But how are parties and balls going to convince men on the other side of the continent—"

"Rumors, Madame," said the Baron quietly. "He hopes that he will cause the high society of San Francisco to endorse him to those in power." He shook his head at the folly of it. "He has spent a great deal of money entertaining the army officers posted here. I understand he has great hopes that Henry Halleck will support his efforts with useful introductions."

"How absurd," said Madelaine, and looked up sharply as a man in uniform stumbled into the ballroom.

Conversation faded and all the guests stared at the unexpected arrival. A number of the ladies drew back.

The young soldier turned deep red, aware that he had committed a serious social lapse. He removed his cap and bowed gracelessly. "Sorry to intrude. But there's trouble. A riot. General Hitchcock, we need men—"

Sherman was already striding forward, his expression animated for the first time in days. "Yes, a riot, we will. What is the trouble, Corporal?"

"Some men. At the wharf. They started a fight with sailors off a ship just arrived from Manila." He looked around. "It's getting bloody. I think they could get killed."

"Which of them?" asked General Hitchcock, watching Sherman instead of the young soldier.

"The toughs from the town want an excuse. To do murder," said the young soldier.

"And we must keep the peace," Sherman declared. "True enough." He stared around the room, pointing to the younger men in turn. "All of you, make your farewells. It is time you all had a taste of the military. There is work to be done tonight. Prepare to leave here at once," he ordered, then glanced at General Hitchcock. "With your orders, Sir?"

Hitchcock chuckled. "Carry on, Sherman. You have the way of it. Let me know if you need my help."

But Sherman was already dragooning the younger men into order. "Those of you who have weapons, get them. Be sure your guns are loaded. We will assemble at the front steps at once." He turned to his hostess and bowed. "I regret that we must cause you distress, Madame."

Missus Hazellet curtsied to him. "Nonsense, Mister Sherman. We must keep the streets orderly, or none of us will sleep safe in bed."

Sherman saluted, and turned on his heel. "Those of you remaining here, pray do not leave until you have received word from me that it is safe. I do not wish to inconvenience any of you, but I would rather do that than see any of you exposed to danger." He went to the ballroom door, and looked about for the servants.

Baron deStoeckl leaned down and whispered to Madelaine. "Not that I wish a riot, but I suspect the action will do him a world of good."

"I am sure you are right," said Madelaine, watching the renewed vigor in Sherman's every move.

"He will do this well," said the Baron. "And I expect that he himself will bring back word when he is convinced it is safe."

"Possibly," said Madelaine as the younger men hastened after Sherman.

Fanny Kent hurried over to Madelaine, her cheeks pale and her splendid bosom heaving. "It is so distressing," she exclaimed as she reached Madelaine's side. "Madame de Montalia, how unfortunate that you should have to see San Francisco at its worst. What you must think of all Americans."

"Given what the Terror was in France, I cannot think why you should believe I would have any lower opinion of Americans than I do of Frenchmen." She saw Fanny's eyes widen with shock, and she went on, "This is not a wholesale slaughter, as we had in France; this is only a riot. No city in the world is immune to them, or so it seems to me."

"You are too kind, Madame," said Fanny, and went off in search of more sympathetic responses.

"I don't think she knows how to justify her country to you, Madame," said Baron deStoeckl. "That is what she wants to do."

"She has no need; I expect no such justification from anyone," Madelaine told him, and noticed that Captain Hazellet had once again taken up the baton and was about to begin an impromptu concert. She sighed and steeled herself against the performance she was sure to come.

"Will you do me the kindness of a waltz?" asked Baron deStoeckl, offering her his arm to lead her onto the dance floor.

How shocking this innocent invitation would have been, fifty years ago, Madelaine thought, recalling the scandal of the waltz when it was new. She put her left hand lightly on his shoulder as he swung into the first step.

At midnight Muriel Hazellet ordered a light supper for her guests, with strong coffee to help them all remain awake. The music had stopped more than an hour before and now all pretense of festivities had given way to anxious conversations.

"I hope there will be no fires," said Joseph Folsom with a worried glance toward the tall windows at the end of the ballroom. "Fires are so dangerous in a wooden city like this one."

"Yes," said one of his companions who owned two commercial warehouses near the waterfront. "I am very troubled."

"There has been no alarm, and no sign of flames. That must be a comfort to all of us," said General Hitchcock in his steady way. "And no other soldiers have come here. If the riot were spreading, that must have happened. We may assume that Sherman is taking the situation in hand." He lowered his chin onto his chest. "A pity he left the army. We need more officers like him."

"He appears to have an aptitude for command," said Folsom, not entirely approvingly.

"He is a very intelligent fellow, and persistent to a fault," said General Hitchcock, and continued more openly, warming to his subject, "He was barely twenty when he was graduated from West Point. There were great hopes for him: he excelled in tactics, engineering, and languages, as I recall, all useful skills. He would have finished top of his class if he had not argued so much with his instructors. But he left the army. He couldn't support his family on peace-time pay, like many other young officers."

"So he's a banker and not a soldier," said one of the men listening at the fringe of the little group around Hitchcock.

"It's the army's loss, I'm afraid," said the General.

"How unfortunate," said Folsom, making it a final statement.

"Not for us, tonight," said Folsom's companion with a sour smile.

Three servants carried trays of coffee cups around the ballroom, making a second effort to provide the guests with the hot, enlivening drink. At one end of the ballroom, two cooks prepared oyster-and-bacon omelettes in chafing dishes set over little oil cooking lamps; at the other, more servants poured champagne into French crystal.

"These omelettes are all the current fashion," said Muriel Hazellet to Madelaine as she once again attempted to coax her foreign guest to join the rest of the party in supper. "They are part of the Gold Rush tradition."

"So I understand," said Madelaine, her eyes widening as she heard the sharp sound of a door opening in the distance.

"You have nothing to fear, Madame," her hostess told her with less certainty than she liked. "If there were any trouble, the servants would alert us."

"No doubt," said Madelaine with a courteous nod.

For the second time that evening all conversation in the ballroom stopped as William Tecumseh Sherman strode in. His evening clothes were in disarray, his tie and collar entirely missing, and a large bruise marred the left side of his face. His red hair stood out in spikes. Dust and blood smirched his shirt and vest and there was a long rent in his trousers. Yet he was smiling fiercely. As he reached the center of the ball-room, he halted and said, "The riot is quelled. We have two dozen miscreants in jail, five with cracked skulls; only three of our men sustained any real injuries, and they are receiving treatment as I speak. The unrest is over. Order is restored. You may leave for your homes without fear."

The announcement was met with a cheer and more than one exclamation of relief. Captain Hazellet hurried up to shake Sherman's hand, and was quickly followed by most of the men in the room. Someone offered him a cigar, and another lit it for him.

Suddenly the ballroom was as noisy as it had been silent, everyone talking at once, trying to be heard above the din.

Baron deStoeckl came up behind Madelaine once again. "He seems to have shaken off the megrims."

"For the time being," said Madelaine with less certainty than the Russian. "I hope he may be in good spirits tomorrow."

"How little faith you have, Madame; a fight was just what he needed," said deStoeckl, and sauntered over to the gathering around Sherman.

Madelaine watched the celebrating, her face clouded with a lingering frown. There could be no doubt that Sherman was in fine fettle, enjoying the savor of victory while he generously praised the efforts of his untried men.

"With training, they could be a formidable force for good in this city. If we are to keep order, we will need such a company, a true militia. We cannot continue to rely on the marshals and sheriff to preserve the peace. Most of the time, they are like foxes among the chickens." He drew on his cigar and looked around the room, pleased that the gathering was listening to his instruction. His steely eyes rested on Madelaine an instant longer than on anyone else, then he turned away and continued to expostulate on the urgent need for a proper militia.

Only an hour later, as the guests were departing, did Sherman approach Madelaine directly. "As you are unescorted, Madame, I will do myself the honor of accompanying your carriage to your door." It was more of a pronouncement than a suggestion, and Madelaine bridled at his high-handed gesture.

"Thank you, but my coachman is armed, Mister Sherman, and I am certain we will manage," she said, reminding herself of the gossip that so troubled him. "He carries a shotgun in the box, and he is prepared to deal with any trouble we might encounter."

"Nevertheless, I will ride along beside your carriage. You are one of the few ladies without male escort, and you are the only one without some other guest with you. As your banker, and, I hope, your friend, I ask that you take no unnecessary risks tonight, and permit me to see you to your door." A flicker of amusement lurked in his eyes though his manner was as correct as possible. "Let me do this for you, Madame. It would relieve me to see you safely within your own house."

Madelaine sighed, annoyed that she had not accepted Baron deStoeckl's offer of escort some twenty minutes before. "Very well, Mister Sherman. I will accept your escort. And thank you for your concern."

Sherman only nodded and called for his horse as Madelaine's coach drew up at the porte-cochere. He held the door for her and handed her up the steps, then went and mounted the handsome Spanish grey he had acquired two months ago. He signaled Enrique, the coachman, and they set off toward Franklin Street.

SAN FRANCISCO, 21 JULY, 1855

To my astonishment, he returned after he had ridden back to his house and satisfied himself that his children were safe and their nurse calm. By that time, Enrique was gone home, Olga and Christian had retired to their various apartments, and all of the city seemed asleep. Even the bands of toughs who often boldly parade the streets at the small hours were gone to ground in the wake of the riot.

It was finally necessary that I explain about the risks that come with loving those of my blood, and he heard me out indulgently, promising me, as if I were one of his children, to consider what could happen if we keep on as we have been. Nothing I said persuaded him that there could be any difficulty coming from our affair. He was jubilant that I wanted him still, given how he has behaved of late. I tried to insist that he take heed of my warning but he was too eager to make the most of the night, and was at pains to end my warnings as quickly as possible, which he did by summarizing all I had said to him succinctly but with a flavor of skepticism that was certainly his most overriding impression of all I told him. Any dread he might have of what might come of this was banished by his desire, which never faltered.

This time he had no hesitation, no awkward beginnings. His embraces were long and deep, and he undertook to follow my lead, to find out how long he could build his passion before spending. He was merry as a boy with a first prize, and he romped with me for more than an hour before fatigue finally overcame him. When I woke him an hour before dawn, he was as refreshed as if he had passed a full eight hours in slumber, and was in good cheer as he left. He promised to come again in three nights, and that he would find good reasons for us to be in one another's company without attracting undue attention and gossip, which pleased me very much, for it is enervating to live with such close scrutiny. I pointed out to him that this would require some careful planning, to which he replied that he was very good at strategy and swore he would relish the opportunity, thinking it worthy of his talents...

THE WARMTH OF THE DAY was quickly fading before the chill fingers of fog that came caressing the hills from the west. As they turned down the steep hill, the wind nipping at their backs, Sherman signaled Madelaine to swing her horse off the main road to the wooded copse, indicating through gestures that they could then dismount and put on their coats.

"The Spanish call those two hills the Maiden's Breasts," he said to her as he lifted her out of the sidesaddle under the trees. He indicated the slope they had just descended. "I like yours better." He took the reins from her hand and secured them to one of the low-growing oaken branches, next to where his grey was tied.

"Less hectic to ride, I imagine," said Madelaine, smiling in spite of herself.

"I wouldn't say that," Sherman whispered to her as he bent down to wrap her in his arms, his lips seeking hers. He took his time about it, feeling her warm to him; it promised well for the night ahead. When he moved back from her, he said, teasing her, "There isn't any other land you would like to inspect, with the prospect of purchasing it, is there? That cove down the coast may prove worth the money asked for it; no doubt there are other promising locations as well. I will find out where land is for sale, so that you can have a look at it. I would have to escort you to advise you and to negotiate for you, wouldn't I? I could not allow you to venture abroad without suitable protection. I would be remiss in my duty if I did." He bent and, moving the thick knot of hair at the nape of her neck aside, kissed her just under her ear. "Where you kiss me, Madelaine. Where you pledge me your bond." His lips were light and teasing, almost playful.

It took her a while to gather her thoughts, and when she did, she struggled to voice them. "That is a good notion, on its own; never mind the chance for privacy it offers us. If you know of any I might like, tell me of it, and I will arrange to see it for myself," she said quite seriously. "I am in earnest, Tecumseh. I want to purchase some land here."

"So far speculation has been very profitable, at least in this area." He nodded, doing his best to fall into his role as banker. "When Congress finally comes to its senses and builds a railroad linking the East coast with the West, then land here may become even more valuable, but it will not happen until there is a railroad. Not even a good wagon road would help as the railroad would. But it would be better than nothing," he said, letting his rancor show. "There is no sense in their reluctance to authorize the railroad other than their usual damned lack of fore-sight. The telegraph link with the Mississippi only begs the question, but it is typical of Congress to settle for half-measures when full ones are wanted. As long as they keep California isolated, it will have little to attract investors beyond the gold fields, and that is not investment but exploitation; and it will continue as long as there is no land con-nection but trails across the continent. Only when goods and people may cross quickly and comfortably will the Pacific come into its own and assume its place in the scheme of things, bringing Occident and Orient together as no gang of Chinese laborers and cooks can do now. Until that time, it will be the last point of escape for the dreamers and scoundrels who seek their own private paradise, and attempt to create it for themselves here. It is short-sighted political chicanery to refuse to unite east and west by rail, I am convinced of it. The trouble is that California is an enigma; not even those who live here understand it." He folded his arms, his shirt-sleeves suddenly too little protection against the encroaching fog. "I will get my coat."

"Bring mine, will you?" She strolled deeper into the little grove of trees, listening to the sounds around her, the rustlings and flutters that reminded her that there were other occupants of the copse, many of which began their day when the sun went down. It was cool enough to be unpleasant, and she was relieved when Sherman came and held her nip-waisted coat for her as she slid her arms into the leg-o'-mutton sleeves. He rested his hands on her shoulders as he stood behind her, then slid them down to cover her breasts.

"How can I give this up?" he murmured, drawing her to him, holding her tightly as he moved his hands down the front of her body; he did this with ease, being slightly more than a head taller than Madelaine. Suddenly he stopped his rapt exploration. "I must be mad."

"For planning to give me up, or wanting me in the first place?" She avoided any hint of accusation in her mild rebuke, but she could not shake off the sadness that swept through her at her realization that she would have to leave San Francisco and Sherman before long.

"Both," said Sherman with utmost conviction, turning her to face him, staring down into her violet eyes as if he wanted to meet her in combat. "I am not a man who loves easily, and I am ... possessed by you. What is it about you? You are more of a mystery than this place." His countenance was stern, his brows drawn downward. "Had I thought I would be so ... so wholly in your thrall, I would never have begun with you."

"Bien perdu, bien connu," said Madelaine, hoping to conceal the sting she felt from his abrupt words.

"But you are not well-lost, that is the trouble. I do not need to lose you to know you, Madelaine." He surrounded her with his arms, his mouth rough on hers. He strained to press them more tightly together, then broke away from her. "But I will not compromise my marriage."

"So you have said from the first," Madelaine reminded him, as much to assure him that she still understood his requirements of her as to lessen his defensiveness. "And I have never protested your devotion. I will not do so now."

"And I meant it. I mean it still." He reached out and took her face in his long-fingered hands. "I treasure you as I have never treasured another woman, and may I be thrice-damned for it."

"Tecumseh," she said gently. "I have no wish to bring you pain."

He released her and moved away, leaves crackling underfoot. His voice was low and his words came quickly. "But you will, and that is the problem. There's nothing that can be done about it now: you are too deeply fixed in my soul for that. Oh, it is no fault of yours; you have been honorable from the first, if that is a word I may use for our adultery. Never have you asked, or hinted, that you want me to leave my wife: it is just as well, for I will not, no matter what sorcery you work on me. Yet when you go, as go you must, you will leave a wound in me that no enemy could put there. When you are gone—" He stared down at the ground as if trying to read something there in the last of the light. "I have never known anyone who so completely won me as you have."

Madelaine did not go after him. "Then we must make the most of the short time we have, so that your joy will be greater than your hurt, and you will remember our time together with happiness." She did not add that she longed for his ecstasy to sustain her in the months ahead.

"How can we?" He met her eyes in the dimness. "Why take the risk? We have been discreet so far, but I must resist my impulse to set all caution aside."

"Why? Who is to know what passes between us? When we are private, there is no reason for caution," said Madelaine, feeling some of his contained anguish as her own.

"No reason? Can you not think of one?" He shook his head, unwilling to look directly at her. "It may be there is the greatest reason of all, for when we are alone together, I have no strength to resist you."

"You are managing to resist me well enough now," she said, more sharply than she had intended.

"Do you think so?" he asked, his voice very quiet and deep, the lines of his face severe.

The silence between them lengthened, opening as if it were a chasm deep as the pits of hell. A scuttling flight in the underbrush as a fox hurried to find his supper provided a momentary distraction, then Madelaine took a step toward him, her hands turned palm up. "Tecumseh, do you recall what I told you of the bond the blood makes between us?"

His features grew less formidable and he reached out to caress her face as if compelled to do it. "Yes, Madelaine. How can I forget?"

"Then believe that when we are parted, we will not be separated," she said as she held out her hands for his.

He put his hands into hers but would not close the gap between them. "What else would you call it?"

For once she had an answer. "Tell me, when you cannot see the sun or stars, do you still know which direction is north?"

48

"North?" he repeated, baffled, and then said, "Yes, of course."

"And how do you know it?" she asked him.

He frowned, hitched up one shoulder. "I ... sense it."

She nodded. "Then understand that I will always sense you, no matter where you are, or where you go. It is the way of those of us who have become vampires."

He winced at this last. "Vampires."

"Yes," she confirmed.

He regained his attitude of skepticism. "For heaven's sake, isn't there another word for it? What a ludicrous notion. Vampires. Legends, for the credulous and childish. Surely there is another explanation to account for what has happened." His statement lacked conviction, but he glowered down at her. "How can you expect me to believe you?"

"I don't," she said wearily. "But it is still the truth. Oh, I have read that Polidori tale, and the little horrors Hoffmann writes, and I cannot blame you for how you think of us, given the model that is presented in such stories. If I were not what I am, I would be inclined to feel as you do, and to scoff at the idea of vampires." She came a step nearer to him. "But I am what you may become, and you need to be alerted to the dangers you may face."

His laughter crackled, brittle as autumn leaves. "Very well, you have warned me. If we continue as lovers, I could become a vampire when I die if my spine or my nervous system or my body is not destroyed. I will have to avoid direct sunlight and running water and mirrors. That covers all the hazards, I think. Yes, and I will need my native earth to sustain me. And blood. Should it come to pass, I am prepared. I will take the precautions you advise, on the odd chance they may be necessary." Then, with a deep sound that was half-sigh, half-groan, he pulled her into his arms again and bent to open her mouth with his own.

SAN FRANCISCO, 4 AUGUST, 1855

At the play last night, during the intermission, I heard discussion of the prospect of fighting in Free Kansas, which they suppose will come to a head within the year. Apparently there is a question if the territory should be a slave or a free state; those who are abolitionists are locked in conflict with those who wish to own slaves, a matter determined by each state, as is their right. Each new state admitted to the Union is permit-ted to decide this for itself and both abolitionists and slave-holders are seeking to gain the balance of power in this regard. A publisher in the East called Garrison has been putting out determined abolitionist tracts in the hope of compelling all the states to outlaw slavery. In the eastern part of the country the debate is a growing one, and becoming more ur-gent with every passing week . . .

Baron deStoeckl expressed hope that the war in the Crimea will soon end. It has been very costly for all the countries involved, as much for the ravages of disease as the terrible depredations of war. The Baron remarked to me that he prays that this country might learn the lessons of war from Russia and England and France and Austria, and seek to negotiate a resolution without a contest of arms.

I am nearly finished with my chapter on the Cheyenne, and in gener-al I am satisfied with the way the work is going; I have recorded enough of their thoughts about the nature of the world that it will be possible for later scholars to have a context for appreciating their legends and tradi-tions. It is frustrating, however, to realize that few scholars will under-stand or share my fascination with these people, for it is not fashionable in scholarly circles to examine the lives of primitive peoples who are thought to have nothing to teach those of us from more advanced civili-zations. In time the fashion will change, but by then the Pawnee and the Cheyenne will not be able to benefit from it.

Saint-Germain has written to me, in care of Lucas and Turner, to say he has been busy in London and Amsterdam, where he read my mono-graph and missed me more with every page he read. It pleased me to know he has read what I have written, the more so because he likes it. And I am moved to know he misses me, for I miss him as I would miss my right hand, if I lost it. How my heart goes out to him, and how much I love him, after so long a time . . . Tecumseh was suspicious of the letter, and spent half an hour quizzing me quite persistently about Saint-Ger-main. I do not know whether or not he has accepted my explanation, though he has apologized for his outburst of jealousy. He told me he has no right to be jealous of anyone, no matter what they are or have been to me. If only I were convinced he believes that . . .

BARON DESTOECKL LIT A LEAN RUSSIAN CIGARETTE and regarded Madelaine thoughtfully across the expanse of his front sitting room.

"You are not often in the habit of making morning calls, Madame, or in seeking confidential interviews," he said in French, and added, "Forgive my ill habit. Most of the Americans think my smoking tastes are too effete, both in my liking for cigarettes instead of cigars, and my smoking in the presence of ladies, but I confess I would like to feel at home in my own flat." The chamber was a testament to the international prosperity of San Francisco: the carpets on the floor were from China, the samovar on the side table was glossy Russian brass. Embossed Dutch bricks formed the fireplace and mantel. Four velvet-upholstered chairs and an Italian divan were provided for guests; Baron deStoeckl himself had an overstuffed Turkish chair with a flexible frame covered in tooled leather, by far the most comfortable article of furniture in the room.

"You may blow a cloud if it pleases you," said Madelaine, indicating the cigarette. "You do not offend me." She spread her skirts over the end of the divan.

"I thought not; you are not easily offended. Though I notice you have taken care to avoid offending the sensibilities of the Americans. Your housekeeper is with you, isn't she?" the Baron said with a favorable nod.

"She is, and it is very good of your cook to entertain her while we talk," said Madelaine in her most cordial manner.

"It is, isn't it? Otherwise she might overhear our conversation, which would be inconvenient for both of us, I suspect." His shrewd eyes twinkled as he made this remark. He studied her for a short while, making no apology for his scrutiny. "I also suspect you are here about our mutual American friend."

"Sherman," said Madelaine. "Yes. I must seek your advice, I fear."

"I am yours to command in any capacity you like," said deStoeckl gallantly. "Permit me to tell you that I can find it in my heart to envy William."

"That is very kind of you, Baron," said Madelaine, trying not to be awkward. "It is a delicate problem, and I would not broach it with you if I were able to convince him of the need of discussing it."

"Ah," said deStoeckl with a knowing nod. "I expected something of the sort. You want to know about his wife."

Madelaine indicated agreement and hurried into her questions before she could convince herself not to ask. "Yes. I want to know about her. I am aware that I have no claim on any information, but I seek it for his sake as well as my own. So if you will, tell me: why has she been away

51

for so long, and why has she left two of her children here with their father?"

DeStoeckl got to his feet and strode the length of his sitting room, his cigarette held between his thumb and first finger. As he spoke, he gesticulated with it for emphasis, leaving little puffs of white smoke in the air. "Very well. I will tell you what I think, with the proviso that this is only my opinion, and I may be in error, for of all those concerned, I know only William as a friend, not his wife. I think she left the children as a pledge of her own return, her promise that she is not leaving him forever. That, and I suspect it may be that she wishes to remain the child of her parents while she is with them, which she could not easily do with three youngsters of her own in tow. She is most profoundly devoted to her father."

"Profoundly devoted," Madelaine repeated, then asked, "What does she think of her husband, do you know?"

"She is deeply fond of him," said the Baron thoughtfully. "Or so it has appeared to me."

"Fond? Not loving?" asked Madelaine.

"Not with passion, no. But I would not expect it of her." He paced back toward the fireplace.

"Why not?" Madelaine persisted, watching his erratic progress about the room. "Is there anything in her nature that would turn her against him as her husband?"

"Not obviously, no." He drew on his cigarette once again, and went on. "Well, they were raised together, from the time her family took him in. As I recall, he was eight when that occurred. So he is more brother to her than lover," said deStoeckl reasonably. "And it has seemed to me that she is not…comfortable with the act of love, as many women of quality are not. She suffers from headaches and boils which cause her to avoid long embraces, or so I have heard; William was bitter when she left and said things…"

"They have three children," Madelaine reminded him.

"I didn't say she does not like having a family, only that the process of getting children is not enjoyable to her," deStoeckl said. "William blames it on her religion."

"He blames everything on religion," said Madelaine quietly. "He says it is the root of war and punitive law, because it forbids reason."

"Who can dispute that?" asked the Baron, showing no signs of shock.

"Those of abiding faith," Madelaine said, and added, "though he would say that abiding faith is only the result of fear."

"So he would. And he and his wife would argue." Baron deStoeckl nodded twice. "I have seen it happen more than once."

"Tell me what she is like, how she conducts herself," said Madelaine. "He will not say much about her except to tell me that his dedication to his marriage is unbreakable."

"Does that trouble you, Madame? His marriage?" asked the Russian, his face growing sharp with his demand as he stubbed out his cigarette. "Given his opposition to religion?"

"Only in that I do not know why he is so determined to ... to keep to a marriage which may not be happy for either of them, since religion is not his reason for it. Oh, not that I wish to be the cause of the marriage ending. Quite the reverse in fact. It would be extremely difficult to see him through any failure, let alone one so important to him as his marriage. If he held me responsible for the end of the marriage, it would be intolerable." This was more bluntly put than she wished it to be, and she did her best to modify the severity of her observation. "I do not presume to know the whole of it. I realize I am not privy to more than one side of the tale, and at a time when his discontent may be higher than it ordinarily is."

"William has a strong sense of duty, Madame, and order," Baron deStoeckl stood still behind the divan where Madelaine sat. He looked at her dark hair as if to penetrate her thoughts. "Why do you want to know?"

"Because I do not wish to add to his distress when I leave," said Madelaine, turning to look up at the Baron, "which will be toward the end of October if Ellen Sherman does not come back to San Francisco before then. If she returns, I will not remain in San Francisco, but will depart at once. I have already made the necessary arrangements and can put them into effect in two days." She regarded him seriously. "It would make things unbearably uncomfortable for him to have both of us here at the same time."

"And for you?" inquired deStoeckl astutely.

"I would not like to add to his unsettled state, which my remaining here would surely do," she said with such candor that deStoeckl could not help but be impressed. "It would not benefit me, or him."

"Dear me. Are you always so noble of heart, Madame?" There was no sting in the question, no hint of condemnation for bad behavior on her part.

"I am not noble of heart, Baron; I love him. And no matter what happens between us, nothing will change it; I will love him until ... I die." She said this matter-of-factly, without any dramatic flourish, and for that reason alone, deStoeckl believed her.

"How certain we are when we are young," murmured the Baron, and made his way back to his own chair.

"This is not the certainty of youth, Baron, but the teaching of experience," said Madelaine with asperity. "I know my face is youthful, but I am not."

"So William has hinted," said deStoeckl.

"What has he said?" asked Madelaine, in spite of her intention not to.

DeStoeckl gave a cat-like smile. "Only that you were more fascinating than any girl could be; he attributes this to your love of study, among other things, including that you are French and have traveled abroad extensively." He leaned forward. "I have given him my word to reveal nothing about his dealings with you, and I will not, not even to you, Madame."

She nodded. "I accept that, and thank you for it," she told him, wondering how much Sherman had confided in his Russian friend. "I hope you will stand by him when I am not here; he will need to confide in you, I think."

"No doubt he will want to. I hope he will do so in the event. Little as he may suppose it now." The Baron folded his hands in his lap, and spoke to the far corner of the room to avoid looking at Madelaine. "For all he claims he is prepared for your leaving, he will miss you more than he realizes when you are gone."

"If he will not resent his missing me, so much the better," said Madelaine, "for I will miss him as I would miss life itself."

"But you will leave, nonetheless?" deStoeckl challenged her politely.

"Yes. It would be too painful to have him come to distrust or hate me, for he would be likely to suffer from dividing his loyalty. And he would come to that, if he felt he had to choose between his family and me. It would be like him to think he had to make such a choice." She got up from the divan. "You have been very generous, Baron, for the time you have spared me."

"Nothing more?" asked deStoeckl. "You have no other questions regarding my friend William?"

"Not at the moment," said Madelaine.

"Then permit me to offer you a few observations of my own," said the Baron, motioning her back to the divan, and scowling with the intensity of his thoughts. "Believe me that I make this suggestion from friendship for you and William, with no other motive than—"

"Well enough," said Madelaine, interrupting him. "I absolve you from ulterior motives, Baron. Say what you want me to hear." She looked over at him, her manner calm and self-possessed.

He lit another cigarette and looked up into the smoke as if he might find answers there. "I think one of the reasons William came here, so far from Ohio, was to try to break the hold that the Ewings have on him and his wife. I think he hoped to show himself capable of being his own man, without need of Ewing sponsorship in the world, which saved him when his father died, and which has nagged him ever since, gratitude often being the most unbearable burden of all. And I think Ellen is afraid of what would happen, should William succeed in winning free of her father's influence." He regarded Madelaine narrowly as he rose and strode around the end of the divan to face her. "You are something he never anticipated in his well-ordered plans, something he desires and dreads. You are freedom from the burden he has carried. You offer release from many obligations, and he is drawn to you for that as much as he is drawn to you for passion. But with you he could never fully vindicate his … honor. He would never truly be free of the spectre of Thomas Ewing, if he cannot prove himself in his marriage." He lowered his gaze. "I do not wish to offend you, Madame, but you came to me …"

"So I did," said Madelaine, no trace of embarrassment in her demeanor. "I am not offended. And I am grateful for your comments."

"They cannot be entirely welcome," said the Baron diffidently.

"No, they are not, but I thank you for them nonetheless," said Madelaine. "Without them, I would be less able to prepare."

"I hope you feel so in time to come," said deStoeckl. "For I have never been more your friend than now."

"I realize that," said Madelaine. "And I am grateful." She cocked her head to the side. "Anything more, Baron?"

"Only that I think you are much too good for him," said deStoeckl directly.

"That's not an issue," Madelaine told him, starting to rise.

DeStoeckl came to her side and took her hand. "He is a most fortunate man, though he may not know it."

"You are most kind, Baron, both to advise me and to compliment me so," she said in her best social form.

"It is always a pleasure to have your company, Madame," said the Baron, going to open the pocket-door for her. "With your permission, I will mention your visit to William when I see him later today, though I will keep your confidence as to our conversation. I don't want him to learn of this visit from other sources. Much as he would deny it, he would be jealous if he thought we met clandestinely."

"Do as you think best, Baron. I have confidence in your good sense, and your tact," she responded as she reached for her short cape, letting him settle it on her shoulders before she looked for her hat, which lay on a table in the entry hall. She fixed it in place with two long pins and smiled at her host, assuring him once more, "It was good of you to talk with me."

"My pleasure, Madame," he said, bowing. Then he rang for his man-servant and instructed him to bring Madelaine's housekeeper from the kitchen. "Tell her Madame de Montalia has finished her business with me."

"Very nicely done," Madelaine approved. As they waited for Olga, Madelaine added, "I doubt he'll tell me when his wife is planning to return; it would be too much like a conspiracy between us. If you hear anything..."

"I will send you word of it at once," deStoeckl finished for her, and raised her hand to his lips.

Olga appeared at the rear of the corridor, adjusting her shawl around her shoulders. "The cook here has shown me an excellent dish," she said in her accented English. "I will prepare it for your next guests, Madame." She had recently given up all attempts at cooking for her employer, and reserved her skills for those few occasions when Madelaine entertained.

"How good of you, Olga," said Madelaine, also in English. "Thank you once again, Baron. I appreciate all your advice."

"I am yours to command, Madame de Montalia," he assured her as he opened the door for her.

SAN FRANCISCO, 19 AUGUST, 1855

*There have been a number of reviews of the garrison. General Hitchcock
organized them, or so I understand, as a way of reminding the people of
the city that order will be kept, no matter what excitement may seize the
populace. These have been greeted with enthusiasm. Even Henry Haight,
who is a very bitter man these days, has said he approves of these elegant shows of force, and cheers with the rest when the soldiers ride by.
Tecumseh watches these displays with his military friends, and longs to
be in uniform once again himself. He has been promoting the idea of a
state militia as the means of policing this city, and a few of the others
where mobs have taken over the control of the streets and the courts.*

*I have found the records of some accounts of the Indians of the West,
and I am determined to read them as I make my plans to travel. I am
told that many of the Indians who keep to their own lands have been
visited by missionaries and teachers, which means that my opportunity
to learn about the traditions of the Indians is fading rapidly. In another
generation the missionaries will have taught the Indians to be ashamed
of their old ways, and it will be difficult for any scholar to learn of the
way they used to practice their traditions without that shame coloring
their remarks and recollections. For a time I thought I was acting too
hastily in my study, but I can see that I could already be too late.*

*... Tecumseh has kept away from me for more than a week, without
any explanation or excuse offered for breaking two of our engagements,
one of which was to inspect land north of the Golden Gate, near the old
Mission of San Rafael; I did not look forward to taking a ship on the
bay, but I was prepared. Yet he did not come. When I task him for his
absence, he tells me he does not want to have any greater risk of compromising me by passing even a part of the night with me, but I suspect
he is feeling the strain of desire at war with duty, as such considerations
have not kept him away before now. For in that sense, I think deStoeckl
is quite right: Tecumseh has a great sense of duty, and I have upset it.
Therefore he denies himself as a way to deny me. I suppose he will punish me for as long as he fears he may be still susceptible to me...*

"ETHAN ALLAN HITCHCOCK, at your service, Madame, and my thanks for your most gracious invitation," said the General as he came into Madelaine's front parlor; he was being escorted by Julian Small, the English butler Madelaine had hired for the evening, taking him from his usual employment as head waiter at the restaurant of the Bella Union Casino. The General shrugged out of his coaching coat and surrendered his hat to the butler's care, all the while smiling at his hostess.

"You're most welcome, General," said Madelaine, and indicated her other guests. "I think you know everyone?"

"Indeed I do," he said, and went to Fanny Kent, shaking her hand as was his habit with married women. "How good to see you all," he told the gathering at large.

"Ungracious people may say any spiteful thing they wish," Fanny declared to General Hitchcock, one hand clasped to her magnificent bosom now splendidly displayed in deep blue taffeta. "I will not condemn Madame de Montalia's party. Where is the impropriety in her entertaining?"

"Good of you," said Joseph Folsom, his irony entirely lost on its object; Fanny beamed at what she understood as a compliment.

General Hitchcock passed on to greet two other officers in uniform, and was not witness to the arrival, soon after, of Baron deStoeckl and William Tecumseh Sherman.

"I am sorry we are late," said the Baron as he kissed Madelaine's hand. "It was unavoida—"

"The children needed my attention," Sherman interrupted gruffly. "I did not want them to be slighted by my departure."

"And you did not like to leave until you were satisfied they were well," said Madelaine, wholly unflustered by his manner.

He stared at her, clearly affronted. "Well, with their mother away, I could not neglect—"

"Mister Sherman," said Madelaine calmly, "We are in agreement. I think it is most laudable that you concern yourself with your children's welfare. How many children would rejoice in so conscientious a father."

He did not respond to this but made his way into the parlor, clearly relieved to see the evening so well-attended.

"Forgive him, Madame. He is most sorely vexed," whispered the Russian before following Sherman into the room. "He says it is apprehension for Lizzie and Willy, but I do not believe him."

Madelaine gestured her understanding, then turned to her hired butler. "Julian, please inform the kitchen that we will want to sit down in
half an hour. Have the staff check the table one last time."

Julian bowed slightly, and left to follow her instructions.

There was another knock on the door, and Madelaine hurried to
answer it herself. She found Colonel and Missus Thomas waiting to be
admitted. "How good of you to come," she said as she held the door
wide for them. "Please, enter and be welcome."

"Had trouble getting here," said Colonel Thomas by way of apology,
and to account for their dusty coats and his wife's disarranged hair. "The
carriage broke a wheel on California Street and crashed; we had to come
the rest of the way in a hired vehicle."

"I'm sorry to hear it," said Madelaine, recalling a few times in the past
when a broken carriage wheel or a lame horse had made reaching a destination questionable at best. "I trust you are not too much put upon?"

Colonel Thomas indicated his wife, who was noticeably pregnant.
"It was more a problem for Amanda than for me. Tumbling out of the
carriage like that has shaken her up quite a bit." He took the cloak from
her shoulders and held it over his arm, not wanting to commit the gaffe
of handing it to his hostess.

"Are you well, Missus Thomas?" asked Madelaine, noticing that under her hat, Amanda Thomas was very pale. "Were you injured?" She
sensed the other woman was bleeding. "Have you been cut?"

"She had a nasty bruise," said her husband, his bluff manner unsuc-
cessful in concealing his worry for her.

"I ... don't think so ... I will be better soon," she said quietly.

Julian came back down the corridor from the kitchen, frowning at
the newly arrived guests. "Let me take the coats," he said, his English
accent very pronounced, as if to add to his disapproval.

Colonel Thomas was more than willing to hand them over; that done,
he gave his full attention to his wife. "What is the matter, my dear? Are
you faint? Shall I get you a cordial?"

"Would you like to lie down?" asked Madelaine at the same time.
"Come. I have a second room where you may be comfortable." She motioned to the Colonel to join the rest in the parlor as she put her arm
around Amanda, and started with her toward the stairs. "You may lean
on me, Missus Thomas; I am not one of those fragile women who totter
under the weight of a shopping basket."

"Madame," said Julian in a repressive manner.

"Seat the guests when dinner is ready, Julian," said Madelaine over her shoulder. "Do not delay serving for me. I will return as soon as I am certain that Missus Thomas will be herself again."

"As you wish, Madame," said Julian, with a nice mix of subservience and disapproval.

"There is no need for you to—" said Amanda Thomas faintly as she made her way painfully up the stairs, hanging onto both Madelaine and the banister for support. Her face was blank but her eyes shone with pain. As she reached the top of the stairs, she clung to the newel post and took several long, uneven breaths. "I won't need long—You do not need—"

"There is every reason for me to be concerned for the welfare of guests in my house," Madelaine countered affably. "I will be much more at ease once I assure myself that you are restored."

"I am doing well enough," Amanda protested weakly.

They reached the second floor, and Madelaine turned Amanda toward the front of the house where she had a room made up for guests. As she opened the door, she moved Amanda to the side of the bed, then went to light the oil lamp on the bedside table. "Here," she said as she lowered the flame to a soft glow.

"What a pleasant room," said Amanda, her breath coming sharply.

Madelaine noted this with dismay; she did her best to appear unruffled by Amanda's worsening condition. "If you will lie down, I will remove your shoes for you. I find I am better when my feet do not hurt."

"Yes, I have noticed that, as well," said Amanda breathlessly as she reached for the brass bedstead.

Madelaine moved swiftly to assist her, her remarkable strength permitting her to lift Amanda onto the bed with ease. "How many months?" she asked as she helped Amanda to stretch out.

"Not quite six," said Amanda, her face shining with sweat. "I think that the fall, when the wheel broke, has...done some damage."

"How severe is your pain?" Madelaine asked at once, coming to Amanda's side and looking down into her face.

"Not...great pain," she lied heroically. "It will go off soon."

"Do you need a composer? I have laudanum and cognac," she offered, thinking that she had something in the cellar that would help more than either laudanum or cognac would.

"Thank you, Madame. It will not be necessary. If I could just lie here for a short while, I will...improve."

Madelaine was not as certain as Amanda was; she put her hand on Amanda's forehead and was shocked to find it very cold. With growing apprehension she touched Amanda's neck, and discovered her pulse there fast and thin. "I think it would be best to loosen your stays, so that you can relax; no doubt it will do you good not to be so tightly bound in. You can have my housekeeper help you dress again when you are rested," she suggested with a self-possession she did not feel.

"Thank you," whispered Amanda, and rolled heavily onto her side so that Madelaine could unfasten her bodice. "I'm sorry to cause you so much trouble."

It was then Madelaine saw the blood which soaked her skirts, turning the dark brown velvet to a matted, dark shine. She knew that it was worse than she had thought at first; there was too much blood and it was still coming. "Missus Thomas," said Madelaine very carefully, "are you suffering any cramping just now?" She busied herself with loosening the bodice.

"A...a little." She turned her head to look at Madelaine; tiny rivulets of sweat ran into her eyes and she made an ineffective attempt to wipe them away. "Don't tell my husband, will you? Say you will not. It will only serve to worry him, and I don't want—"

"Perhaps, but I think he had better be told that you are not well," said Madelaine with as much persuasion as she could muster without adding to Amanda's alarm.

"Please do not," panted Amanda.

"I...I fear I must say something to him," Madelaine said. "There is some sign of blood, Missus Thomas, and I think your husband would want your doctor to see you."

"Oh." Her voice was very soft. She sighed once, and asked in an undertone, "Is it really necessary?"

"I am afraid it is," said Madelaine, adding, "Take off the bodice. You will feel better once I get your stays—" Amanda stifled a cry and bent double at the waist, her face contorted with pain. "It...it...too soon."

"I fear you are right," said Madelaine, trying to ease Amanda onto her side once again. "Once your stays are undone, you will be able to rest," she promised, adding as she hurriedly worked the laces, "I will ask my man-of-all-work to carry a message for you to your doctor."

Amanda just nodded, too consumed with suffering to speak.

Now that Amanda's stays were released, Madelaine gave her attention to the blood that continued to spread through the muslin petticoats and into the velvet of her dinner gown.

A tactful cough from the door claimed Madelaine's attention; Olga stood there, her face somber. She held a second oil lamp in her hands, and she carried a large towel folded over her arm.

"Olga, you come in good time," said Madelaine, relieved that she would not have to leave Amanda alone. "Missus Thomas has injured herself, as you can see, and I am urging her to send for her doctor." She gestured to Olga, encouraging her to second this notion.

"It might be best. So I think," agreed the housekeeper with a significant nod toward Amanda's bloody petticoats. "You will need help with this." And she handed Madelaine the towel.

"Indeed I will," said Madelaine with feeling. "First, I want Christian to go fetch Missus Thomas' doctor." She leaned over the stricken woman. "Who tends you, Missus Thomas?" she asked.

"Uh … Doctor Lowrey. He is on Sacramento Street, near the corner of Yerba Buena, at the crest of the street." She moaned and her teeth began to chatter. "I'm sorry. I didn't mean to cause such trouble."

"You heard her," said Madelaine. "Doctor Lowrey, on Sacramento, near Yerba Buena. He should be able to get there in fifteen minutes. If the doctor moves quickly, they could return within the hour." She looked directly at Olga. "Tell Christian to leave at once. When you return, bring the tall, amber bottle from the basement. It has a seal on it impressed with the shape of a hippopotamus."

"Yes, Madame," said Olga with a quick, short curtsy before hurrying off to carry out Madelaine's orders.

"I should be better shortly. You need not stay … " Amanda whispered as Madelaine handed her a comforter to pull around her shoulders. "Oh, thank you. I am so cold."

"You wrap up in that; it should serve you well enough. Lie back." Madelaine had no doubt that the woman was miscarrying, but did not know how to tell her. More important, she thought, was to keep Amanda from bleeding to death. She took the toweling and pressed it into a thick bolster, then said to Amanda, "Let me put this between your legs. It will ease the cramping."

Amanda held the comforter tightly under her chin, and nodded.

As carefully as she could, Madelaine loosened Amanda's sodden petticoats and lifted them so that she could place the bolster between Amanda's legs. "Like getting into the saddle astride," she remarked as she heard Amanda groan with the effort. "It will lessen the discomfort shortly."

"I ... feel so ... dizzy ..." muttered Amanda.

"Hardly surprising," said Madelaine, doing her best to keep the grimness out of her voice. "Lie still, Missus Thomas. My housekeeper will bring you something to ease your pain directly."

A short while later, as she frowned with the effort of keeping the rolled towel in place, Amanda asked, "Is there ... any more ... blood?"

"Yes, some," Madelaine answered, knowing it would be senseless to dissemble.

"Oh, dear," whispered Amanda, and began to cry, her sobs more like whimpers. She pressed the knuckles of her free hand to her eyes as if to keep her tears from coming. "I will ... lose the baby ... won't I?"

It was difficult for Madelaine to answer. "I am afraid so," she said, not at all certain it would be possible to save Amanda Thomas.

"Don't ... don't tell ... Colonel Thomas," Amanda said, her words barely audible. She pressed her face into the pillow and began to weep in earnest.

Madelaine put her hand on Amanda's shoulder. "I'm very sorry, Missus Thomas," she told her.

All the answer she received was more tears as Amanda Thomas began to mourn.

A few minutes later, Olga returned, carrying a tray bearing the bottle Madelaine had asked for as well as a crockery basin of steaming water, a pile of clean cheesecloths, a bottle of spirits, and a china cup. "Christian is on his way, Madame, and your guests are just sitting down to eat. I told Julian to announce that you are still attending Missus Thomas. If you wish me to carry a note to Colonel Thomas, I will have Julian hand it to him."

"Very good," Madelaine approved. "And thank you for all you have done." She reached for the bottle and pried off the seal, then glanced at Amanda once more. "I will need to give you something to drink, Missus Thomas," she said, speaking carefully. "It will make you feel better."

Amanda turned a tear-mottled face to Madelaine and regarded her with a passivity that worried Madelaine more than the rest of her symptoms combined.

"Drink?" she asked, almost lazily.

"Yes. To stop the bleeding. It has a sharp taste that you may not entirely like, but it will help you, if you will drink it," Madelaine went on,

63

knowing she was nattering. She poured out some of the pale golden liquid into the small cup Olga had brought, and leaned down to help Amanda sip from it.

"Dreadful," complained Amanda before she took a second sip, and a third. Her eyes were slightly unfocused and she moved awkwardly, as if her limbs were not wholly her own.

"Finish it, Missus Thomas," Madelaine urged, and tipped the cup to a steeper angle.

Olga put her tray down on the dresser that stood beside the window. "What do you want me to do, Madame?"

"Bring me notepaper first," said Madelaine, watching Amanda narrowly. "Much as I would rather not, I must inform Colonel Thomas what is happening." She wiped her forehead, smoothing her coffee-colored hair back. "He will have to authorize Doctor Lowrey to treat his wife when he arrives."

"I have the paper here, and a pencil for you." Olga took both from the capacious pocket in her apron.

"You are a godsend," Madelaine declared. She spread the paper on the nightstand next to the lamp and scribbled two hasty sentences: "Colonel Thomas, I regret to inform you that your wife has miscarried. I will remain with her until Doctor Lowrey arrives. M. de M." This done, she folded the note twice and handed it to Olga. "Here. Tell Julian to deliver it to Colonel Thomas at once."

"Of course, Madame," said Olga, and went off immediately.

Madelaine stood beside the bed, her thoughts in turmoil. How long would it take the liquid to work? And Saint-Germain had never said how long it would be effective. What if Amanda Thomas was too far gone for any help? Madelaine had seen enough blood over the last century to know that the woman lying in her guest bed was dangerously depleted of it. She reached out and put her hand on Amanda's neck again, noticing how erratic her heartbeat was. It would be sensible to look at the toweling between Amanda's legs to see how much more she had bled, but it seemed to be impossible to make herself do it.

When Olga came back, she told Madelaine that the note was being handed to Colonel Thomas as they spoke. "Julian wanted to know if there is anything you need him to do."

This offer surprised Madelaine, who had not thought that Julian had any sympathy for his fellow-creatures, let alone this unfortunate woman. "Not yet. Doctor Lowrey may require his help, however. I would appreciate it if you would tell him. Not just now," she went on reluctantly. "Now I think we ought to see how … the bleeding is."

Olga paled but ducked her head. "Yes. We will have to wash Missus Thomas's legs if she is to be ready for Doctor Lowrey's care."

"Yes," said Madelaine, and moved the wad of petticoats aside. She saw at once that part of the towel was saturated with blood. Carefully she moved it, saying, "Let me check this toweling, Missus Thomas."

"Go ahead," she murmured, and feebly lifted her leg.

Madelaine dreaded what she assumed she would see; to her astonishment there was very little new bleeding. Quickly she checked the pulse in Amanda's neck; satisfied that there was still a faint beating of her heart, she withdrew the towel and asked Olga to hand her the cheesecloth. "This is better, I think," she said, trying to recall everything Saint-Germain had told her about the golden liquid in the amber bottle.

"She isn't …" Olga's voice was very low, and she averted her eyes from the bloody towel.

"I don't think so, not now, in any case," said Madelaine. "Put this aside so that Doctor Lowrey can examine it when he arrives." She folded the cheesecloth tightly and slipped it back between Amanda's legs. "This will be less … intrusive," she said as she pulled the petticoats away and set the comforter in place around Amanda.

Then a sharp knock on the door demanded her attention. "Madame de Montalia?" called Colonel Thomas from just outside the door.

"Colonel," said Madelaine, a curious mixture of apprehension and the desire for extrication welling within her. "Do you wish to come in?"

"Would it help?" asked the Colonel uncertainly.

"No," said Amanda quietly. "No."

Madelaine indicated to Olga she should come to Amanda's side. "I will have a word with her husband. I won't be long," she said, and slipped out of the room to confront Colonel Thomas. She knew her appearance would not reassure the man, so she did her best to behave as if nothing were out of hand. "You had my note."

"Yes," said Colonel Thomas with consternation. "You alarm me greatly." He looked into her face. "I don't suppose you can be mistaken about …"

"The miscarriage? I fear not. I am very sorry." She coughed once, softly. "Her doctor will tell you more when he has had a chance to examine her."

"Certainly," said Colonel Thomas, trying to grasp what he was being told. "How is she?"

"Very weak," said Madelaine.

"Not...beyond remedy?" It was more a plea than a question.

"No, I don't think so," said Madelaine, trying to infuse optimism into her voice. "I have hope for her."

"Thank God for that," exclaimed the Colonel, his voice catching with the force of his contained emotion; then went on with greater propriety. "I am very grateful to you for all you have done."

"No, no," said Madelaine hastily. "I am sorry I was not able to help save the child." It was true; Madelaine was not yet used to the brevity of life as most lived it, and when so directly confronted with mortality, she could not help but feel it as a sadness that carried a portion of guilt that she should continue her life while countless others lost theirs.

But Colonel Thomas was speaking. "...any woman so young could deal with so great an emergency."

Madelaine motioned him away. "I'm sorry, Colonel. I have to get back..." And with that, she slipped away from him, returning to sit with Amanda while she struggled to live.

SAN FRANCISCO, 30 AUGUST, 1855

Amanda Thomas has asked me to call upon her next week; I have accepted her invitation, only because I have been told it would be thought a slight if I refused; as if I blamed her for the supposed failure of my dinner party. How could she think that? So I will go and reassure her that I do not hold her accountable for what happened. As if she could determine when she would miscarry, and did it deliberately for the sole purpose of causing me social embarrassment...I do not want her to burden herself with so ludicrous a notion, so I will visit her, although she probably should not be receiving guests yet. She is said to be recovering slowly, which is to be expected after such an ordeal.

I do not yet know if I have recovered from the experience. It was as if I had never seen anyone die before, or was cognizant how fragile life can be. That poor woman, who wanted only to have a child, lost it and very nearly herself along with it. How harrowing it was, watching her become more and more pale, knowing that she could easily die and noth-

ing I could do would change it. For two days afterwards I was rattled, and even now, I find myself harkening back to that evening, my thoughts wholly preoccupied with what transpired. This has slowed my work on my book. I have not yet completed my chapter on the Utes, which I had thought I would have finished by the end of this month, and which I now realize is impossible.

Fanny Kent has called here twice since that evening, determined to renew her sense of shock and amazement. At each recounting, her horror increases; one would think that she endured more than Amanda Thomas. Luckily she has only fainted once, and that was the actual evening of Missus Thomas's miscarriage; she collapsed when Doctor Lowrey arrived and without ceremony inquired of Julian where his patient was and if she was still alive. If I did not know how great Missus Kent's distress was that evening, I would have to suppose she was enjoying herself, so eager is she to relive it.

I have yesterday received from Colonel Thomas copies of maps of the former Mexican Territories now in United States possession. He has given them to me as a token of gratitude for the aid I rendered his wife, and to aid me in my travels through the wilderness when I resume traveling in another two months. He has also warned me that great expanses of the territory have not been explored, and that he cannot tell me what dangers might be encountered in those places. I have taken time to study these maps in order to acquaint myself with the trails I might reasonably expect to travel as I go south and east.

... In the last ten days I have seen Tecumseh once, and that was in his carriage with his children, taking them on an outing to the Chinese market where Willy had purchased a paper kite in the shape of a dragon's head, which he was attempting to fly off the back of the carriage. Tecumseh was meticulously polite, doing nothing that anyone could construe as paying untoward attention to me, but his eyes were haunted. Why he should be so distant now, I do not know, but it saddens me ...

RAIN WAS TURNING THE STREETS from dust to mud as the afternoon wound down toward night. Along the streets, lamps were being lit early to stave off the coming darkness as the first storm of autumn whipped over the hills.

Madelaine sat at her desk, busying herself with writing, when she heard the knocker on the front door. She looked up, annoyed at the interruption, recalling that Olga had taken the afternoon and evening off in order to talk with a man who claimed to know where her sister and her sister's husband had gone; she hoped he would be able to tell her how to reach them. Clicking her tongue impatiently, Madelaine blotted her half-finished page and reached to pull a vast woolen shawl around her shoulders before hurrying to the front of the house to answer the urgent summons.

"Madelaine," said William Tecumseh Sherman as the door swung open. He was wet and bedraggled, his hair quenched of fire and rain-slicked to his skull. He glanced over his shoulder at the street. "May I come in? Will you let me?"

"Tecumseh," said Madelaine, holding the door wider. "Welcome."

His head continued bowed; he hesitated, and asked in a whisper, "You are willing to speak to me? After my inexcusable behavior?"

Perplexed, Madelaine stepped aside to admit him. "Certainly. Come in. You have done nothing that would keep me from knowing you. What do you want?" It was the only question that came clearly to mind, and it was out before she could soften or modify it in any way.

He pressed the door closed quickly. "I don't think anyone saw me," he said cautiously.

"Possibly not," said Madelaine, her bafflement increasing as she looked at him. "You are soaked to the skin."

"It doesn't matter," he said, squaring his shoulders and daring to look directly into her violet eyes. "I have been a fool and a coward, and I wouldn't blame you if you tossed me out on my ass."

Had she truly been as young as she looked, Madelaine might have taken advantage of his offer; as it was she shook her head. "No. I have a few questions I hope you will answer before I do that." She indicated the way to the parlor.

"Thank you, Madame," he said with unwonted humility. He turned and locked the door himself, leaning against it as if he had been pursued by the hounds of hell. "Let me say what I must, Madelaine; if you stop me my courage may fail me and then I will be thrice-damned." He looked directly at her, but kept his voice quite low. "I have chastised myself every day for not coming to you, and with every passing day it grew more difficult to act at all. I have all but convinced myself that you do not wish to see me because of my cravenness. So I must come to you now, or mire hopelessly in my own inaction. Poor Hamlet had to bear with the same trouble, in his way; I don't think I ever grasped the full range of his predicament until now." He passed a hand over his eyes. "I'm maundering. Forgive me; I don't want to do that." He straightened up, and moved a few steps to stand directly in front of her. "I'm no stranger to suffering. I have not yet fought a war, but I have seen men fall of fatal wounds in Seminole ambushes, and I have held my comrades while they bled to death, so that they would not be wholly alone."

"What has that to do with you and me?" asked Madelaine, growing confused.

"Let me continue," he said forcefully. "There are things I should have said to you days ago."

She realized how determined he was and made a gesture of acquiescence. "If you think it is necessary, go on."

Sherman took a stance as if to fend off attack. "It was the loss of that unborn baby that flummoxed me. You would think that one who is...or, rather, has been a soldier would not have such weakness, but I have no resources against that loss. It is the most unbearable of all losses to me, the loss of a child." He held up his hands to stop any protests she might make. "Oh, yes, it was not yet a child, but it had come far enough that their hopes were fixed on it. And that is bad enough. When I try to think of how I would feel if ever I should lose Minnie or Lizzie...or Willy, I have no words to express it, so utterly despairing is the prospect. What the Thomases endured routed me as superior force and material could not." Now he looked away, unwilling to let Madelaine see the shine of tears in his eyes. "I...could say nothing to console them, or to support your purpose. And I became ashamed, because I fear that, in the same situation, I would not have had the presence of mind to do all you did."

"Tecumseh..." Madelaine said gently, searching for a phrase to end his self-condemnation.

He fixed her with his gaze, determined to admit all his faults. "You were so cool and self-possessed all through the calamity, that I—"

"I may have appeared that way to you, but I was far from feeling so, believe me," she said, hoping to turn him away from his continued abasement. "You have no reason to cast me in such an angelic role. I am still unnerved by what happened."

"No one would have known it," he said with feeling that was partly disbelief, and partly pride. "If that's true, you conducted yourself like a good officer, Madelaine." This was the highest praise he could give her.

"If that's true and it's useful, then it pleases me." She tried to smile and nearly succeeded. "Well, I will consider myself fortunate that I have some poise, and I will tell you I am grateful to you for holding it in high regard. Let me get you a cup of coffee, or something to eat."

"No," he insisted. "I am not yet finished, and I am not hungry." He put his hands together so that he would not be tempted to reach out to her. "It was inexcusable of me not to offer you any succor I could provide; it haunts me every hour that I failed you. You cannot blame me more than I blame myself."

"Doubtless," she said dryly.

"My only excuse is that I was filled with anxiety about my own children, and have kept close to them these past several days, so that I can guard them from all harm. Don't tell me that their dangers are nothing like the misfortune that befell the Thomas's baby. I know that. I know that, but knowing means nothing when one fears for his children. That fear is all-encompassing, and knowledge has no weight against it." He stopped abruptly, then said more formally, "I am sorry I deserted you. I should have been here to uphold you. I regret that I did not give you the consolation I might have been able to provide." He faltered, struggling to finish. "I . . . I was tremendously proud of you for all you did, and how well you did it."

It would have been easy to give him a facile answer, Madelaine realized; it would also shut him away from her as no barred door would do. She considered her response carefully. "I know it is hard for you to say these things to me."

"As it should be," he agreed with self-disgust.

"The more so because you have taken all the responsibility upon yourself, as if you were the only person who might have aided me," said Madelaine, her understanding of him making this a precarious revelation.

"But I am . . . your lover," he protested. "You yourself say there is a bond between us."

"And so there is," she said, "Which is why I do not hold you in the contempt you dread and hope I might. My sensibilities are not so delicate that I must have constant reassurance for my—"

His supplication gave way to aggravation. "For heaven's sake, Madame, get angry with me. Denounce me for my desertion. Rail at me for not coming to you before now. Tell me what a poltroon you think me."

"But I don't wish to do any of those things," she said reasonably as she attempted to move nearer to him without upsetting him. "I think you are what you say you are; a father who is worried about the mortality of his family. I think you have taken the Thomas's loss very much to heart and it has made you apprehensive and fretful on your children's behalf."

He nodded, the first dawning of hope in his steel-colored eyes. "There is some truth in that."

"The more so because you have castigated yourself for things I had not held against you. The accusations you made against yourself are of your own creation, not mine. I do not hold you to the account you hold yourself. And just as well, given the catalogue of offenses you have conjured for yourself." She went and stood next to him, not quite touching him. "You have assumed I would not recognize your desire to protect your family, and would expect you to devote yourself to me."

"As I should have done," he interjected harshly.

"You may think so; I do not." She put her hand on his shoulder, noticing again how wet he was, then looked up into his face. "Tecumseh, listen to me: I will not deny that I would have liked you with me, for I would have. I was … distressed by Missus Thomas's loss, and it upset me that it should happen at my house, and I could do nothing to prevent it, or to spare her any—"

"Robert Lowrey said you saved her life," Sherman told her. "Without your care, she would surely have bled to death."

"Possibly," said Madelaine, her doubts returning full force. "I had little or no opportunity to consult Doctor Lowrey, and so tried to do what I could without guidance or instruction of any kind." This was less than the truth, for Saint-Germain had long since tutored her on the use of the medicaments in the urns, jars and bottles he had provided her three decades ago; she had not been put to this test before but was better prepared for it than most qualified nurses.

"Not without guidance, according to Lowrey: whatever you gave her saved her life." He favored her with gruff approval. "At the time, I wanted to say how wonderful you are, and how proud I am of you. But that would have revealed far too much. It would be poor recompense to tarnish your reputation while crediting you with uncommon bravery." He put his hand over hers where it rested on his shoulder. "I am taking a chance coming here now. Your housekeeper might—"

"My housekeeper has the day off, and will not be back until later this evening. I have told her she does not need to look in on me; she may go directly to her apartment and retire. My man-of-all-work is dining with his cousin's family." She smiled at him.

71

He did not return the smile. "You mean they have left you alone? With all you have been through?" he demanded. "What kind of servants do you have, Madame, that they will leave you by yourself?"

Now Madelaine grew impatient. "What nonsense you talk, Tecumseh," she said with asperity. "You would think I am a hot-house flower, incapable of fending for myself, when you should realize I have managed on my own for decades."

"Visiting Indians," he said, determined to make his point.

"Among others," she responded, refusing to be dragged into another dispute with him.

"Oh, yes; those travels in Egypt," he grumbled. "Hard going, no doubt."

"They were," she said. "Some of the time. The expedition was a small one, and we were four hundred miles up the Nile." With these few words, she recalled the heat and the endless sand that was everywhere; she remembered the Nile at flood, and the profusion of insects and vermin that came with the water; she saw the faces of Falke and Trowbrige and the Coptic monk Erai Gurzin, and the death of Professor Baundilet.

"What is it?" Sherman asked, reading something of her memories on her face. "What's the matter?"

"Nothing," she said. "It's all in the past, all behind me." She shook off the hold of the memories and made herself pay closer attention to him. "Your hand is like ice," she said, noticing how chilled he was becoming. "You're wet to the skin. You may not want any food, but you need to get warm and clean once again."

"It doesn't matter," he claimed.

"It does if you are taken ill because of it; I have had my fill of medical crises, and want none of that from you," she said briskly, and slipped her hand from under his, but only to seize it and lead him through the gloom of her house to the curtained alcove off the kitchen where her bathtub was kept. "I will start heating the water right now," she declared as she went to the stove and stirred the embers to life. She pulled two sections of wood from the box near the stove and put them, one on top of the other, on the glowing coals. "This will be hot shortly, the kitchen will be warm, and your bath will be ready in half an hour." She paused to hold out her hand to him again. "Do this for me, Tecumseh."

Sherman regarded her tenderly. "A bath. I wish I could stay for it," he said ruefully, his fingers lacing through hers.

"Do you tell me you will not?" she asked.

"I fear I must," he said by way of apology.

She closed the stove grate and put her hands on her hips. "And why can't you? And no farragoes, please, about my reputation. No one saw you come, and only I know you are here."

He looked somber. "My children are—"

"Your nurse is more than competent to care for them," said Madelaine, who had met the woman three times and had been impressed each time with her good sense and reliability. "And don't tell me you have never gone home later than expected."

"But—" he began, only to be cut short.

"You need to get warm and dry before venturing out in that weather; I will supply you with an oilskin against it. You would tell me the same if I had paid you a visit, and well you know it; you need not bother to say otherwise, no matter how you wish to persuade me." She looked hard at him, waiting for his answer.

"What would be the point?" Sherman said. "You wouldn't believe me if I did. And neither would I."

"Good; at least you will admit that much: we make progress," said Madelaine as she lifted the side of the curtain and took the first of four large pots from the shelf next to the bathtub. She carried this to the pump at the sink and began to work the handle to fill the pot.

"You're never going to be able to lift that," said Sherman, reaching out to lift it for her. "Let me carry it for you."

It was tempting to let him take the pot, but Madelaine kept her hold on the two handles and lifted the eight-gallon pot from the sink to the stove without effort. "Unnecessary; I can do it, thank you. I told you that those of my blood acquire extra strength, and this pot is a minor thing," she said, unwilling to permit him to claim otherwise, even if it were for no reason other than good manners.

"But it isn't fitting," Sherman protested as Madelaine reached for the second pot. "No, Madelaine. No; I can't allow it. You should not have to do such menial work, not while I am here to help you."

"Why not?" Madelaine asked, setting the pot in the deep sink and starting to work the pump handle once again. "What is the vice in menial work that you think I should disdain it? Why should anyone feel shame at doing necessary work? Don't tell me you have never filled a pot or carried one before now?"

"Of course I've done both," he blustered. "That's different."

"Because you did it?" Madelaine guessed, and shook her head. "Where did you learn such intolerance?"

He glared. "It is what everyone expects of well-bred men and women."

"Isn't that a bit extreme?" Madelaine asked. "To ask well-bred men and women to become dependant puppets requiring the labor of servants to make their way in the world?"

He did not answer her question, and stood, with an expression of distant blankness, staring at the two windows at the rear of the kitchen. The anemic light filtering into the kitchen banished most of the colors in the room, turning the figures of both Sherman and Madelaine a ghostly, washed-out shade of brownish-gray with pale beige faces. As if to banish this perception, Sherman shook himself and found the nearest of the kitchen lamps and a box of lucifers to light it with. As the flame rose, the kitchen seemed to warm with the return of colors. "There. That should make your task easier."

She did not point out that the increasing dusk made little difference to her; she saw in darkness almost as well as she saw in moderate light. Instead she nodded her thanks and carried the second pot to the stove while Sherman took the third from its shelf and set it in the sink under the pump, starting to ply the handle with vigor.

"The wood is catching, that will make everything warmer," she remarked as she glanced at the tinderbox of the stove.

Sherman continued to fill the third pot with water, then carried it to the stove, setting it in place without splashing a drop. "Since you are determined to do this, I suppose I ought to lend you my assistance."

"If you like," said Madelaine, handing him the fourth pot, and saying, "Just fill it with water." She tugged the curtain aside so that the bath alcove was completely open, revealing the large, enameled-copper tub and a wall of shelves where various requirements for bathing were placed. "I'll set out bath salts, if you want them. And I have a razor and shaving material, if you have need of them."

"You are always prepared," he said, intending it as a complaint, but making it into a compliment. "Yes, I will rid myself of this stubble," he said, and went on slyly, "or I might have to explain where all the scratches on your body came from. Since you insist on doing this. Perhaps I should grow a beard again."

Madelaine could not stop herself from smiling, knowing now that he would remain with her for several hours, if not all night. The weight of his absence lifted from her, and she said playfully, "In fact, given the circumstances, shaving would be the prudent thing to do."

"Prudent," he repeated ironically. "What a word to use for anything pertaining to you and me, Madelaine."

"All the more reason it is necessary," she said, satisfying herself that the tub would be ready when the water was hot. She set out two large sponges and a rough washing cloth on the rack next to the tub, and then pulled out a brass towel-rack. "I'll get a robe for you from the linen closet."

He extended his arm to block her progress and pulled her to him, bending to kiss her as his embrace enfolded her.

She shifted against his arm, then gave herself over to his caresses as if she had never before experienced them. Finally when she could speak at all, she said softly to him, "Tecumseh, I have no wish to compel you to do anything that displeases you."

"I know that," he said indulgently as he stroked her breasts through her clothes.

"You're distracting me," she objected without any determination to stop him.

"Good," he approved. "It's supposed to." His kiss was light and long, full of suggestions that made both of them breathless. "Why don't you let me help you out of that rig you've got on?"

"Tecumseh," she said again, making a last-ditch effort to keep from giving in to him. "You will not be angry, will you? For my turning you from your purpose?"

"Why should I be angry?" He kissed the corner of her mouth. "And what purpose do you mean? I wanted only to apologize for failing you."

"You mean you had not resolved to break off with me?" she asked.

He stared at her, a hint of defiance in his answer. "After what I have done, I am shocked that you are not angry with me." He reached up and pulled the long pins from the neat bun at the back of her neck. "That's better," he said, as he loosened her hair.

"I could not be angry with you, not when I have tasted your blood," she said.

"That again," he muttered; he became patiently courteous, all but bowing to her. "And why is that, Madame Vampire?"

"Because I know you, and I know what you are." She looked up at him, and read vexation in his eyes. "I know that you despise weakness, especially in yourself, and you often regard your feeling for me as weakness."

He looked at her in mild amazement. "How the devil—"

"It is your nature," Madelaine said swiftly. "It is intrinsic to your soul. You have decided that if you love me, you are weakened. I don't know how to make you see that loving is a strength, not a weakness, and that it takes courage to love because love's risk is so great."

Sherman shook his head, scowling down at her. "If I were not married, what you tell me might be true, for there truly are risks in loving. But as I have a wife, and you, my dear, are not she, I must look upon this as an indulgence."

Madelaine used her one reserve piece of knowledge. "But you don't," she said softly, "look upon this as an indulgence."

The stern light in his eyes warmed and softened, and he drew her tightly against him. "No; I don't."

Their kiss was deep, passionate, and long; it was the strangest thing, Madelaine thought in a remote part of her mind, but it was as if Tecumseh wanted to absorb her into himself, to pull her into him with the intensity of his appetence. Then she let all thought go and gave herself over to the desire he had ignited in her.

When they broke apart, Sherman had to steady himself against the table, laughing a little with shy embarrassment. "Sorry. That was clumsy of me. I was … you made me dizzy."

"You weren't paying attention," said Madelaine as she ran her hands under the lapels of his jacket and peeled it off him.

He did not protest this, but set to unfastening his waistcoat and the shirt beneath it, working so precipitously that he got the shirt tangled in his suspenders and had to let Madelaine disengage them for him, which she did laughingly. "It isn't funny," he grumbled.

"If you say not," she told him, with a smile that pierced his heart.

He caressed her hair as she continued to unfasten his clothing, and said dreamily, "If I were truly a brave man, I would take you and my children, and we would sail away to the Sandwich Islands together, and live there, the world well-lost. But I'm not that brave."

She interrupted her task and said very somberly. "And you would come to hate me within a year or two, for making you forsake your honor."

"But you don't ask that," he said, holding her face in his hands and scrutinizing her features.

"In time you would persuade yourself I had," she said with grim certainty. "And I am not brave enough to sustain your loathing."

"How could I?" he asked her, marveling at the forthrightness she displayed in the face of his examination.

"You would," she said, and stood back to let him step out of his trousers. "I will fill the tub for you; the water is nearly warm enough." She could see the first wisps of steam rising from the large pots. "Then you will bathe and we will have time together." She reached for the potholders and lifted the first of the pots from the stove. As she emptied it into the bathtub, a cloud of steam rose, made tangy by the bath-salts.

Sherman was down to his underwear and shoes; he started to protest her labors, but stopped and said, "Shall I help you out of your clothes, as well?"

Madelaine emptied the second pot. "No. I will do that once you are in the bath," she assured him.

"Where I can watch," he ventured.

"Of course." By the time she had poured the contents of the third pot into the tub, Sherman was naked and shivering. "Hurry. Get in," she said, gathering up his clothes and setting them out on the butcher's block to dry.

"It feels so good it hurts," Sherman sighed as he sank into the water, gathering up the sponge and soap from the stand beside the tub.

"Then enjoy it," said Madelaine, reaching to release the fastenings of her bodice as she moved toward the bathtub.

SAN FRANCISCO, 8 SEPTEMBER, 1855

A second letter has come from Saint-Germain, who tells me he is moving once more, this time to his house in Antwerp. He writes he will put his business in order there and then go on to Switzerland. I cannot describe how the sight of his handwriting wrings my heart; he is like music heard from a long distance, tantalizing and unreachable, not quite definable and the more entrancing for that. My love for him is like a deep note on the organ, more felt than heard, but essential to all the melody above.

I am almost finished with my chapter on the Utes, which pleases me tremendously. I tell myself I have captured the spirit of their legends and other teachings clearly enough so that the most opinionated of universi-

*ty-bound scholars cannot misinterpret what I have said. But I know that
is impossible, so I must be willing to accept my own satisfaction with my
efforts as sufficient.*

*Two days ago there was a slight earthquake, which I am informed
happens frequently on this coast. It was not so destructive as the one I
experienced in Turkey, twenty years ago, but I found it disquieting nonetheless. Poor Olga was in hysterics for the greater part of an hour, and
Christian claimed that he knew it was coming because the dogs of the
neighborhood howled before it struck. I have heard there was some minor damage in one of the grand casinos; their imported crystal chande-
lier fell into the lobby, injuring half a dozen patrons. The Chinese have
set off firecrackers to keep the evil spirits of the earthquake away . . .*

*Tecumseh has been with me five nights out of the last ten, and he al-
ternates between anguish at his laxness and joy for our passion. When
he is not berating himself he tells me that he has never been so moved
before, that I have revealed pleasures and gratification he thought did
not exist until now. But this is always accompanied by the warning
that he will not shame his wife any more than he has already, and that
he will never leave his family. He refuses to be convinced that I do not
wish him to run off with me, and nothing I have said to the contrary has
made any lasting impression on him.*

*Tomorrow I go to an afternoon party given by Mister Folsom to cel-
ebrate the tenth anniversary of the marriage of Captain and Missus
Kent—or so reads the invitation that was delivered to me last week. Baron deStoeckl has offered to be my escort, and I suppose I will accept . . .*

"HOW IS YOUR BOOK COMING, MADAME?" asked the Baron as he
handed her up into his carriage.

It was sunny but windy, and the fur rug waiting for her was welcome.
"Very well, thank you," she answered, taking her seat with her back to
the coachman. "I suppose that Sherman has told you what a bad idea
he thinks it is."

They moved off in the direction of California Street. "I know his opinion of Indians, and so put little credence in his objections," deStoeckl
said, his eyes glinting merrily. "I do find it amusing that he becomes so
outraged at your interest, however." As diplomatically as possible, he
added, "He may not be alone in his notions."

"He isn't," said Madelaine crisply.

Baron deStoeckl nodded wisely. "It is good you are aware of the reception your work is likely to receive."

"You mean that it is more apt to be ignored than anything else," she said, feeling world-weary. "Yes, I know."

"Then you will not be disappointed," the Baron said with a nod of approval.

"I can't promise that," she replied with candor. "It would please me more than I can say to have this work read for what I hope it is, and given a thoughtful acceptance. But there are fashions in the groves of academe as there are in all things, and the old ways of the Indians are not as fashionable as the wilds of Africa just now." She was able to laugh, but there was sadness in her voice.

"Ah, Madame, I am sorry." He noticed his coachman was slowing down, and called out, "Michael, what is the trouble?"

"There is a wagon overturned at the next corner," said the coachman.

"Then take the next street." The Baron snapped his fingers. "We are expected to arrive on time."

"But if there are injuries—" protested Michael.

"We will only add to the confusion, which will not assist the injured," said the Russian testily.

"But perhaps Madame—" the coachman suggested, turning on the box.

"God help us all!" burst out deStoeckl. "Will you drive on, or are you unhappy in my employ?"

"But Madame saved Missus Thomas' life," said Michael, pausing to job in his leader, who was pulling at the bit.

"Yes, she did," agreed deStoeckl. "But that does not mean she must minister to all of San Francisco. Drive on." He ended the matter.

Michael sat with a very stiff back all the rest of the way to the Folsom house just off California Street; he exchanged no more than five words with the Baron when he let him and Madelaine down, then drove off with a strong attitude of disapproval.

"It appears that stories of your heroism have spread," said deStoeckl as he handed over his hat and cloak to the servant who opened the door for them.

"Servants talk," said Madelaine with a philosophical gesture.

"Almost as much as their employers do," deStoeckl agreed, and offered Madelaine his arm for their walk into the garden where a great buffet was laid.

Fanny Kent was radiant in a flounced gown of peach-colored tarlatan over petticoats a la Duchesse; her eardrops were baroque pearls surmounted by rubies, and she wore a necklace of diamonds and rubies, the gift her husband had given her for this occasion.

Beside her, Captain Kent was in a claw-tail coat of dark-blue superfine over a waistcoat of embroidered white satin. He was beaming with pride as he lifted his champagne glass to his wife and thanked her for "the ten happiest years of my life." He was delighted by the applause that followed.

"I won't bother to bring you wine," the Baron whispered to Madelaine after they had greeted their host. "But excuse me if I get some for myself."

"Please," said Madelaine, returning the wave Fanny Kent gave her. "You do not have to wait upon me, Baron."

"You are gracious as always," said deStoeckl, and went off to have some of the champagne.

Madelaine had no desire to go sit with the widows and dowagers in the kiosk, nor did she want to join the younger wives, all of whom seemed to spend their time talking about the unreliability of their servants, the precocity of their children, and the ambitions they had for their husbands. She would have nothing to contribute to their conversation and her presence would not be wholly welcome because of this. Instead, she went to where a new bed of flowers had just been planted; she occupied her time identifying the leaves of the plants, her thoughts faintly distracted by the realization that she would have to make more of the compounds Saint-Germain had taught her to make nearly a century ago, which would mean she would have to gather plants, barks, berries, and roots and do so without attracting undue attention. She did not hear Fanny Kent's light, tripping step behind her.

"Oh, Madame de Montalia," she enthused, prettily half-turning so that the tiers of her skirt fluttered becomingly around her. "I was so happy to see you arrive with Baron deStoeckl."

"Why, thank you so much for inviting me," said Madelaine, adding, "My felicitations on your anniversary. And may all those to come be as happy."

"Thank you," said Fanny, a smug half-smile showing her delight in this occasion. "I am a fortunate woman; my husband is devoted to me."

"Yes, you are fortunate," said Madelaine. "The more so that you are fond of him."

Fanny clasped her hand to her throat. "Dear me, yes. I have seen marriages—well, we all have—where the partners do not suit, and one is forever trapped in trying to win the other, with flattery and gifts and other signs of affection that gain nothing but the aggravation of the other, or make more pronounced the alienation between them. The greater the effort, the greater the failure in those sad cases. Luckily, I am not of their number."

"Which must please all your friends," said Madelaine, thinking that festive small talk had not changed in the one hundred twenty-nine years she had been alive. She made up her mind not to be bored. "I see the Captain has given you a beautiful remembrance."

"So he has," she preened. "How good of you to notice." She looked around, then moved a step nearer to Madelaine. "I mentioned Baron deStoeckl just now, in the hope that there might be some... interesting announcements from him."

Madelaine realized at once what Fanny sought to know; she chuckled. "Do not let his affianced bride hear you say that, or he will never lend me his escort again."

Fanny's face wilted. "Oh. An affianced bride, you say?"

"So he has informed me," said Madelaine, her good humor unaltered. "Dear Missus Kent, you must know that with your best efforts few of us can become as happy as you are with the Captain. Although I appreciate your wish to see me thus." She regarded Fanny, trying not to lose patience with her.

"Yes," said Fanny naively. "It is true that happiness like ours is rare. But I think it is necessary for a woman to have a husband in this world. Life is quite impossible without one." Impulsively she put her hand on Madelaine's arm. "And I hate to see you so alone."

"I deal well enough with my single condition," said Madelaine, knowing that Fanny intended the best for her, but offended by this intrusion in spite of it.

"But the future; think of the future, Madame." Her pretty face was now puckered with distress. "What will become of you? I cannot bear to think of it, not when I know you to be a prize any man would be glad to win."

"Please, Missus Kent," Madelaine said, her manner less conciliating than before, "do not think that you must make arrangements for me. I am capable of caring for myself; I value your interest as I ought, but I must ask that you do not pursue the matter."

Fanny dabbed a tear from her fine eyes with a lace handkerchief. "If you insist, I will do it, but why I should, I cannot grasp. Surely you must know that we all wish you well, and are grateful for your saving of Amanda Thomas's life. Nothing would please us more than to see you well-situated. Not for that act alone," she appended in some confusion. "Any man would be more than satisfied to win you for himself had you done nothing so noble as that."

Madelaine held up her hands in a gesture of supplication. "There is no reason to think that I have done anything remarkable. It was what anyone would do in the same situation."

"Do you think so?" Fanny inquired, genuinely surprised at the notion. "I would like to believe you, but I already realize I am incapable of dealing with any such tragedy." She lowered her gaze to the flower beds. "This will be so splendid next spring. Don't you look forward to seeing it?"

"Yes," Madelaine answered, "and I regret that I will no longer be in San Francisco when they bloom."

Fanny's expression was shocked now. "What are you saying, Madame?"

"Only that my purpose for being in this country will take me away from here before much more time goes by; I will be leaving before winter sets in and makes travel too hazardous," said Madelaine, trying to make these statements calmly so that Fanny would not be too inquisitive about her plans.

"Gracious," said Fanny, nonplused to the point of silence for a moment. "What purpose do you have, Madame de Montalia?"

"I am making a study of America; the United States are part of my subjects." It was not a lie, Madelaine reminded herself, though it was not quite the truth.

"But why would you want to do that?" Fanny marveled. "Why should a wellborn woman like you undertake so dangerous a task?"

"Curiosity," said Madelaine. "Women are supposed to be more curious than men, aren't they?"

"Well, I suppose so," said Fanny dubiously, then turned as she heard her name called. She waved in response, then looked guiltily at Madelaine. "Oh, dear. You must excuse me, Madame; my husband needs me."

"By all means," said Madelaine, and went back to her perusal of the flower beds. But she could not bring herself to concentrate on what she saw now, for Fanny Kent's well-meaning interference niggled at the back of her thoughts, and she remembered how Saint-Germain had cautioned her against making herself too noticeable in society. At the time, she had thought it the advice of someone being too protective, but now she could perceive the reason for his warning, and she tried to think of how best to undo the damage she had done.

A short while later, Baron deStoeckl found her once more. He carried a glass of champagne and he smiled broadly at her, his manner wholly amiable, his eyes shrewd. As usual, he addressed her in French. "How are you faring, Madame?"

"Well enough," she said, taking care not to appear too interested in him. "Fanny Kent was hoping that she could make a match with us."

Baron deStoeckl chuckled. "And did you tell her of my promised bride at home?"

"Yes," said Madelaine. "I think she was more disappointed than shocked." She indicated the half-grown cypress at the end of the garden. "Those will be fine trees in another ten years or so."

"True enough," the Baron agreed, making no attempt to return to the subject of Fanny's match-making. He strolled along beside her toward the trees, content to say little as they went. Finally, as they reached the foot of the garden, he remarked, "I hope you will not allow yourself to worry about what she said to you."

"It is not my intention, no," said Madelaine, trying to sound unconcerned.

"Because most people here know how to take what she says. They realize that she is of that kind of temperament, and give credence to her words with reservation. Also, at such an occasion as this one, it is all but expected that the celebrating couple will want to see all their guests happily disposed."

"You're doubtless correct," said Madelaine, and went on impulsively, "but it galls me to think I have been foolish enough to expose myself to her ..."

"Scrutiny?" suggested deStoeckl when Madelaine did not go on.

"Something of the sort," she admitted. "Though that may be too strong a word," she added an instant later.

They started back to where most of the guests were gathered. DeStoeckl gestured to indicate the expansive garden. "You know, at the rate this city is growing, holdings of this size will soon vanish. I predict that in another three years there will be four houses here."

"Do you think so?" Madelaine inquired.

"Only consider how rapidly the city has expanded since the Gold Rush. Ask William what it was like when he was in California the first time. It was nothing like the place you see now. Once the Rush was on, San Francisco mushroomed. And it is mushrooming still." He grinned impishly. "William learned a great deal then, and it has stood him in good stead now. In fact, he was one of the first to know about the gold discovery. He claims that at the time, he paid little attention to it, having other things on his mind. Ask him why they called Monterey Bay 'Sherman's Punch Bowl,' six years ago."

"I didn't know," said Madelaine quietly, thinking that she needed to know much more about Tecumseh than she did. "You may be right about the city," she went on with more verve. "Though it would be a pity to lose this garden."

"The price of land is rising steadily," deStoeckl reminded her. "And buildings are going up everywhere. I venture to guess that the city will one day stretch from the Bay to the Pacific."

This struck Madelaine as unlikely and she was about to say so when Colonel Thomas came up to her, an eager expression on his face. "Good afternoon," said Madelaine, who wanted to forestall any effusiveness.

"To you as well, kind Madame," said Colonel Thomas, shaking hands with the Baron before giving his whole attention to Madelaine. "I hoped I might find you here. My wife is still not sufficiently recovered to be with me today, but she asked me, if I saw you, to extend to you again her heartfelt thanks for all you did on her behalf."

"Colonel Thomas, we have said enough on this head already," she protested as cordially as she could, fearing that their encounter was the subject of general attention. "Give your wife my good wishes for her continued recovery."

"I will, and she will thank you for them." He bowed slightly. "I don't wish to cause you embarrassment, Madame, you are so modest a female. I will take myself away now. But if ever I can be of service, or any of my family, you have only to let me know of it."

"You're kindness itself," said Madelaine, beginning to feel oppressed by the occasion. She looked around and noticed that deStoeckl was deep in a discussion with four men she had not met. It was all she could do to contain her irritation; she wanted to leave the anniversary party, though it was much too soon, and would draw notice to her departure, which was the last thing she wished to do. So she went into the house

84

and looked about for whatever passed for a library; the chance to read would calm her and diminish her anxiety.

There were two small shelves of books in the withdrawing room. With a sigh she resigned herself to the limited fare, and taking the copy of *Bleak House* from the shelf, she sat down to read, hoping to find what it was that Sherman so admired in Dickens.

"I wondered what had become of you," said a voice from the door; a young importer stood there, smiling fatuously at Madelaine. "No fair, running off the way you did."

"It is too bright in the garden; I fear I do poorly in the sun," she said, noticing that the fellow looked a bit flushed. "As do you, it would seem."

"The sun don't bother me," he boasted, and held up his glass to toast her. "But not looking at you does. You're better than the sun any day of the week."

This flattery was more alarming than complimenting; Madelaine began to wonder if the high color in the young man's face came from too much champagne rather than too much sun; there was a certain glaze to his eyes that suggested it. A quiver of alarm went through her as she recalled other unwelcome encounters: Alain Baundilet in Omat's garden, Gerard le Mat on the road to her estate in Provence, Ralph Whitestone in her box after *The Duchess of Malfi*. "Thank you for the pretty words," she said automatically, continuing with great deliberation, "I think, perhaps, it is time we rejoined the others."

The young man gave her a lupine grin. "Not so fast. I thought we could have a little ... talk all on our own."

"Did you?" Madelaine closed the novel and slipped it back into its place on the shelf. "I fear you were mistaken." She rose and started toward the door, not so quickly that she would seem to confront the young man. With all the composure she could muster, she said, "If you will let me by?"

He extended his arms to block the door. "I don't think so."

"Mister..." She could not bring his name to mind; it was something simple, uncomplicated, not as obvious as Smith. Although she was concerned, she continued to maintain her outward calm. "There is no reason to do this."

"There's plenty of reason," said the intruder, enjoying his position of advantage. "And a Frenchwoman shouldn't need to be told what that is."

Madelaine frowned. She could always scream, but that would defeat the whole purpose of her withdrawal—to remove herself from observation and the occasion for comment—and give new fodder to the scandal-hungry gossips. "I don't think you want to do this," she began reasonably. "Please stand aside." She thought she sounded like a schoolmistress with a recalcitrant pupil.

"Not on your life," the young man said, swaying toward her. "Not while I have this chance." He drank the last of the champagne in his glass, tossed it away without paying any notice to its shattering, then reached out for her.

Madelaine thought to get around him and was about to reach for something she could use for a weapon when Sherman abruptly forced his way into the withdrawing room, grabbing the young man by the front of his shirt to back him up against the wall, leaning hard against him, pinning him to the wainscoting. "You didn't hear the lady, sir. She asked you to stand aside."

The young man blanched and sweat broke out on his forehead. "I … I …"

"And you will do it, won't you?" Sherman demanded through clenched teeth.

"I …" Though bulkier than Sherman, the young man was terrified, and he squirmed in an attempt to escape; Sherman leaned harder. "Oh, God."

The relief and gratitude that had filled Madelaine a moment before vanished in a wash of exasperation. "Mister Sherman," she said crisply, "I think he has taken your meaning."

Sherman kept his relentless grip on the fellow. "You will apologize to the lady, sir," he ordered.

"I … sorry … I didn't mean …" He stopped as Sherman released his hold and moved back. "I … just a mistake. Never meant anything … untoward. Upon my word, Madame." He was shaking and kept glancing quickly at Sherman, then at the windows, anything to avoid looking directly at Madelaine for fear of the banker's wrath.

"And because it was a mistake, you will say nothing to anyone, will you?" Sherman pursued, giving the younger man no chance to capitalize on his gaffe through boasting or smugness.

"No. No, I won't. Ever." With that he bolted from the room. His hasty, uneven footsteps were loud.

The withdrawing room was still, neither Madelaine nor Sherman being willing to speak first. She relented before he did. "Mister Sherman. I didn't know you were here."

"I arrived not long after you did," he said, keeping his distance.

She had nothing to say to that. "How did you happen to follow that young man in here?"

"Winters? I heard him boast that he would get a better taste of France than champagne. When I saw him come into the house, I followed; I had an idea he might attempt something of this sort." He looked at her directly. "I'm sorry I was right. I would not have you subjected to . . . such things for anything."

"Thanks to your intervention, I wasn't," she said bluntly, and could read shock in his face. "His intentions were . . ."

"If he had touched you, I would have killed him," said Sherman with quiet certainty.

She achieved a rallying tone. "Now that would have been a grand gesture. And neither of our reputations would survive it, so it is just as well you arrived when you did." She managed to keep her hands from shaking as she slipped out the door. "Speaking of reputations, it might be wise if we did not leave this room at the same time. I will go back to the garden now; follow when you think best."

He nodded, and before she could turn away, he blew her a kiss.

SAN FRANCISCO, 22 SEPTEMBER, 1855

There has been more rain; I am told this is earlier than is usual in this part of the country. Some of the farmers on the outskirts of the city are complaining bitterly that their crops will have to be sacrificed to the rain, and none are more distressed than those whose orchards are not yet fully picked.

Olga left this morning on the stage coach, bound for Sacramento, where she has been informed her sister can be found. She is distraught because it appears her sister's husband has deserted her, and this, she claims, has never happened in their family. I have paid her to the end of October and given her an excellent reference, which is all she would take from me. I am now left with trying to decide if I should find another housekeeper for another month, or fend for myself. I cannot see that I need to have the housekeeper, but Tecumseh informs me that I could easily be compromised if I do not have a woman living here to provide adequate chaperonage.

I have warned him of my coming departure, but I doubt he believes I truly mean to go, not with winter coming on, though I have reminded him that winter is the wisest time to cross the deserts to the south and east of here. He will not ask me to stay, nor would I, but I think he would like to delay my leaving, no matter how difficult that would become for us both…

Tomorrow I will be speaking to a Diego Gilez, who is said to be a fine guide, familiar with all the trails south and eastward as far as New Mexico Territory. He has a group of six men with him, two of whom I understand were once friars and were sent to minister to the Indians of the deserts, and therefore can assist me. I hope he will be able to undertake the journey this autumn, so that I may not have to winter here, or even in Monterey or San Diego, which I am convinced would be a mistake for many reasons…

Now that my book is nearly complete, I will have to employ a copyist to ready it for publication. I will send one copy of the work to Amsterdam, and keep the other with me, as I have done with the earlier excerpts I have prepared as monographs. This will be the fourth copyist I have seen. None of the others were satisfactory, wanting to interpolate their own style atop my own. I trust that Missus Stephens is as capable as I have heard…

EUPHEMIA STEPHENS WORE WIDOW'S BLACK, including a veil over her face. She shook Madelaine's hand and said, "I had no idea you were so young." Since Euphemia herself was well past fifty, her shock was more excusable, or so Madelaine thought, than if the other woman had been nearer her own age. "Pardon me; I had no right to say that." She made no effort to unbutton her coat, but held it closed, showing she did not want to be rid of it, nor did she attempt to take off her hat, though she did lift her veil.

"You have every right," Madelaine countered. "I would prefer you speak your mind, whatever my own opinions may be. We shall get on much better if you do." She indicated the withdrawing room where her desk stood; there were two chairs near it. "Please sit down," she offered.

"Thank you." Very properly Euphemia Stephens sat down in the straighter-backed of the two, opened her large handbag and drew out several sheets of papers tied with a plain blue ribbon. "These are my recommendations, if you wish to examine them."

Madelaine took them and glanced through them, noticing that all of them were in different hands, and on dissimilar paper-stocks. "They seem genuine enough."

"You did not read them," said Euphemia, sounding disappointed.

"Why should I? You said yourself they are recommendations. It does not seem likely that any of these letters would register complaints." Madelaine smiled quickly. "How long have you been a copyist, Missus Stephens?"

"I began the work when my husband fell ill, six years ago, and have been at it ever since." She looked down at her gloved hands. "He died not quite two years ago."

"And you are still in mourning," Madelaine said in some surprise, for it was not often that women in California wore formal mourning for more than six months, if that long.

"We were married thirty-eight years, he and I; at my age it would be foolish to set my weeds aside." She coughed delicately. "He was a school teacher, at first at a secondary school in Baltimore which failed in thirty-nine; when we came here he worked in Fort Ross and Sonoma and then here for some time. We came to California in forty-one, John Sutter hired Mister Stephens to establish a school in what he called New Helvetia."

"You must have seen many changes in that time," Madelaine observed, thinking that at another time she would want to hear more of these events from Euphemia Stephens, but now she could ill-afford such curiosity.

"California was a change from Baltimore, that was the single greatest obstacle," said Euphemia Stephens. "I was never more homesick in my life than those first two years in Fort Ross and Sonoma. Fort Ross was the strangest place of all, because it had been Russian." She coughed delicately. "Mister Stephens felt the change more keenly than I did, though he never complained of it."

"It must have been hard, making so great a change," said Madelaine.

"Yes, it was," agreed Euphemia without any trace of self-pity. "But it was preferable to living off the efforts of our son, which was the only other possibility at the time." She looked speculatively at Madelaine. "Your note indicated you have a manuscript you wish to have copied. How long is it?"

"In my hand it is slightly more than three hundred pages." Madelaine saw that Euphemia was surprised at this number, and went on, "I think you will find that in a regular copperplate hand, that will become closer to four hundred than three."

"A work of some…length, I perceive," said Euphemia, doing her best to sound undaunted by this prospect. "And how long will I have to copy it?"

"Just under four weeks, if my plans are not disrupted," said Madelaine. "A challenge, I know, but not an impossible one." Her smile this time was light with amusement. "Yes, I look like little more than a child, I know, but I assure you that my appearance is deceptive."

"Not that it is my business, in any case," Euphemia said hastily. "It is not for me to question your capabilities, beyond the capability to pay my fee."

"True enough," said Madelaine. "And for that, you may consult Mister Sherman at Lucas and Turner, who manages my funds for me. He will assure you that you will have your money in full when your task is complete. I will leave it up to him to decide if he will give you a portion of payment at the start of your employment." She spoke pleasantly, without any hint of apprehension, and then indicated the work to be done. "I have ink and pens of several sorts at hand for your use. If you have other tools you want, you have only to ask for them."

"It will take me a day or two to learn what is necessary in this instance." She coughed delicately. "I would appreciate a fire in the grate. These cold mornings do not favor my old bones."

"Certainly. I have a man in my employ who will see to your comforts. I have other demands upon my time. You will not find me looking over your shoulder, Missus Stephens. I will rely on your competence to enable you to complete your work without any urgings from me." Madelaine regarded the older woman with interest. "Is that satisfactory to you?"

"Very much so," said Euphemia. "I am not one who wishes to be closely observed at my task." She inspected the materials set on her desk and nodded her approval. "Yes. This is quite satisfactory. You need only provide me with a rolling blotter and I will be prepared to set about the work." She lifted the paper on the desk and felt it. "A fine grade."

"So I hoped," said Madelaine, knowing that paper of this quality was not often found so far west.

She inspected the manuscript she was to copy, flipping her way

90

through the loose pages. "Your text appears to be very clean; few lines are overwritten and you are very specific in your notes regarding changes."

"There is no advantage in confusing you, which would only serve to slow your work and annoy me," said Madelaine, her expression serious without being somber. "It would benefit neither of us."

Euphemia Stephens turned toward Madelaine, the first sign of a change in her proper widow's reserve becoming apparent as she did her best to smile. "Does that mean you are willing to give me a chance at this job?"

"Of course," said Madelaine, surprised that Euphemia was startled. "Is there any reason why I should not?"

"No," Euphemia answered, coloring to the roots of her hair. "But so often a man is wanted for this ..."

Madelaine sighed. "I know of no reason why a man should be a superior copyist to a woman, especially when working for a woman; in the past I have found that men were more likely to attempt to interject their own observations and opinions onto my work than women have been. Since I dislike disputing my own work, I believe that this is the most practical way to avoid such an impasse." She touched her manuscript where Euphemia Stephens had placed it. "I have worked for several years to prepare this. I do not want to be discouraged about it now."

Euphemia nodded. "Your point is well-taken, Madame," she said formally. "I will strive to abide by your wishes in preparing the copy."

"Excellent," said Madelaine, holding out her hand. "At what rate do you charge for your work?"

"I have usually charged twenty cents for a completed page, with a guarantee of recopying a page without cost to you if any error can be found upon it." She was clearly aware that her price was higher than the current standard rate, but her promise of corrections made free was a rare offer.

"I will give you twenty-five cents for a completed page, and meals at this house, if it will speed you," said Madelaine.

Euphemia stared at her. "That's ... very generous," she said at last, turning toward Madelaine with increased respect. "Are you sure you can afford to do this? If the manuscript is to be as long as you believe it will, then upon its completion you will owe me"—she calculated rapidly, eyes squinting—"one hundred dollars."

"At least," said Madelaine. "And given the high expenses in this city,

91

it will not last you long, no matter how reasonable the costs at your rooming house may be."

"It is true that San Francisco is a very expensive place to live," said Euphemia. "And I will not claim that your offer is not welcome. But I do not wish you to make yourself poor on my behalf. I will be satisfied with my usual charges."

Madelaine shook her head. "I would prefer you let me give you this incentive to do your work with dispatch," she said crisply. "It will ensure that I have the opportunity to require effort from you."

"I suppose that's reasonable," said Euphemia after a short pause to consider what Madelaine said. "I will have to leave at sunset every day, but I will contrive to be here soon after sunrise, so that you will have the most of my labors." She glanced toward the windows. "You have excellent light here."

"And lamps if they are needed," said Madelaine. "If it turns out that you must stay beyond sunset, I can arrange for a carriage to take you home."

Euphemia shrugged. "I have no wish to inconvenience you."

"It would be a greater inconvenience to have the manuscript unfinished before my departure," said Madelaine, and cocked her head in the direction of the stairs, visible through the open hall door. "I have a great many things to do before I leave, and I will have to rely on you to work with minimal supervision. If that is satisfactory to you? ..."

"My dear Madame de Montalia, I could not arrange things more to my liking," she said, and took Madelaine's proffered hand to seal their bargain.

SAN FRANCISCO, 7 OCTOBER, 1855

How still it is this evening. After a week of wind and fog it has turned bright and hot. I was surprised at this sudden change, and coming when it does in the year, though I now understand that it is not unusual to the region. I was told that this is one of the reasons vintners have been flocking to the inland valleys north of here, where they can plant vines with a reasonable hope that their growing season will be long and warm ... Euphemia Stephens has proven most adept at her work, and I am pleased that she is so willing to do this task quickly and with so little need of my tutoring; I was concerned that the names of the Indians, and some of my transliterations of their words would cause her problems, but she has assured me that her work among those Russians remaining at Fort Ross inured her to variant spellings and language. I am confident that she will finish her work in the time specified...

Diego Gilez has broken his arm and will not be able to guide me on my travels. He has recommended a man called Dutch Hagen, whose accent is faint but without doubt Austrian, not Dutch. He has been in the West for nearly thirty years, or so he claims. He is a slight, stringy fellow, not quite six feet tall, and that all sinew and bone, with long, white hair and pale blue eyes; his skin is leathery, his face filled with hard wrinkles. He has agreed to guide me, and though the sum he demands is high, Tecumseh tells me the man's reputation, as far as he can determine, is very good in an occupation over-run with rogues and worse. He advises me that if I must go at all, I should content myself with Mister Hagen's terms. So I have consented to give him one third of his fee at the start of the journey, with the assurance that my bank draft will be honored in St. Louis at the end of it. Hagen has accepted Tecumseh's word that I have money enough to do this, and has arranged to purchase supplies over the next two weeks against our departure. He claims he will need to have another three men with him, and has reluctantly agreed to bring along one woman to cook, at Tecumseh's demand for propriety; once again he is determined to preserve my reputation.

It is arranged that we will depart no later than 10 October, no matter what the weather. It is tempting to delay, but I must not, for my own sake as well as Tecumseh's...

"I KNOW IT IS WHAT MUST BE DONE, and I hate it," Sherman whispered, his hand tangled in her hair, his leg between hers, his body replete, tired, and yet unwilling to sleep; it was after midnight and the city beyond the house on Franklin Street was quiet.

Madelaine shifted her position so that she could lift herself up enough to look into his face. "I will miss you, Tecumseh."

"I will miss you, too, and be damned for it," he said softly, the usual tension gone out of his features, making him look younger than he was. The hand in her hair moved down to brush her face lightly, and he stared into her eyes, wanting to pierce more than the night. "I should never have let myself become..." He drew her down to kiss her searchingly.

She gave herself over to his mouth, opening herself to his growing renewed need, lying back as he made his way down her body as if by passion alone he could take the whole of her into himself. As he moved between her thighs, he gave a harsh sigh, then lowered his head. Madelaine caught her fingers in his fine red hair. "What's the matter?" she asked, sensing the return of his ambivalence.

He raised his eyes enough to meet hers. "It has nothing to do with you," he told her, touching the soft, hidden folds of flesh and relishing the shiver that went through her.

"If it impairs our loving, it has something to do with me," she said as gently as she could.

"Later," he muttered.

"Now," she insisted, concern more than determination coloring her inflection.

"Very well," he said, and brought his elbows under his chest so that he could more easily look at her without moving from his place. "Since I cannot truly grasp the enormity of your leaving, I was thinking that this is one delight—one of many—I will lose with you. If I could contain myself, I would do this for hours, to have the pleasure of your transports." He laughed once, chagrined. "But I am not patient enough for that, and so I have to make the most of our desires and be content with memories."

Madelaine reached down and stroked his shoulder. "You are a generous lover, Tecumseh, more than you know, and you have learned—"

"To be less precipitous?" he ventured. "To increase our gratification by postponing its fulfillment?"

She touched his neck, feeling the strong pulse there. "It grieves me that you cannot be as generous in your marriage as we are together."

To his acute discomfort, he blushed. "Not all women have the capacity to enjoy these things." He rested one hand on her thigh, caressing her with delicious languor. "And many who claim to are suspect, since it is their profession to please men." He moved to adjust himself more comfortably between her legs, saying, "If I had been less infatuated, less off-guard, I would have kept away from you, arranged things with one of the whorehouses for discreet—"

"Servicing," Madelaine supplied for him. "If that was your only alternative to me, then I am gratified your infatuation was—"

He stopped her. "It isn't infatuation," he said in a flat tone. "And you know it."

She looked at him, deep into his steel-colored eyes. "I know."

94

This time when he sighed, he slipped away from her, ending up at the foot of the bed, naked and cross-legged, with a mess of sheets in his lap. "I should not have permitted this to happen. My life ought to be better ordered than that. But what proof am I against you—you, with a face filled with light, and all the sweet delirium of the world in your body. No wonder I could not reason myself out of my fascination. It is mad of me to love you."

They were both silent for a short while, then Madelaine shivered and sat up, facing him down the length of the bed. "I cannot help but love you, madness or not."

"Because it is your nature," he said, repeating what she had told him so often. "Because you have tasted my blood."

"Yes," she said, trying not to fear his response.

"Yes," he echoed, wanting it to be an accusation and hearing himself make the single word a vow.

"And you accept it." She felt a surge of rapture go through her as no physical act would bring. That he finally recognized the bond between them! She would have laughed with utter joy had she not understood that would offend him.

"How can I not?" he asked in mock capitulation.

Certain his resistance was crumbling, she went to him in a single, sinuous motion, sweeping the sheets and comforter aside; she would not let him turn away from her. "Then tonight must stand for all the nights to come that we will not share, Tecumseh; why waste it in anticipating our separation when we may yet be together for a few hours more?"

It was more than he could bear, having her so close. With a sound that was not quite a groan, he reached out and pulled her tightly to him, his carnality igniting afresh as he embraced her. At last he took her firmly by the shoulders and held her back from him. "How can you endure parting?" There was pain in his voice and his body was taut.

"I can because I must," she answered, not resisting him. "Those of my blood do more parting than anything else. Or at least it seems that way to me."

"And when you have gone, there will be others, won't there?" He meant this to hurt; his long fingers tightened on her shoulders.

"Yes. There will." She looked directly at him, unflinching in the face of his accusation. "As you will have your wife, and those women you seek out for … didn't you call it necessity and amusement?"

He released his hold on her and looked away. "You are right, Madelaine; I have no basis for complaint. I, after all, made the conditions of our liaison; how ill-mannered of me to protest them now."

She took his hand. "Stop berating yourself," she said in discomfiture. "If you must know, I find your jealousy unrealistic but … flattering."

"I am not jealous." In spite of his forbidding demeanor, he could not stop a quick burst of rueful laughter. "Fine pair we are," he told her at last. "It would serve us both right if we lost the whole night in bickering."

"If that would make parting easier, then—" she offered, only to be cut off by his lips opening hers.

He seemed determined to press the limits of their passion, for he went at her body as if it were territory to be won. He lavished attention on her face and mouth, on the curve of her neck and the swell of her breasts, using every nuance of excitation he knew to evoke a desire in her as intense as his own, all the while reveling in her tantalizing ministrations and ecstatic responses to the onslaught of his relentless fervor; it was an act of flagrant, erotic idolatry. "Now. Let me have. All of you," he whispered to her as he drew her onto his lap, guiding her legs around him, shuddering in anticipation as she sheathed him deep inside her. His kiss was as long and profound as his flesh was frenzied; while she nuzzled his throat, he clasped her as if to brand her body with his image until their spasms passed.

They were quiet together for some undefined time afterward, neither wanting to make the first move that would break them apart. Then he shifted, changing how he held her. "My foot's falling asleep," he apologized.

"Does it hurt?" Madelaine asked, moving off his lap entirely. In the pre-dawn umber gloom her bedroom looked more like a sketch in charcoal than a real place; no birds yet announced the coming of the October sun, but Madelaine saw it heralded by more than the muting of darkness.

"No; it tingles," he said, wrapping his arm around her shoulder. As he pulled her close, he said, as he flipped his foot to restore circulation, "What a prosaic thing to happen."

"It might have been a leg cramp," said Madelaine as levelly as she could; she was still filled with the glory of their consummation.

"That would be a different matter, wouldn't it?" He chuckled once.

She turned her head and kissed the lobe of his ear. "Oh, entirely."

He ran his hand down her neck to her breast, cupping it and brushing her nipple with his thumb. "I hope you won't have bruises."

"No," she said. "I won't."

"Another of the things those of your blood don't do?" he asked deliberately lightly. "As you do not eat or weep?"

"Yes," she said quietly, and kissed the angle of his jaw where it met his neck.

"Is it difficult, not to eat or weep?" he asked, still holding on to her.

"Occasionally," she admitted, aware that she would have welcomed the release that weeping would bring her upon parting. She was about to move away from him when he tightened his arm, pulling her back close to him.

"Oh, God, Madelaine: I cannot give you up. I must, but I cannot." This was wrung from him, a cry of such utter despair that she was rendered still by its intensity.

"I know," she said, moved by his anguish; she sought to find some consolation to offer him, but could think of nothing.

His eyes were frenzied as he pulled her around to face him. "I will not let this end. If I took you with me, if we left right now, we might be anywhere in the world in a month."

"If that is what you want, Tecumseh, then I will do it," she said, amazed at how deeply she meant what she said.

"It is, it is," he insisted. "It would be the joy of my life to have you at my side. Think of all the places we might go, and all the time we would have." He tried to smile, but succeeded only in stretching his lips over his teeth.

"That might not be the advantage you assume it would be," said Madelaine, a sadness coming over her that surprised her more than it surprised him. "You would grow old and I would not. You might not mind this year, or next year, but in time it would vex you. To say nothing as to what your children would think."

He stared at her. "My children?"

"Well, you would not leave them behind, would you?" she asked reasonably, and knowing what his answer would be.

"No," he admitted after a moment. "I could not do that."

Madelaine kept on. "They would see what you would see: they would grow older and I would not."

He did his best to deny what she told him. "If I could have you all to myself, then I would be happy, no matter what became of us. Or what my children might suspect."

"And how long would you be content?" Madelaine bent to kiss the fingers of his hand on her shoulder. "Even with your children along?"

"I would be thankful to the end of my days," he said with profound conviction.

"Do you think so?" Her voice was soft and poignant. "You tell me this is how you feel, but it is not. You would not like to face age as the living do, while I would hardly change at all."

"I wish you wouldn't say it that way," he protested.

"How would you like me to say it?" she challenged. "You would grow old, and I would appear not to. Vampires age very, very slowly. I have hardly changed in the last century. How would you—"

"I would accept it," he insisted, his fingers digging into her flesh, driven by the force of his emotions. "I might not like it, but I would be willing to accept it."

"Would you? What of the lovers I would have?" She made her question blunt deliberately.

"You wouldn't need them. You would have me," he told her firmly.

"For a time, perhaps," she responded, continuing with great care, "But I would need to find others, or you would soon be exhausted and come to my life." This was not quite the truth, but it was near enough that she knew she had to make him aware of what was likely to happen.

"Then we would carry on in vampire fashion," he said, his emphatic tone shoring up any doubts that might trouble him.

"But vampires cannot be lovers of vampires," she said, and felt him go still.

"And why not, pray?" His tone was harsh, sarcastic, as if he expected some self-serving answer.

"Because vampires must have life. It is the one thing we do not have to give, and the one thing we need above all others," she said quietly. "Once you come to my life, you and I will not be able to—"

"It's not true!" he exclaimed, pushing her away.

"But it is," she said.

"So I must share you or lose you," he said thoughtfully.

"Yes," she said.

"Are you certain?" he demanded.

"If I weren't, I should never have met you; I would not have come to this country." She touched his face. "It is too hard to remain with those we have loved when we can love them no more as we did when we lived."

"And I take it there is no alternative to this?" He reached out for her hand. "Can we not devise some means to allow us to remain together without having to become estranged?"

"We can never be estranged," Madelaine said.

"Because you have tasted my blood," he said, a wistful note creeping into his statement.

"Yes, Tecumseh; because of that."

He had a sharp retort in mind, a single, pithy remark that would show his skepticism was flourishing; the words never came. Instead, he turned, took her face in his hands and scrutinized her features, memorizing them, before he kissed her with the sudden, harsh misery of parting. As he rose abruptly from the bed, he said "Stay there. Please, Madelaine. Don't come to the door. I won't have the courage to go if you do."

"All right," she said, watching him dress, her violet eyes filled with anguish. Only when he was ready to leave did she say to him, "You are part of me, Tecumseh. You will always be part of me."

He paused in the door but would not look around. "And you of me." He waited for her to say good-bye; when she did not, he strode out of the room and down the stairs.

SAN FRANCISCO, 8 OCTOBER, 1855

Tomorrow I will be gone from this place. It is a harder parting than I would have thought possible, for I am torn between my certainty that I must go and my reluctance to leave Tecumseh. I find his hold upon me quite astonishing, for I have been resigned from the first—or so I thought—to going before his wife returns. I had not thought I would find leaving so arduous, or the wrench of separation as painful as it is proving to be...

The two buck-board wagons are ready, one carrying my books and papers and personal things, one carrying four crates of my native earth. I have bought two horses to ride, and mules to pull the wagons, and I have paid off those I have hired. There only remains the closing of my account at Lucas and Turner; I have decided to do it as I am departing tomorrow, my last stop in this city before we turn to the south-southeast. It may be that Tecumseh will not handle the matter himself, but will deputize one of his assistants to tend to me...

"WE'RE SORRY TO SEE YOU GO, MADAME," said Jenkins as he held open the low gate, admitting Madelaine to the realm of desks and files.

"I am sorry to leave," said Madelaine with as much sincerity as good manners. "I have truly enjoyed my stay here."

"Yes," said Jenkins, going on a bit too smoothly, "Mister Sherman has your account information ready, if you'll just step into his office?"

Madelaine was a bit startled to hear this. "Very well," she said, and turned to walk toward the door at the end of the aisle between the desks. She had to steel herself against seeing Sherman this last time, and she waited a long moment before she knocked on the door.

"Enter," came the crisp order.

She obeyed, leaving the door open by a foot and making herself smile as she went up to his desk. "I've come to say good-bye, Mister Sherman. And to pick up my account records and traveling money."

Sherman had risen but he did not take her proffered hand; instead he rummaged through a stack of papers on his desk. "I have your account information here, Madame de Montalia, and the funds you requested," he said in a voice that did not seem to belong to him.

"Thank you," she responded.

"I wish I could persuade you to carry less gold and cash with you." Concern roughened his tone. "You are not on the boulevards of Paris, Madame, and any signs of wealth are likely to attract attention you cannot want." His face was set in hard lines, but his eyes were full of anguish.

"I know something of the dangers of travel, Mister Sherman, although I am grateful for your warning. I will heed your admonitions to the extent that circumstances allow." How formal and stiff she sounded in her own ears; she wanted so much to weep, and could not. It would not be seemly, she told herself, even if it were possible, and added aloud, "I will take all the precautions I can."

"Yes," he said. "Be sure you keep a loaded pistol to hand at all times. If you need one, you will need it instantly."

"I'll do that," she said, delaying taking her file of material into her hands, for that would be more final than closing the door.

"You will be wise to learn as much as you can about those you hire to guide you. Many of the men in that profession are scoundrels and not to be trusted." He spoke crisply, yet all the while his eyes revealed suffering he could not admit.

"I will be careful, Mister Sherman," she promised him.

Sherman coughed twice, short, hard coughs that might signal an asthma attack. "Don't trouble yourself, Madame," he said brusquely, waving her away, although she had not moved. "It will pass. And I have a vial of your medicine, if it does not."

Madelaine had to stop herself from going around his desk to his side, to comfort him. "Well," she said rallyingly, "do not let pride keep you from using it."

"I won't," he said, and stared down at his desk in silence for several seconds, then asked, "Do you think you will ever come back to San Francisco, Madame?"

"Ever is a long time, Mister Sherman," she pointed out. "I do not plan to now, but in time, who can tell?"

"Who, indeed," he said. "And we knew when you came that you would leave, didn't we?"

She nodded. "Sooner or later, I would go."

"Off to study America," he said, trying to be jaunty; his voice cracked.

"Yes." She bit her lip to keep from saying more. With an effort, she remarked, "I suppose your children must be glad that their mother is coming home."

"Oh, yes," he said, grateful to have something safe to say. "Both of them are delighted."

"I'll think of them kindly," said Madelaine.

"You're very good." He fumbled with a square envelope, then held it out to her. "Here. I want you to have this."

"What is it?" Madelaine took the envelope cautiously, as if she expected something untoward from it.

"A sketch I did. Of you." He looked her directly in the eye, a world of longing in his gaze.

"Oh!" Madelaine said softly. "May I open it?"

"Not here, if you please," he said, his stand-offishness returning. "I couldn't keep it with me, much as I wanted to. It...it is very reveal-ing—oh, not of you, of me. If Ellen ever saw it, she—" He cleared his throat. "It is enough that one of us should have a broken heart. I will not chance giving such pain to her."

Madelaine nodded, unable to speak; she slipped the envelope into her leather portfolio, which she had brought to contain her account records.

"This is too difficult," Sherman whispered as he took the file and thrust it toward her. "If you do not leave now, I don't think I will be able to let you go. And let you go I must."

"Yes," said Madelaine as she took the file and put it into the portfolio.

"And your cash and gold," he went on with ruthless practicality, handing her a heavy canvas sack with Lucas and Turner stenciled on its side. "Be careful where you stow this."

"I will," she said, and turned to leave.

"Madel—am," he said, halting her. "I wish, with all my heart, you ... your stay here wasn't over."

"You're very kind, Mister Sherman," said Madelaine, struggling to retain her composure.

"As it is," he went on as if unable to stop, "I will think of you each ... often."

"And I of you," said Madelaine, wishing she could kiss him one last time and knowing she must not.

"If only you and I ..." He let his words falter and stop.

Madelaine backed away, reaching behind her for the door. "Our ... our friendship is not at an end simply because we part," she told him, forcing herself to speak steadily. She pulled the door open, readying herself to leave the bank.

His reply struck her with the full weight of his constrained emotions, as if he wanted to impart to her all that he could not say: "I know, Madelaine; I know."

* * *

PRESIDIO DE SANTA BARBARA, 14 NOVEMBER, 1855

We have found an inn near the Presidio itself, and I am assured we will be safe here ... This part of California is much more Spanish than the north, more like Mexico; I suspect it is because there are fewer men willing to prospect in the deserts than in the mountains. Perhaps the hold of the Spanish landlords is stronger here than in the north, as there are fewer newcomers to challenge their rule and their Land Grants. Thanks to gold, San Francisco has become quite an eclectic place, what with miners arriving from every part of Europe and America. But here, I am told, it is not so dramatically changed. For the most part, the Camino Real, which our guide calls the Mission Road, is well-enough main-

tained that we made good progress along it, and lost only one day to rain. Our average progress has been a respectable ten to twelve miles a day, although we did slow in our climb through the mountains around San Luis Obispo. Generally, however, we have traveled swiftly, and at this pace we should reach San Diego by Christmas, from whence we will turn east.

I have sent two letters back to Tecumseh, though I have had no replies and expect none; I have not yet found a way to thank him sufficiently for the sketch he made of me and gave me the morning I left. He is right: it is too easily read for him to keep it by him, where it might be discovered and understood. In execution it is simple enough: he has drawn me seated on a fallen log, my hat in my hand, in all considerations a most innocuous pose—but there is something about it that smolders, so that I half-expect the paper to burst into flame. He included a short note which said he would have to carry my likeness burning in his heart; that is very gallant of him, as well as being very nearly accurate, if this sketch is any indication of his sentiments. I am surprised to discover how strong the bond between us is, though why I should feel so, I cannot think.

I wonder if Saint-Germain is right, and I am developing a weakness for Americans.

The
Santa Fe
Trail

YUMA, NEW MEXICO TERRITORY, 9 JANUARY, 1856

*I have never seen so much dust as I have coming here, and that in-
cludes the sandstorms of Egypt. It is silky, and it gets into everything:
hair, nose, underwear, tack, the lot of it. My clothes are worn from it,
and I have decided to do as some of the women in these remote regions
do—wear trousers of sturdy canvas. It is better to shock a few of the settlers than to continue as I have been doing. At this rate I will have no
clothes, but the single ball gown I have brought with me, left in a month
or so ... Mineata San Ardo, our cook, has much the same complaint, but
she would rather rub herself raw than go so much against tradition that
she don trousers. I have attempted to convince her that other women in
the world wear trousers and would think it strange not to, but she will
not entertain so radical a notion ...*

*In the four days since we have arrived here, I have been the object
of local curiosity. Women who travel as I do are an oddity—European
women alone are apparently so much an oddity that no one knows what
to do about me. I am to speak to the alcalde of the town this evening. I
hope my explanations will satisfy him.*

For the last week there have been warnings of sudden floods, for during the winter they say this is a great hazard. It would appear that rain falls in the mountains, and fills the creeks and rivers so suddenly that whole villages may be washed away in a matter of minutes ... I have asked Mister Hagen to use all reasonable precautions, but thus far he is not worried, though he agrees that these floods are a risk here.

I have sent a packet of notes back with a military messenger from Taos bound for San Francisco, as General Hitchcock arranged for me; these are to go to Euphemia Stephens for transcribing and shipping on to Amsterdam to the publisher. Tecumseh has my authorization to pay her for this, and little as he may approve of what I am writing about, he will make sure she receives her fee for her work. There is a note to Tecumseh with the rest, saying once again that I miss him. It is not wise of me to send that to him now that his wife has returned, for I am convinced she has, but I find I cannot quite give up the links that are our bond ...

Tomorrow there is a market to be held, and I will want to attend it, with the hope of seeing what Indians are there, in the hope that I can persuade them to permit me to learn from them ...

YUMA, NEW MEXICO TERRITORY, 14 JANUARY, 1856

I am getting used to being here on sufferance. I don't know what I shall do if I am asked to leave while I am writing on the Yuma Indians ... From them I have learned of a tribe living in a deep canyon to the north of here, in a beautiful, deep gorge with great waterfalls and natural protection against all comers ... When I broached the matter to Mister Hagen, he said that all this part of the country is full of legends of lost peoples and great cities hidden in canyons. But he is willing to go upriver with me if we have a reliable Indian with us, and I can meet his price. He tells me that he will not put himself at risk for less than two hundred dollars a day, which he himself considers outrageous and thinks will discourage me.

So now I must find a reliable Indian ...

LOS OSOS, NEW MEXICO TERRITORY, 22 JANUARY, 1856

Carlos Nisachii is half-Indian and half-Spanish, what is called a mes-
tizo here, I think. He has said he will find the Havasupai people for us.
Mister Hagen tells me that Carlos Nisachii is regarded as reliable, and
will probably not guide us into a trap where we will be made slaves
or held for ransom or killed or any of the rest of it. He has made sure
his men are well-armed, ostensibly to hunt; but I don't think anyone is
fooled by that assertion...

    The trousers are quite satisfactory.

AT NIGHT THE DESERT WAS COLD, the moonlight making the
vastness of it appear corpse-like. Dutch Hagen sat by the fire for his
portion of the watch, his fully loaded Smith and Wesson Volcanic
Repeater resting against his knee. From time to time he put more dry
wood on the fire, watching abstractedly as the flames leaped up; he
could hear the rush of the river not far away.

Madelaine lay in her tent staring up at the ridge-seam, missing Tecumseh. She had resisted the impulse to write to him once more, knowing it would serve no purpose but to bring pain to them both. So she
thought back to their times alone, letting the incompassable vastness of
the night return her sense of perspective. She had finished her entry in
her journal while the men had eaten. Only their cook, Mineata, knew
that Madelaine did not, in fact, eat separately with her as the men supposed; she had reluctantly accepted Madelaine's explanation that she
had taken a vow to eat alone to avoid the sin of gluttony, as it was the ridiculous sort of thing a European would do. Madelaine drew her watch
from its double pocket in her jacket and looked closely at it. Not quite
one in the morning. She sighed, thinking what nonsense it was that she
could not be permitted to stand guard—she slept so rarely and her night
vision was the most acute of the entire party's.

From a short distance off came the yapping howl of a coyote, and for
a moment all the desert was still.

Madelaine rolled onto her side, recalling the young American missionary she had visited in sleep, only three nights ago, just before she
left Yuma. He had luxuriated in his dream so intensely that he doubtless

spent the next morning plagued with guilt. It was not the same as being with Tecumseh, of having him desire her in full knowledge of her nature. For the next few years she realized she would have to content herself with the fare of dreaming men and the memory of all she and Tecumseh had shared.

There was a sudden flurry of activity near the campfire, and Dutch Hagen cursed.

Madelaine opened the flap of her tent. "Is anything wrong, Mister Hagen?"

"Something bit me," he replied, laughing enough to show he did not consider the bite anything serious. "It's uncomfortable. I'll put salve on it before I go to sleep."

"What was it?" Madelaine asked, aware of how little she knew of the dangers of this region, and nothing at all of the poison of plants and venom of animals here.

"I didn't see it, and I didn't get to squash it," he answered. "I don't know. Maybe a bug. Maybe a spider. It'll be fine."

"All right," said Madelaine, disliking the thought of anyone being hurt out here, where only the few jars she carried could treat injuries or illness; and in a place like this she did not want to have to deal with more pressing emergencies, such as gunshot wounds or broken arms.

"Go back to sleep, Madame," said Dutch Hagen softly. "You'll need your rest tomorrow."

This was more true than Madelaine liked to admit. "I agree; and I wish you would consider my suggestion that we travel at night. There are many desert-living people who do." Night would be easier for her, not compromising her strength and endurance as the battering daylight did. She would have less of her esurient hunger if she could travel at night.

"So you say. And maybe we'll do it, if we don't reach that canyon soon." He shied a small rock into the night and listened to the scuttlings where it landed.

"Very well, then. Good night, Mister Hagen." Madelaine closed her tent flap and resigned herself to drowse for the next watch.

GOING UP THE COLORADO RIVER, 25 JANUARY, 1856

*It has been getting more difficult to travel, for the river is faster and the
banks are higher. In an overwhelming way it is impressive. Carlos Nisachii informs me that this is only the beginning and that our journey will
become arduous in a day or two. I am pleased now that we had the good
sense to hire mules for this journey, given the state of the land...*
*Mister Hagen has developed a large, open sore on his shoulder where
he was bitten a few nights since. He claims it does not pain him much,
but his eyes and movements tell another story. I have offered to treat the
bite, but he will have none of it. So I am constrained to watch him suffer
and know that he could soon develop an infection severe enough to cause
irreparable harm. The men with us sense this as well, and they have become wary of Carlos Nisachii and of me...*

"IT WOULD NOT BE SO BAD if they had not taken three of the mules,"
said Carlos as he stared about the camp. "With just three left, we will
not have an easy time of it." He glanced significantly toward the tent
where Dutch Hagen tossed in the fierce grip of fever.

"I understand," said Madelaine, who did not want to spare one of the
mules to carry Hagen, but knew it was necessary. "It might be best if we
waited here today, and pressed on tomorrow."

"Or we could go back to Yuma," said Mineata dryly. "I would like to
go back to Yuma." She indicated the forbidding landscape around them.
"This is no place for the likes of us."

"Possibly not," said Madelaine, permitting herself to feel discouraged. "But we have come such a long way, and we may need Mister
Hagen's services if we are to make it back without trouble. He must improve, and quickly." She sighed. "I have a poultice for hurts of this sort,
to draw out the infection and ease the pain. I will treat him with it today
and hope that he will be better tomorrow."

"He cannot be much worse," said Carlos Nisachii. "The fever will kill
him soon if it doesn't break."

"Yes, it will," said Madelaine.

ON THE BANKS OF THE COLORADO, 29 JANUARY, 1856

*Mister Hagen continues to improve, but slowly, and our progress is cur-
tailed because of it. I doubt we have covered more than five miles today,
and much of that in the early morning... I continue to treat the festering
bite on Mister Hagen's back and take some reassurance in its continued
draining. It will not be long before it will begin to heal, if he does not
cause renewed inflammation.*

*If I can find a few crucial herbs, I believe I can stimulate his capacity
for healing, but many of the plants of this barren land are unfamiliar to
me, and I must proceed with care.*

NIGHTFALL CAME EARLY TO THE SANDBAR in the canyon; above
the sky was unsullied blue, and the rocks glowed in the long, slanting
rays of the sun where they touched them. But the direct light penetrated
no more than half-way down the walls, making the twilight beneath the
more oppressive for the brilliance above.

"How far does this canyon reach?" Madelaine asked as she slapped
dust from her canvas trousers.

"No one knows, señora," said Carlos, bowing a little in deference to
her.

"But it does reach the tribe I'm seeking? The Havasupai people?"
She found this place beautiful in a stark and dangerous way, though the
quantities of running water so near her gave her a persistent touch of
vertigo.

"It is said that it does." He looked around. "I have not been to their
land, myself, but I have been told how to get there. And you may be sure
they know we are searching for them."

"Oh?" In spite of herself, Madelaine felt apprehensive.

"They always watch those who come into the canyon. If they approve
of us, they will come to us and guide us to their place. If they do not
approve, they will drive us away with rockslides and..." He crossed
himself. "They can summon the spirits of those who have died here to
fight for them."

"And you think they will?" Madelaine asked.

"If we are not to their liking," said Carlos.

110

"What do they like?" It was an obvious question, and Madelaine did not expect much of an answer.

"Quien sabe?" Carlos replied: who knows.

THE COLORADO RIVER CANYON, 5 FEBRUARY, 1856

We have managed to cover another four miles today. Near the rim of the canyon I can see patches of snow, and the wind that whips through these towering stone walls is an icy knife.

Mister Hagen is improving noticeably, which is a great relief. In a few more days he will regain some of his strength, or so I suppose now. Mineata has been feeding him rabbits and wild fowl, and it seems to help him. I think she is very taken with him, for she fusses over him and smiles when she looks at him.

I have three chests of my native earth left, enough to last me well into next year if I am circumspect in what I do. It will take time to get more, either from San Francisco or St. Louis, and I must keep that in mind...

Carlos Nisachii has told me that the number of Indians watching us has increased, and earlier today we came upon the footprints of half a dozen flat-shod feet, which tends to support Carlos's claim...

THERE WERE THREE OF THEM STANDING at the end of the narrow sandbar, their faces stoic, neither frightening nor welcoming. They waited for Carlos Nisachii to approach them, and when he did, they let him speak first.

Madelaine continued to make her notes in her journal, taking care to do nothing that would give the newcomers reason to strike out. She glanced toward Dutch Hagen, who was squatting next to their cooking fire, helping himself to the last of the stew Mineata had made.

"Three of them, four of us," said Hagen quietly. "It means they're probably not going to kill us."

"Good," said Madelaine, equally softly. "Then we and they are in agreement. It is not in my plans to be killed here."

"I would guess not," said Hagen with a curt laugh. "My Volcanic is still in my tent, curse it."

"I think it is probably just as well," said Madelaine. "I doubt those three men would be here if your gun was in sight."

"That might not be a bad idea; we better not look too worried," said Hagen, taking his skinning knife and using it to pick up the hunks of meat on his plate. "Beans and goat. Not too bad for a place like this."

Carlos glanced over his shoulder, indicating Madelaine, then resumed his hushed conversation with the other Indians.

"They have knives," said Mineata, making it a simple statement. "I don't know if they intend to use them."

"So long as it is not on us, I don't care," said Madelaine, and went on writing. When she finished her paragraph, she closed the book and put it back in the canvas-and-leather dispatch case she always kept with her.

Hagen looked at her sharply. "We could be in a great deal of danger."

"We could," she agreed. "But I doubt that you will make it better by acting as if you expect them to kill us at once. They may well decide that you are intending harm to them, and then it will be…what is the expression? Dicey?"

"That's one expression," said Hagen. "Who knows how the dice will roll this time? It depends on them." He cocked his head in the direction of the strangers.

Carlos came hurrying toward Madelaine. "Señora, they want to find out if it is true that you are the one who is seeking them."

"And how do they plan to do that?" Madelaine asked, looking toward the three Indians. She wanted to address them directly, but lacked the language to do it. She also suspected that these men would not take kindly any direct contact with a foreign woman; few, of all the Indians she had met, did.

"They will ask you. They have ways of detecting lies, or so they say," Carlos told her, crossing himself at the end.

"Fine," she said, and rose, her dispatch case slung over her shoulder. "Lead me to them."

"I will," said Carlos, taking his duty very seriously.

Madelaine followed after, wondering how she would answer their questions, and what they would ask.

------◆------

WITH THE HAVASUPAI PEOPLE, 26 FEBRUARY, 1856

... The canyon where they live is isolated as it is beautiful; the water-
falls are unlike any I have seen, appearing to be a luminous blue-white
due to the way light falls in the steep rock walls rising around us. It does
not surprise me that these people are not much known, even by those
tribes that live nearby ... A woman named Flower Wisdom has been
given the task of trying to make the way of the people known to me.
Carlos serves as translator, but as he knows very little of the Havasupai
dialect, it goes very slowly. I do not know how much of her teaching is
actually what Carlos is telling me. I am going to have to learn some of
their tongue myself...

Mineata has put herself into Dutch Hagen's care, and keeps herself
isolated with him. He appears satisfied with the arrangement, though he
has not spoken of it directly to me...

MADELAINE HELD UP THE PLANT Flower Wisdom had just dropped
into her gathering basket. "What is this for?" she asked in the Havasupai
dialect, one of the few phrases she had learned.

With Carlos to translate, the Havasupai woman answered, "That is
for the illness-of-seven-days. It lessens the harm of the malady."

"How is it used?" asked Madelaine, reverting to Spanish.

"It is dried and pounded to powder, which is mixed with pure water,
and given to the sick person in the morning and the night."

Madelaine wrote down the information as Carlos relayed it to her. "I
thank you, Flower Wisdom," she said when she was done. "Is the virtue
of the plant the will of your gods, or is this plant like the cactus—one
that was punished for some error?"

"This one is favored by the south wind," said Flower Wisdom. "It is
the warm and pleasant vitality that comes from the south, with the main
river." She did not smile—her people, Madelaine realized, where chary
of smiles—but her face changed subtly to show how she felt on the matter of these beneficent plants and the kindly south wind.

As Madelaine finished her notes, she remarked, "It is good that you
are willing to let me know these things. I will honor your teaching."

"There are other plants that help us," said the Havasupai woman as if she had not heard or understood the compliment as Carlos translated it for her. "And roots, as well. And things in the water."

"Anything you are able to teach me of your knowledge, I am willing to learn," said Madelaine, and listened to Carlos repeat her words, a trace of fatigue in his voice; he was finding Madelaine's interest in Havasupai traditions and practices dull as well as possibly heretical.

"If you will listen, I will tell," said Flower Wisdom, and pointed to a clump of low-growing grasses. "These will be next," she declared. "They are for the fever and watery bowels. They are gathered when the trouble begins and are made into a thick tea, boiled down several times to something very dense."

Madelaine prepared to write.

ON THE TRAIL TO THE ZUNI PEOPLE, 31 MAY, 1856

… It was necessary I leave; I could not risk visiting another of the Havasupai men in dreams, for these people put great importance in the messages of dreams, and from their dreams they glean understanding which places me at risk. They have legends of those like me, and they know how we are to die the True Death. It is too great a hazard to remain now that they are alerted…

The country here is arid and becoming scrubby, making hunting more difficult. Occasionally we come across a small party of settlers in wagons bound for whatever place they are seeking… Many of them are European, often driven away from their homelands by war and persecution; most are poor, with all they own piled into a single wagon. They must be desperate beyond conception to come to this stark place for refuge.

IT WAS CARLOS NISACHII who broached the matter to Madelaine first. "It is the Apache," he said as they sat at the long plank table at the coaching inn at Santa Fe, two days after their arrival in late July. Outside it was hot in the keen, cutting way of high altitude; masses of clouds piled over the parched land, as if mocking the mountains, mottling the ground with their shadows. "The Apache are not like the Zuni or the Tewa or the Hopi or the Havasupai. You were fortunate with them; they allowed you to live beside them for a short time and did not demand anything of you beyond the respect you offered them. The Apache are less cordial. They want no one asking questions of them, least of all a foreigner like you. You will not be welcome among them. They will treat you as a foe, and will not change."

"That's possible. Yet I was not very welcome among the Zuni, either, when we first arrived there, but they soon realized I was not dangerous to them and left me alone to go about my studies," Madelaine pointed out, wondering where all this was leading.

"But the Apache are not the Zuni, or the Hopi, or the Tewa. It would be an unwise thing to stop in their company for long. They do not like white people. They do not like Mexican people. They do not like most other Indians unless they are compelled to, and they do not wish anyone to study them, and would not be content to leave you alone if you tried," said Carlos, trying to make his point as deliberately as he could. He stood very straight. "If you must go among the Apache, I will not be able to remain with you, nor will Mister Hagen or Mineata."

This announcement held Madelaine's attention. "Surely it is not so bad as that."

"It may well be," said Carlos, looking miserable to have to say such things to so kind and generous an employer. "I know good men, strong men, who will go no nearer to the Apache than we are now."

"But we are a good two or three days from their camp, and in a Spanish town," protested Madelaine, beginning to wonder if Carlos had concocted a tale. "They cannot leap that distance in an hour."

"No, but they will be watching us. The Zuni living near Santa Fe have told me that they have seen Apache scouts on the ridges." He indicated the well-ordered surroundings outside the adobe inn. "These people, the Spanish and the Zuni as well, have found a way to keep peace with the Apache. So have the Hopi and the Tewa. They give the Apache no cause to become suspicious or angry, no reason to hold them responsible for their ills. This is very wise, and I hope you will learn to behave in the same way." He folded his hands, not quite prayerfully. "I beseech you, Madame, do nothing that would put all these good people at risk. They are already uncertain as to what course they should take in regard to newcomers. You, staying here and studying them, alarm the others."

"You mean the Apache are not pleased that we have come here? I would think they would rather have us here, with the Spanish, than with the Zuni or the Tewa or the Hopi, if matters are as delicate as you suggest." She set her writing case aside. "Why should I have anything to fear from the Apache that I would not have from the Zuni or the Hopi?" She smiled slightly. "I have already dealt with many Indian peoples, the Cheyenne and Pawnee, among others. They have sometimes questioned my motives, but I have never felt threatened by them."

"Never?" asked Carlos, his eyes becoming keen. "That is not what you said to the Zuni medicine man. Do you tell me you were foolish enough to lie to him?"

"No, I did not lie," Madelaine admitted. "But I meant that in another way."

"Then you do know that you could be in great danger among Indians," Carlos said, his face brightening. "Good."

"Of course I do. But there is danger in living and the Apache are a very important nation among the Indians. They reach from the forests of Louisiana to the middle of New Mexico Territory. Surely they are aware that they need an advocate with the white government in America? Don't they realize that their refusal to allow anyone near them is working against them?" Madelaine asked this with a strong expression of indignation; this was the argument she intended to use with the Apache themselves. She braced herself to defend her position only to have her hopes dashed with Carlos' laughter.

"The Apache want no part of any government, Madame," he said when he could speak. "Other than their own, they do not think any authority is worthy of notice. The treaty they signed here four years ago means little to them, señora, for their raids continue; the major clan of this region, the Mountain Clan, has no reason to respect the treaty. Their Chief Mangas Coloradas has not required that the terms of the treaty be honored. They are independent in their own groups, as well—"

"But I have been among the Kiowa people already, and they have long associated with the Apache. Surely with the good word of the Kiowa—" Madelaine protested.

"Which Apaches?" asked Carlos sharply. "The Little Basket Clan, which is called Jicarilla, or the Mescal Clan, called the Mescalero, or the—"

Madelaine held up her hands. "All right. I will consider what you tell me," she said, already trying to think of reasons why she would not have to heed the warnings.

"And, señora," said Carlos with a faint, warning wag of his finger, "I will not accompany you to these people, nor will Señor Dutch. We will not help you to this madness. It would be senseless to ask us."

Madelaine sighed and capitulated. "All right."

———◆———

SANTA FE, NEW MEXICO TERRITORY, 29 AUGUST, 1856

Between the arguments of Mister Hagen and Padre Bernardo Lopez, it seems necessary that I give up my intention to study the Apache, at least for the present time. Padre Lopez has promised to arrange for me to speak to one of the chiefs of the Chiricahua and the Mimbreno, the local clans. I will have to content myself with this, I suppose, and leave the study of these fascinating people for another time, when it will be possible to be reasonably safe among them.

TUCKED AWAY BEHIND THE LITTLE CHURCH was a small, three-room adobe house where Padre Lopez lived; its furnishings were spartan but for the elaborate antique crucifix which hung over the long plank table at the end of the main room nearest the kitchen.

"I fear that Mangas Coloradas is not convinced of your goodwill," said Padre Lopez as he offered Madelaine a bowl of fruit. He smoothed the front of his cassock and sat down on the bench across the table from his foreign guest, and did his best to soften the blow he felt obliged to deliver. "I did what I can, but he holds all of us in suspicion."

"You mean whites in general? Or of me in particular?" asked Madelaine, politely moving the bowl aside with a small shake of her head.

"Yes, of all whites. It is the way of the Tinde, as they call themselves; Apache is a Zuni word for them, from their word for foeman," said Padre Lopez. He folded his hands and looked beyond her to the long, glowing shards of sunset light. "He also required that this meeting be at the end of day, so that they can observe this house and the church and be certain that this is not a trap. This house has been watched for hours."

"And if it is a trap, they can move against it under cover of darkness," said Madelaine, who had seen similar tactics used over the last century.

"True," sighed Padre Lopez. "Of course, you are a foreign noble-woman, and that makes you a curiosity as well as a danger, which may or may not be to your advantage. It is uncertain which will be stronger—his suspicions or his inquisitiveness." He crossed himself and fidgeted with his amber-and-silver rosary. "At least your hair is dark. They distrust all those with fair hair. A pity your eyes are that strange shade of blue; that will be considered a bad omen."

"An old friend of mine said that the Chinese once, long ago, thought all those with fair hair were ghosts." Even this oblique reference to Saint-Germain had the power to cause her a pang of longing, which she reminded herself was as useless as it was unavoidable.

"Is something the matter?" asked Padre Lopez, his weathered face creasing in concern.

She shook her head. "I may have had too much sun today."

"That is easily done in this place," said the priest, not aware of the irony of her comment. "Those with such fine skin as yours, señora, if you will permit me to say it, are in the greatest danger."

"I thank you for your concern," said Madelaine. She was concentrating on listening, aware only that the evening was unusually silent, a condition that made her very uneasy. She adjusted her shawl around her shoulders more to conceal her nervousness than to keep warm, for the evening was still hot from the relentless sun of the day.

A sound at the door brought Padre Lopez to his feet. With a fastidious gesture he adjusted his pectoral crucifix, then went to answer the summons.

The man in the door was not young; probably at least forty, judging by the depth of lines in his face and the first few white strands in his hair. He was in traditional Apache dress, but with a frock coat over his patterned cloth shirt, as a concession to the occasion. He stepped into the candlelight and made the sign for one who comes with peaceful purpose. "Good evening," he added.

Madelaine knew better than to let her surprise show. She smiled and offered him a slight curtsy. "Good evening."

"Mangas Coloradas sent me," he went on, his English stilted but far from inexpert. He regarded Madelaine with stoic calm. "I am here to talk with you on his behalf."

"So I hoped," Madelaine responded. "I am very pleased that he was willing to do this, and that you would undertake his commission."

The Apache paused and looked directly at Padre Lopez. "Must you remain here?"

"Ah ..." The priest looked from his new guest to Madelaine then back again. "It is not suitable to ... to ..."

"I will not kidnap the woman," said the Apache in Spanish. "I am here to answer her questions so long as it is proper for me to do it." He glanced at Madelaine, and added in English. "Unless you need the priest here? You are not afraid of Indian demons, are you?"

"I may need his help in translation," said Madelaine, having decided to leave her knowledge of Spanish a secret. "I want to be as accurate in my understanding as is possible."

The Indian shrugged. "If that is necessary."

"Only when I cannot understand you," she said, "otherwise I am content to speak with you in private."

"Then let us talk alone," said the Apache.

Padre Lopez bowed his head. "I will go to my study; it is the next room, and if you need my help, you can summon me easily." He gave Madelaine an uncertain stare. "Are you sure you would prefer this?"

"Yes, I think I would," said Madelaine. "But I thank you for your concern, Padre." What could she tell him that would not increase his trepidation? It would be folly to demonstrate her uncanny strength or her ability to resist all but the most destructive hurt. So she contented herself by adding, "I think we can trust to the honor of Mangas Coloradas, and his lieutenant."

"His son-in-law," the man corrected, and noticed that Padre Lopez started in recognition.

"All the more reason," said Madelaine, who decided she would persuade the priest to tell her the Apache's name if he would not volunteer it himself. "Come," she went on to the Indian. "There are chairs by the hearth. They aren't very comfortable, but they are tolerable." She held out her hand to the visitor as she gave Padre Lopez a covert signal to depart. "I am Madelaine de Montalia. From France."

"France," the Indian said, shaking her hand once as if operating a pump handle. "I have heard of it. That is over the water, isn't it?"

"Yes," said Madelaine as she drew him with her toward the chairs, her manner a nice blend of the formal and the attentive. "Far to the east."

PADRE LOPEZ'S HOUSE, 8 SEPTEMBER, 1856

We talked for the last time tonight, Mangas Coloradas's son-in-law and I. He still refuses to tell me his name, for fear of giving me power over him, though he says when he becomes chief he will have to let the world know it. I find I like him, in spite of his forbidding nature and his abiding suspicions ... He told me he learned English while working for a group of lumbermen to the east of here. It was useful to know what the white men said among themselves as well as what they said to the Indians ... He has told me a fair amount about his people and why they keep so much to themselves, and I am willing to respect it.

Before the first storms begin, we will travel; I would like to reach Indian Territory before winter comes, for I am told it is often harsh and bitter on the plains, which does not please me.

Mister Hagen has decided to marry Mineata, and will go on to St. Louis after guiding me to the Cherokee and Choctaw. He believes he can hire out as a guide west now that Kansas is being opened to settlers. Some will want to go further, into the mountains and perhaps all the way to the Pacific on the Oregon or California Trails. Mineata will travel with him, and that satisfies them both profoundly, it appears.

At the suggestion of Mister Hagen, we will travel the new route sometimes called the Cimarron Crossing, for it permits us to avoid going through Raton Pass on the Santa Fe Trail, which, I am told, can be dangerous once the rains begin. After what I have seen in crossing to the west, I am willing to believe this. It would not be pleasant to be stranded in these mountains through the winter because a road has washed away ...

MANY OF THE TREES WERE SPANGLED with leaves bright as gold coins that glinted whenever the wind touched them as Dutch Hagen led the way on the narrow track along the steep slope of the mountain. He sat his mule with the alert posture of a man wary of his surroundings. Behind him, Madelaine drew her cloak more closely around her, and patted the neck of her mule by way of encouragement. She could hear Mineata singing quietly behind her, and the clap of the pack mules farther back, behind Carlos Nisachii, who brought up the rear of the party. It was more than a week since they had left the town of Las Vegas, to the east of Santa Fe, and they had not covered as much ground as Madelaine had hoped they would.

"There's a spring up ahead," Hagen announced. "We can refill our water jugs there." He sounded relieved at his own announcement. "Make sure all of the jugs and skins are filled. It's a long way to the next spring."

They had drawn up the nine mules at the well when there was a distant, ominous rumble.

"Thunder?" asked Madelaine, knowing it was not.

"Avalanche," said Hagen as the last of the sound died away, several seconds later. "A way up the trail, I'm afraid. I hope I'm wrong."

"Is that bad?" Madelaine asked, anticipating his answer.

"It isn't good if it cuts us off here," said Hagen bluntly.

Mineata put her hands to her face in terror. "What will we do?"

"I suppose we'll have to find another way," said Madelaine coolly. "We cannot remain here." She made herself shrug. "And it may be that the avalanche is not on this trail at all; the way these mountains echo, it could be miles away from where we are going."

"That's right," said Hagen, much too heartily.

Mineata crossed herself, unwilling to believe them.

THE CONNERS' MINE, NEAR THE CIMARRON CROSSING, 17 NOVEMBER, 1856

I suppose we shall have to make the best of this. We cannot travel again until spring, not with the ice everywhere and snow coming. It is already in the higher peaks, and the wind is unforgiving...

There are nine families here at the mine, six of them Irish, the others from Holland; all are Protestant, and wary of us, because Mineata is Catholic, and they fear I may be, as I am French, and from the wrong part of France to be Huguenot. I have implied that some of my people are followers of Peter Waldo—and so they were, centuries ago—which has served to ease their worst fears. I have offered good pay for shelter for the winter, and they have set their apprehensions aside to take us in. With the hunting skills of Mister Hagen and Carlos Nisachii added to the bargain, they are inclined to overlook our religious affiliations, and we do not force the issue...

We have been given a two-room wooden house, the outer walls packed with sod. It is warmer than I thought it might be, but it is also dark and smoky, and impossible to keep clean. Mister Hagen has pronounced himself satisfied with the arrangements and is constructing new stalls in their stable for our mules...

CONNERS' MINE, 25 DECEMBER, 1856

Being good Protestants, the people of this little community have passed this holiday in Bible reading and feasting. The fare was hearty enough: goose and venison, bread pudding and potatoes in an onion sauce. I explained that those of my blood fast at this time, which is close enough to the truth to make it credible. Mineata prepared a sweet of sorts using dried berries and cream whipped into a froth and then put in the snow to chill . . .

Of late I have been longing for Tecumseh, and not only for our shared gratification; I can sense a discontent in him that wears at him, which serves to make me want to be with him, though what I could do about that restlessness, even if I were with him, I cannot guess . . .

I have discovered that two of the men here are eager to be visited in dreams, which thus far has sustained me. They are filled with simple desire and strong appetites that they admit only in sleep. Yet I dislike having to live in such close and continual proximity to them, for it might well lead to trouble if they come to make the association between the images of their dreams and me.

A CRUDE WASHROOM AND LAUNDRY had been constructed at the back of the stable, and it was here that large barrels were used to melt snow to provide water for all those at the Conners' Mine. The premises were presided over by Zenobia Bliss, whose husband served as sapper for the mine; she was a formidable woman of middle years, thick-bodied and rugged-faced with her curly faded-russet hair contained in an untidy bun. She was boiling shirts in the main tub when Madelaine came into the steamy room, and she looked up as if she resented the intrusion.

"I have a few things I would like to wash," Madelaine said.

"With hands like yours?" scoffed Zenobia, her brogue rich and musical. "You'd have a maid do it, if you could, or were you planning to ask me to?"

"I am fortunate in my skin," Madelaine allowed without bristling. "It stays soft through no effort of mine. But I require no maid to tend to my needs, just a good tub and hot water. I have my own soap."

Zenobia regarded her with patent disbelief. "There's tubs against the wall, and a washboard, if you need one. We're all out of blueing, and we're low on bleach. Won't have more till spring."

"Thank you, I have what I need," said Madelaine, annoyed to be wearing skirts again; it was worse than being hobbled.

"I hope you don't expect me to help you. You're going to have to tend to yourself here. Ladies like you don't often bother getting their hands wet, I know. But I got my own work to do," she said, indicating the boiling pot and a stack of trousers and jackets on the floor.

"I know you do. And though I appreciate your ... concern, I will manage for myself, thank you." She set about her task efficiently, doing all she could to stay out of Zenobia's way. Once she had enough hot water to begin her work, she said, "Do you mind if I use that stool?"

Zenobia shrugged, and stirred the boiling shirts with a long wooden paddle. "If you want."

They worked side by side in the steam-filled room, saying nothing as the evening dark closed in around them. Just as Madelaine was leaving, her wet wash gathered up in a canvas bag, she was startled to hear Zenobia say something to her.

"Pardon?" she asked, feeling foolish for not paying attention.

"They tell me you're writing a book," she repeated in condemning accents.

"I am." She spoke more firmly, aware that most of the people at Conners' Mine were illiterate and preferred to remain so.

"What about?" asked Zenobia, with a trace of interest.

"Indians," answered Madelaine.

Zenobia considered this response. "So long as it's not about slavery," she said at last, and went back to her work.

CONNERS' MINE, 4 APRIL, 1857

The roads are clear enough for us to leave without mishap, though not all the snow is gone from the mountains. It is warm in the day, but cold at night, with a nasty wind, making our tents slight protection. Mister Hagen is tending to the mules, and Carlos is fixing the tack for us; he is planning to shoe the mules tomorrow, having kept them barefoot all win-

ter, to prevent disease of the hoof. We will be away in three days…

It is clear that the miners will be glad to have us go, in spite of the money they have received. And I will be pleased to visit other men in their sleep than these, not only to lessen my risk but to find greater variety in my fare…

KANSAS JUNCTION, 19 MAY, 1857

At last we have reached a place where I may send my papers on, though it is nothing more than a wagon supply stop with what passes for a hostelry in this part of the Kansas Territory. And what a lot of pages there are, since I had so much time during the winter to expand my notes; in a sense the time I have had here has allowed me to do my work without distraction. This leaves me in a dilemma, for I can send my pages back to San Francisco to Euphemia Stephens, or I can send them to St. Louis, to Lucas and Turner there with instructions that they be sent on to Amsterdam.

I cannot write that name and not think of Tecumseh, and I wonder how he is faring in San Francisco, if indeed he is still there, for I have sensed a change in him of late. Whatever he is doing I hope it will bring him the satisfaction which thus far seems to have eluded him. He has such turmoil within him. I want to know what has become of him, though it is foolish of me; he is still married and would not want me disrupting his life again.

Carlos Nisachii has told me he will be turning back in a few days, hiring on as an extra guide for a group of settlers bound along the old Santa Fe Trail. He has said he would carry my work to Yuma and see that it was handed over to one of the more reliable shippers to be taken to San Diego or San Francisco, as I wish… One way or another the pages will be sent.

Mister Hagen has assured me he will see me into Indian Territory; with all the fighting going on in the Kansas Territory, he does not think it safe for me to attempt to travel without escort, so bitter is the dispute over slavery in this place. I have tried to comprehend the argument between the slave-holders and the abolitionists, but the proponents of each position seem terribly muddled, resorting to Biblical quotes when reason fails them…

A CLOUDBANK GATHERED OVER THE WESTERN SKY, dark and massive; to the northeast the Cimarron River wound toward the Arkansas and then the Mississippi. "You won't have to go all the way to the old Father of Waters," said Hagen as he recalled the land ahead of them from his previous journeys. "Once we reach the Arkansas, we'll be pretty near your destination. That is, if you're still determined to study the Choctaw."

"I would like to study them all," said Madelaine with feeling.

"What about the ones who don't want to be studied?" asked Hagen, relishing their ongoing debate. Now that they were in less hazardous surroundings than the mountains had been, or the bloody plains of Kansas, he had taken to intellectual fencing with Madelaine as an amusement.

"You mean the Apache?" Madelaine shifted in her saddle to be a little more comfortable.

"I mean them, and the Seminole, and probably a couple dozen others who want to keep to themselves." He chuckled, enjoying himself. "What makes you think that the others wanted to be studied, anyhow? How do you know they told you the truth when you asked them questions? Why should they tell you the truth? Can you be certain that you did not change their ways simply by being there?" He glanced at Mineata and smiled at her, and was rewarded with her most profound look of gratitude.

"I don't," Madelaine conceded.

This was not the response Hagen was hoping for, and he scowled. "Then how do you justify what you do?"

"I don't," she said a second time. "If we had to justify curiosity, we should all be still building pyramids and worshipping the sun. America would remain undiscovered, except by the Indians, and—"

"All right, point taken," said Hagen, and shaded his eyes to check the horizon. "We're going to have rain in an hour or so. Do you want to stop or keep on?"

"Is there shelter ahead?" Madelaine asked, her tone cool and practical.

"I think there's a way-station about eight miles on. If we pick up the pace, we should make it." He signaled to Mineata. "We'll have to press the mules."

"They won't like it," said Mineata, who had had a lot of experience

125

with the animals.

"Too bad," said Hagen, and pushed his mount to a bone-jarring trot.

"This is when I miss horses," said Madelaine, using a military post to break the worst of the jolting. "Mules were never intended to trot."

"They would agree," said Hagen merrily, refusing to be aggravated by the gait.

Madelaine gathered her reins and prepared for a hard eight miles.

CHOCTAW NATION, INDIAN TERRITORY, 30 JUNE, 1857

To the north are the Cherokee and the Creek, to the west are the Chickasaw, to the south is the Red River and Texas, to the east is the state of Arkansas. This is the place the United States gave the Indians when they were removed from their traditional homelands in the states of Georgia, Louisiana and Mississippi. The Cherokee come from further north, from the Carolinas, or so I am told by Joseph Greentree, who has agreed to answer my questions. In regard to the uprooting brought upon his people some twenty years ago, he informs me that not all his people left their lands when the government demanded it, that there are still small settlements in remote areas of their old lands, and that there is continuing contact between the Nation and these isolated Choctaw.

These people have made many concessions on certain points to the whites, but have remained sternly uncompromising on others. Joseph Greentree has told me that he will never reveal his Indian name to any white, for only Choctaw may know it, and I am content to honor his determination. He is part of the Greentree clan, and so accepts it as a family name as is the way of Europeans. He is an interesting man, about thirty-five, well-schooled and clever, with an excellent understanding of the many difficulties confronting his people. His wife has given him four children, which pleases him because all four are alive and well. I am to call her Sarah...

Mister Hagen and Mineata have departed for St. Louis, and I wished them happiness together and gave them a wedding present of fifty dollars and three mules. They are carrying my notes for me. They will deliver them personally to Lucas and Turner, and inform them where I may be reached for the next year or more. I will contact them myself as soon as I

know how I intend to go on here, which will depend more upon the Choc-
taw than on me ... It was tempting to ask for news of Tecumseh, but I
resisted, to a point: I did ask how business was going in San Francisco as
part of arranging transfer of my remaining funds there back to St. Louis.

I have also instructed that all but two of the reserve chests of my na-
tive earth be shipped to me here, for once I have been allocated a house,
I will need to prepare it, and I have just the one chest left ...

SHORTLY AFTER MOONRISE, Joseph Greentree came to the door of
the simple frame house the Choctaw had set aside for Madelaine's use.
He held his lantern up as he knocked so that she would be able to see his
face plainly when she opened the door. "I don't mean to disturb you," he
said as soon as she answered his knock. As was correct, he did not use her
name, for that would be an unacceptable invasion of her privacy.

"I was making notes; you don't disturb me, Joseph." Madelaine
recognized his courtesy, and knew that so long as she used his public
name, she would not offend him. She held the door a bit wider. "If you
want to come in?"

He shook his head. "Thank you, but it would be considered ... odd."

"You mean it would be improper for you, or for me, to do this," she
corrected him gently. "Many of the other Indians I have studied have
had similar restrictions, and I will respect them. And I appreciate your
concern. It is awkward for you, I'm sure, dealing with me, since I am
foreign and a woman. I hope that your teaching me the language of the
Choctaw will not make trouble for you." She kept the door open, and
studied him, noticing how serious he looked. "Tell me what is bothering
you." It was hot and close in the way of summer, though it reminded
Madelaine of the steaming winter laundry at Conners' Mine.

"It is nothing so important that I would call it a bother. No, it is
something I believe you should know for your own protection, so that
you will not be drawn into a dispute, which could go badly for you. It
is a thing that is worrisome to the people here." He cleared his throat
and spat, to show that he would not allow a lie in his mouth. "We are all
troubled by it. It is the matter of slavery. We must come to a decision."

Madelaine cocked her head and looked at him. "Yes?" Why did he
come in the night to tell her this, she asked herself. What had her studies to do with the Choctaw debate on an institution that was not of
their making? She remained quiet, giving Joseph Greentree the time he

needed to answer.

"We have had a long meeting, the other Greentree clan members and I, and we have decided that we do not want slavery any more. Not for Greentree." He regarded her with a direct look. "It is an incorrect thing." The word he used in Choctaw implied shame and loss of face as well as incorrectness.

"And what has that to do with me?" asked Madelaine, truly puzzled.

"There are those in the Nation who do not agree, who, like the Cherokee, keep slaves, or have had them before. But if we are ever to be allowed to be our own state, we must agree on slavery as a condition of our statehood." He coughed once, and rubbed his chin with his free hand. "It is not the way of Choctaw people to make another man property, even if the man is black, unless he has been defeated in battle, and we do not fight the blacks. To buy a slave is not honorable, for there is no contest to see who has the right to rule the other; that is our way. These blacks are purchased like sheep and pigs, and that is not our way."

"As you understand it, you of Greentree," Madelaine added for him, sensing what was coming now.

"Yes, as we of Greentree understand it. It is not what all Choctaw accept." He turned his head away from the lantern to conceal his frown; without success, for Madelaine's vision was keener than he knew. "It may be that you, as our guest, will come to hear of these things. I do not want you to believe we ask you to take our position, but it would not be wise for you if you were to disagree with us among the rest. Such things are not understood here as they are in your world. It would appear that you disdain our hospitality."

She listened to him without comment, and when he stopped talking, she took a short while to reply. "I do not think my opinions are needed in this matter." Not, she added inwardly, that they would pay any attention to her in any case. "It is because I am French, that you think I will know things you do not?"

He stared at the line of her roof. "Some might suppose this to be so."

Madelaine made a gesture of dismissal. "I am here to learn from you, not to teach you. I am not like the missionaries, who bring you reading and the Bible at the same time, with the intention of using the skill they teach to bend you to their faith. My purpose here is to record as much as I am permitted to discover about you, not to persuade you of my correctness. Whether or not the United States are agreed upon slaves or whether the central government has the right to decide these things for all states is nothing to me if it does not have meaning to you."

He nodded, only his eyes showing his relief. "I will tell the others."

"As you wish," she said, and prepared to close the door.

Joseph stopped her. "Certainly you may believe slavery is acceptable, if that is your way. I will not try to persuade you, either."

"Ordinarily it would not be appropriate for me to tell you. However, if you are curious," Madelaine added pointedly, "like you, I do not favor slavery, not after all I have heard of it." She did not say that the accounts she had received had been from Saint-Germain and had concerned his centuries in Egypt, and his later misfortunes in Tunis and Spain, not the published catalogues of the plight of the blacks in America, which she had only encountered once.

Joseph Greentree managed a slight smile, as a concession to her European manners. "It is a good thing to hear of you. I would not have expected anything less from you."

Madelaine regarded him steadily. "Is it going to get unpleasant? For your people?"

"I don't think so. The Americans will have to change their laws, but we have nothing to do with that. Their laws are theirs, and they will maintain them or change them according to their understanding." He made a gesture that took in the whole of the Choctaw settlement. "It is not our way to fight over such things."

"But the … the Americans are fighting, already, from what I have seen and read. In the Kansas Territory." She looked directly into his eyes, and made no apology for her affront to his position.

"They are. But it is their fight, not ours." He hesitated, then went on with some awkwardness. "Many of them want it to end there, in the Kansas Territory. That is why the army does not stop it. As long as the army plays no part, the matter can be resolved peaceably. Otherwise, they fear there could be war."

"Not a great one, surely," said Madelaine, recalling all she had heard in her travels. "And not over slavery. That is still decided by the states, is it not? How can that be changed?"

"Yes, the states decide, and they do not agree," said Joseph Greentree. "But it might not always be." He lowered the lantern; the wavering light cast his face into stark, low shadows.

"That is for some time in the future, and for the Americans," said

Madelaine, her demeanor mildly distant. "Neither you nor I will be consulted when the time comes." She knew it would be sensible to thank him and close her door before it could be noted that they had been speaking for longer than was seemly.

"No, we will not," he said, and stepped back to wish her good night. As an afterthought he said, "Allan Riverman is leading those who favor slaves."

In spite of her best intentions, Madelaine looked startled: Allan Riverman was one of the men she had felt drawn to and had already once visited in his sleep. "He is?" She wondered if she blushed at this outburst.

"Yes," said Joseph Greentree, his face revealing nothing of his thoughts. "You ought to know it."

"All right; thank you," she said, and went back into her house.

WITH THE CHOCTAW, 3 SEPTEMBER, 1857

... How anyone contrives to work in this heat, I cannot think; it drains the will as well as the strength. The last two weeks have been one continuous roasting in the worst of sweltering dampness I have encountered anywhere. Egypt was an oven, but its heat was the desiccated heat of aridness, not this rich, green, strength-sapping enveloping moisture. Saint-Germain described this to me from the time when he went into the jungles in South America, but I never supposed I would endure it here on the plains of the North, where there is a sea of grass, and no vast green umbrella overhead to hold in the heat. It cannot have been this miserable when I was with the Kiowa, or Cheyenne, or Ute peoples, or I would have given up skirts then. How I miss the summer chill of San Francisco fog now ...

I have arranged with Darius Jones of New Orleans to have books shipped to me as regularly as possible; I have deposited two hundred dollars with him, on account, to ensure his quick service. I have missed having something new to read, and I find my own writing grows stale if I am not exposed to new authors. I am planning to make a similar arrangement with William Harris of Philadelphia, who has had a business there for twenty years and more, and who is reputed to be most reliable ...

*Joseph Greentree has told me much of the history of his people,
though I notice he does not go farther back than when the first white
men came here, and I have been unable to coax anything earlier from
him. Still, what I have will undoubtedly be useful, the more so because
he has taught me so much of the language of these people... He has
agreed to arrange for me to talk with a number of the clan leaders,
though he has warned me that it is not likely I will be able to get information from them he has not supplied already.*

*I am still not allowed to talk with the women of the Nation. Appar-
ently the missionaries have convinced the men here that I, and all foreign women who are not missionaries, may be a bad influence on these
women, tempting them to turn against the traditions and virtues of the
Choctaw, though why I should want to do that, since it is their tradition
I have come to study, I cannot imagine...*

IT WAS THE FIFTH TIME MADELAINE had met with the clan leaders,
and she found that the talk would not go any more easily than it had the
first time she tried to speak with them. They tolerated her as a stranger
more than they did as a woman; Simon Wright, who at sixty-eight was
the most senior of the leaders, had yet to say more than two words to
her.

The men sat in a circle around a low and unnecessary fire; a few
of them were smoking pipes, and all were listening to Nathaniel Hill
recount in their language, interspersed with English words where the
Choctaw had none suitable, the meeting he had had with the Creek
leaders three days ago. Insects droned in the still afternoon, and the
first hint of autumn was in the long shadows cast by the pines. "They
are inclined to the federalists, as the position best suited to their aims,
and the one most likely to gain them statehood. They would rather not
maintain their posture alone, for that would make it appear that dissention existed here in regard to the government. I told them I would
broach the matter with you." As Hill concluded his report, he sat down,
giving Joseph Greentree the opportunity to speak.

"I say it is to our advantage if we support the Creek," he declared. "If
there is one government in charge of all, then we have just the one to
deal with instead of four states and four governors. It is easier to get the
ear of one president than to force four governors to agree, for they are
jealous of one another and will not do anything that they suppose will

131

advance the others." He moved aside.

"That supposes that the president will give better justice than the governors," protested James Pearce, one of the younger leaders. "If we are granted statehood, we will not want to be answerable to the president for everything. If the president is oppressive and unwilling to hear our petitions, is it not better to have governors who can be appealed to? Perhaps not every one will honor our requests, but if we persuade one, it will be easier to persuade the others, and if we can persuade only one, we will have something for our efforts. If we cannot convince the president, we will have nowhere to turn, and no autonomy of our own, for the rights of states will not exist." He glared suddenly at Madelaine. "We should not speak in front of her. Who knows what she will tell the officials."

Joseph Greentree got to his feet once more. "We have already agreed to permit her to listen, and I do not want to deny her what we have agreed she may have. I will stand for her reliability." He folded his arms, watching Simon Wright for his response. "I believe she will not betray us."

"Good," said Pearce. "It would not be fitting to be compromised by a woman." He shot a quick look at Madelaine, his dislike showing well beyond acceptable bounds.

"We are not unkind to our guests," said Simon Wright, very quietly.

James Pearce did not take this reprimand well. "How is it that we are her hosts? She came to us. We are not obliged to her."

"We do not dishonor those who come to us in peace," Simon Wright said, not willing to look at Madelaine.

"She came here in good faith," said Joseph Greentree. "She has abided by the requirements we have made of her—"

"Hah!" Pearce countered. "What white woman comes to Indians in good faith? She wants something from us—"

Knowing it was unthinkably rude, Madelaine stood and said, in faltering Choctaw, "Yes, I want something from you. James Pearce is right. I have said this from the first. I want to know all you can tell me of your people, so that I may set it down."

Four of the men stared at her, two of them so shocked that Madelaine began to feel embarrassed for her outburst. Finally Joseph Greentree began to smile. "She is a good student."

"Too good," muttered James Pearce. "We should not allow her to listen if she understands so much. She is worse than a spy among us."

"I do not think she is a spy," said Allan Riverman. "I think she may be something much more dangerous than a spy." Since the death of his wife in childbirth, two years ago, Allan Riverman had been suspicious of all women, as if his wife had touched all females with the potential of death; all those listening, except Madelaine, knew this.

"She is too impetuous," said James Pearce. "She lacks judgment."

"It is wrong for her to speak," said the half-blind William Taylor.

Five of the leaders nodded their concurrence, but Joseph Greentree said, "She is not one of our women, who must live by our ways. She is a visitor here, not Choctaw. If we permit the missionary women to speak to do their duties, then we must allow her to, as well, no matter what the missionaries tell us. She may listen to us and not trouble our women with her foreignness. It is not fitting that she be accused and have no one to speak for her."

"Better she were gone," said James Pearce.

Allan Riverman made a sign that gained the attention of all the leaders. He rose from his place and regarded Madelaine with a direct stare, apparently unmindful of the implied insult in his steady look. "You say you record what you learn of us. What do you do with your records of what you have learned?"

It took a moment for Madelaine to calm herself sufficiently to answer. "I write them as ... detailed reports on what I have seen and been taught, and when they are ready, I send them to my publisher, who is in the Dutch city of Amsterdam. That is across the ocean, far to the east—"

"I know where Amsterdam is," said Allan Riverman. "And I know where France is, as well. We may not travel about the world as you do, but we know something of it." He indicated she should continue.

Now Madelaine was feeling slightly flustered. "Well. My accounts are printed and published from there, in French and English. Most of the copies of my work are bought by scholars at universities. Some are sold to those interested in America." She stared down at her hands, and tried not to appear nervous as she laced her fingers together. "It is rare that more than a thousand copies are sold, over a period of three or four years."

Riverman was concentrating on everything she said. "A thousand copies. So many."

"It is actually not a large figure," she said, wishing she knew how much any of these men had read. "My publisher calls it respectable." For an instant she saw Saint-Germain standing before her, elegant and compelling, his dark eyes glowing with pride in her. She felt her self-possession return. "I have not offended any of those I have written about thus far."

"Are you certain of that?" asked Allan Riverman, regarding her with determination. "Do you have any direct knowledge of this from any of those you have written about?"

Finally Madelaine smiled. "Yes, as a matter of fact, I have a letter from the administrative head of the Kiowa, thanking me for recording the working of their calendar. His name is Running Cat, and he is an old man, much-honored by his people. I can bring the letter to you—he wrote it in English."

"In English," repeated Allan Riverman. "How convenient."

"It is, for the sake of my publisher," said Madelaine. "Running Cat reads the language better than he speaks it. There are times he claims he does not speak it at all, and there are foolish people who believe him, to their sorrow."

Simon Wright gave a single crack of laughter and motioned with his pipe. "It is well that she has given us her word. I would not like to be opposed by this one." He looked away, and it was understood that he accepted Madelaine's presence for the time being.

"Why do you allow this?" demanded Allan Riverman of Simon Wright. "She is a foreigner. She is a woman!"

Simon Wright turned back to Riverman. "Why allow it? Because she is foreign and a woman. If anyone questions what we have said, she is the best witness we can produce, for she has no direct interest in our people, and no hope of reward from us for supporting us. What she reports can help us." He put his pipe back in his mouth and once again stared off through the trees.

Allan Riverman heard him out in astonishment. When the old man fell silent, he turned to the others. "I no longer object. She can stay."

———◆———

WITH THE CHOCTAW, 22 JANUARY, 1858

Winter continues bitter, but not as hard as the one I passed with the Cheyenne. With the considerable information on the Choctaw I have amassed, I am busy every day, which pleases me, especially now that Simon Wright has agreed to tell me more of the history of his people, including events before Europeans arrived here from Spain and France. Since I provided his widowed daughter with a draught to ease her stiffening fingers, which the Choctaw herb-healers have not been able to do, he has been convinced that I mean his people no harm, and has made certain that the other leaders do not slight me ...

Now that I am half-way through the first load of books, I am beginning to hunger for more; in a month or so I should have a carton of them from Harris in Philadelphia. I find it strange that I should go without them for more than a year and miss them only occasionally, but once I have a dozen in my hands, I long for another twenty ...

Reverend Sampson is still here, and is still determined to "bring the Gospel" to all the heathen in Indian Territory. I have rarely encountered anyone with so narrow a mind as the good preacher possesses. He is distrusting not only of anything he does not believe is Christian, but of any Christianity that does not conform to his notions of it. He regards me as dangerous because I am obviously a Catholic, and therefore suspect. He strongly endorses the prohibition that prevents me from speaking with the women here. If he had any notion of my true nature, he would most certainly resort to the Church's methods of dealing with those of my blood, and burn me at the stake ...

I wonder if I should risk visiting Allan Riverman in his dreams again with all the disturbance Reverend Sampson is causing. Little as Allan Riverman trusts me, he is drawn to me, and it gives his dreams a potency that I am grateful to have, since I cannot have knowing passion, as Tecumseh gave me ...

THE NIGHT BREEZE SMELLED OF APPLE BLOSSOMS, and the sound of the nearby stream, now running full, added a gentle melody to the darkness. The Riverman house was at the front of a small grove of pine, the door facing south as tradition demanded.

Madelaine approached the building from the side, coming through the edge of the pines, moving with the shadows. Finally she stood beneath the window of the room where Allan Riverman slept. With a faint sigh, she began to climb up the tree nearest the side of the house, choosing hand- and foot-holds that had become familiar to her in the last months. She reached the branch that came nearest the window, and made her way with care along it, aware that her position was precarious. At last she was as near to the window as the branch came, and the most dangerous part of her journey. Without her extraordinary vampire strength and pliancy, this next maneuver would have been impossible. She stretched out her left leg, and secured her foot over the lip of the roof. Then she reached out her arm, sacrificing her firm hold on the branch to do this. With a quick shift, she swung her weight from the branch to the edge of the roof immediately below the window. Then, very carefully she eased her right arm and leg onto this narrow perch.

For an interminable instant she teetered there, unable to scrabble for purchase because that would risk waking Allan Riverman inside. Then she regained her balance, and started to open the window, taking care to move slowly and carefully so that no sound would alert him. When she had enough of a gap in the window, she slipped through and stood in the shadows, letting the sense of the room come to her before she moved toward the pallet where Riverman slept, his cotton night-shirt open at the neck, his blanket drawn half-way up his chest.

Madelaine watched him, assessing the depth of his sleep. When she was satisfied that it would be safe to approach him, she moved forward carefully, speaking his Choctaw name that he had told her in an unguarded moment a few days ago. She kept her voice low, saying "How beautiful is sleep. In your sleep you are enveloped in the beauty of all things, and you know your sleep makes you part of all things. Your sleep is so sweet that you want nothing more than to enter more deeply into its realm, where you may seek the serenity of the beauty given in sleep, which encompasses all things. Your satisfaction in sleep is so great that you will not be taken from it while the beauty of your dreams engulfs you. You know the richness of your dreams, and honor them with your sleep." She reached his side. "The great beauty is life, to see all around you filled with life," the rich cadences of the Choctaw language turning this to poetry. "It is an honor to embrace life, to walk in the beauty of life." Now she was standing next to his pallet, and she knelt beside him, moving with greater care than before. This was the crucial part, where her risk of waking him and facing discovery were greatest. It was also where she longed most poignantly for the acceptance of her nature and her self that would make his dreams unnecessary. "You are part of all the beauty, which fills you with its own joy. You enter into the whole of life, and you are beautiful with it." She touched him, her fingers lighter than a passing breeze. "You are endowed with life; it stirs you."

Allan Riverman moved slightly, his breathing becoming slower and more regular as he fell more profoundly asleep.

"You are surrounded by all things beautiful, and you seek them with all your heart, with all your soul." Her voice was hardly a whisper now; she kissed his chest where his nightshirt was open, and waited to see if he would waken. When she was certain he would not, she went on, "You are sustained by the beauty around you. You are part of it, joined with it, taken into the First Ancestor, and made one with all the world." She felt his excitement increase, and she wished he would embrace her, accept and know the gift she imparted. But that was folly, an invitation to disaster. Long experience had taught her to accept the limitations of her nature. As she enflamed his desires to the height, she pressed her lips to his neck, sharing in his ephemeral exaltation.

When he was once again deeply lost in sleep, she left the way she had come, satisfied but unfulfilled.

WITH THE CHOCTAW, 7 JULY, 1858

Two letters today, and another three chests of my native earth.

Saint Germain has written to me from Bavaria to tell me that he is going to London again, to settle business there. It is wonderful to know what he is doing; I miss him with all the strength of my love for him ... He tells me that copies of my second monograph have been well-received and he is eager to see the next; he is proud of what I have done ... He went to the premiere of a new opera by Verdi at La Fenice in Venice, a work called Simon Boccanegra *which he says was not much applauded. How strange it seems to me, attending opera premieres and going to museums, though I enjoy such things. Now I think it must have been a lifetime ago that I did such things, though it is less than a decade. In time I will want to do these things again, but at present they seem an encumbrance, an obstacle to learning ...*

The second letter brings me the funds I have requested, and the news that Tecumseh is no longer in San Francisco, that he has left the bank for other work. I wonder what has become of him? I can sense discontentment in him, but that has always been with him, as have his dark moods. It is not surprising that his restlessness finally prevailed ...

Simon Wright has agreed to review all my notes on the Choctaw, and if he is satisfied, he will permit me to contact some of the small com-

munities of his people still living in Louisiana, Alabama, Mississippi and Georgia, so that I may see how they keep to the old ways. That would be an accomplishment.

SARAH GREENTREE LOOKED UP from her weaving and nodded to Madelaine. That done, she resumed her task as if nothing had passed between them. It was a mild autumn day, with enough of a chill in the air that both women wore jackets, Madelaine's in wool, Sarah's in antelope hide.

"Sarah," Madelaine said, coming nearer to her, yet not so near that it would insult the woman; she spoke in Choctaw, "I know you have been told not to speak with me. I know the leaders have insisted on it. I wish you would tell me why, because it baffles me that I should learn from the men and not the women."

"It is not the wish of my husband," said Sarah quietly in English, her eyes fixed on her work.

"But why is that?" Madelaine persisted.

"You must ask him," said Sarah, her English becoming more accented than when she first spoke.

"I have, and he will explain nothing," Madelaine said, not liking to admit she was troubled by this refusal.

"Your ways are strange to us," said Sarah, clearly determined to end the conversation.

Madelaine moved nearer, looking at how quickly and expertly Sarah worked her loom. "But yours are strange to me, and I want to learn from you, so that the strangeness will lessen, and our understanding grow."

"It is not the wish of my husband," Sarah insisted a second time. "I will obey him."

"Yes, I know that," said Madelaine with asperity. "But why does he refuse to permit me to learn from you?"

"If he will not tell you, I will say nothing." She stared once at Madelaine. "Some of the old women on the old lands might talk to you, those whose husbands have died. But no woman here will." With that she resumed her weaving with silent determination.

"I will speak with your husband," said Madelaine, and expected no response.

"He will not tell you," said Sarah unexpectedly. "It is not advisable to ask."

"Perhaps not," Madelaine responded to lessen Sarah's discomfort, "but I will speak with him nonetheless."

WITH THE CHOCTAW, 5 MARCH, 1859

It is growing more difficult to remain here, for there is burgeoning tension within the Nation concerning affairs in the United States. Some of the Choctaw fear that the opportunity for the Nation to become the Choctaw State rather than a portion of Indian Territory is slipping away from them as debate in the United States over states' rights becomes increasingly heated, though Minnesota has been admitted to the Union and I am told Oregon is about to be, in fact, may have been by now and word of it has not reached us ...

Joseph Greentree has advised me to take the offer Simon Wright has made and go to the communities of Choctaw in the United States, to Louisiana and Mississippi, perhaps. From any of those states it would be possible for me to depart for Europe, which Joseph Greentree recommends I do, for he fears that war is coming, though the others disagree ... While I do not wish to leave with so much more to learn, I know that it would not be wise to remain much longer, not only for my own sake, but for the sake of these good people, who have got a rift in their Nation now that seems insurmountable, separating those who support the Union from those who support the rights of states over those of the Union. If the debate among the Americans is half as intense as it is here with the Choctaw, it could prove more difficult to resolve than most hope it will be.

I still have not been given a reason why it is wrong for me to speak to the women, only that the traditions will not allow it. Joseph has repeated what Sarah told me, that perhaps one of the widows in the old land will be minded to break with tradition and discuss the women's lore with me. It would be more easily done here, where I am known and trusted to a point, but it may not be possible. I want to respect the traditions, but I also want to have the information. Thus the dilemma of the scholar ...

Now that Allan Riverman has taken a wife once more, I do not visit him at night. And while I am saddened that our meetings are ended, I hope that the time will come when I will again meet a man who is willing to know my true nature and love me without the aid of dreams ...

139

"YOUR NOTIFICATION TO YOUR BANK will be sent with the next courier, along with your instructions for shipping your goods back to France." said Joseph Greentree as he helped Madelaine finish the last of her packing. "This is not man's work," he remarked for the third time.

"But you offered to do it," Madelaine reminded him. "And I thank you for it."

"You will not tell anyone I have done it, will you?" His eyes smiled, though his mouth remained stern. "Especially not Sarah."

"She would not believe me if I did," said Madelaine seriously, and saw his slight, single nod of agreement.

A short while later, Joseph Greentree said, "My brother Luke will take good care of you. He is an experienced guide, and he knows where all our people are who remain in the old lands. He goes there often and knows which ways are the most safe. You may trust him with your life, for he would not dishonor our hospitality by taking you into danger." He allowed her to pour him a cup of coffee, the last gesture of friendship she would make in this house. "I have to admit it will be odd to have you gone. Many of us have grown used to you being with us, asking questions. You have made us think of things we might not otherwise have considered." He put his hands around the mug she offered, and looked down into the hot, dark liquid. "There are few things the white men have brought us that are as pleasant as coffee."

"To the white man's shame," said Madelaine with feeling.

"No; it is not for shame, it is for ignorance, which they will not admit. White men are quick to feel shame and to be angered because of it. That is one of the reasons many of our leaders do not trust them." He patted the table left in the main room.

"How strange that you should call white men them to me," Madelaine said with a rush of pride. She had succeeded as she had hoped she would, after all.

"Well, it is not wrong, is it?" He cocked his head as he waited for her answer.

"How do you mean?" she asked, realizing that he intended more than he told her. "What is it, Joseph?"

He did not respond directly. "There are sometimes animals born white, when all the rest are the color of earth. They are noted for this, and we do not hunt them, for fear of bringing too much of their medicine upon us, for they are sent to make the spirit known. It is not fitting that such creatures should die." He took a long sip of coffee. "Some similar things happen with men, from time to time. Or so the old tales teach us."

"Yes," Madelaine agreed carefully.

"And those who are born white like the animals are more comfortable in the night, under the stars, whose color they share." He patted one of the chests that contained her native earth. "And they are often more closely held by the land, are they not? They are part of it and not part of it, of it and beyond it. And it is the same with certain people, as well."

Madelaine could think of nothing to say. She nodded once, slowly, wondering what Joseph Greentree would add, if anything.

Eventually he finished his coffee and put it aside, and then he indicated the door. "Come. It is time you were leaving."

LEAVING THE CHOCTAW NATION, INDIAN TERRITORY, 14 OCTOBER, 1859

I am beginning to appreciate how kind Joseph Greentree was in sending his younger brother Luke to serve as my principal escort and guide, though there are three other men accompanying us. It is enough of an escort to convince the Choctaw that I will not be dishonored or come to harm. My first traveling with these men has gone well, I think. Luke Greentree has a remarkably detailed memory, and his ability to find our way through what appears to me to be trackless countryside is astonishing. Like many of the Choctaw, Luke Greentree is a man of few words, and I suspect he does not approve of what I have been doing among his people, for I assume he is afraid that I will show no lasting respect for the traditions of his people. However, he is more suspicious of Reverend Sampson, which gives me hope . . .

My single regret is that I was not able to learn from the Choctaw women directly, so that all the information I have on them has come second-hand. The decision to keep me from speaking directly with the women has remained firm against all persuasion. I will hope to have another opportunity to learn of them before all the old knowledge is subsumed by the teachings of missionaries, so that all the traditions are shifted and altered to fit the demands of the preachers.

In two weeks we will cross the Father of Waters to Memphis, in Ten-

IN THE FACE OF DEATH

nessee, which I do not look forward to. They would have chosen a less obvious place, but they have agreed to do this for my benefit. I have asked that I be allowed to lie down while we are on the water, and said that arrangements must be made for this, though I gather it is inconvenient. I have claimed that the motion of the current makes me ill, which is not as far from the truth as I would like ... Luke and his three companions regard this as ludicrous, but as I am a European woman, they will do what they can to indulge me in my caprice, which is something ...

The
Tennessee
River
and
Cumberland
Plateau

MEMPHIS, TENNESSEE, 23 NOVEMBER, 1859

Today I purchased three more horses to replace those we left on the western bank of the Mississippi; the breed is called Foxtrotters and they are valued for their stamina and the rapid gait which gives them their name. I also bought two large mules with tack, to augment those we have already for our journey eastward along the Tennessee River; I was warned that it might be difficult to buy more of this or any mount but a plow-horse in a month or so, not only because winter is coming but because there are many Southerners who do not want to sell anything to foreigners for fear it will aid the Yankees. There is much speculation about the Yankees, and consensus is that they are not to be trusted, for they are sly and clever and they are said to want to ruin the South. I am at a loss to know how the purchase of a two or three animals would make any significant difference in this dispute, but I will take the warning to heart...

Luke Greentree wants to be away the day after tomorrow, once we have finished restocking our provisions. This evening he warned me against wearing my trousers here, telling me I will give the white settlers offence if I do not wear skirts, no matter how much of an encumbrance they may be. I know of these biases, but I find it difficult to take them seriously. Nevertheless I suppose I must put on petticoats once again, little as I wish to, and climb back onto a sidesaddle.

This town is all caught up in reports of a tragic incident at Harper's Ferry in Virginia: it appears that an abolitionist named John Brown, with a small company of followers, took over an armory there to protest the continued legality of slavery. They held the place for three or four days, to the anger of the townspeople. He and his followers were captured after a company of U. S. Marines under a Colonel Lee overpowered them a few days later. As I understand it, they are now to stand trial for treason against the state of Virginia. Sentiments here are for hanging, though apparently many abolitionists feel Brown should be released, and a few regard him as a martyr to the abolitionist cause . . .

I have received a letter of credit from Lucas and Turner, brought very quickly from St. Louis, telling me the current state of my account and providing such traveling funds as I may need. They tell me they are shifting my funds to another bank in Brooklyn, New York, in case there should be war; apparently they are doing this service for many of their larger depositors. While I doubt it will come to open hostilities, I can see it would be sensible to transfer the account, and have sent the necessary authorizations.

My new dresses will be delivered tomorrow, since fashions have changed while I have been with the Choctaw. The skirts are now more voluminous than two years ago, and the waists more tightly nipped with corsets; sleeves are often tiered, which is most impractical for my endeavors, but I have seen women at all sorts of tasks in these new fashions, so I suppose I will learn in time. Day dresses show less shoulder and bosom, but the evening gowns are nearly as revealing as those of eight years ago, and done in opulent fabrics. I will not have any ball gowns, of course, but there are three riding habits and two day dresses and a dinner gown with a second crinoline for special occasions. These clothes are not as heavy as I would like for winter, but when summer comes, I doubt I will complain. I do not relish having to accustom myself to these changes, but I suppose I must, at least to some extent . . .

RAIN WHIPPED THE TREES to bending submission as the little party wound their way along the slope above the small river Luke Greentree called the Daughter of Rainbows; it was no more than mid-afternoon but the day was already darkening as the clouds massed over the vault of the sky, jostled along by the wind. Madelaine and her escort had left Memphis behind two days ago, but their progress had been slowed as the weather worsened, and now, with a storm driving up from the southeast, they were still barely twenty miles from the city, near the little lumber town of Gazette.

"Madame," Luke Greentree called back to her through the rain, "I think it would be best to take shelter for the night. It will only get worse as the day fades, and we might not reach Bradley's Station before nightfall."

"You may be right," said Madelaine, her face all but aching from the pounding of the rain. "Is there a place in that town below where one may rent a room for the night, do you know?"

"There is an inn, for those traveling to and from Memphis; it has ten rooms, as I remember," said Luke Greentree, pulling his horse to a halt and motioning to the rest to stop. "You could stay there, though they do not like catering to women alone. It is a dangerous thing for women to do, traveling alone. We will find a place at the livery stable."

Madelaine shook her head and the water from her hood ran down her neck and into the high collar of her riding habit, making her shiver. "I don't understand why it is that such restrictions are placed upon you," she said, although it was not wholly true, for she had seen enough of white contempt for Indians that she felt embarrassed for her race.

"I do not like inns. They are too closed in," said Luke Greentree. "It is better that we sleep in stalls tonight."

"With your horses?" said Madelaine, though she already knew the answer.

"Yes. So they will be there in the morning, and no questions asked." He spoke without inflection, but it was apparent that he knew of old the practice some stable-keepers made of taking Indian horses and claiming them as their own, since the Indians did not brand their mounts. "These are white horses, and they might leave them alone." He did not sound very confident.

"If you think it best," said Madelaine, her dismay concealed unsuccessfully. "I will abide by your choice."

"It is not you who would take our horses. You bought them; they would not sell us such mounts as these if you had not paid for them," said Luke Greentree, knowing what bothered her.

"And I have the bill-of-sale along with a record of their brands, not that these men would pay much attention to a woman, if they were determined to steal the horses," said Madelaine with a trace of bitterness. She let her own argument convince her. "Very well, I will take your advice and do as you suggest, for all our protection. Lead the way." She thought that it would not be easy to get down the slope in the wet. "At the walk."

"Yes," agreed Luke Greentree, with a glance at Madelaine's sidesaddle. "It would not be safe for you to go faster."

"It is a ridiculous thing," Madelaine agreed. "But if we are to go among white people, it is necessary." She disliked the way she sounded, too proper and stuffy, so she added, "Another foolishness."

"That it is," agreed Luke Greentree, and started his strong clay-bank chestnut Foxtrotter down the shoulder of the hill, zig-zagging to stop from sliding into the trees.

It was not easy for Madelaine to keep up with him; her balance in her sidesaddle was more precarious for her and her mahogany-chestnut Foxtrotter, and the constant shifting made her legs ache. She longed to be back in trousers, with legs on both sides of her horse and a good strong hold with her lower legs. But that would not be acceptable to the good people of Tennessee, and she knew it. She resigned herself to the discomfort of her ride, and struggled to keep up with the Choctaws.

As they reached the outskirts of the little town, an old man with a forty-year-old Pauly double-barreled sporting-gun came out of the nearest building, ordering them to halt. "Or I'll shoot you all, like the varmints you are. Don't come no nearer, any of you redskins." He wore a wide-brimmed hat that shed rain over his shoulders. He hoisted his sporting-gun to his shoulder and made a show of sighting down the double-barrel.

"We're looking for a place to stay the night, a safe place out of the rain, so the horses can dry off," said Luke Greentree, one hand up, the other controlling his mount.

"Not here you're not," the old man insisted, seeming to be about to fire. "Move along, all of you."

Madelaine pushed her horse to the front of the group. "It would be a kindness," she said as if there were no danger from the old man. "We have been traveling all day."

The old man stared. "What in tarnation?" He lowered his sporting-gun and peered at Madelaine as if he did not trust what he saw. "Come nearer. Let me have a look at you."

Obediently Madelaine nudged her gelding ahead and stopped him less than six feet from the old man. "I am Madelaine de Montalia, from France," she said as cordially as she could. "These good Choctaw are my escort. They have brought me safely all the way from Indian Territory, and will guide me to Charleston, where I intend to take ship for Amsterdam."

"You said yourself you're no Dutch woman." He hefted his sporting-gun once again. "And what's a white woman doing in the company of redskins, anyway?"

"I am French, as I told you. But my blood relatives are in Holland, where they went during the Revolution, and I will return there to join them once again." It was near enough to the truth that Madelaine knew it was a plausible tale; many French had fled their country during the Terror seventy years before.

"Oh. One of them." He made a point of mulling over what she had told him. "Well, it's right peculiar, you coming here with Indians and all, but I suppose, you being French…" He trailed off.

"Thank you," said Madelaine and taking advantage of his confusion, said, "I understand there's an inn here."

The old man hitched one thumb to indicate the main street. "Fifth house along on the right after the lumber mill, two stories. You can't miss it—has a sign with a rooster on it." He regarded the Indians suspiciously, his gunbarrels angling upward. "Four all there are?"

"Four men and four mules," said Madelaine, indicating the pack animals they led. "I own the mules and the horses." She said this last, recalling Luke Greentree's warning.

The old man showed his opinion by hawking and spitting. "They won't take savages at the inn."

"We will stay with our animals," said Luke Greentree with an irony the old man did not appreciate.

"Well, see that you do," he said, and retreated back into the plain storefront building he had emerged from.

"They were more reasonable in Memphis," said Madelaine as she put her horse to the walk again. "If you will stop at the inn first, I will make arrangements for a room, and for a meal to be provided to you." With the amount of money she now carried in the lining of her corset, she supposed she could buy the inn, and the livery stable as well, without putting herself at a disadvantage; meals and shelter should be no trouble to purchase.

147

Luke Greentree said nothing, but his bearing became straighter. "You are good to us. My brother said you would be."

"That is high praise, indeed," said Madelaine with great sincerity as she watched for the inn with its sign of a cock. Little as she wanted to admit it, she was looking forward to resting somewhere dry and warm.

* * *

MOULTON, ALABAMA, 7 JANUARY, 1860

We arrived at this place on Big Nance Creek, which flows north to the Tennessee River, two nights ago, amid the worst sleet I can remember in decades, though I am told it is not uncommon in this part of the state. We found a family here who was willing to take us in for a reasonable fee. They have even allowed the Choctaw to stay in the house, albeit in the slaves' quarters, where there is room for six and they have but two; the quarters have a stove in one room only.

The family is named Montgomery; there are seven of them: Lamont and Auralene, with his spinster sister Mary Anne living with them, and the four children: Bethune, 11; Russell, 8; Pansy 7; and Clifford, 3. Mary Anne has been serving the town as schoolteacher and librarian, tasks which are not entirely to her liking, but she says that in Alabama a woman without a fortune and having a prominent facial birthmark such as she has must make her way as best she can without a husband.

This house is one of the three fanciest in this little town, which is not saying a great deal, and the Montgomerys are one of the most important families in the town, and have been here for more than forty years. Mary Anne said that the only reason we were given shelter in this town is because Lamont feels a debt of gratitude to the Choctaw for saving his father's life, thirty years ago. Most people in Moulton and the towns in this region do not like or tolerate Indians and would refuse to house them no matter what the weather, but the Montgomerys are not so unkind, which is why Luke Greentree brought us here, or so I suppose.

On another front, Luke Greentree informs me that we will not be able to reach a small group of Choctaw living deep in the hills to the south of here until the weather improves, which may mean spending the winter here. It is unfortunate that we cannot continue on at once, but I know that the next six to eight weeks are apt to be hard. I will try to contain my restlessness and turn the time to good purpose.

148

THOUGH THE FIRE WAS ROARING in the little Franklin stove, the schoolhouse was unpleasantly chilly; it was the first time it had been opened in more than two weeks. Now that the storm was over and the roads marginally passable, class would be resumed. Mary Anne put her books on her desk and pointed to the chalkboard behind her. "My brother bought this for the school. He had to go all the way to Chattanooga to get it." She turned her face away so that her smile would not be marred by the strawberry mark the size of her palm that dominated most of the right side of her face. "I can't tell you how grateful I am to you for agreeing to talk to my students. They have so little opportunity to expand their knowledge beyond these mountains."

"It is my pleasure," said Madelaine.

"France is exciting enough for me," said Mary Anne. "But to think that you have been to Egypt, and you so young. What that must have been like." There was a wistful expression in her eyes, and another, less generous emotion.

"I am not as young as you suppose; and Egypt is a furnace." Madelaine regarded the schoolroom with a mixture of curiosity and dismay. It was so small and had so little to offer. There were two shelves of schoolbooks under the shuttered windows, and perhaps four hundred volumes in the cases at the back of the room, which she understood was the town library. She did her best to show approval. "This is probably the best school for miles around."

"Probably," said Mary Anne, "since it is the only school." She made a gesture that was at once self-deprecating and satisfied. "For where we are and what is to hand, we do well enough. I'd like to buy more books, of course, but we already have more than many of these small communities can boast. Still, it would be wonderful to have more to read, and more modern references." She looked at the clock hanging on the wall and frowned. "The children should start arriving in the next ten minutes."

"How many do you teach?" asked Madelaine.

"In good weather, about thirty-five, but on a day like this, I will be surprised if more than fifteen or sixteen come for lessons, and they will leave at mid-afternoon." She set out making stacks of notebooks on her desk. "I try to give them exercises they can work on without my constant supervision, but it isn't a very satisfactory way to go about it." Again she glanced at the clock. "I am going to boil some water for tea. Would you like a cup?"

"No, thank you," said Madelaine, and went to the back of the schoolroom to inspect the volumes there. "I have brought many books with me. Would you like to have a few of them when I leave?"

Mary Anne beamed. "Oh, yes." Then she recalled herself. "That is, if it is no imposition on you. I would not like to ..."

Madelaine spared her further confusion. "It would be my pleasure to return some of the kindness you and your family have shown me," she told the other woman. "I will look at what I am carrying and set aside titles you may find of use."

"That's wonderful," said Mary Anne. "Living here, where we do, it is not often that we have such an opportunity. The plantations in this region do not favor these towns, and so it is not an easy thing to get books. They usually come in from Georgia, or from Chattanooga."

"It must make your teaching more difficult, being so isolated." Madelaine thought of the Choctaw, off in Indian Territory, or the Havasupai, hidden in their magnificent canyon, or the Apache, deliberately seeking to be left alone, and she decided isolation was a relative matter.

"I fear so," said Mary Anne, with no trace of emotion in her voice. "From time to time my brother pays for the supplies we need, and the parents are supposed to give their children notebooks and pencils, but—" She shrugged.

Madelaine recalled her days in Turkey and the hostility her desire to learn engendered, before she was declared persona non grata for her attempts to teach her native staff to recognize a few words in French. "But not everyone approves of learning," she finished for Mary Anne.

"No, they do not," said Mary Anne, and turned her head as her two oldest nephews came rushing into the schoolhouse, banging the door closed, their faces rosy above mufflers. They carried their notebooks in canvas grain bags, and set these on their desks at once.

"Take your places, Bethune, Russell. And no misbehaving." Mary Anne used the same stern tone with the boys as she used for the rest of her students, or so she intended. "I will want to have your essays on Texas before class begins."

The two boys made a show of disgust, but both brought out scrawled pages of exercises and carried them obediently to Mary Anne's desk.

"Isn't Pansy coming to school?" asked Madelaine, thinking that the little girl should have arrived with her brothers.

"No," said Mary Anne tonelessly. "She's being tutored by her mother. She doesn't come to school."

"I see," said Madelaine.

"Lamont believes that women should be protected from the harsher truths of the world. He prefers that Auralene teach Pansy so that she will not be exposed to any of the unpleasantness a general education too often requires." She said this as if reciting from memory, and there was a futility about her attitude that revealed this was an old family dispute that Mary Anne had consistently lost. "Auralene was taught the same way. It makes for docile wives, or so they claim."

"Yes," said Madelaine, her memory of the Ursuline nuns who had provided her first, properly genteel education coming back to her in a rush. "And she spends as much time learning to set a perfect seam as reading and mastering her numbers."

"She does; and how she will manage when the world changes, I dread to think," said Mary Anne with feeling,

"Then you expect the world to change? That is wise of you, but uncommon," said Madelaine.

"Of course it will change. Look what is happening with railroads, and that is the least of it. In twenty years, who knows what invention will bring to us? We are at the beginning of a new age, and we must prepare." She was about to go on when more children burst into the schoolroom, their mittened hands holding their schoolwork. Mary Anne turned her attention to these new arrivals, and left Madelaine to her own devices for the next half hour. When a modicum of order was established, Mary Anne announced, "Miss de Montalia is here from France, which is her home. She has graciously agreed to tell us something about her country and the places she has visited, including Egypt. Say good morning to Miss de Montalia."

The class rendered an uneven chorus of "Good morning, Miss de Montalia."

Madelaine came to the front of the room and faced the children. There were eighteen of them, ranging in age from seven to sixteen, fifteen of them boys. Madelaine sighed, and began, "My family home is in the south of France, as yours is in the south of the United States. It is near the border with Italy, which is how we got our name, de Montalia, the Italian mountain. I still have a house there..."

TWELVE MILES NORTHEAST OF AURORA, ALABAMA, 18 MAY, 1860

Fox Woman has decided she will take me as a guest here at her little holding in the mountains. She is a widow of about fifty with five grown children, three daughters and two sons. She lives alone by preference and keeps two goats and a flock of chickens, though she does not make cheese, for she claims it makes her ill. Many Indians have the same complaint. She uses the goat hair for weaving and from time to time buys a young one and slaughters her oldest for food. She is a capable hunter, as well, and knows every edible plant in the region, which information she is willing to impart to me ...

Finally I will learn some of the teachings the Choctaw women have gathered over the years. Fox Woman has agreed to let me be her student in exchange for all I can tell her of Europe and Africa. She claims that none of the missionaries she has met have been willing to tell her anything of these places, and she told me she doubts they have any authentic information about them, including the place called the Holy Land. I find her skepticism refreshing and I am delighted to discover another woman who loves knowledge for its own sake. As curious as I am about Indian peoples, she is about whites. And blacks as well, for that matter. I have warned her that I have seen little of Africa beyond Egypt, but she is willing to forgive this lapse in exchange for what I have seen in Turkey and Greece.

Luke Greentree and his three companions have decided to remain nearby at a small Indian settlement, so that next spring they can escort me to Charleston or New Orleans and so fulfill their commission from the leaders of the Choctaw Nation. The reason they are staying in the settlement is less clear: I gather they are looking for wives, though one of the men has said he wants to find a militia commander to take him on if there is war.

LIGHTNING FLICKERED IN THE CLOUDS like sparks on flint. Fox Woman looked up from where she had been digging, and remarked to Madelaine, "It is the heat that brings the thunderstorm. Heat is the fire in the sky. The clouds are there to keep the fire from consuming the earth, though they cannot stop its heat. Sometimes sparks escape, and the thunder comes."

Madelaine rubbed her face, hoping that Fox Woman was not too aware that she did not sweat in this appalling weather. "How does the fire get into the sky?"

"It comes from the sun, of course," said Fox Woman, pointing down to the root she had exposed. "This will help stiffened muscles and re-store vitality. It is best when pounded to a paste and then boiled into broth. In times of famine, it will be one of the last plants to die, and therefore it will feed those in danger of starving. It does not dry very well, and should be used fresh." She dug out the root with her wooden trowel. "Here."

As Madelaine took the root, she turned it over in her hand, saying, "Where does this grow? Only in these mountains?"

"How should I know the answer to that?" snapped Fox Woman. "I have lived all my life here."

"But surely," Madelaine said with all the respect she could muster, "the women's teachings record if this root is found in other regions." She slipped the root into the capacious front pocket of her apron.

"Oh. Yes, it is found more often in the mountains, but it can be found in forests from here to the sea." She rocked back on her heels, then pushed herself to her feet. "In the lowlands, the plants do not grow as tall, and you must look for them in hollows and under trees. In spring, the plant puts out a pale blossom." She cocked her head. "I have shown you the honey-tree already."

"That you have," said Madelaine. "You smoke out the bees the way the people in my part of France do."

"Just as well. Bees tax us with pain for taking their bounty." Fox Woman pointed along the trail to a cluster of bushes. "Those are not to be touched."

Madelaine went a bit nearer and looked at them. "Nettles," she said.

"That is what the whites call them," Fox Woman said in her direct way. "They may be cooked and used as a poultice or a tea." She raised her head suddenly. "Horses coming. Three or more." With a quick mo-tion she pulled Madelaine back with her into the shadows of the trees. "Say nothing. We do not know who they are."

Madelaine obeyed, knowing better than to dispute any of Fox Wom-an's orders. They remained in the shelter of the trees for some time, and then Madelaine touched Fox Woman's sleeve. "Is it safe?"

Fox Woman answered indirectly. "They were not Indian people. They were whites. Sometimes they come here, looking for runaway slaves." She scowled. "There are more runaways now than before."

"You mean more of them try to hide here? With the Choctaw?" Madelaine asked, her curiosity mixed with apprehension.

"From time to time," said Fox Woman evasively. "There are tales of Choctaw guiding some of the slaves to the Shakers in Tennessee. What becomes of them after that, I do not know. It may be only tales."

Madelaine heard this out with growing interest. "Are you saying that some of the Choctaw help runaways?"

"I am saying that it is said that some of the Choctaw help runaways. I have no proof that it is so, not as the whites demand proof." She started along the path toward her house. "There are some of our people who do not wish to do anything that might bring the ire of the whites upon us. There are others who say it is a dishonor not to help a slave seeking to be free if the slave was not taken in battle." She stopped and indicated a low-growing, broad-leafed plant. "That is very good to eat. It has a taste like good peppers."

"Shall I gather some?" Madelaine asked, starting to reach for the plant in question.

"There is no reason. We have plenty food at the house. And you do not eat it, do you?" She squinted upward as another spatter of lightning laced the clouds. "It will rain shortly."

"How shortly?" asked Madelaine, looking upward as thunder muttered in the distance.

"In twice the time it will take us to walk back to my house," said Fox Woman, her eyes bright with amusement, though there was not a trace of a smile on her lips.

"That is well enough," said Madelaine. "It might be best for us to turn back."

"Not quite yet," said Fox Woman. "We do not want the slave-hunters to find us. They do not use women alone well." All the mirth faded from her eyes. "I had a good friend, who kept to herself as I do, and she was taken by the slave-hunters and used shamefully."

"You mean raped?" Madelaine asked, dreading the answer.

"I mean that was the least of it. She was dragged by the horsetail until her legs were ruined, and then they left her beside the road. The rot took her." She recited this as if it meant little to her, but the stiffness of her back and shoulders gave her away.

154

Madelaine decided to keep silent. "It would be well to find shelter, in that case," she said.

"There is an abandoned mill not far from here. We can go there. Those men have already searched there. They always look there first. No one hides there any more, but they always look there, in case the runaways have been stupid. It is the men who look for them who are stupid." She started off, away from the trail through the undergrowth, taking care to avoid the densest thickets and brambles. She paused once to point out a small, purple berry just forming on a trailing vine. "This is good for those with great swellings. You make a paste of it and smear it over the swelling. It is not good to eat it."

"I will remember, Fox Woman," said Madelaine, keeping behind her mentor.

"And well you should," she answered, lengthening her stride so that her long, soft, deer-hide skirt slapped the underbrush aside.

Madelaine followed after her, matching her pace easily to that of the Choctaw woman; as she walked, she pondered what she had been told.

WITH FOX WOMAN, NEAR AURORA, ALABAMA,
2 SEPTEMBER, 1860

When I returned from town today, I found Fox Woman in great distress. It appears that there has been a rift in her people over the matter of states' rights and the Union, and the damage this has done to the Choctaw Nation is most upsetting to her.

From what I heard in Aurora, it seems likely that there may be some kind of open hostilities between the North and the South on the same issue. At least the men in town were eager to have a fight with the North ... The resentment they feel toward the political weight the North has acquired runs very deep with these people and many of them want to show their disgust with the high-handed way the North has handled Southern matters ... Luke Greentree has asked me to consider leaving America, in case the rancor between North and South should erupt into open conflict. He tells me he would like to escort me to Charleston so that I could arrange for a berth on a ship bound east. I have informed him I will wait until spring so that we will not risk getting caught in bad

*weather, for I would not like to have to establish myself in a new loca-
tion for the winter when I have managed so well here. He does not like
my decision, but he has given me his word he will not try to persuade me
to change my mind.*

*There was a new box of books waiting for me. Mister Harris has fi-
nally caught up with me again. He was good enough to enclose some recent newspapers from Philadelphia and New York, and one from London
as well. It seems that King Oskar of Sweden died last year and his son
Charles is now reigning. The rulers have changed in the Two Sicilies,
and King "Bomba" is no longer alive to harass his own people, though
Garibaldi and his Redshirts may become a force to deal with before
long... Tecumseh must be pleased with the discovery of silver in Washoe,
Nevada, for it must increase the likelihood of the rail link of east and
west which he thought so necessary. With the pony express started, at
least mail is moving between St. Louis and Sacramento in rapid order,
much faster than by sea. Ten days to cross two thousand miles is an
enviable performance... The papers are all several weeks old now, but
I was pleased to have a glimpse of the cosmopolitan world again, and
read accounts of developments, editorial opinions, and commentary on
the political climate... Who knows, in a year or two, I will probably
miss that world enough to return to it...*

*One of the books sent by Mister Harris is Charles Dickens's new
novel, A Tale of Two Cities, which I have found unreadable. Such deliberate sentimentalizing of so unsentimental an event as the French Revolution, and a heroine with no sense about anything, a perfectly mawkish
creature. Her only accomplishment, it seems, is fainting, and as for her
taste in men... I know Tecumseh admires Dickens, but I cannot fathom
what he likes in this ill-conceived drivel...*

*I have sent on to Amsterdam another portion of my manuscript on the
Choctaw, about two hundred pages of material this time, on the subject
of the lives of the Choctaw who remain in these isolated places on their
traditional lands. I do not know if Saint-Germain will want to publish
it separately now, or wait until I have finished the thing and bring out a
large, single volume...*

*I am always shocked at how much I miss him, as if I had suddenly
remembered I had lost a hand. It might not be so acute if I had a knowing lover now, but lacking one brings my love of Saint-Germain into
sharp relief and I cannot put him wholly from my mind... I find myself
wishing to see Tecumseh again, and though I know it is folly, I want to*

embrace him again. But I have no strong idea where he is, though I sense he is nearer to me than he was a few years ago…

GREGORY HOLT REGARDED MADELAINE askance as she picked up another of her huge boxes of books. Beyond the windows of his general store, Aurora looked lost in faded and blurred images as rain turned the street to mud and colored all the houses a uniform shade of dun. "You going to carry that back with you?" he asked as Madelaine, to his astonishment, hefted the box in her arms. A little thing like her, slinging about a box he had had trouble lifting… He looked to where her horses were tied. "You'll get wet, trying to get that onto the pack saddle. Or are your Indians here to do it for you?"

"Luke Greentree is not my Indian, but, yes, he and his friends are escorting me, as you say." She had warned Holt before that she disliked his way of referring to the Choctaw men, and so had no hesitation in speaking sharply now.

"But they're not here, are they?" asked Holt.

"No. They have skins to sell at the tannery. I will meet them there." The tannery was two miles outside of town so that its stench would not overwhelm the residents of Aurora.

"But what about these boxes?" Holt inquired.

"They're no problem, Mister Holt, but thank you for your concern," said Madelaine, then recognized the unvoiced suspicions behind his solicitous manner. "But it would be useful if you will have the two boxes of provisions loaded onto my pack saddle."

"Jimmy'll see to it," said Holt, and called sharply to his slave. "Put those two boxes on the lady's pack horse." He glanced at Madelaine again. "And the box she's carrying. Put that on the pack saddle, too. Let him have the books, ma'am."

"Very well," said Madelaine, who realized that her ability to handle such weights might bring undue attention on her. "How kind of you. I will. It is… heavy." Making it appear an effort, she lowered the box to the floor. "And thank you, Jimmy," she added to the middle-aged black man, reaching to hand him a coin for his trouble.

"No call to do that, Ma'am. Just gives him ideas," said Holt, and signaled Jimmy to go on about his work. "Not that it's any of my business," he went on once Jimmy had stepped outside, "but isn't it kind of dangerous staying with an Indian woman now that there's been more fight-

157

ing? I don't know if you heard, but the Indians attacked Fort Defiance in New Mexico Territory. Shows how risky it is, being around Indians. You wait until John Breckenridge is president. He'll know what to do about the Indians."

"Mary Fox," said Madelaine, using Fox Woman's name among the whites, "is a Choctaw, not a Navajo, and unlike the Navajo, she is not being denied food by the army." She had read about the incident in the St. Louis paper and had thought that the army had bungled the whole of their dealings with the Navajo. "The army ought never to have shot the Navajos' sheep."

Gregory Holt scoffed. "You got to keep the Indians in line, ma'am. Look what happened during the Seminole Wars."

Madelaine recalled Tecumseh's tales of fighting the Seminoles; even the Choctaw had little good to say about the aggressive Floridian people. "I don't know that the situations are similar. The Navajo did not attack the fort until the army killed their sheep. The Seminole have a long tradition of war for war's sake, or so the Choctaw have told me." She drew on her gloves and pulled her cloak around her in preparation for stepping out into the rain. "Oh, and I trust all is well with your family, Mister Holt." This was an afterthought, for she realized she had not seen Amanda Holt in the rear of the store today or the month before. "Will you give Missus Holt my regards? And all your children?" She had only met four of them, but was aware of another two at least.

"My wife's doing poorly, thank you for asking, Ma'am, and stays to home, most days. She's of an age when women take up humors; you know how it can be for some women when they come to that time in life." He shrugged, slightly embarrassed that he should mention so delicate a matter to this stranger. "Doctor put her on beef-broth-and-cream for a month. We'll see how she does."

Against her better judgment, Madelaine said, "I have a nostrum with me that might ease her condition, if you would like me to send some to her. It is not unpleasant, I assure you, and I have seen it do good many times. Luke Greentree will bring it, if you will allow..."

The marked distress with which Gregory Holt met this offer would have been comical if he were not so clearly frightened. "Ma'am, it wouldn't be right, taking anything from Indians. Best not."

"Not from Indians, Mister Holt, from me," said Madelaine patiently, watching Jimmy put the last of the three large boxes onto the pack saddle of her second horse and went to work securing it in place with wide leather straps. "Or are you worried that because I am French, there might be Papist contamination in the remedy? I can promise you that—"

"I don't think about those things, ma'am. I leave it to Preacher Johnson. He knows what to do." He looked around uneasily. "Don't get me wrong. I think it's right kindly of you to want to help my Missus. Not saying anything against you, but everyone knows you're staying with Mary Fox, and she's one of those Indian women who make potions. I don't reckon my wife would be willing to take a chance on something you gave her. No offence. Sorry, ma'am." He indicated the messy street, and said, "Jimmy's holding your horse."

"Thank you, Mister Holt," said Madelaine, saddened that she would not be allowed to aid the man's wife. "I will see you in a month, if the road is passable."

"You got enough food to keep you for two months, it looks like," he said, trying to make polite conversation once more.

Madelaine smiled distantly. "Yes. I suppose I do," she said, and went out into the storm.

WITH FOX WOMAN, NEAR AURORA, ALABAMA, CHRISTMAS DAY, 1860

We have kept a special fire burning for the last two weeks, made of dried blossoms and fragrant wood. We will keep it lit for another six days, to ensure the return of the sun and the reawakening of the earth. How strange that so many people throughout the world should light fires at the winter solstice to bring back the sun. Or perhaps it is not strange at all, only a human wish to influence things beyond their powers to affect...

I have been reading On the Origin of Species by Means of Natural Selection *by Charles Darwin, and I certainly understand why the book has been considered so controversial. I must write to Saint-Germain to find out what he thinks of this theory; I am much persuaded by the arguments presented in the work. Surely, if what Darwin is saying is valid, Saint-Germain, with his four thousand years, will have seen much the same thing as the adaptations described in these pages... I mentioned the thrust of the work to Fox Woman, but she is not interested in speculations of this sort. For her, the First Ancestor is responsible for all life, and there is no reason to look further for explanations...*

The people in Aurora are outraged at the election of Abraham Lincoln to be president of the United States. When I visited the town yesterday, there was a general air of angry unrest that is troublesome ... They say Lincoln is a dangerous, untrustworthy lawyer who will bring shame on the country. Most of them would have preferred John C. Breckenridge, or even the more radical Stephen A. Douglas, Lincoln's long-time political rival, to Lincoln. All the town is alive with rumors, though there is no reliable news as the roads to Blountsville, Gasden, Murphree's Valley, Guntersville, and Lebanon are nearly impassable, and those are the only places where real news may be had ... There is talk of secession in the town, and the belief that a challenge to the North must come soon, before the abolitionists bring ruin on the South. Some of the men are saying that the slaves will be encouraged by Lincoln to rise against their masters and make the masters the slaves ...

With so much excitement, I have found it more difficult to visit men in their dreams. Most are easily roused now, and their sleep is restless, no matter how carefully I lull them into that profound slumber. Twice I have almost been discovered ...

FROST HUNG ON THE LEAVES and glittered on the path to Fox Woman's door; it was early on an icy February morning, and Luke Greentree's breath ghosted his face. "I wish you would reconsider," he said to Madelaine. "There is still time to get you to the Choctaw Nation and away from any chance of fighting."

"I doubt a place like Aurora is going to be under fire, even if war does break out," said Madelaine as she wrapped her thick woolen shawl more tightly around her. "I think it would be best to remain here until the trouble is resolved. This place is isolated, and I don't think we'll have much to worry about. If there is fighting, everyone says it will be over quickly."

Luke Greentree coughed once. "We will have to leave you here alone, Madame. It is not what we promised to do."

"I realize that," said Madelaine, and determined to provide him some respite from his own demanding conscience. "And when you made me your promise, neither you nor I could have anticipated that secession would come so quickly, or spread as far as it has. You cannot hold yourself responsible for what has happened."

"Still, I do not want to leave you here," he said slowly. "I don't know when I'll be able to return." He looked up into the brightening dawn. "What will I tell my brother?"

"You may tell him that you did your best to convince me to leave before secession began, and I did not heed you; it is my fault that you are not able to fulfill your promise," she said, pleased that it was the truth. "I will not hold you accountable for what may happen now. It is beyond anything you or I might do. Your honor is not in question, Luke Greentree, not by me, and not by your brother, I am certain of it."

"I am not so certain," said Luke Greentree, his face revealing little of the anxiety that colored his voice. "My brother placed you in my care."

"But he had no reason to think that war would break out," said Madelaine reasonably. "And he cannot hold you accountable for it." Had he been European, she would have rested her hand on his arm, but she knew this familiarity would not be welcome to him, so she deliberately spoke more softly, leaning slightly toward him. "You have a right to do as you think best in this matter without regard to my situation. If you truly support the Union, then it is best that you should go with your friends and volunteer for the army in the North. You need not remain here on my account, when so many of your Choctaw men are determined to support states' rights and the secession."

"It is a bitter thing when a nation is divided," said Luke Greentree.

"Yes, it is," Madelaine agreed, thinking back to the days of the Revolution in France, and recalling how deeply the wounds of that event had struck. She did not like to think of the United States being similarly torn.

"I do not know when the Choctaw Nation will be whole again." He fell silent.

Madelaine tried again. "Listen to me, Luke Greentree. You cannot remain here, no matter what I do, so let me urge you to do as your honor requires, and act with the forces you favor. I will manage well enough. I have come this far without serious mishap." She added inwardly that the only exception to that was Tecumseh, and he had nothing to do with the conflict. "And when it is over, you may return and give me the escort you promised. Will that do?"

He almost shrugged, and allowed her to convince him. "After the war. If all goes well, by this time next year, I will return and take you to Charleston, or all the way to Baltimore, if that is your wish."

"I hope to see you by the end of summer, in happier times," said Madelaine, and held out her hand to him. "I wish you good fortune in your battles, Luke Greentree."

"And a speedy end to them," he added, and turned away from her, going into the mists that draped the barren trees, vanishing before the sound of his steps had faded.

Fox Woman appeared in the door of her house. "That was a foolish thing. You may come to regret this gesture."

Madelaine swung around and looked directly at Fox Woman. "What was I to do? He could not remain here, not with so many of the Choctaw men here favoring secession. There is no way he could guide me to any harbor now, not in safety. The only sensible thing was to release him from his obligation."

"Sensible, you call it," said Fox Woman, her expression sharp. "You are taking a chance, staying here. True, this is isolated, and that creates a kind of safety as long as nothing happens here. But if it does, you will have no haven left to you, and escape would be difficult."

"But you Choctaw have been able to manage in these places, away from important roads and big towns, where there is nothing to gain that would interest an army, and where you can hide with ease." Madelaine recalled the devastation she had seen in Paris and Lyon in the wake of the Revolution, and she added, "It is safer here than in cities, that much is certain."

"Until the fight comes here," appended Fox Woman. She motioned. "Come inside. It's too cold to remain out there."

Madelaine realized she was shivering, but knew it was from something other than cold.

NORTH OF JACKSONVILLE, ALABAMA, 8 MAY, 1861

This is a more remote place than Fox Woman's house near Aurora. She has insisted we come here because feeling was running so high in Aurora she feared the men in town would take it into their heads to practice war on the few remaining Choctaw. Where we are now is rugged country, and Fox Woman thinks that with luck we can wait out the war here.

Assuming the letter I left with Mister Holt was actually delivered to my bankers, I will be able to gain access to my money as soon as it is safe for me to travel north . . . I am troubled that I will be unable to reach my bankers directly due to the recent outbreak of fighting. I may have to make do with the money I have with me, which is little more than three thousand dollars, not an inconsiderable amount, but in these uncertain times, who

knows how long it will have to last me? Since Lucas and Turner trans-
ferred my money to the Williamsburgh Savings Bank of Brooklyn, New
York, I have had only a few dealings with the bank, which I am told is
a flourishing venture. No doubt Lucas and Turner were prudent in their
decision to transfer the funds, given how things are going in the United
States. Nevertheless, it would be more comforting to have some direct
means to reach the bank so that I will not have to depend on the mails to
the extent that I must now.

I have brought five horses and three chests of my native earth, along
with four cartons of books, and Fox Woman has brought most of her
supplies with her, along with her goats, so it is my hope that we can
continue on in the studies we have begun. She tells me that she wants to
prepare a number of places where we can retreat in case soldiers invade
the region. Given the remoteness of this location, I cannot believe it will
come to that, but I am willing to do as she wishes.

There is game in the woods, which will suffice me for a short while, but
I am beginning to wonder how I will find nourishment ... Little as I wish
it, I may have to venture nearer a town in order to sustain myself ...

"IF YOU ARE CERTAIN YOU MUST DO THIS," said Fox Woman, frowning at the cases Madelaine had just finished packing.

"Yes, I am afraid I must," said Madelaine, holding up her hand to stop the protest she knew was coming. "And if I do not leave now, I will certainly be here through the winter, which would not be wise."

Fox Woman regarded her thoughtfully. "It will be dangerous for you in a town."

"Yes," Madelaine said again. "But hunger is a greater danger still."

"There will be enough for both of us, given how little you take," said Fox Woman, cocking her head to the side. "Or are you afraid that if the winter is hard, we will starve?"

"Something of the sort," said Madelaine indirectly. "I have no wish to abuse the hospitality you have shown me, and I fear it could come to that, in the winter."

Again there was a short silence between them. "I do not wish you to go because you are worried for my welfare," said Fox Woman, choosing her words carefully.

"But I must," said Madelaine. "I cannot argue with you about this. It is my nature to need ... the things I need."

Fox Woman nodded slowly. "In that case, let me give you some names. I have cousins who work near the town of Buchanan, in Georgia, just over the line the white men insist is there, though no one has ever seen it. They have a white father, these cousins, and so are allowed to live there. They are respectful people, and will not dishonor the family or the Choctaw."

Madelaine sighed in gratitude. "You are very good to a foreigner, my friend, and I thank you for—"

"It is not a question of goodness," said Fox Woman with asperity. "You have done me honor, and I will honor you."

"Call it what you will," said Madelaine, feeling the first pangs of separation from this knowledgeable, good-hearted widow, "I am grateful for all you have done for me, and for all you have taught me. I will miss you."

"You have taught me many things, too," said Fox Woman, her bright eyes now glinting with appreciation.

"How is that?" asked Madelaine, thinking that Fox Woman was not referring to the few medicaments Madelaine had shared with her in exchange for Fox Woman's expertise.

"I have seen that though you are a stranger, you do not seek to overturn the ways of the Choctaw. I have seen also that you keep to yourself. That is an admirable thing; few whites know how to do it. They withhold themselves, and think it is the same thing." She reached for a deerskin cape and held it out to Madelaine. "You will need this, I think."

Madelaine looked at the wonderful garment and hesitated. "It is yours, Fox Woman."

"Then you will have something of me with you; and you are leaving me a horse," said Fox Woman, and all but shoved it into Madelaine's hands. "There. Now, let me tell you how to find the road that leads to Buchanan. It will not do to have you lost in these mountains."

"No; I would not like that," said Madelaine, not wanting to contemplate what her hunger could do to her if she were forced to wander the hills for any length of time. It had happened to her once before, and the memory was repulsive to her.

"You will go to Jacksonville, and take the road east that goes to Rome," Fox Woman began, very businesslike. "About five miles after the road swings north, there is another road that comes in from the southeast. There is a farm there, and a church called Bethany. Turn onto that road and follow it. Once you cross the Tallapoosa, you will have about eight miles to go until you reach a narrow road going north. That will take you to Buchanan. My cousins live a mile to the east of the town, on a farm called New Springs. Their name is Selbie: Walter, John, and Susanne. Show them the cape and they will know you come from me."

So, Madelaine thought, the gesture was not entirely selfless as she had first supposed. "I will do it, Fox Woman," she said.

"You should have escort," said Fox Woman, her sense of propriety offended by Madelaine's solitary departure.

"It can't be helped," said Madelaine, her curtness concealing a welling sadness. "And when Luke Greentree returns, tell him where I have gone, in case he should want to escort me to the coast."

"You may be sure I will," said Fox Woman, suddenly made awkward by the burden of farewells. She looked at the cartons stacked by the door. "Let me help you with those."

"I will manage them well enough, my friend," said Madelaine.

The canny look was back in Fox Woman's eyes. "So that I will not discover how heavy they are? I have seen you lift things that no woman—or man—your size should lift without effort." Her manner turned brusque. "Go on. Load your pack saddles."

Feeling disquieted by this abrupt change in Fox Woman, Madelaine faltered. "It…it was not my intention to deceive you."

"Good. You didn't," said Fox Woman, and went back to her household tasks while Madelaine busied herself with loading her chests and crates onto the pack horses.

When everything was loaded and strapped into place, Madelaine swung up into her sidesaddle, disposed her skirts in the approved way, secured the deerskin cape to the cantle of the saddle, and called out to Fox Woman, "I thank you again, my friend." She waited, hoping that the Choctaw widow would come to the door, or make some other gesture for good-bye, but it did not happen, and after a few minutes, Madelaine picked up the reins and the leads of her three pack horses, and rode away through the autumn-bright trees toward Jacksonville.

ON THE JACKSONVILLE-ROME ROAD, 17 OCTOBER, 1861

The dun is going lame on her off-front. I have slowed the pace to a walk and moved all the load from her pack saddle to the other two, but I can see no improvement. It will probably be necessary to leave her here, at Bethany Church, so that she will have a chance to recover…

I have encountered a number of young men on the road, some of them wounded, who are going home for harvest, leaving the army for the winter … They are all full of tales of the great deeds of Generals Beauregard and Johnston, whom they believe will rout the Yankees completely before the end of the year. They are less pleased about a Yankee general named Butler who has taken several coastal forts in the Carolinas …

The minister here is an odd young man, full of zeal and the rhetoric of religion, but also filled with passion he does not recognize for what it is. He believes completely in the Last Judgment, and that it is coming very soon. He has warned his small congregation that they will have to answer for their sins before God in the next few years, basing his assumption for this on some of the stranger verses in the Apocalypse of Saint John, which the Protestants call the Book of Revelation … While I can understand why it is he is afraid, with war breaking out everywhere, I doubt it is the trumpet of the Last Judgment. He is very worried about the souls of his flock, thinking it necessary that he save all of them, though why he should think he has such a right or obligation, I cannot fathom, for his ordination is self-imposed. And although he refuses to keep slaves, he is certain that whites are a superior people to blacks, and men superior to women; the Bible confirms this, or so he insists. Abolitionists are anathema to him, the embodiment of devilishness he cannot sufficiently condemn. He has only a sketchy knowledge of Africa, taken mainly from his interpretation of passages in the Bible, which he accepts as the sole authority on all matters. If he found a passage in the Bible he decided meant that righteous men should wear their shirts back to front, he would do it at once. While castigating me for my "vain and unfeminine intellectualism," I saw that he desired me. This condemnation is the price of his charity for a place to stay, though I have paid him for a traveler's room at the back of the church. I wonder if I dare to visit him in his sleep? Or am I seeking to best him at his own game? Better him than one of the soldiers on the road, I suppose.

Georgia

NEW SPRINGS FARM, NEAR BUCHANAN, GEORGIA, 1 JANUARY, 1862

Walter and John have left the farm today to join the army, which surprises me, given their Choctaw mother; but apparently there is less stigma in having an Indian mother than a Negro one, though the latter are far more common than the former. Also, having their mother Choctaw and their father white is apparently less dreadful than the other way around. Their departure leaves Susanne and me to tend the place, for the Selbies have no slaves and do not like to hire hands except at harvest time. Many of the farms in this region have suffered the same fate, with most of the men gone to fight, and the women, children and old people left to manage the land for them.

There have been fewer claims of a quick conclusion to the war than I heard last spring. Then everyone supposed that it would not last long or have many losses. But that is turning out not to be the case. There have been rumors that a Northern general was invalided out of the army for saying the war would be long and bloody because he was thought mad for saying it. It gave me a start to hear about this, when I learned the general is named Sherman, and he has been serving in Kentucky. I cannot help but wonder if he is any relation to Tecumseh, for he has brothers—John and Charles, if I recall correctly—and other relations, and surely he isn't the only member of his family to have had a military education. No one in Buchanan seems to know more than his last name, and while they scoff at what they have heard of him, they say it serves the North right to have such an officer.

The hero of the day is a General Thomas Jackson who is being called Stonewall, apparently for not retreating in battle. He, along with two generals called Johnston, one Joseph and one Albert, have been quite successful in battle. Most of the people in Buchanan are impressed that Jackson is a fervent Christian, and are convinced that will aid him greatly in his campaigns...

Not long ago the Wilsons, a family three farms away, learned that two of their sons were killed in combat at a place called Ball's Bluff. Everyone in the town is shocked that this has happened, and they all hope that the two Wilson boys will be the only losses Buchanan will suffer. I say very little, because I cannot share their certainty that no more Buchanan boys will die...

MADELAINE USED A PICK TO BREAK THROUGH the ice on the water trough this cold morning of the last day in February. The small barn was hardly warmer than the outside, and the sheep, for all their wool, huddled together; the two cows at the far end of the barn chewed at their fodder and waited to be milked. Between them, Madelaine's four horses, stalled European fashion, waited for their morning oats.

"I'll take care of the chickens and turkeys," said Susanne, hoisting up her skirts as she went out in the direction of the coops. A large metal scoop, clutched in her left hand along with a mass of skirt, dribbled grain as she walked, calling out to the fowl that breakfast was coming. She was a handsome woman of twenty-four, fairly tall, somewhat angular, dark-haired and dark-eyed with strong features and flawless skin. In another place she would have been considered a very eligible woman, but here in Buchanan, Georgia, no one could forget her mother, and she was considered an old maid. To find a husband, she would need to settle in a city where men were not so particular as they were in Buchanan.

"I'll start milking," Madelaine called after her as she reached for a pail and the three-legged milking stool. The nearer of the two cows was a soft brown color and her milk was very rich. Outwardly placid, Sheba had the disagreeable habit of putting her foot into the milk pail as soon as it was full; Madelaine was now familiar with her tricks and anticipated her mischief. She moved the pail aside just before she finished milking and squeezed the last into a skimming pan, which she set aside for the half-dozen feral cats who made the barn their home.

The second cow was a tawnier color, with darker head and ears and a dark stripe down her back; called Lilly, she had the perpetual dazed air that gave the word *bovine* meaning. Madelaine filled the second pail quickly, wondering, as she often did when milking this cow, if Lilly realized she was there at all. As she prepared to carry the pails back to the pantry, she heard the sound of recklessly cantering hoofbeats on the road outside, and a moment later a large, dark horse filled the barn door, a young man, enveloped in a three-tiered cape, exhausted, hanging onto the reins. There was a bull's-eye lantern clutched in one hand, the wick still lit, mute testimony to his long ride. "Don't mean to disturb you," said the young man in a hoarse voice. "This New Springs Farm?"

"Yes," said Madelaine, neither cordial nor hostile.

"Miz Selbie?" he panted.

"No; she's around at the coops. I'm Miss de Montalia. Is there anything I can do for you?"

The young man shook his head. "Got to see Miz Selbie," he insisted.

"She will be here directly," Madelaine told him. "You might want to get down and give your mount a rest. I have to get this milk to the creamery. I will be back in a few minutes. There's water for your horse."

The young man nodded several times, then all but dropped from the saddle, dragging the reins over the big horse's head and leading him toward the water trough.

One of Madelaine's horses whinnied; the newcomer neighed back.

"Don't do that," the young man ordered his horse. "Sorry, ma'am."

"It's nothing," said Madelaine, and lifted the pails, carrying them off to the rear of the house to the creamery. She emptied the pails into larger cans, worked the pump to rinse out the pails, and then made her way back to the barn, calling to Susanne as she went.

The young man was in earnest conversation with Susanne, his soft cap clutched in his hands. "He made sure you'd want the news about Walter. I gave him my word I'd let you know."

"Where is he?" asked Susanne, doing her best not to appear upset.

"In Tennessee. He got that far. There's a ... place run by the Shakers. They took him in. They've been nursing a lot of sick and wounded, both sides. Doesn't matter to them. They won't fight, not for North nor South. They say the Good Book won't let them."

"How sick is he?" Susanne's trembling lip betrayed her emotion, though her voice was level.

"Very sick. His lungs is putrid." He looked away. "He took a bad chill after that river crossing, and cutting his back, and what with the snow

169

and all, it settled in his chest. He was doing poorly for more than a week before anyone got him help, and his cut worsened."

"And John is with him?" Susanne spoke more urgently now, as if she could not contain her worry much longer.

"He was. But his company needed him back. They need good farriers, you know. They couldn't let him bide with his brother for long, not with the Yankees pressing in." The young man was apologizing for the army now, and his face showed how difficult he was finding this interview. "Sorry, Miz Selbie. I got to get on my way. I got letters to carry to Atlanta."

"Where did you say Walter is, again?" Susanne asked, as if she were having trouble understanding the words she heard.

"With the Shakers, Miz Selbie. They're up between Woodbury and Smithville. They got about a thousand acres. Don't worry. They'll take real good care of him. They're good at nursing, and they take all comers. They're godly folk, the Shakers, but a mite peculiar. Not that that's anything to hold against them." He reached for his lantern and indicated the two large saddle bags on his horse. "You can get word to them from Rome, if you want."

"You say John's all right?" Susanne said as she watched the young man prepare to vault into the saddle once more.

"Oh, he's fine. I hear Colonel Crowder wants to promote him to sergeant." He sprang aboard his horse and pulled hard on the reins, swinging the big animal around, so that he had to address Susanne over his shoulder. "You get a letter down to Rome, and they'll see it finds your brother."

"I will," said Susanne as the young man set his horse trotting out of the barn.

When the sound of hoofbeats had faded, Madelaine came forward. "Well," she said, regarding Susanne with mixed concern and curiosity. "What do you think?"

Susanne put her hands to her face. "I don't know what to think." She was shaking now, and unshed tears welled in her eyes. "His lungs ... people die of rotten lungs."

"Yes, they do," said Madelaine. "But they don't have to, or some of them don't." She set the empty pails back on their pegs and came toward Susanne. "We will take a couple days and go to Rome."

Susanne looked around. "But how can we? The stock can't be left in the dead of winter, and we have too much work. There's no one who can be spared to look after the place, not around Buchanan." She wiped her eyes. "I will have to ask someone who is going there to take a letter for me."

Madelaine smiled at Susanne. "I'll do it." She hurried on before Susanne could protest. "I have the horses, and the road is easy. I know at this time of year it is hard going, but I have traveled worse roads before." For a moment she was back at Conners' Mine, in the impossible grip of a mountain winter. "I can go there in a day if the weather clears, and be back at sundown the next day." She held out her hands to Susanne. "You don't need me to churn for you, and you told me yourself I am useless on your loom. So let me do this for you."

Susanne looked dismayed. "I should not allow it, but..." With a sigh she capitulated.

"Good," said Madelaine, and went on enthusiastically. "We will write the letter tonight, and I will leave tomorrow morning at first light, if the weather is good."

"It isn't right..." said Susanne, shaking her head, but unable to make a greater protest than that.

"In these times, we cannot be bothered with what is right, not if it means more unhappiness." Madelaine busied herself putting out the last of the morning feed, letting Susanne collect her thoughts. With the simple chores finished, she gestured to Susanne to return to the house with her. "You need something hot inside you, to steady you."

"You must have something, too," said Susanne, her thoughts more collected than before.

Madelaine did not respond to this as she made her way along the frozen mud path to the house once again; she thought that her traveling would give her the chance to find some nourishment.

But the day ended with freezing rain, and it was not until four days later that Madelaine was able to set out to the north and the small city of Rome, along a road that was now eight inches deep in mud. Madelaine longed to ride straddled, and wished she did not have to use her sidesaddle, for on such treacherous roads, she needed all the control possible to guide her mount along them. She rode the strongest of her Foxtrotters, a nine-year-old dark bay mare with a blaze on her face and two white stockings which were quickly lost in a coating of mud.

"Are you sure you want to go?" Susanne asked, shielding her eyes from the bright, early rays of the sun. "You could wait a day or two, until it is drier."

"And watch you fret every hour?" Madelaine countered. "No thank you."

"But there will be a great deal of mud," Susanne warned her.

"Of course," Madelaine answered. "It may take a little longer than I planned, though, because of the mud." She thrust her gloved hand into her fur muff, and put her hand on the little Bell revolver she had concealed there. "You don't have to worry about me. I will manage well enough."

"Well then," said Susanne, clearly relieved that Madelaine would not be dissuaded. "Go with God."

Madelaine accepted this with a nod and a salute with her crop, then set her mare off at a springy trot. By midday, Madelaine had gone seven miles, not quite able to enjoy the wooded hillside in the harsh winter wind; but she found the ride invigorating, and she felt satisfaction to be doing something more than milking Sheba and Lilly. She was congratulating herself on making such good time with the condition of the road and the severity of the weather when she saw a carriage up ahead, its wheels mired, and a black coachman standing at the head of the team, tugging at the leaders' heads while a woman in the carriage urged him to use the whip.

"Not gonna do that, Miz Warren. They be no good with bloody shoulders. You just wait while I coax them out real gentle-like." The coachman, hearing the approach of Madelaine's horse, called out as she grew nearer, "There's a bog the next couple miles, where the road is low."

"I can see that," said Madelaine. "But I appreciate the warning."

A middle-aged woman wearing a widow's cap atop a profusion of curls clustered at her ears, that made her look more like a Cocker spaniel than a fashion plate, stuck her head out of the window and stared at Madelaine. Her greeting was formal. "Good day to you, young lady."

"And to you, ma'am," said Madelaine, puzzled by the disapproval she heard in the woman's voice.

"Where are you bound?" There was no hint of invitation in the question, and she plainly disapproved of young women going anywhere unescorted.

"To Rome. To get news of a soldier who is ill. I should get there day after tomorrow, if this road remains a mire, or tomorrow evening if it improves." She touched the brim of her fashionable hat with her crop. "I hope your journey goes well."

"Lord have mercy," cried the woman, and disappeared back inside the coach.

172

"You go right on, ma'am," said the black coachman. "It's gonna take some time for us to get out of this."

"Thank you," said Madelaine, and let her mare mince by, avoiding the ruts with water standing in them.

Two miles further on, Madelaine came upon a flat-bed wagon loaded with sacks of flour that had been abandoned, the team unhitched and taken away. A solitary slave of about sixteen years sat on the driver's box, his cloth coat hardly enough to keep him from shivering, looking forlornly down the road. He took off his cap as Madelaine rode by, and warned her that it was another six miles to a roadhouse where she could sleep for the night.

"Six miles. I should be there before nightfall," said Madelaine, and asked if she should inform anyone at the roadhouse of the wagon. "Do you need someone to come for you tonight?"

"No, ma'am. My massa's gone back to the mill on the Little Coosa. Should be along with a new team of mules real soon now. We got to get the flour to the railroad at Kingston. They want it for the army." He glanced apprehensively at the sky, as if trying to guess the hour.

"All right," said Madelaine, and went on, thinking that it was dangerous to leave a load of valuable flour in the care of one unarmed man. She let her mare choose the places on the road she wanted to walk, and patted the revolver she had tucked into the muff on her arm.

The roadhouse was not promising, being little more than a two-room frame house with sleeping compartments in the loft and communal dining at long plank tables in front of the hearth. Madelaine decided to continue on, though she realized her mare was tired; it was late afternoon and it was possible to cover another three or four miles before the horse would have to rest.

It was dark when Madelaine resumed her journey, letting the mare walk steadily. The special vision of her blood made the night brighter than for the truly living, and she took satisfaction in making the most of the increased energy the night gave her. Finally, an hour or so before dawn, she drew up at an empty auctioneer's barn and found a stall where the Foxtrotter could rest; it was time to give the mare her well-earned oats and a bucket of water; a short while with her saddle off her back and the bit out of her mouth. Madelaine gave the mare a cursory grooming and used the next several hours to stretch and nap, so that when she once again was back on the road, she was as refreshed as her mare.

Rome, when she reached it the following afternoon, was bustling with men in butternut uniforms, most of them mud-caked, in a general air of confusion that made her wonder how they had managed their successes in the field. By the time Madelaine arrived at the station-house, where mail was handled and tickets were sold for the stage coach that linked Rome with the railhead at Kingston, she understood from the talk among the soldiers that the new Southern Confederacy had lost two strongholds in Tennessee: Fort Henry and Fort Donelson, though there were rumors of a great victory coming in the west.

The stationmaster greeted her with suspicion when he heard her accent. "You're not a Georgian, are you?"

"No. I am French," she said. She knew her riding habit needed brushing and her coffee-colored hair was no longer neatly secured at the nape of her neck, for she could feel long strands of it against her skin. "I am here on behalf of a friend, who has received news that her brother in the army is ill." It struck Madelaine that the stationmaster probably thought she was acting on her own, and that the friend she mentioned was a convenient fiction. She held out the envelope Susanne and she had addressed with such care.

"Tennessee," said the stationmaster critically. "Shakers."

"Is something wrong?" asked Madelaine, feeling the man's hostility in the way he looked at the envelope.

"This'll have to go to Kingston, and from there to Chattanooga. It will cross the river on the ferry to the McMinnville Road, and go from there to Woodbury. That's as close as we can carry it." He rattled this off, and moved a little, revealing a newspaper pinned to the bulletin board behind him. It was an issue of the *Cincinnati Commercial* sporting the headline: GENERAL WILLIAM T. SHERMAN INSANE.

Madelaine stared at it, reading the words with complete disbelief, as if they were in a foreign language she had never encountered before. Though she had speculated that the Union officer she had heard about might be Tecumseh, she had not actually supposed it could be true. Reminding herself that she had been wondering about the officer named Sherman who had been discharged from the army, she made herself focus on the page. She found it difficult to breathe, as if the act of comprehending the headline was wholly enervating. It said William T. Sherman, just as the plaque on his desk in San Francisco had; there could be no doubt that this was Tecumseh. She indicated the paper, and trying to appear little more than politely curious, asked, "Pardon me, but how old is that? The Cincinnati paper?"

174

"Date's December 11th. Got it down here a week later. Had copies shipped all over the South." He spat a brown stream of saliva and tobacco into the brass cuspidor. "Yankees. Just goes to show. They're all insane, if you ask me. Word is, they're giving that fellow another command, back in Kentucky again, where they know all about him. How're they going to win a war with such generals?" He hitched his thumb in the direction of the displayed newspaper, adding derisively, "And even the Yankees know he's crazy."

"A command? In Kentucky?" said Madelaine, feeling suddenly very foolish. She decided she had to account for this lapse, and began, "I am afraid I don't understand very much about how the—"

"Yankees'll lose Kentucky if they ain't careful," the stationmaster informed her with a chuckle. "Sending a crazy man there. You'd think they want the South to win. Probably do. Most of Winfield Scott's officers are Southern."

"You expect the North to lose? Because of this General Sherman?" said Madelaine, recalling how Tecumseh had reveled in his success that night he and his volunteers had restored order to San Francisco's streets. What could have thrown him into such despair—for she had no doubt he had been overset by one of his fits of desolation—that he was thought crazy?

The stationmaster smiled and made a serious mistake with Madelaine. "This ain't nothing for you to bother yourself about, ma'am. You got nothing to fear from that crazy man, or any other Yankee soldier ever coming here. Don't you worry about it, you're safe."

For an instant Madelaine wanted to shout at him for daring to try to placate her; she wanted to defend Tecumseh, for she knew with the certainty of their bond of blood that no matter how dark his mood might be, he was not insane. Something of this must have shown in her violet eyes, for the stationmaster drew back a little and muttered about not wanting to give offence. "But you probably don't know how things look to us, you being French and all."

Madelaine accepted this with a single nod of the head.

"But the thing is, ma'am, a lot of folks around here are worried that we won't have this thing settled before the end of summer, and that makes them fretful." He leaned forward, his manner more conciliatory. "Once England comes in on our side, the Yankees'll give up."

"Do you think England will do that?" asked Madelaine, schooling her features to an expression of sincere interest.

"It seems hopeful, at least that's what they're saying in Atlanta. England, and maybe France, too. With England on our side, those New York bankers won't want to pay for any more guns, that's for certain." He held up the letter Madelaine handed him. "I'll make sure this gets off today. You tell your friend that he should get it in a week or so, when the Shakers come into town for their mail." He nudged her arm with one wide finger. "They say that the men and women marry but they don't live as man and wife. Those Shakers. They make good, plain cloth, and good, plain furniture. I'll say that for them." Again he spat. "You got Shakers in France?"

"Not recently, and not by that name," said Madelaine, who recalled a few of the more austere Christian communities of the past. Saint-Germain had seen some of them for himself; she had only read of them or heard his accounts.

"Then you wouldn't know," said the stationmaster. "But chances are they'll take better care of him than any army doctor could." He smiled deprecatingly at Madelaine. "Just remember. You got no reason to worry about the Yankees. We'll have them running for home before August."

Madelaine handed him a small, gold coin. "Is this enough for the letter?" She did not want to hear anything more about fighting, not with this news of Tecumseh to ponder.

"You get change for that," he said, handing her two badly-printed bills. "Jeff Davis is making sure we're a real country now." His pride was obvious.

As Madelaine accepted the banknotes, she found her eyes drifting back to the headline: GENERAL WILLIAM T. SHERMAN INSANE.

AT NEW SPRINGS FARM, NEAR BUCHANAN, GEORGIA,
29 APRIL, 1862

Word has come from Fox Woman that she is leaving her traditional home for the Choctaw Nation in Indian Territory, because she is afraid of what this war may do to her if she remains where she is and the fighting spreads. She is not the only one of her people to make such a choice ... Her nephew says that she would rather face disunity among her own people than continue here, where both sides are her enemies ... I am saddened to know she is in such desperate straits, but it is not within my power to assuage her ... As someone who fled the Revolution in France, I cannot castigate those who are doing now what I did then.

176

Five more Buchanan boys are dead. They were killed on the 6th of this month at a battle on the Tennessee River. General Albert Johnston also died there, and many of the reports I have read consider his loss a dire thing for the South. A messenger brought back what effects of the dead soldiers could be found, though none of the bodies has been sent back here for burial. The messenger, who stayed with the Thatcher family, is hardly of an age to shave yet, but he has the eyes of an old and frightened man...

I have learned from this messenger that Tecumseh was also part of that battle. I know he is alive still, but I begin to fear for him. We are hearing accounts of terrible slaughter and frightful injuries, wounds that no man would want to live with, and men who welcome death to end their suffering, knowing it for a kindness. Those condemned to linger in agony know better than anyone how cruel survival can be... And many of the dead are now being embalmed, so that their bodies may be returned home without overmuch decay. I do not know what embalming would do to one of my blood, for embalming does not destroy the nervous system, and as such, should not be fatal. None of the Pharaohs ever rose after embalming but their brains were gone as well as their blood. Yet since embalming drains the body of blood, and for us more surely than any other, blood is life, it could be that it would be sufficient to bring the True Death... If Tecumseh falls in battle and is embalmed, I fear he will be lost forever... I must write to Saint-Germain and find out what embalming might do to one of us... How I may get a letter to him in these times, however, with the North blockading Southern harbors, I cannot guess, and once I have such information, how do I convey it to Tecumseh?...

Army suppliers have come to Buchanan, as they have to many of these small towns, requisitioning supplies, and leaving behind documents stating the value of what has been taken, all this with the promise that the full value may be redeemed at the end of hostilities, or on the first day of the New Year, whichever comes first. All these farmers will have to do is journey to Richmond, Virginia, to claim the sums owed. Susanne has admitted some irritation in that regard, for who, she asked me when the suppliers were gone, is going to leave a farm in the beginning of winter and travel all the way to Richmond and back again while Yankees are abroad in the land?

She has had a second letter from Walter, who is gradually improving but is by no means well yet. He tells his sister that the Shakers are very good people, who have the strongest faith he has ever encountered...

I am planning to leave shortly on another ride to Rome. This will

*make my third time on that road, and I begin to hope that I now know
all the places I may safely stop for rest. I will have to ride the blood-bay
gelding this time; the mare has yet to recover from the bruise to her hoof
and she is not up to the rigors of the trip. I hope she improves enough for
my next journey to Rome... Perhaps I should look to purchase another
horse or two while they are available...*

IT WAS A HARD RIDE FOR MADELAINE, for she was delayed
by a large company of soldiers on the road, many with bandages
and make-shift splints protecting wounds which showed signs of
festering. Occasionally she would see a man borne on a stretcher,
one trouser-leg pinned up or cut off, the stump still oozing from
the recent amputation. Watching these men filled her with pity and
revulsion, and she had to resist the urge to offer to tend the more
severely injured. By the time she reached Rome, she was unsettled,
and resented the time she had to wait in line for the stationmaster
to serve her. Only the realization that the *Cincinnati Commercial* had
been taken down brought her any satisfaction; at least she did not
have to read those damning words about Tecumseh. In its place was
a list of casualties arranged by regiment, dead first, wounded second;
those missing were listed last.

"It's you again," said the stationmaster as Madelaine reached his cage.
"I thought you might be along one of these days." He gave her a familiar
smile, his wide face spreading wider than she thought possible. "What
can I do for you this time?" The innuendo was so obvious it was as
comical as it was annoying.

"I have another letter," Madelaine said, trying not to notice the welcome the stationmaster offered her.

"For Tennessee, to the Shakers," he said, shaking his head in feigned
disappointment. "Sorry, little lady. The couriers have been ordered to
carry military dispatches only, and letters if there's room left over. Unless you have a little extra to pay, so the courier will tuck it in his shirt."
He indicated the open place behind the stationhouse where coaches
and wagons were loaded. "But it won't be long now. A month or two at
most, and we'll have trains here. The army needs it for their supplies,
or we'd've had to wait until the Yankees are whipped. Once the railroad
spur is complete, things'll be different."

"You mean because of your unfinished railroad you can't accept this
letter for delivery," said Madelaine, very coolly.

"Not right now. Unless you want to give the courier something to make it worth his while, if you take my meaning."

"That I do," said Madelaine, allowing her temper to show. "But I don't suppose it would be wise for a foreigner to bribe a postal courier, would it? Not during a time of war. Both of us could get into trouble." She had made just such an error in her effort to leave France at the height of the Terror and the memory of it still burned.

The stationmaster was taken aback. "You're wrong. I didn't mean anything like a bribe," he blustered. "I only wanted to make things easier for you."

Madelaine glared at him. "How considerate you are."

"I aim to please," he said, making an attempt at creating a better impression. "There's lots of ladies who get lonely with their men away at war. You're foreign, it must be worse for you."

With deliberation, Madelaine gave the stationmaster a hard stare. "I will manage, sir."

The stationmaster rolled his eyes upward. "Don't blame me for wanting to make your nights a little easier. You're all alone, ain't you? Think I don't know? Ladies need someone to look after them, someone who knows what ladies like. You know you would—"

"How can I get this letter into Tennessee?" Madelaine demanded, no longer willing to accommodate the stationmaster's clumsy advances. "You say it cannot be delivered from here. If not here, then where may I give it to a postal courier? There must be some place where they are handling mail for your citizens as well as the army."

"Nearest place'd be north of here, La Fayette. It's another thirty miles or so up the pike." He shook his head, his expression one of polite incredulity. "You don't want to go all that way for one letter, do you?"

"If I must," said Madelaine, stepping away from the window. She disliked the thought of more travel, but she resigned herself to the necessity. Stepping out onto the boardwalk again, she looked up and saw the Confederate flag on the pole over the station house, and found herself again recalling the chaos in France before Napoleon came. Not, she added to herself, that Napoleon turned out to be an improvement, but at least the carnage he created had not been in the streets of Paris. With a shrug she went to her blood-bay and swung up into her loathed sidesaddle, and set the horse off at a trot for La Fayette.

———————◆———————

BETWEEN CEDARTOWN AND DALLAS, GEORGIA,
31 AUGUST, 1862

I hate Nathan Bedford Forrest, bold and dashing hero though he may be. Not content with taking both of Susanne's cows and all seven of my horses, including the ones I purchased only last week; he and his men raided all the supplies at New Springs Farm, leaving only half a dozen chickens to last for the rest of the war. Blankets and cooking utensils were claimed for his men, with the excuse that they do worse to the Yankees, and that this would speed a Southern victory. He was unthinkably crass in his manner, and justified everything by saying it was for the Confederacy. A fine achievement, when you win your campaign but reduce your own people to beggars ... We have been forced to abandon the farm entirely, and have sought out this old mill, located in a fold of the hills called here a hollow, which faces to the south-southeast, closer to Dallas than Cedartown; the place is sufficiently isolated, that I can hope it will be a safe haven until this madness is finished. My only concern in that regard, for we are roughly thirty miles from Atlanta, is that if the war should come here our sanctuary will end. Of course, everyone says that the Yankees will never get to Georgia, let alone Atlanta, but should it happen, we will have much to contend with, and Yankees may well be the least of it. If the army is greedy now, it will be voracious then.

This move is an act of desperation, and one that Susanne deplores. She has said that she will send word to Walter, so that he will not fear the worst ... We hope that the letter will reach him in good time, so that he will know where to come when he is fit enough to travel ...

Luke Greentree, who has been serving as a scout for General Braxton Bragg, has joined us here as of two days ago, having lost his left arm in fighting near Corinth in Mississippi at the end of May ... He located us through reports gleaned from other Choctaw scouts, and has declared his intention to stay out of this fight from now on ...

LUKE GREENTREE DROPPED HIS HAMMER and swore in English, a comprehensive oath that would have earned a private soldier a strong reprimand; the door he was repairing lay at his feet, the bent nail sticking up from it in mute testimony to his inaccurate aim. "I ... I didn't mean that," he told Madelaine after realizing what he had said. "It just came out, from the army."

"Of course you meant it," said Madelaine with good humor. "You're feeling frustrated, and who can blame you?" She came to his side. "Let me help you."

"No," he told her curtly, then said, "You will not be here to help me at all times, will you?"

"I suppose not," said Madelaine, accepting his decision. "But do not make too high demands upon yourself, Luke Greentree, not until you have had more time to grow accustomed to—"

"My loss?" he asked sarcastically, and made another attempt at driving a nail. Madelaine left him to his task and went into the mill, stopping to shake her head at the broken millstones and the shaft from the ruined wheel in the millrace. What sense was there in wrecking this place? she asked herself. What did the soldiers who did this expect to gain?

"They say that the miller hid runaway slaves," Susanne remarked from the top of the stairs, as if she had discerned the questions in Madelaine's mind. "The loss of the mill was nothing compared to recapturing runaways." She unfastened the scarf tied around her hair. "At least it is cooler than it was."

"Yes," Madelaine agreed. "And we have two horses now, unless Forrest comes and takes them, too. I doubt he'll want draught horses, though. They're not fast enough for his purposes." She wiped her hands on her skirts. "I am going to speak to the farmer at Powder Springs, the one with the new slaughterhouse. He might let me purchase a pig or two, or some sheep, and, if we're lucky, a mule. I have some gold. He should be willing to accept it." She glanced at the case containing her books and her manuscripts, trying to convince herself that here she would have more time to work on her treatise on the Choctaw.

"We do not need them," said Susanne quietly. "We need soap and thread and blankets.

"Yes. And you will need livestock before winter arrives. You will not be able to live on what you forage in the hills," Madelaine said with grim confidence. "So, chickens and pigs as well as soap and thread and blankets. A couple sacks of oats wouldn't hurt, either. I'll take the wagon, to bring the goods home. The horses will stand going that far."

"You do not have to do this," said Susanne, her expression bordering on defiance.

"But I want to," said Madelaine. "We have discussed this already. You are not beholden to me. You have given me your hospitality, and this is the least I can do in return." She came to the foot of the stairs and looked up.

"But you don't eat pork. Or anything else, for that matter," Susanne declared, her voice rising.

"No, I don't, except in private," said Madelaine, unflustered only because she had been expecting this challenge for the last week.

"That isn't the way of the French, is it?" Susanne said, summoning all her courage.

"It is the way of those of my blood," said Madelaine.

Susanne shifted her gaze to something on the second level of the millhouse. "I saw you carry that table up here."

So that was the reason for these remarks, thought Madelaine. "I see," she said. "I suppose it would be useless to tell you—"

"Anything," Susanne finished for her. "You need not explain. It would be wiser if you didn't, so I would not have to deny knowledge I possess. But you must know that I have seen things, observed them carefully, and I know you are not simply a rich and adventuresome foreigner."

"Well enough," said Madelaine, her fear diminishing. "What else do you think I may be?"

This time Susanne's expression softened a bit. "As long as it brings no danger to me and mine, there is no reason for me to know more."

"If you wish," said Madelaine.

"It is not a matter of wishing, it is a matter of knowing," said Susanne, and motioned to Madelaine to come up. "My kinsman, Luke Greentree, is certain that you are not what you seem." She indicated the table Madelaine had carried up the stairs. "With both arms, if he had them, he could not lift that."

"You two have spoken of this?" Madelaine asked as she selected a chair and sat down, trying to maintain her composure.

"This morning," said Susanne with a single nod. "He told me of how much strength you showed getting from our people's Nation in Indian Territory. He has seen strong women, but nothing to equal what you are, little as you look it. He worried at first that he might be in danger from you, but soon realized that was not the case."

"Neither of you have ever been in danger from me," said Madelaine with slight emotion. "You have my word that you will not be."

Susanne made a sign of acceptance. "And my brothers?"

"No danger," Madelaine assured her. "Even if they were both here."

She adjusted her skirt, studiously arranging its folds as she continued quietly, "I am not a ravening beast."

"You have been most kind to us," was Susanne's response as she sat down opposite Madelaine. "And the animals do not fear you."

"There is no reason they should," said Madelaine candidly. "It is not my way to injure them."

"No, I did not think so," said Susanne, not quite able to meet Madelaine's steady gaze. "Fox Woman told us that much. She would not have sent you to us if she had thought you would bring harm with you."

Madelaine sat very still. This confirmed her sense that Fox Woman had suspected; it should not be surprising, but it was, and it took a while to digest this. Finally: "What did she say?"

"That you were not what she thought your kind would be. That she had been afraid, when she first came to understand about you, but her fear ended quickly when she understood that legends are not always truthful. She said you had taught her much." She moved back in her chair, though her shoulders remained stiff. "It has pleased me to have your trust, Madame."

"Yes, you have it," said Madelaine. She felt terribly awkward and ill-at-ease, for she could not guess what more might be demanded of her. With an attempt at lightness, she said, "At least I will not be a burden if food runs low this winter."

"Truly?" asked Susanne, revealing some of the trepidation she had not entirely conquered.

Madelaine did her best to laugh, and very nearly sounded convincing. "I will not take advantage of either you or Luke Greentree. Neither of you have sought that from me. Nor will I impose upon your brothers, should either of them come here." She waved her hand toward the window and the wooded slope beyond. "I will not obtain what I need near this place. There are farms out there, and occasionally one of the men who work them will have a sweet dream, and I will have sustenance for a while. It is all I can do in safety for them, and for myself." She cocked her head, and did her best to ignore the longing she felt to be known and welcomed as a lover once again. "You may rely on my discretion, Susanne Selbie. I will do nothing to bring any blame or condemnation upon you."

"Is that why you have been so willing to carry letters for me? Because it would take you to ... uh ..."

"Somewhere I may discreetly feed?" asked Madelaine, being deliberately blunt. "Yes, that is part of the reason. In Buchanan I had to be very circumspect."

"Yes," said Susanne, nodding twice in a decisive way. "I can see that. You would have to be careful, wouldn't you? If the men you—"

"Visit in dreams; it is the most prudent way," Madelaine supplied, wishing she had Saint-Germain with her to explain; he did it so well. But then, she reminded herself, he has had four millennia to become good at it, while she had had less than a hundred-fifty years.

"Visit in dreams. All right," said Susanne. "If they realized that their dreams were... shared, it could go badly for you."

"Or if they decided that their dreams pointed them in the direction of the woman they want, it could be... difficult, particularly if they were not willing to recognize my nature," said Madelaine, recalling the determination of Professor Alain Baundilet who had tried to seize her in his arms even while he died. "Some men can only love a thing if they possess it."

"White men," corrected Susanne.

"If you say so," Madelaine granted, not wanting to argue the matter when it was all going so well. She folded her hands in her lap. "Let me make one promise to you: no one who is on this property who does not actually seek me for himself will have anything to fear from me."

Susanne made no effort to hide the relief she felt at this assurance. "Thank you, Madame. It quells my... concerns."

Madelaine did not want to question this last word, certain that the first that had come to Susanne's mind was dreads, not concerns. She ventured her best smile and rose. "Thank you. For all you have done for me." Her gesture cut short the protestations Susanne started to offer. "You don't have to say anything."

"All right," Susanne told her, satisfied with the promise Madelaine had given so willingly. As she stood, she declared, "There are many more crates to unpack."

"I'll manage my own," Madelaine said quickly.

Susanne gave no answer.

AT THE OLD MILL, EAST OF CEDARTOWN
AND NORTH OF DALLAS, GEORGIA,
11 NOVEMBER, 1862

It has been very wet these last several days, and when there has been no rain, a thick mist has taken its place, clammy as a winter day in Venice. Everything is permeated by dampness. I have gone out twice with Luke in search of game, and will go out again shortly, so that there will be meat at the mill. Finding game is not as easy as it was once; when I have gone alone at night, I have discovered fewer deer and more hungry people in the woods. The army is demanding more food, and those with small holdings are suffering.

Another group of men from the general area—Cedartown, New Hope Church, Dallas, and Pumpkin Vine—came to the mill early this afternoon, ostensibly to learn who is here, and whether the mill will be restored to operation, but actually to try to determine if run-away slaves are still hiding here, waiting for guides to take them north. One of the men had the grace to be apologetic, a wagon and coach-maker, who has had most of his business taken over by the army. He did not have the air of contempt so many of these men show to anyone with non-white blood, which is to his credit.

From them we learned that the war is going well for the Confederacy, at least according to what these men chose to impart to us. They spoke of victories in Maryland and Virginia, but made no comment on the battles along the Mississippi, which I infer have been more often Union successes. I did not press for anything regarding Tecumseh, thinking that if he had been wounded or killed, these men would surely have mentioned it, and gleefully, as they crowed with pride recounting how Generals Lee, Jackson, Johnston, and Longstreet routed the Union commander, General McClellan... They could not find enough invectives to sufficiently condemn a proclamation Abraham Lincoln has issued, going into effect the first of next year, freeing all the slaves in the Confederacy...

ON THE RIDGE ABOVE THE MILL there had been a dusting of snow during the night, and its freezing breath came on the wind. The ground was hard enough to crunch when walked on, and the empty branches

185

made brittle music when the wind moved through them. Only the pines sighed, as if relieved to have dawn come again to this remote stretch of hillside.

Madelaine huddled at the foot of a hawthorn bush, strangely exhausted, her deerskin cloak drawn close around her. The man she had visited during the night had troubled her, for his dreams were filled with scattered bodies and torn flesh and the chaos of battle. He had succumbed to her with a peculiar numbness that shocked her, and it lingered as she made her way back toward the mill, sapping her strength. The man, she realized, was a deserter, a harness-maker's apprentice who had seen too much of war and had fled its horrors.

The first sounds of birds warned her to hasten on her way, for the hills had become dangerous in the last few months as more people were displaced from their small holdings and forced to seek a living away from the fighting. If she were discovered by one of these groups, things could go badly for her. That was one of the reasons she had avoided the narrow road and had chosen to climb the hill through the underbrush.

A distant sound of hoof-falls attracted her attention, and she shrank back in the shadows, squatting down low where a rider was unlikely to look. She remained very still as she listened to the approach of eight or nine horses, the creak of tack revealing they were mounted.

Suddenly a deer burst from cover and bounded noisily down the hill. Two of the men swore as their horses shied at this unexpected activity.

"Keep in order," said a curt, low voice with the soft accents of Alabama.

"My horse—" a protest began.

"And quiet." There was great authority in that soft, determined voice.

"We'll get caught," one of the others moaned; this voice had the distinctive timbre of a black.

"If you make another sound, we may," insisted the first.

The horses came nearer, and then one faltered on the icy footing and was only kept from falling by the quick, expert ministrations of his rider. "Watch this part. There's ice."

Madelaine tried to make herself smaller, trusting that the mounted men would not be carrying more than a single lamp.

"When we get to Reverend Singleton's church," the first voice said quietly, "you two'll go into the attic. He'll arrange the next part of your journey. You do like he says and you'll do fine."

"Yes, sir," said a second black-timbred voice.

"Singleton'll get you as far as Chattanooga; he'll tell you who takes over there." This was in a reassuring tone. "Remember, the Union says you're free. Get there and you will be."

"Praise God," said the first black voice.

The horses were abreast of Madelaine now, and she looked away from the mounted party; Saint-Germain had long ago taught her that watching a person's head or hands increased the likelihood you would be noticed by him. Recalling that lesson now, she watched the legs of the horses as they minced across the stretch of black ice.

"It's gonna be light soon," said a new voice, one with a greater twang than the leader had.

"All the more reason to be careful. Singleton's church is only two miles away from here. We'll get there in half an hour, that's plenty of time." The leader sounded wary and exasperated at once.

"If you say so," said another of the men uncertainly.

"Penvy, if this bothers you, go home," said the leader, raising his voice a bit. "No one forced you to do this."

"But, Chance..." The objection faded.

Madelaine waited until she could not hear the sound of the hooves any longer, and then slowly stood up, filled with astonishment. She had heard rumors of antislavery Southerners who helped runaways to get safely out of the South, but had never before witnessed their work herself. She felt intense curiosity about the men and for an instant had the urge to go after them, to ask them why they had undertaken such dangerous work. Then she realized the folly of such an act, and resumed her trudge up the slope to the ridge which ran above the hollow where the old mill was located.

THE OLD MILL, NEAR DALLAS, GEORGIA,
8 APRIL, 1863

Today three children came to the mill looking for food and shelter. They are such pathetic little creatures, ragged and thin, their father and older half-brothers gone to war and their mother dead of fever... Susanne asked me what I thought—should we take them in. How could anyone turn them away? It will mean finding more food, but it would be intolerable to have them suffer more.

They are called Jesse, Melissa and Eliza, and I would guess their ages at eight, seven and five. They said they had been walking for six days, and I can believe it, they are so worn. As to where they come from, they say it is a farm across the Chattahoochee from Franklin, which Susanne tells me is south of here by some distance. They are looking for their mother's brother whom they were told is in Dalton, perhaps, if he has not joined the army.

War always means orphans.

THERE WAS A LARGE SACK slung over Luke Greentree's shoulder and he grinned as he entered the mill. "Nothing fancy. A few chickens and some greens. It'll make a passable stew." He dropped the sack onto the broken millstone and signaled to the children who had followed him through the door. "You take this upstairs to Miss Susanne, and tell her I'm going out for more."

"Sure," said Melissa, who was the most communicative of the three. She grabbed for the sack, then stopped to say to Luke Greentree, "I never knew Indians could be nice. Pa says they'll scalp you soon as look at you."

"Not all of us," said Luke Greentree, no emotion on his face.

"That's good," said Melissa, and led the way up the stairs with the neck of the sack clutched tightly in her hands, Jesse and Eliza trailing behind.

Luke Greentree went out again to put his thick-bodied draught horse in the makeshift barn, where he found Madelaine sorting herbs. "More of your potions, I see."

"When I finish the preparation, yes. It would be good if you could find me more moldy bread." She did her best to smile encouragement. "I know. People don't throw much away any more, and with the price of flour as high as it is—"

"And getting higher," Luke Greentree interjected.

"And the army requisitioning everything it can lay its hands on, well, I suppose I will have to make do with whatever you can find." She smiled at him, and went on with her work, thinking as she did that her dress was sadly stained and faded. Considering the wear it had been given, she was not surprised it was not as fine as it had been when she purchased it.

"Oh. While I was hunting today, I found an empty house, set back in the hills. Just an old farm. Nobody for miles around, and nobody working it." Luke Greentree worked over the coat of the draught horse with a handful of straw.

"Has anyone . . . been at it yet?" Madelaine asked in an off-handed way.

"Not that I could see." He paused. "If we returned there, we might find a few of the things you want." His voice was level but there was mischief in his eyes. "I think it would be worth the time to go there."

Madelaine shrugged. "Surely there is no livestock."

"No, but I think there is a root-cellar and maybe a few blankets." He let himself smile at her. "There are clothes, too, and sheets and pillows. With the children here, we should have more for them."

"You're right," said Madelaine, making up her mind. "We'll take both horses and load them up as best we can. How far is this place?"

"Ten miles or so, but the ground is rough." He came to her side. "The signs are for summer being hotter."

"So you've told me," said Madelaine.

"It will mean illness." Luke Greentree regarded her narrowly. "If there are herbs you would like me to get for you, I will do it. So we will not have to fear growing ill here."

This offer took Madelaine aback, for she knew Choctaw fighting men did not gather herbs, and she did not answer at first. "That would be very helpful, yes."

"Then show me the ones you want, tonight while we are on our way." He nodded once, to signal their agreement was struck, then turned on his heel and walked out of the barn back toward the mill.

<hr>

AT THE OLD MILL, NEAR DALLAS, GEORGIA, 11 JUNE, 1863

A letter has come from Walter, who is now well enough to travel and is planning to come here before the end of summer. He informs Susanne that he will be traveling in the company of two Shaker women, who will serve as his nurses if he should suffer another setback while traveling. While I am certain it is a kindness for the women to do this, I understand that there has been more fighting in Tennessee, and they may well wish to remove themselves from the paths of advancing armies.

With the letter came other news: Van Dorn and Forrest have had some successes against the Union troops, but it is not going as well for the South as they tell themselves it is ... Whether they like it or not, the North has taken on the task of reuniting the country, and they will not be turned from their purpose ... Tecumseh is with General Grant, hoping to break open Vicksburg, and though they have encountered stubborn resistance, with so much of the Mississippi River controlled by the Union, it is only a matter of time. Daring generalship and military dash are all very well, but an army is only as good as its supplies, and the Confeder-ate states are running low on supplies...

The herbs brought by Luke Greentree yesterday are quite useful and will permit me to make a few more tinctures for injuries and sick-ness...A few of the remaining Choctaw to the west of here have sent herbs to me, as well, and I am most heartily grateful to them, and to Fox Woman, for without her approval, I would see none of these.

I have finished the two cut-down dresses for the girls...How odd, that the needlework taught me by the Ursuline Sisters should stand me in good stead now, in this place...I am glad we found cloth at that de-serted house, as well as the other supplies, for we certainly have need of it, simple muslin though it is...I will return to my manuscript when I have finished the dresses for Susanne and myself.

BOTH HORSE AND RIDER WERE SWEATING as they rode up to the old mill in the midday heat. The man rose in his stirrups and called out, "Hallo! You in the mill."

Madelaine, who had been lying on her earth-filled mattress at the top of the mill, lifted her head, wondering where she had heard the voice before. As she fussed with her skirts, she rose and went to the window and leaned out. "Hallo, rider."

The man doffed his hat and bowed in his saddle. "Good day to you, ma'am. I wasn't certain anyone was here."

Madelaine decided not to tell him that Susanne had taken the three children down to Dallas to see if she could find any supplies they might need; Luke Greentree had gone hunting at first light and had not yet returned. "Well, we are."

"Aha," said the man. He was good-looking, pampered, russet-haired, with a glint of easy humor in his light-blue eyes. His horse was well-bred, in top condition and well cared for. "Would you mind giving a thirsty stranger a drink of water?"

It was a reasonable request, and one it would be suspicious to refuse. "Of course not," Madelaine answered, and added, "I will be down in a moment." She did not wait for his answer, but hastened down the three flights of stairs to the ground floor, still trying to place his voice.

The man stood in the door when Madelaine drew back the bolt, his hat still in his hand. "And if I may let my horse drink down at your millpond?"

"Certainly," said Madelaine at once. "If you want to give him a chance to cool, it might be best."

"I have him tied up to that tree," he said, gesturing toward the oak in question. "I saw a ring and used it."

"Good," said Madelaine, and motioned him into the mill.

"This is awkward," the man continued. "I reckon I had better introduce myself, since there's no one else to do it for me. I am Chauncy Howard of Twin Oaks." He bowed to her slightly. "Chauncy is such a silly name. My friends call me Chance."

Now she knew the voice. This was the leader of the men she had watched from the thicket last winter. Startled by the recognition, she hesitated before saying, "I am Madelaine de Montalia. That's in France."

Surprise registered on his mobile features. "It would be ungentlemanly of me to inquire what a Frenchwoman is doing here," he said, a speculative lift to his brows.

This was not something she was willing to discuss with him. "Let me get you a glass of water," Madelaine offered, retreating to the pantry and reaching for a glass before starting to work the pump handle. "It comes from the millpond."

"Fine," said Chauncy Howard, who had followed her to the pantry. "You have supplies." He glanced at the shelves, noting what he saw.

"Not as much as we need, either for this summer, or the winter to come," she told him, holding out the filled glass to him.

"It's much the same everywhere," he said, shrugging. "Thank you, ma'am," he told her when he had taken his first sip. "It's pretty fierce out there."

He was older than she first supposed, perhaps thirty or thirty-five, and his charm seemed more studied than she had thought; his boots were dusty and scuffed, testament to hard riding. Madelaine began to wonder why he had come. "We don't see travelers up this way very often."

"Things could change," Howard remarked, "if they find out what's up here."

"We're not restoring the mill," said Madelaine. "That's what most people would come here for."

"Don't be so sure of that," Howard said.

Madelaine wondered if he intended to flatter her with that observation or was simply making polite small talk. "Well, this is a long way for anyone to come out of curiosity."

"You may well find out otherwise," said Howard. "There's a lot of people on the move, and some of them stay off the main roads." He chuckled once, as if his comments were a private joke.

"And if war reaches here, there will be many more," she said, studying his response from the tail of her eye.

"The war won't come this far. We'll have a treaty long before fighting can spread here." He was very sure of himself, and his grin bordered on cocky.

"You're convinced of that?" Madelaine ventured.

"Doubtless." He took another long sip. "You're lucky to have the millpond. This creek dries up some summers; that's one of the reasons the mill was abandoned." He finished the water and held out the glass. "It's probably a good place to swim."

"Would you like another glass?" asked Madelaine. "If you have far to ride, you will be thirsty again."

"Yes. Another glass would be welcome," he said, favoring her with a sudden flirtatious smile. "How good you are to a stranger."

She did her best to respond in kind. "Given that I am a stranger myself in this country, it would be odd if I—"

"And you could be much better if you wanted to," he added, winking.

"I'm sorry," she said, glancing toward the shelves of the pantry. "I can't spare any food for you—"

"Don't be stupid. It won't fadge." Without any warning he touched her shoulder. "I have heard that you Frenchwomen are very knowing." His insinuation was eloquent. "In all kinds of ways."

Madelaine stopped working the pump-handle and stared at him. "Mister Howard?"

"I told you my friends call me Chance," he said, making this an imposition. "Say it. Say 'Chance'."

"Mister Howard," she said firmly, "I do not want this attention. If you are a gentleman, you will not do this to me." What had happened, she wondered, that had brought about this change in him? And why had it happened? What had changed? One moment he was engaging in polite banter, the next he was treating her as if she were bought and paid for.

"They say that you are taught the ways of pleasing your men," he went on in determination, his smile still fixed in place. "Is it true?"

"All women are taught to please their men," said Madelaine abruptly. "And I will thank you to take your hand off me."

"That's not real pleasing of you," he cajoled her.

"It isn't intended to be," she said. "Stop it at once, Mister Howard."

Howard's eyes brightened. "Why? What will you do? Scream? There's no one here but you and me and the horse. Why not take what's offered?"

"If you do not want me to scratch your face, you will stop. Now." If it came to that, she could best him in a fight even in daylight, she knew, but she did not want a fight; there would be too many questions to answer.

"Why'd you want to do a thing like that?" he asked, his tone light and teasing, but his hand still on her shoulder, the fingers digging in as if he wanted to fix claws in her flesh. "You don't have to take on this way. This can be real pleasant for us both. No reason for either one of us to regret it. Nobody'd have to know but you and me."

"Just as nobody has to know you help runaway slaves get north?" she countered, and felt his fingers tighten more cruelly. Now he would either come after her, or the shock of her question would make him retreat.

"What are you saying?" he demanded, stepping back from her, releasing his hold on her. "What runaways?"

She finished filling the glass a second time. "You and a few others guide runaway blacks north. Don't deny it: I've seen you at it, very late at night. You were guiding the runaways to a Reverend Singleton. If people in this area found out about it, what would they say?"

His laugh was unconvincing. "No one would believe it. Especially your being out at that hour. What were you doing when you saw us? If you saw us?"

"Why would they not believe me? There are groups of men who hunt the runaways to recapture and punish them. They have no love for any abolitionists, and I suspect they like the Southern ones least of all. They would probably be glad to discover who is helping the runaways escape." She could feel his anxiety mounting and pressed her advantage; she did not want him to renew his questions about her nocturnal wanderings. "If I were to add that you forced your attentions on me, you might not fare very well at their hands."

"Don't be absurd," he said, his voice two notes higher than before. "You wouldn't do that. You're the one at this mill. Everyone knows that this place was used by runaways."

"Yes. A group of men have already come to warn us about that." She held out the glass, noticing that there was sweat on his upper lip. "Here."

He took the glass and drank it down quickly, all the while watching her as if he expected a trap. He handed the glass back to her, taking care not to touch her fingers as he did. Then he made the effort to smile again, and produced a grimace. "You don't have to ... There's no reason for you to ..."

"Mister Howard, I have no wish to bring embarrassment on myself or on you." She spoke as if to a naughty child, and saw at once it was a mistake.

"It'll be our secret," he said forcefully, his confidence returning. "Just between us."

"No, not a secret. I do not say this for your benefit. I respect the work you do with the runaways. I have no wish to endanger that. But if you do anything or say anything that impugns my reputation, you will sorely regret it." She felt her anger course through her, as if it scoured her veins.

"What would make me do that?" he challenged her.

Madelaine gave him a level stare. "This is no idle threat, Mister Howard."

"It's not? What would you do to me?" he asked in a show of bravado. "Sue me in court? What witnesses do you have? It would be your word against mine, if you tried that. And who do you think they'd believe—me or you?" He rocked back on his heels, satisfied that he had escaped all hazard.

"I am not so foolish," said Madelaine.

"Then what? Give me away to the men you said came here?" He was close to jeering now.

"No, Mister Howard; that would endanger the runaways. No, I would break your spine and leave you crippled," she said flatly.

Now it was his turn to stare. "You?" He raked his eyes over her, repeating incredulously, "You?"

"Yes, Mister Howard," she said with cold certainty.

He took a step back from her, his mouth turning sulky. "It won't come to that."

"I hope not." She indicated the door. "Your horse must be cool enough now to drink safely. Take him down to the millpond. You can leave from there."

AT THE OLD MILL, NEAR DALLAS, GEORGIA, 3 SEPTEMBER, 1863

Walter arrived today, with his two Shaker women. They came in a very handsome dog-cart, with a hinny pulling it. From what these two women tell me, Shakers have a reputation for breeding good hinnies and mules ... I have asked Sister Bethesda and Sister Leah to tell me about their sect, and they have said they would once Walter is safely established ... Both women are widows, though not from war: Sister Leah's husband, who was considerably older than she, died of heart failure two years ago, and Sister Bethesda's husband froze to death four winters ago while tending stock. Sister Leah is thin as a stick and has a childlike prettiness her austere clothes cannot conceal; Sister Bethesda is a hale, large-framed woman of sixty years who thrives on work ... They are willing to remain here to tend Walter for as long as he needs them. Susanne has not said if this is agreeable to her, though I am sure that she cannot care for Walter alone.

There is sad news from that dreadful battle at Gettysburg, in Pennsylvania. John Selbie was wounded there and three days later, died. Susanne has done what she can to bear her grief but I fear she may be overcome by it ... Walter received the news a month ago, but felt it would be better to wait to tell Susanne until he could do it in person, so that she would not have to suffer her loss alone.

As for Walter himself, he is not strong and I suspect he may never be so again. His wound has left his back damaged, and though he is able to walk with crutches, it is not likely that he will improve beyond the need of them. I have no medicaments that can repair the injury, though I have given him an anodyne to reduce his pain, and a poultice for when his wound swells ...

There is no word of Tecumseh, and I dare not ask for any, given the sentiments of those around me ... How I have come to miss him. I remember the taut lines of his body, his passion, the weight and taste of him ... It has been too long since I had his knowing love.

"HOW DO THEY FIND THIS PLACE?" Susanne asked, flinging her hands in the air as she saw two unfamiliar children wander into the hollow, their faces pinched with hunger and fatigue.

"I don't know," said Madelaine, setting the stoneware crock aside and glancing out of the barn. "They may sense it," she suggested, half in jest.

"Well, we can't turn them away," said Susanne fatalistically. "They have endured so much already. It is cruel enough that they are cast adrift. We must not refuse them haven."

"As you wish," said Madelaine, brushing dried leaves off her muslin skirts. "Look. There's Melissa." She laughed once. "That child has the makings of a grand society hostess."

As Susanne and Madelaine watched, young Melissa came rushing from the back of the mill, her braids flying behind her, one hand stretched out to the newcomers. "Hello," she caroled as she ran. "Welcome to the Old Mill." She seemed unaware of the dazed stares of the two arrivals. "You must be hungry. And tired. Come with me," she said as she reached them. "I'll show you where you can rest, and then we'll get you some stew. It's just lamb, greens and onions, nothing fancy. But it fills the belly."

The taller of the two, a tow-headed boy, made a half-hearted attempt to pull away from her as she linked her arm with his. "Don't."

"You'll feel better when you're rested up," Melissa informed him, paying no attention to his rudeness.

"We better tell Luke Greentree to make the rounds of his traps again," said Susanne as she started out of the barn. "This makes nine children we're feeding."

"And I can ride to Dallas to get some supplies," Madelaine offered, aware that her supply of gold was getting low as prices were rising. "More soap, and blankets, if I can find any." She watched Susanne hurry toward Melissa, who was escorting the new children into the mill, thinking that they would not be able to accommodate more than another three or four, given their current resources. Perhaps, she thought, they should look for a better location. But where would that be? she asked herself. With fighting coming nearer all the time, this small, protected place might be the best location possible. With a short sigh, she left the barn and went toward the mill to find out about the latest additions to their community.

Sister Leah was just ladling stew into heavy white bowls when Madelaine came into the kitchen. She looked up, murmured a lukewarm greeting, and went back to her task, saying to the new children, "Now make sure you thank God for giving you this food, and guiding you to this safe place.

So much could have happened to you, and you've been spared. You're here because He is merciful. Let Him know you're grateful."

The taller child said, "Shan't," as he took the bowl and spoon.

"Will too," said the shorter.

Sister Leah was about to deliver an admonition to them; Melissa stepped into the breach, saying, "They can thank God when they're done eating. God must know how hungry they are. He'll understand."

"All right," said Sister Leah. "Just see that you thank Him right and proper." She avoided looking directly at Madelaine as the children sat down to eat. "Miz Selbie's making up a bed for them."

"I thought so," said Madelaine, aware of the Shaker woman's distrust of her. "Do we know who these children are and where they came from?"

"Not yet," said Sister Leah. "They aren't very talkative."

"So I gathered," said Madelaine, and went over to the table where the two youngsters were gobbling down their stew with as little chewing as possible. "I'm Madelaine de Montalia. Who are you?"

The taller boy glowered. "Ain't supposed to tell."

"Why not?" asked Melissa, who had taken a chair across from the newcomers.

"Cause that's what Ma told us." The shorter boy made a face and went back to the serious business of eating.

"Where is your ma?" Madelaine asked.

"Gone," said the shorter boy. "His, too."

"Then you're not brothers," Madelaine asked in surprise, for the two had a marked resemblance and she had assumed they must be siblings.

"Cousins," said the taller. "My pa's his ma's brother." Satisfied that was settled, he picked up his spoon again.

"Well, it's very clear you're related," said Madelaine, hoping to draw them out. "Your families live near each other, do they?"

"Yep," said the taller around a mouthful of lamb.

"Where is that?" asked Madelaine.

"Not supposed to say," said the shorter.

"Shut up, Seth," said the taller, then blushed so intensely that his scalp glowed pink through his pale hair.

"Is that your name? Seth?" Madelaine asked, pressing her advantage with the shorter of the two.

Looking guilty, the boy nodded, and pointed to his cousin. "He's Daniel."

"Seth and Daniel," said Madelaine. "Those are good names." She turned to Melissa. "You'll make sure Seth and Daniel meet the others, won't you?"

Melissa nodded with bright-eyed enthusiasm.

Suddenly Daniel said, "The soldiers took our mas." His face tightened up. "Just took them."

"Took them?" Madelaine repeated. "Took them where?"

"Don't know," said Seth.

"What about your fathers? Do you know where they are?"

"With General Taylor," said Daniel. "My pa is, anyway." He looked down into his stew as if expecting to discover news of his father there.

"And yours? Seth?" Madelaine said, encouraging the boy as much as she could.

His face darkened. "Got shot fighting with General Mitchel. Serves him right."

"General Ormsby Mitchel? Do you mean that General Mitchel?" Madelaine guessed, realizing the reason for the boy's taciturn answers; his father was with Union troops.

"Yeah," said Seth, going on as if driven against his will. "Had a ball in the face. Made him blind."

"I'm so sorry," said Madelaine, putting her hand out to the child.

"I'm not," growled Seth, though his knotted face belied his words.

"I'm sorry for anyone hurt in war," said Madelaine gently. "I don't care what side they're on, it only matters that they're hurt."

"Yeah," muttered the unhappy boy. He went back to eating, and would not look up from his bowl.

Sister Leah heard this out with growing concern. "Poor lad," she said. "Don't make it worse than it is by forgetting to honor your father. If you don't honor your father, you break one of God's rules."

"His pa broke the rules," said Daniel firmly. "Going over to the Yankees like that."

"He must have felt he had to," said Madelaine, trying to find a way to mitigate Seth's misery.

"Well, he shouldn't've done it," Seth said, his face still scarlet with shame. "God should've made him fight for us if He wanted me to ... to keep His rules."

"Child!" Sister Leah shook her head. "Do not say such things. They injure your soul."

"Do not," said Seth truculently.

"Sister Leah," Madelaine intervened. "Perhaps we should let these two young men get some rest before we worry about their souls? The body needs care as well."

Whatever objection Sister Leah might have had was lost in the loud whoop as Luke Greentree came through the door, Eliza wrapped around his leg, giggling.

"Indian!" cried Daniel, almost overturning his bowl as he jumped to his feet, his face going white with dread.

Madelaine saw that the child was terrified; she rose and went to his side. "Yes. This is Luke Greentree. He helps us out here, since he can't do any more scouting now that he's lost his arm." She kept her voice low and steady. "Luke Greentree is a Choctaw. His people were here long before any white men were."

Luke Greentree was disengaging himself from Eliza's frantic hug, but he turned around to look at the cousins. "New faces."

"This is Daniel. And this"—Melissa reached out to him—"is Seth. They just got here."

"I guessed that," said Luke Greentree, standing upright as Eliza finally let go. "How far have you come?" he asked them.

"Long way," said Seth, looking wretched.

"They haven't said where they came from," said Melissa, obviously interested to find out.

"Give them time," said Luke Greentree. "You don't have to find out everything all at once." He gave Sister Leah a respectful nod, then approached Madelaine. "If you have time, there are a few things we must discuss."

"Certainly," she told him. "When would you like—"

"What about now?" Luke Greentree suggested.

As he said this, Jesse hurtled into the room, his square face set in rage. "Benjamin," he announced in terrible accents, "says the Yankees are going to win the war. He's lying. He's LYING!" He stared around for someone to take this out on.

Susanne appeared at the top of the stairs above the kitchen. "What's this?" she called out, as if she were unaware of the outrage being expressed.

Jesse was about to start in again, when Seth said very quietly, "Yankees won't win."

Astonished at finding an ally, Jesse looked over at the newcomers, and goggled. "Who're you?" he demanded.

"Now," said Luke Greentree to Madelaine, indicating the outer door. "It won't take long."

Madelaine nodded and followed him, hoping to attract as little notice as possible. "What is it?" she asked when she got outside.

"I found ... something today while hunting," he said.

"You're being deliberately obtuse, aren't you?" Madelaine asked him.

"Yes. It is something … you will have to decide." He stared out toward the millpond.

"Whatever it is could be dangerous," she said, knowing his reasons for hesitation.

"Yes, I think so," said Luke Greentree. "If you will decide … I can't. And neither can Miz Selbie." He made an attempt at explaining. "I don't know if the war getting nearer makes it better or worse."

"And it is getting nearer, isn't it?" said Madelaine.

"There's been fighting in Tennessee before," said Luke Greentree indirectly.

"But it's coming nearer. Bragg is at Chattanooga, or so they say; Rosecrans is in pursuit." It was what the recent papers reported, and both of them were aware that this could mean a collapse was coming, though neither of them said as much. "Does this make your problem worse?"

"It could," said Luke Greentree. "If you will come with me. I've saddled one of the horses for you."

"Now?" Madelaine asked, a bit surprised that the need was quite so urgent. "Very well," she said as she read his expression. She looked down at her dress. "I will need to change my shoes for boots. Let me have a few minutes."

"I will be waiting," said Luke Greentree.

Madelaine went back into the mill, and discovered that peace had been restored; Jesse and Seth were in deep, low-voiced conversation about all the powerful secrets the South had to defeat the Yankees. As she reached the next level, she saw Susanne. "I'm just going with Luke Greentree. I'll be back in a while, probably by nightfall."

Susanne frowned. "Is something the matter?"

"Luke Greentree thinks there is. He wants my opinion." She was halfway up the stairs to the next level where her room was.

"Will you tell me the whole of it?" asked Susanne.

"I usually do," Madelaine replied, and went up to get her boots.

Luke Greentree led her away from the mill in silence, up over the ridge at the back of the hollow to the north, along the side of a dry creek bed. "That old sorghum shack? That's where we're going."

Madelaine heard this, and said, "It's runaways, isn't it?"

It took Luke Greentree the better part of a minute to answer, "Yes."

OLD MILL, NEAR DALLAS, GEORGIA, 9 DECEMBER 1863

*I am in a quandary. I have reluctantly spoken to Mister Howard in re-
gard to Daisy Buford and Jacob Dent, for it is increasingly apparent that
they must get north of here or be discovered, which would bring danger
to all of us at the mill. I had hoped to find others who would be willing
to help, but only Mister Howard is considered reliable. So I must deal
with him, and on his terms, or risk bringing raiders to this place. That
would be intolerable. With fifteen orphans here now, it is all we can do
to care for them here...*

*I wish I knew of some other way to insure the safety of these two
brave black people, because Mister Howard has made very plain what he
wants from me... I find it ironic that I, of all women, should balk at the
bargain he has proposed, but much as I yearn for knowing caresses, the
thought of Chauncy Howard's hands on me sickens me... But if I must
do it, so that we may abide in safety here, then I suppose I must... What
I fear is that he will demand more when it is done, and use what he
knows to the discredit of everyone sheltering here at the mill. If I thought
he would not use me so, I would be more sanguine...*

*The word is that the South achieved a victory at Chickamauga, two
months ago, but matters have gone badly since then. Our last news was
that Chattanooga was in danger of falling. Union General Rosecrans
has been replaced with a General Thomas, who is said to be a stubborn
fighter... Is this the brother Colonel Thomas spoke of in San Francisco,
almost a decade since? What became of Colonel Thomas, I wonder?
The name is not so uncommon, but many families have a tradition of
military careers, so it is not unlikely, either, that this may be his brother... The papers report that Tecumseh is in Tennessee, as well, and has
become the right hand of General Grant... It is hard to think of him so
close and yet completely unattainable.*

*Tomorrow Mister Howard returns and will require an answer. What-
ever I tell him, I dread what my decision will mean I must do...*

"I CAN GET THOSE TWO SLAVES headed north tomorrow; just give
the word," said Chauncy Howard, smiling at Madelaine's distress. It was

evening, and a light, blowing rain dashed along the sky. He was still in his oilskin coat as he stood in the barn door, enjoying the way the lamplight played on Madelaine's face. "You're very pretty, Madelaine. I can call you that, can't I?"

"Thank you," she said, resenting that good manners demanded so much of her. "Where will you take them?" She forced him to return to their business at hand, wishing now that she had more than a woolen shawl to keep her warm; the wind through the half-open door was cutting.

"There's a place outside Stilesboro, a small plantation. The owner never kept slaves, and likes to help runaways. He has a smoke-house where they can rest the night." He achieved a warm smile. "Think about it. They'll be out of danger. And so will you." This last was said with heavy emphasis. "No one will learn of what you've done, not what you do with me, nor why. You won't have any of those runaway hunters coming here, searching everything." He came a step nearer. "The last place they looked, they burned down when they were done, just to teach everyone a lesson. You don't want that to happen here."

"No," said Madelaine in a small voice. She wanted to throw him off a mountaintop, to batter him with a maul, to flay him and leave him hanging from a hook.

"Those children you've taken in, you and that half-breed woman, they could be back wandering the roads, and winter's closing in." He unfastened his coat. "That's up to you."

"Is it?" she asked, wanting to keep him talking. If he continued to boast, she had more time to plan. He was so proud of himself, and she intended to use that pride against him.

"I told you that from the first. You're the one who can save everyone or ruin them. Is what I want so much, compared to all those lives?" He grinned. "And what about that poor cripple? He won't get far in the cold, Shaker women or no. He doesn't have enough strength to take the cold."

"He was wounded fighting for the South," Madelaine reminded her tormentor.

Howard laughed. "You think I'm so low, a snake wouldn't ripple going over me, don't you? I know he was fighting for the Confederacy. Hell, I'm fighting for the Confederacy. If we don't stop slavery, there won't be a Confederacy to fight for." He made a sudden sweep of his arm. "So don't hold me up as a man without patriotism. I love my country. I want to see it survive. And it won't if we try to hold on to our slaves." The color had mounted in his face. He came three steps closer. "So if you want to do your part, you know how."

"Mister Howard—" she began, keeping her sorting counter with its stack of herbs between them.

"Chance," he corrected her.

"Mister Howard, if everything you say is true," she said, trying to sound calm and reasonable, "then why do you put me in this position? What do you gain by it? Why do you want to coerce me when you have reason to help the runaways?"

"Because I can," he answered, gloating openly. He unfastened his coat and tossed it away, paying no heed to where it landed. "I can make you bend to my will. I can make you do whatever I want."

This pronouncement brought Madelaine to a keener sense of her precarious situation. "You want to have slaves," she said harshly.

"I wouldn't call it that," he responded with anger, stung by her accusation.

"You might not," she said, growing braver. "But it is apparent to me that it is what you seek to make me."

He looked ugly now. "A woman owes it to her man to—"

"Cringe?" she suggested. "Detest him? Loathe him? Despise him? Well? Which is it?" She read increasing wrath in his demeanor, and she went on, goading him. "What do you think a woman owes her man?"

"Devotion!" he shouted. "That's what she owes her man!"

"And you will demand it by holding her friends and innocents hostage to ensure her devotion," said Madelaine with feigned approval. "Very wise. She might not be willing to endure you otherwise." She reached over and lifted the oil lamp, watching the wavering flame. "It is a coward's way of courtship."

"I am not courting you, woman," he snapped. "We're making a ... contract here. I will arrange for the runaways you're sheltering to get north to safety, and I will make sure nothing happens to this place for doing it, and in exchange, you will lie with me when I like, as often as I like." If he had hoped to shock her, he was disappointed.

"Come now, Mister Howard. You must know better than that." She made herself look amused. "You cannot risk that, and we both know it."

He reached across the counter and seized her arm. "That's a lie. I can make you do anything I want."

She winced at this treatment, but only said, "Mind the lamp. We don't want a fire, do we?"

He took the lamp away from her, hanging it on a hook at the edge of the first stall. "You can't put me off this way, Madelaine. I know what I want, and you will give it to me."

From the direction of the mill came the sounds of children singing in uncertain unison the old hymn "Come, Holy Redeemer." Howard swung around, pulling on her arm as he did, then turned back to her. "You won't distract me that way," he promised her.

"I didn't think I would," she answered, using her free hand to reach into her capacious apron pocket for her revolver. As she drew it out, she said, "I hoped I wouldn't have to use this."

Howard did not see the weapon at first, and when he did, he laughed. "You'll never tell me that's loaded."

"Yes, it is," said Madelaine coolly. "And I know how to use it. At this range, I can hardly miss." She lifted the gun. "Now, release my arm and step back."

"You wouldn't dare. You don't know what to do with the runaways." He laughed, and made a snatch for the revolver.

She used the barrel to strike his wrist, listening to the metal crack against the bone and his brief howl of pain. "You told me where you take them," she reminded him as he lurched back from her. "It is a start."

"You conniving bitch!" he burst out. "You're nothing but an Indian's whore. Who are you to—" He had started toward her once more, but she waved him back.

"Stay where you are, Mister Howard," she advised him. "I will not hesitate to kill you if you force me to." She made her way around the end of the counter, taking care to keep him in the line of fire the whole time. "You have told me what you want me to do, and now I will tell you what I want."

"I'm not going to help you," he said, holding his injured wrist carefully. "Look what you did to me."

"Yes, you will," said Madelaine firmly. "Or you will be left in Dallas with a note saying what you have been doing." She hated the thought of losing anyone who had helped so many runaway slaves to freedom, but she was not willing to be in this man's power in any way.

"You wouldn't," he said with contempt. "A woman like you—"

"I might do anything," said Madelaine. "Now, will you hear me out, or shall I plan to carry you down into Dallas tonight? It's up to you, Mister Howard."

He lowered his eyes, not in dislike or embarrassment, but to be able to watch her without being watched himself. "Tell me. I might get a laugh out of it."

"You will take the two runaways north, and you will go with them as far as you are able. Once you have reached a Union-held city, you will surrender to the military authority, with the offer of guiding them back into Georgia." She smiled at him. "They are giving handsome rewards for such service. You should not suffer too badly for doing my bidding."

"The North will never get into Georgia." He cleared his throat then, and added, "Chickamauga was only a flanking action for Chattanooga, everybody knows that." He lifted his head and spat. "I will not go to the North to save my hide, or my reputation; no ma'am. That for your orders."

The children were now singing the *Doxology* in the old form, with the half-speed second half of each cadence.

"All right," said Madelaine with a sigh. "Then I will have to ask you to turn around and put your hands behind your back."

"Ask all you want, it won't happen." He had regained a little of his sureness, and was doing all that he could to provoke her. "I won't let you truss me up like a hog for the butcher. You could shoot me, though. That's right. I forgot that part." He winked at her. "The gun's loaded, you said."

Madelaine was neither flustered nor amused. "That's right, Mister Howard." She did not want to kill him; she hated the way killing made her feel, the memories it brought back.

"And you know how to use it," he went on with a condescending smirk. "I bet you shot men before now." This was in patent disbelief.

"As you will discover," she said, starting to lose patience with the man. "Turn around and put your hands behind you."

"No 'please'?" He gave a devil-may-care shrug, then began to swing around. In the next instant he seemed to trip, for he started to fall, arms flailing, first to the side, and then backward, grabbing out for support. He slammed into Madelaine with his upper body, using his momentum to carry them toward the floor.

Although Madelaine had expected mischief from him, she was unprepared for this abrupt action; she fell heavily, her shoulder striking the rough boards of the floor, jarring her and leaving her shaken. Pain sawed at her shoulder and chest as she held on to the revolver. She cursed herself for not anticipating this move, for assuming he would not fight her here, in the barn, with the others close by.

He grappled with her, trying to wrest the revolver from her hand, and swearing steadily. He smashed into her jaw with his elbow, then brought his fist down on the side of her head. "Give. It. Up." He took hold of the bun at the back of her neck and used her own hair to help him pound her head onto the floorboards. His breath was ragged with anger and effort.

Madelaine stopped fighting long enough to brace herself, and then, with all of her preternatural strength, she rose against him, shoving him aside as easily as she might an obstreperous child. As he struggled to regain his advantage, Madelaine got to her feet, her eyes set on him, her face blank with concentration. She still had her revolver in her hand and she raised it once more. "Now, Mister Howard," she said in a cold, level voice, "you will get to your feet, please, and place your hands behind your back."

He goggled at her, as if he could not believe the evidence of his senses. He crouched as if preparing to rush at her a second time, his face as flushed as if he suffered from a fever. "I will not."

"Then you force me to knock you out and tie you up afterward," she said with no trace of distress at this notion.

"How you gonna do that, Miz Fifi?" He indicated his size. "You couldn't move me if I was out cold."

"You forget I am not alone here," said Madelaine, more than confident that she could and would move him handily without any help whatsoever. She glanced around, looking for a board of sufficient size to wield against him.

He moved as her eyes flicked away from him. He grabbed her around the legs and tumbled her to the floor once again, reaching to take the pistol from her. His fingers wrapped around her arm, tugging.

She kicked out, but was hampered by her voluminous skirts. She concentrated on keeping him from reaching her revolver as she strove to reclaim her advantage.

"You can't stop me," Howard said through clenched teeth. "I'll kill you first."

Madelaine had no doubt that he meant it. She renewed her resistance, twisting away from him and trying to roll free of him.

He grabbed her breast, deliberately fixing a deep grip on her, chuckling as she gasped against the pain. "Don't like that, do you?" He dragged himself nearer to her again, using his hold on her for leverage.

"I'll do more before we're through." His intentions were clear already, and Madelaine had one great surge of energy left to her. "Keep struggling, dahlin'. It makes it better for me."

She did not waste her strength in responding to this; with all her might she shoved him off her, dislodging him in a single, enormous effort. As she rolled free of him, she felt him reach out for her revolver, trying to yank it out of her hand.

There was just one shot, and for a moment everything in the barn was still. Then the animals, already made fretful by the fight, protested, and the singing from the old mill faltered.

Chauncy Howard stared down at the blood pumping from the inside of his leg, just above the knee. "Do something," he muttered, and fell heavily to his side, the blood continuing to pulse from the wound.

Madelaine went to his side, and stared down, aware that there was very little she could do now. A tourniquet would slow the bleeding, but his leg, with muscles shredded and bone cracked, would not be saved. "I'd have to amputate it," she said, her anger vanished.

"No," said Howard. "Don't touch me." He floundered, trying to get away from her, then grew weak. "I won't... Don't..."

But Madelaine was already searching for tools that would permit her to remove his leg. The thought made her feel cold, but she knew she had to make an effort. She threw him a stirrup-leather, saying, "Here, put this around your thigh. Tight. Above the bleeding. Do it now."

He held the stirrup-leather uncertainly, then did as she ordered, sighing with effort as he attempted, with the last of his fading strength, to put the thing in place. When he passed out a few moments later, Madelaine finished tightening the belt. Then she moved the man to the counter where her herbs were, and set him there. She had a polling saw and farrier's tools within easy reach, and she drew her lantern closer, then steeled herself and set to work.

THE OLD MILL, NEAR DALLAS, GEORGIA,
7 APRIL, 1864

Today the last of the children left with Sister Bethesda to join the rest at the place Luke Greentree found for them in Jasper, to the east of here, where they will be safe... They have taken all the stock but one of the horses, which they have left to me. So only Mister Howard remains, and he is almost recovered sufficiently from his amputation to be able to leave here at last, for which I will be heartily glad. Let someone else endure his bouts of self-pity. In another two or three days, I will see that he is taken down to the church at Dallas. They are welcome to him. If he complains to me again that he would rather have died than lost his leg, I may let him prove it...

It has been a cold spring and cold longer than usual; it is said that planting will have to be late this year, and the harvest will probably be thin. With the threat of more fighting, it may be that there will be little to harvest come fall, and it will not matter how far the Confederates forage; they will find nothing to sustain them, nor the Union soldiers... Farmers are saying they are living on what little they have left from previous years, and sending many chickens and turkeys to the smokehouse early, to save on grain and to ensure that there is something to eat. I presume the rest of the region is similarly afflicted...

I have seen no newspaper for more than two months; I am assured they are still being printed, though many are now sporadic. Few people come here, so no rumors have been repeated, but if the Union still holds the advantage, they would be foolish not to make the most of it... Skirmishes over supplies are probably coming...

... How has Tecumseh fared through all this, I wonder? He has been in Tennessee, that much is true; I learned that much from Mister Howard. But where? And when will he move again? In which direction? I know he is nearer to me than he was a year ago, but is this favorable or unfavorable? I have such mixed emotions that I do not know if I want to see him again, or to avoid him, if he and I are to cross paths once more. It has been a decade since we were together in San Francisco, and it was difficult for him to love me then. Now, in the face of war, what would he think of me? All this time I have yearned to see him, aware that he has kept me in his heart. But what if he prefers me as a memory? I have no answers to my own questions, but I rehearse them every night I go to find sustenance, which is now no more than once a fortnight, for there is too much risk in wandering abroad at night, even for those of my blood...

Many preachers have been going through the land, and the spirit of conversion and revival is very strong in this part of Georgia... No doubt many are hoping for God to save them now that it is apparent that the South will not win this war...

HE WAS WEARING A FRAYED JACKET that revealed his rank as sergeant; he staggered into the mill-yard with the last of his strength, dragging his rifle by the barrel. He was thin and his beard had not been trimmed in a month. He stared up at the old mill and called out, "Hallo!"

Madelaine had heard him approaching as she tended to her herbs in the barn. She came out smartly, no longer shocked by the conditions she saw when wounded soldiers arrived here. "Good afternoon, Sergeant." She went toward him without hesitation.

He was staring at her. "They told me I'd get help up here. Down in town they told me." He blinked as if he expected her to vanish when he opened his eyes.

"They have been saying that to many soldiers. I have not yet turned any-one away." She went toward him, trying to assess the extent of his injuries.

"How many have come?" he demanded.

"At the moment, I have seven men here." All told, there had been twelve; only one had died, at least so far. She waited while he thought her answer through. "Two are Union, the rest are Confederates."

"You take in Union men! What kind of place is this?" the sergeant burst out, his eyes getting wild.

"I take in wounded soldiers," Madelaine corrected him. "They cannot fight here, so it does not matter which uniform they wear."

The sergeant straightened himself, his head held a bit too high. "It matters to me. I won't lie down with no Yankees. It was Uncle Billy's men did this to me," he went on, lifting the edge of his tunic and reveal-ing a long, angry gash along his ribs; the tissue was inflamed, swollen and an unhealthy color.

"Let me take care of that for you," said Madelaine, moving closer.

"I want to see your doctor," the sergeant announced suspiciously. "Let him tell me what my chances are."

"Sadly, the doctor is not here at present; he has many other patients to tend to," said Madelaine with rehearsed smoothness. "I will do what I can for you until he returns." She gave an encouraging smile. "Don't worry, Sergeant, I have had a great deal of experience, and I know what I am doing. You may ask the others if you don't believe me." As she said this, she once again felt relief that Chauncy Howard had been gone for more than a month, for his sense of outrage would have diminished the confidence of anyone.

"I will," said the sergeant with great weariness, accepting her lie and looking toward the old mill. "In there?"

209

"At the top of the first flight of stairs. It's nothing fancy, but you will be able to rest comfortably. I will treat you until the doctor comes back." She was less than a dozen steps away from him now, and she knew she could close the gap quickly, but knew it would not be wise.

Fatigue and injury won over indignation. He sagged and stared at her. "I need some sleep. And if you have food..." He dared not hope for much.

"I have a strong broth you can take now. Later I'll have pork-and-onions and a little bread." She had salvaged two barrels of flour in Dallas, and paid a staggering price for them. But it was worth it, she decided, as much to secure herself some source of medicinal mould as to have unleavened, flat, Egyptian-style round loaves for the wounded to eat. She indicated the entrance to the mill. "Go ahead. I'll come after you."

He cast a dubious look in her direction, but made his way unsteadily toward the door.

"The pantry is straight ahead of you. Let me give you broth first, before you go upstairs to find a bed. Some nourishment will help you to husband your strength." She was keenly aware that he stood in need of a bath, as well, but knew it would accomplish nothing to mention it.

He looked about the dark, cool chamber and sighed. "It's been a long walk," he admitted.

"And why did you come here? It is a long walk, and there are other places where you can get help." She went to the pantry and took down the large crock of rabbit broth and ladled out a generous portion into a white bowl. "Here. There are spoons on the table."

"Thank you, ma'am," said the sergeant, sagging onto the bench at the table and propping himself there with his elbows. "Silas Wainwright, Forty-fifth Alabama, at your service, ma'am," he remembered to tell her before he reached for a spoon and all but plunged bodily into the thick broth.

Madelaine introduced herself, and, as she had before, explained she was French, which satisfied Sergeant Wainwright in regard to her practice of taking in wounded soldiers of whatever army.

"You can't be expected to know how things are here, I guess, you being French and all. Just remember that the Yankees can't be trusted, not any of 'em," he said, trying not to yawn. "Sorry, ma'am, I can't keep going. Point me to a place to sleep, will you?"

"Up those stairs. There are cots. Choose one that is empty," she said, taking his bowl and setting with it others in a pan of cooling water.

"My thanks again," he said, and began his climb.

As she watched him go, Madelaine again thought she had done well

210

to put willow bark and pansy in the broth she made; a slight lessening of pain could bring annealing rest for those not requiring immediate attention. She would make a poultice for his wound while he slept, and prepare to stitch the gash closed when he wakened. She had other patients to worry about; Private Dillon was not improving, and Private Hall would need a new binding on the splint holding his broken leg in place. And there was young Lieutenant Cameron, who was in need of the same tincture for asthma she had given Tecumseh almost a decade ago.

Thinking of him reawakened her memories of him, and her awareness of his advance along the Western & Atlantic Railroad. It was hard not to want to seek him out, to discover at last if he wanted her as more than a memory of loneliness and passion, more than two thousand miles to the west, and nearly a decade ago. But in the middle of a campaign, it would be foolish to make such an attempt, for the chance of reaching him unscathed was ridiculously low. And he would never receive her in front of all his officers and men. She sighed once, and ordered herself to return to the barn to finish her work with herbs and poultices and bandages.

THE OLD MILL, NEAR DALLAS, GEORGIA, 26 MAY, 1864

The battle has been raging less than a mile from here. I can hear the sound of it, like constant thunder, and from time to time soldiers pour through this mill-yard, most of them cavalry, though a small contingent of infantry riflemen came this way not an hour since, and left two of their number here for treatment.

I have almost no food left now, and little hope of getting any with the fighting around me. Most of my bandages have been taken as well, and the wood I've used for splints ... Any game in these hills has long since fled or ended up on a spit over a fire ... I will have to arrange something for the twenty-five wounded I now have in my care, so that they will not starve while they mend their wounds.

These are Tecumseh's men, these soldiers who take our supplies and leave the wounded behind.

THE HORSE COMING HAD A STEADY, FAST WALK. Madelaine could hear it over the low conversation and the occasional moans of the men she tended, and with it came another sensation, one she had anticipated for more than a year. She paused in changing the improvised dressing of rags on Corporal Snow's scalp wound, listening intently.

"Just the one horse, ma'am," said Private Wainwright, who had appointed himself her orderly. "Nothing to worry about."

Madelaine shook her head, and handed the soiled tattered cloth to Wainwright. "I had better go down."

Wainwright shrugged. "I can do it, if you like," he volunteered.

"And if the man is Union, what then?" Madelaine asked, indicating the last remnants of Wainwright's Confederate uniform.

He pursed his lips. "You're right; and he won't be expecting a woman, will he? You can deal with him proper."

"I suppose I might." Realizing her hands were shaking, Madelaine moved back from Corporal Snow. The air felt alive around her, crackling. "You know how to fix the dressing." She was feeling distracted now, and as she heard the hoofbeats slow, she made herself hurry down the stairs, rushing toward the door so eagerly that it took all her self-control to keep from flinging through it. She forced herself to stop, to gather her thoughts and her whirling emotions.

"French Mill!" The voice was a bit rougher and just now husky with fatigue, but she would have recognized it in the fury of battle.

She stood deliberately in the shadow as she swung the door open. "I understand that's what they're calling it now," she said, and saw him bring his head around sharply, then make a swift gesture of dismissal.

"May I come in?" He paused again, as if testing the air. "I'm not holding a gun. I understand you have some of my men here; I'd like to see them. Steady, Sam"—this to his horse—"And I suppose you could use more supplies," he said as he swung out of the saddle, his single spur ringing as his shoe touched the earth.

"Please," she said, hardly trusting herself to speak; she was grateful for the concealment the shadows provided her so that she could absorb the shock of seeing him before he saw her. A jolt of longing, painful in its intensity, went through her as she stared at him.

Something of her feeling must have reached him, for he narrowed his steel-colored eyes, frowning with concentration. Then he coughed twice, and secured Sam's rein to the low rail at the front of the mill; squaring his shoulders he strode through the door, tall, whip-lean, all bone and sinew, more grey in his short beard and red hair than she remembered, and his face more wrinkled in that hard, paper-like way those with fine, tough skin sometimes acquire with age. His tunic was too short in the sleeve so that the bony knob of his wrist showed plainly as he removed his hat. "General William T. Sher—"

"I know who you are," she said, stepping out of the shadows at last, her hands extended to him.

He stood absolutely still, as if he could not believe the evidence of his eyes, or feared a single motion on his part would deprive him of a treasured illusion. "No," he muttered, and then could not go on; he made an attempt to speak, but no other words came.

She marshaled her courage and went up to him, daring to smile. "Hello, Tecumseh." It took all her strength of will to look directly into his well-remembered face. "I knew you were coming. I have felt you coming from hundreds of miles away. And you're here at last."

He found his voice. "You! In this place! You are the French Angel?" His outburst bordered on accusation, and his expression was daunting.

Fighting off rising panic, Madelaine managed to keep her smile in place. "I've missed you, Tecumseh."

"You? Here?" He dropped his hat and took both her hands, bending toward her with the intensity of his concentration. There was little friendliness in his demeanor. "I must have run mad. Tell me."

"Yes, I am here. I don't know about the French Angel part, but it is Madelaine." She wanted more than anything to be drawn into his arms with the kind of desperate tenderness he had shown her so long ago, but all she felt was a tightening of his long, lean fingers.

"How?" he demanded.

She realized he would require an account of her presence. "I had thought to leave America before war broke out, but I waited too long. So I have done my best to wait it through."

"Not a very wise choice of locale, if you ask me," he said bluntly. "And you so clever."

"How was I to know that when we came here?" She saw the quick compressing of his lips and added, "The others have gone. I remained."

"To care for the wounded, no doubt, as you did for Missus Thomas." His eyes hardened. "You have better sense than that."

"No, not to tend the wounded; I started out with lost children and had no thought of the toll of battle," she agreed readily enough. "Though it has to be done." She decided to tell him the truth, the truth she had not

213

fully admitted to herself until now, when she was with him once again. "I thought I made it plain: I was waiting for you."

He attempted to scoff at her revelation, but the sound caught in his throat, and the glint in his eyes turned liquid; he glowered to conceal his emotion, unwilling to risk ridicule or condemnation. He shook his head sharply once. "You are in the Confederacy—"

"Not precisely," she corrected him.

"Oh? How could you be in Georgia and not—" He broke off, remembering her studies. "You've been with Indians, I suppose," he said sharply.

"Choctaw," she confirmed, and attempted to interject their old familiarity into this reunion. "They were as divided on the issues of this war as most of your countrymen seem to be."

He nodded, and then the rough timbre of his voice changed, and he touched her face with the tips of his fingers; it was a tentative caress, given to assure himself that he had not been deluded. "You," he said again, and stared at her, his demeanor softening. "You haven't changed."

Her expression became somber. "No. I said I would not—"

"No," he interrupted, amazement dawning in his eyes. "You haven't changed at all. Most people, when they say 'you haven't changed' mean you have aged no more swiftly than they. But you." He took a step back from her. "You are unchanged. Truly unchanged."

"And will be until the True Death," she said quietly.

"So you said, in San Francisco. When you loved me." His voice was hardly more than a whisper.

"I love you now, Tecumseh," she said with a calmness that was at odds with her inner turmoil.

He sensed the latter, for he gave a quick, fierce smile. "Do you." He glanced swiftly over his shoulders in both directions, and, satisfied they were alone, abruptly embraced her, his mouth hard on hers.

Now it was Madelaine who was startled; as much as she had longed for this, his sudden ardor took her aback. She steadied herself against him, and held him to return his kiss, which passed from a kind of fury to all-enveloping urgency that staggered them both.

Sherman was the first to move, but only far enough to be able to look down at her. "Good Lord, Madelaine," he murmured, smoothing a few wisps of dark hair back from her brow. "I had forgotten."

"I haven't," she responded, looking up at him.

Suddenly self-conscious, he moved back from her. "How many men are you treating here?" he asked, attempting to establish a distance between them.

"At the moment, there are twenty-seven men here, eleven Confederates, the rest Union soldiers," she answered, smoothing her skirt, hoping that this simple action would restore her sense of reality. "I despair of saving three of them, but the others should survive, if we can get food."

He was brushing the front of his tunic, having bent to retrieve his fallen hat. "I will arrange for some to be sent," he said, trying to be remote, and all the while his eyes ached at her.

"Thank you," she said, doing her best to accommodate his shift in mood. "Would you like to see the men? Most of them are on the floor above, though I have two in the barn. I'm running out of room." She did her best to look apologetic, and succeeded only in gaining a kind of primness that made him chuckle.

"You will never persuade me that way," he said, managing to smile quickly.

"I wasn't trying to persuade you," she countered, and indicated the stairs. "My assistant is a Confederate. Don't be put off by his uniform."

"I won't be, as long as he makes no move against me, or to take advantage of you," he assured her, then added crisply as he started upward. "I suppose it is foolish to ask if you have a surgeon here."

"Thus far we have managed without one," she said as she went after him.

"How like you," he said to her, and then gave his attention to the wounded soldiers.

<hr />

FRENCH MILL, NEAR DALLAS, GEORGIA,
18 JUNE, 1864

We now have thirty-five men to care for, and though Tecumseh has ordered supplies sent to us, our need outstrips our available medicines and bandages ... I have used Saint-Germain's recipe for a cleaning solution because we have no carbolic acid and are not likely to get any soon. I have asked for ether, but I despair of being provided any ... Food is also, and continually, in short supply, as much because of the cold spring and late planting as what the war has done. How am I going to keep these men alive if they have nothing to eat? Not that I have any time to cook ...

215

Tecumseh has been back here twice, but has not been able to remain for more than half an hour. I can see his need in his eyes, but he has done little more than steal long kisses from me when he dares. He has promised to return again in three days. I hope he will be able to keep that promise, for I have spent the last several months yearning for him, and it is torment to see him and feel his need as strong as my own and yet be able to do nothing . . .

Wainwright is proving an apt pupil, and as he recovers he has shown himself to be a cheerful and tireless assistant. In another time, with different circumstances, I might find him of abiding interest. But in another time, with different circumstances, we would probably have no reason to meet, and so the question is moot at best . . .

IT WAS JUST AFTER MIDNIGHT that Madelaine at last saw Sherman coming up the narrow road on Sam. He rode straight in the saddle as if impervious to fatigue, and he fixed his eyes on the dim path without the aid of a lantern. When he dismounted, he led Sam down to the millpond to drink, taking care to walk softly as he stripped off his gauntlets and tucked them into his belt.

Wrapped in her deerskin cloak in spite of the heat, Madelaine remained in the shadow of the trees, watching the mill with her night vision, making sure they would be unobserved before she called out his name in a voice hardly louder than the deep breathing of Sherman's horse.

"There you are." As he came to her side, he frowned, attempting to see her clearly in the gloom of the trees. "I might as well chase a will-o'-the-wisp," he complained before his mouth came down on hers. He held her tightly, his body taut with hunger for her, his breath coming harshly as he broke from their kiss. "I should not be here."

Madelaine read the anguish in his face and did not offer the sharp response that came to her mind; she knew how ambivalent his feelings were. "You are not my prisoner, Tecumseh. You came because you wished to be with me. If you are now reluctant, then leave. If you are willing, then stay."

Sherman cocked his head and regarded her closely, trying to pierce the darkness with his will alone. "How can I want you now? How dare I want you now?" He held her face in his hands and stared down into her eyes. "How dare I?" he whispered before he again opened her lips

216

with his, letting his hands roam down the cloak she wore, sighing as he strained her nearer.

The buttons and buckles of his uniform pressed into her flesh as she opened her cloak to him, revealing the promise of her nakedness beneath the deerskin. "If not now, when?" she murmured, challenging him deliberately.

He made a sound between a sob and a moan, then reached out for her, plundering her with his hands, making no apology for his urgency or the roughness of his caresses. For caresses they were—a curious mix of passion and tenderness that had been his from the start. He knelt before her and explored her body with his mouth, pausing now and again to wrestle free of another item of clothing, which he tossed aside in a heap. He said nothing, and when she tried to speak, he silenced her with a single, abrupt gesture. Only when he drew her down beside him did he utter a few disjointed phrases. "God. Oh, dear God. So sweet, so sweet." He bent his head to her breast, his beard rough on her skin, his tongue exciting her as he moved above her, and at last, deeply into her.

"Slowly, Tecumseh." Madelaine rode his ardor with him, matching his growing frenzy with the release of her own long-pent desire. "Savor it."

His rhythm changed, becoming steadier, and now his kisses were long and wet, with the searching quality she remembered from San Francisco; he was still seeking the whole of her, embracing his quest even as he wrapped his arms more surely around her and she brought her lips to his neck.

The enormity of his fulfillment was overwhelming. After years of stolen dreams, her esurience was gratified beyond anything she had experienced since leaving him. She trembled with the force of his rapture, and was rewarded by a soft, reverent oath from him as he finally lay still atop her, his sweat running over her, his breath no longer harsh in her ear. "My God, Madelaine," he said softly, his elbows keeping his full weight from her. With one hand he curled a loose tendril of her hair beside her ear. "How can anything so profane be so ... so ..." He managed a rueful smile that softened his features and smoothed his wrinkles. "I've never had the right words to say what you are to me."

She returned his smile. "You do not need words with me, Tecumseh, though it is lovely to have them."

He kissed the corner of her mouth where a red smudge remained. "You know that way, don't you? The way of your kind."

"Yes." She freed her hands and fingered his close-cut beard. "That is a change."

"Do you like it?" he asked without apprehension, the question rough music now that the tension had left his voice.

"I'm not used to it." She studied him. "It suits you."

"It conceals some of the lines, anyway," he said a bit more brusquely. "I don't look like somebody's lawyer."

"Does that concern you, the wrinkles?" she asked lazily, relishing the companionable closeness between them in the warm darkness.

"Certainly," he answered, and rolled off her, lying beside her on her cloak, one arm across her body just beneath her breasts. "It would you, too, if you had any."

"I don't know," she said seriously. "There are many times I wish I did not look quite so much like—"

"A girl just out of school?" he suggested, his eyes glinting with amusement. "You do have that air about you, Madame. Still."

"Exactly," she agreed, and seeking to extend their intimacy added, "Speaking of girls in school, how is Lizzie? She must be ... what, thirteen or fourteen by now?"

Sherman looked away and some of his awkwardness returned. "She is with her mother. And our other children."

There was something amiss here, Madelaine knew; perhaps he still did not like talking about his family with her. "And how is Willy?" she persisted, aware that the boy was his favorite.

In a flat voice Sherman said, "Willy died last year. In the autumn." He looked away from her, into the trees. "He and my wife had come to visit me on campaign."

Sympathy went through Madelaine in a sharp tide. "Oh, Tecumseh. I am so sorry."

"He took a fever," Sherman went on in the same blank way. "At the end of September."

"And you grieve for him," she said, putting her hand on his shoulder.

Overhead, an owl hooted as it flew on silent wings, searching for a night's prey.

He shook his head. "How can I? In the midst of all this? He was one child, and there are thousands of men dying around me every day." He turned back toward her with a suddenness that startled them both. "What sort of monster would I be, to put a boy ahead of all these brave men?"

218

"A loving father," said Madelaine quietly, recalling the delight Sherman had taken in his oldest son. "As I know you are."

He nodded once, looking away from her again. "And when this is over, I will mourn my boy. But not while this war goes on. I must not." He pulled her up against him, his long-fingered hands spread wide on her back. His words were laden with despair. "And I have other children."

"They are not Willy," Madelaine said as gently as she could, aware now of some of the inward source of his need for her.

"No, they are not," he responded, and coughed.

FRENCH MILL, NEAR DALLAS, GEORGIA, 9 JULY, 1864

Tecumseh has returned twice since we lay together, but not at an hour or for long enough to have more than kisses between us, and those hurried. He is concerned about his wounded men, and is as eager to see them and assure himself they are properly cared for as he is eager to visit me. Today he sent a cartload of medical supplies to us, prepared by the Sanitary Commission, with a note of thanks for helping so many Union soldiers.

One of the wounded brought here yesterday is a drummer boy, no more than thirteen, if he is that old. He comes from Illinois, as he told me, "The same as Mister Lincoln." I fear we will lose him in the next two days, for he has a badly swollen abdomen and he suffers from fever and nausea. If Saint-Germain were here he could tell me what has happened to the boy, and he might have skill enough to save him, but without such skill and proper medication, I do not think he will survive ... As I watch this Timothy Rawlins, I think of how Tecumseh must feel at the loss of Willy.

If only he would mourn the boy. It is fixed in him like a Minié ball or a thorn. But he refuses to acknowledge it, and it eats at him with the tenacity of ivy, and it will exact a price from him ...

We are still treating men wounded in the Kenesaw Mountain assault. Union casualties were very high, and direct attack has been abandoned for more flanking maneuvers; it may prolong the march, but overall there will be fewer men wounded and killed, and for that I am heartily grateful. There are now forty-one men at this place, and I have set Silas Wain-

wright the unenviable task of seeing that the men who die here are prop-
erly buried. We have set a small dell near the mill aside to serve as our
cemetery. When it has been possible, I have written to the families of the
dead men, and turned the letters over to Tecumseh when he has been here,
to be carried with other dispatches...

How hard it is to see these young men die with so much promise in
them, and so little chance in the world. It would be easier, perhaps, to
resign myself to their losses if I were as mortal as they. But to have the
luxury of time for myself and to see these men deprived of it—I cannot
accept the very thing I must if I am to be able to continue as I am...

"THREE THIS WEEK." Silas Wainwright leaned on the simple grave-
marker, his face dripping. "It's getting worse," he said to Madelaine. "If we
have so many casualties, think how bad it must be in the camp hospitals."

"Horrible," said Madelaine with feeling. She looked at the tattered
New Testament in Wainwright's pocket. "Do you want to read anything
for him?"

"I guess I should," Wainwright said, sounding too tired to do it; the
sweltering afternoon had been enervating, and the task itself was dis-
heartening. "It's only right."

"Would you rather I did?" Madelaine offered, and took the New Testament Wainwright handed to her. "Is there anything you would prefer
I read?"

"I know it should be 'I am the resurrection and the life,' but somehow
that don't seem right..." He thought about it a short while. "Matthew
twenty-four, verses six through fourteen."

"All right," Madelaine said, trying to recall what was contained in those
verses from the lessons of her childhood at the hands of the Ursuline Sisters. She located the chapter and began to read: "'And ye shall hear of wars
and rumors of wars: see that ye be not troubled: for all these things must
come to pass but the end is not yet. For nation shall rise against nation and
kingdom against kingdom: and there shall be famines, and pestilences, and
earthquakes in diverse places. All these are the beginning of sorrows. Then
shall they deliver you up to be afflicted and shall kill you: and ye shall be
hated of all nations for my name's sake. And then shall many be offended,
and shall betray one another, and shall hate one another. And many false
prophets shall rise, and shall deceive many. And because iniquity shall
abound, the love of many shall wax cold. But he that endure unto the end,

the same shall be saved. And this gospel of the kingdom shall be preached in all the world for a witness unto nations; and then shall the end come.'" She closed the little book and handed it back to Wainwright.

"Says it all, doesn't it?" Wainwright asked after a certain silence.

"I suppose so," Madelaine replied, and started back along the narrow path to the mill. "Do we have an address for Private Ritter?"

"He said his family was in Michigan, a place called Copper Harbor. But he couldn't read nor write, and probably his folks can't, either. It wouldn't do no good to write to 'em." He looked back over his shoulder to the glen that was filling up with graves.

"There must be a church there. I'll write to the minister and hope he can find the family." There was an abiding sadness in her now, and a fatalism that few things other than the company of Sherman could shake off. "I hope for their sake he was not their only son."

"Amen," said Wainwright.

They were almost in the mill-yard when the sound of heavy guns stopped them. "Another skirmish," said Madelaine as the man-made thunder faded. "We'd better be ready for more casualties."

Wainwright sighed. "Where can we put 'em? The barn's as full as it'll hold without turning the animals out."

"Maybe we can put up tents," Madelaine suggested. "Or sheds for shelter. Or make pens for the animals."

"Maybe," said Wainwright, clearly doubting it. He pointed in the direction of the sound of canon. "With General Johnston gone, there's bound to be harder fighting. Hood won't fall back just to suit Uncle Billy Sherman." The look he shot Madelaine was uneasy.

"That's unfortunate. No general wants to lose men. A loss of men means a loss of a war." She remained unperturbed, though she knew Wainwright wanted to discover the reason Sherman had been willing to supply her little improvised hospital, since she treated soldiers of both sides.

"They say that three of Sherman's right-hand men were classmates of Hood's at West Point," Wainwright persisted. "Lieutenant Caufield told me about it."

"In this war all the generals appear to have been each other's classmates or teachers and pupils," said Madelaine, refusing to be drawn into the matter. "Did you give Lieutenant Caufield the poultice I prepared?"

Wainwright gave up for the time being. "I did. But I don't like the color of his wound."

"Why?" she asked as they entered the mill. There were cots everywhere, and the men who lay on them were suffering from the heat as much as their injuries.

"It's got inside flesh sticking out, all purple." He swallowed hard, and looked around him. "Corporal McMasters needs another drink for pain."

"I'll take care of it," Madelaine promised as she went to the pantry to see which of her medicaments needed replacing. She noticed that the tincture for asthma had been only a little depleted, and all by Sherman. It might have afforded her some amusement at another time, but now, with so many men needing her help, she could do little more than make a mental note of her supply of the tincture as she continued her hasty inventory.

FRENCH MILL, NEAR DALLAS, GEORGIA,
20 JULY, 1864

Generals Hooker and Thomas have repelled a Southern attack, and the casualties are here to prove it. It is approaching midnight, and I have not had any time to write until now...

Tecumseh has not been here much; the fighting is growing more intense and demands his time. He has also told me that there are rumors floating among his men that he has a mistress, so he has become more circumspect in his dealing with me. Speculation is that his mistress is black and that he is hiding her for that reason. He is worried for my reputation, it would appear...

Luke Greentree reached here today, saying that so far the new location is safe. He was going west, to try to return to the Choctaw Nation. He is in complete despair regarding the war, and wants to move as far away from it as he can... In the morning he plans to resume his journey.

"HE IS IN A TERRIBLE STATE," the young lieutenant told Madelaine for the fifth time since he had summoned her from the old mill to Sherman's camp. It was now after two in the morning, and most of the Union army was lost in exhausted sleep as he guided Madelaine toward the ruined house where General Sherman had temporary headquarters and was spending the night. It was warm and close, the air hardly moving. Both horses were flecked with foamy sweat. "He has been up and sleepless, since they brought McPherson's body back. The Army of the Tennessee has needed support, and he has exhausted himself with the task. He hasn't been breathing right since mid-afternoon. He put General Thomas and General Schofield on the attack."

"McPherson was killed this morning?" Madelaine asked, hoping to get some sense of the order of events.

"Yesterday morning, yes, ma'am," the young lieutenant corrected her.

Madelaine said nothing; she could feel the agony of spirit which held Sherman in its relentless grip, and had since early the previous afternoon. Her draught horse mount whickered as they approached the house, recognizing Sam among the other officers' horses. "Is he alone?"

"He was when he sent for you. He would let no one near him, said the surgeons had enough to do without wasting their time on him," the lieutenant told her, pointing to the entrance of the half-burned house. "In there."

She dropped out of her sidesaddle and reached for the case strapped to the cantel. "Tell me where to find him."

"I'll take you there," said the lieutenant. There were deep circles under his eyes and when he dismounted he moved as if every joint was sore. "I am grateful to you for coming. Someone has to help him."

"He's right. Your surgeons do not have time or the supplies to treat his asthma. Fortunately, I do," she said briskly, hoping to convince the young man that her summons had nothing more to it than medical necessity.

The lieutenant hesitated at the foot of the short flight of stairs. "He...was not himself. When General McPherson was killed...They brought his body back here, laid it on a door for a table." He rubbed the stubble on his chin. "I never saw Uncle Billy cry for anything before. But he sure did for General McPherson. He paced the room, shouting orders, and all the while the tears ran down his face. I don't think he knew he was doing it. The crying, that is."

"They were friends," said Madelaine with what patience she could muster, her anxiety increasing. "Where is he? The sooner I can treat him, the sooner he will be himself again." She saw a worn-out corporal come to take the horses, and she told him, "Give him water and a handful of oats. It is a long ride back to the mill." And one she suspected she would have to make in sunlight; at least she had lined the soles of her boots with her native earth the morning before.

"Come with me," said the lieutenant, at last going up the stairs and motioning Madelaine to follow him.

They climbed to the second floor, past two posted sentries, along a hall with one wall charred and stinking. At last they reached the last door, and the lieutenant knocked. "General? The Frenchwoman is here."

The voice that answered was so distorted with wheezing it was difficult to hear what he said. "Go away!"

The lieutenant was about to knock again, but Madelaine moved him aside and touched the door twice, very lightly. "You sent for me, General Sherman."

This time there was the sound of hasty steps and the door was flung open. Sherman had removed his tunic and his shirt was open to the middle of his chest. His wild eyes were hollow, lividly shadowed and bloodshot, and his red hair was in disarray. His breathing was strident and labored. He stared at Madelaine for a few seconds, then grabbed her by the shoulder and abruptly tugged her into the room, slamming the door behind her at once to shut out the lieutenant. He shoved the bolt home to guarantee their privacy, then glared at her, unacknowledged tears on his face. "You came."

"How could I not?" she asked, trying to hide her distress. Nothing she had anticipated prepared her for the sight of him, his face mottled, his chest straining visibly as he gasped for breath. She put down her case and opened it, doing her best to remain calm; she removed three glass vials. "I knew you would need this." The room smelled of charring nitre paper; a single lamp burned on the gate-legged table standing near the center of the chamber. "Why did you wait so long to send for me?"

"I had other things to do." He regarded the vials suspiciously, wariness in his stance and inflection. "Ah, that same concoction you gave me in San Francisco. When you told me you were studying Indians?" He could barely get the last words out.

"Yes," she said, opening one of the vials and holding it out to him.

"It will work?" he demanded, glowering at her.

"It did before. It has for others." She was not intimidated by his stare; she put the vial into his hand. "Here, Tecumseh. Drink it."

He took it without comment and tossed it back as if it had been whiskey. Then he coughed—deep, wracking coughs like sobs that made him whoop for gulps of air as he began to exhale at last.

Madelaine set the other two vials down on the table and went to his side. "How long have you been suffering like this?" She had rarely felt as helpless as she did now, and it made her testy. "Tecumseh? Answer me."

224

He bent over at the waist, retching, one hand moving to show he would say something directly. He dropped to one knee, still hunched over, the veins in his neck standing out with effort. Slowly the struggling subsided and finally he drew a long, steady breath, let it out fully without wheezing, the mottling faded from his face and then he straightened up, refusing her offer of a supporting arm as he fussed with the open front of his shirt. He directed his gaze at the far wall, and spoke distantly. "My thanks, Madame."

She would not be put off by his formality. "How long, Tecumseh?"

"A while," he answered indirectly, then gave her a long, appraising stare.

"You should not have waited. Asthma can be dangerous," she reminded him.

"It doesn't matter," he said, reaching for her, determined, cool lasciviousness showing in his demeanor.

"The attacks have been getting worse, haven't they?" she asked with certainty.

"From time to time," he answered. "I am better now." He reached out and took her arm, pulling her closer to him.

"Until your next tragedy, if you will not mourn Willy and McPherson now," she said, confronting him. "Then it will be worse than this time."

"I will manage." He ran his hand down the front of her body, hard anticipation shining in his steel-colored eyes. There was no kindness in him now, no suggestion of the tenderness he had offered her before.

"Tell me how long you have been suffering with this," she insisted, not quite resisting him, but not acquiescing, either. She made no attempt to stop his calculated assault on her, yet she made no indication of capitulation to his desires.

He was unbuttoning her bodice, working steadily as his breathing continued to deepen. "Not important. How long." His kiss was an act of possession, ferocious and arrogant, driven by despair. He gripped her clothes and tore at them, opening her bodice and exposing her camisole, then tried to haul himself out of his shirt, leaving it hanging beyond his suspenders. "A night of debauch—what do you think? A better cure than nostrums. I've seen to my men already, and they are prepared for tomorrow. But tonight? A bout of excess to lend forgetfulness. A balm against dying. But you don't die, do you? No corsets. That's providential." As he pressed his mouth to hers again, she could feel his teeth on her lips.

Knowing he was expecting denials and a fight, she put her arms around him and held him, accepting his kiss, taking in the rage that hid his anguish. When he tried to break away from her she clung to him, unwilling to allow him to retreat into his self-imposed isolation and loathing. She opened herself to his grief and his engulfing shame, the sorrow he would not recognize, and she gave him her constancy and love to take its place.

Sherman pushed back from her, his face aghast. "Madelaine." He looked down into her face as if seeing her for the first time. "What have you done to me?"

She embraced him, leaning against him. "Nothing that is not in you to have done," she answered, and drew his head down to her, their lips barely touching for many long seconds, then meeting fervently. When they drew apart she said, "You are part of me, Tecumseh. Nothing can change that, not war, not distance, not age, not death itself."

"But...how?" His eyes glittered with tears. He tried to wipe them away but she stopped him. "Don't. It isn't fitting."

She answered him without hesitation. "What has that to do with it? Know your sorrow, Tecumseh, or you will sink into black desolation again. It is like a festering wound and you must lance it or it will spread its poison through you. Grieve, for your son and your friend, I beg you, and I will comfort you; my word on it." There was only the table, two chairs and a cot in the room; she took him by the hand and drew him toward the cot.

Now he hung back, refusing to look at her. "No. No. I cannot. Not here, not yet. I haven't the right to mourn yet, not for McPherson, and certainly not for Willy. Don't you understand?"

"But you must; I understand better than you do. Mourning is not a privilege to be earned; it is the cost love exacts from us for loving." She took both his hands and lifted them to her lips, kissing the prominent knuckles and long fingers. "Accept the pain of your losses. For my sake, if not for yours."

"Why for your sake?" he asked, startled at her plea.

"Because of my bond with you. Your life touches mine, including your torment. If you contain your pain, it must be mine, as well. Be free of it, and you will release me from its grip." She sank onto the cot, still holding his hands, so that he had to bend over her or break their touching. "The blood is a bond that cannot be severed." She could see the doubt in his face. "I told you this at the first, and nothing has changed."

226

"Nothing has changed?" he echoed, incredulity making his voice rise. "How can you say that? You see for yourself daily how the world has changed."

She met his eyes steadfastly. "Nothing between us has changed, Tecumseh, nor can it."

He shook his head in adamant rejection of her perseverance. "There is a war that brings us back together. We meet over the corpses of the fallen, over oceans of blood. Surely that is a change? Or do those shattered men at your mill mean nothing to you but fodder?"

Madelaine recoiled as if struck. "What do you think me?" she asked, shocked but determined not to be goaded to anger, for she realized that he was trying to thrust her away from him, to put himself beyond her concern and his own wretchedness.

"Why," he said archly, "you told me yourself, Madame. You are a vampire. And what better place for one than in the midst of this unspeakable carnage? And that we have in abundance."

"You know that I seek no one who does not want me." She said it quietly, without countering his challenge. "And I would not prey on the helpless." Deliberately she added, "The dead have nothing I can use."

"You do not prey on the helpless, you say?" Sherman inquired sardonically, and put one knee on the cot so that he could loom nearer to her, tempting himself with her accessibility. "And what would you call me?"

"Hardly helpless," she answered with asperity, stung to a hasty reply. She sat rather straighter, feeling unjustly attacked.

"Ah, there you are wrong." He leaned closer as if compelled by something beyond his power. "I am vulnerable to you, Madame, as I am vulnerable to no other woman. And I am twice-damned for it; for adultery and for—" His fingers closed on the twist of hair at the nape of her neck. Using this, he pulled her head around so that he could kiss her again, this time roughly, as if to prove he could do it and feel nothing.

"Tecumseh, Tecumseh," she whispered as he broke away from her and paced the length of the room, pausing as far from her as the confines of the chamber would permit. "It isn't me you wish to escape."

"How astute of you," he snapped, then stood very still, his back to her. As she watched, his shoulders, held so rigidly, drooped and trembled as the first terrible sobs shook him.

Madelaine went to him, standing behind him, pressed against his back, her eyes sore with tears she could not shed. For that instant she envied him his weeping as much as she knew he despised it. She could feel him shudder with the intensity of his misery. For several minutes they remained that way while he cried himself out.

When at last he turned to her, he caught and held her as if to staunch a bleeding wound. His face was wet. "I cannot bear it," he murmured, as if seeking her pardon for his lapse.

Her soul went out to him. "You don't have to, Tecumseh, not alone," she said softly.

"You will take my burden? You?" He managed a single bark of devastated laughter. "For all this cruelty?"

Her arms remained firmly around him. "Must it be cruel?"

"Of course it must be," he said with a trace of his usual force of character. "It is war."

"But to what purpose must it be cruel?" she asked reasonably, feeling a little of his strength returning.

"Why, to end it!" His finger dug into her sides. "This cannot drag on another year, or deteriorate into constant regional skirmishes, and if it isn't settled soon, that is what will happen. Neither North nor South could survive that. There is no kindness in such protracted fighting. It must be stopped. Now. For good and all." He looked down suddenly to where he clasped her body. "I've hurt you," he whispered.

"Not that way, not with your hands," she responded, and pressed close to him once more. "You hurt me by denying our bond, and by refusing what succor I offer."

His chuckle was brief. "Succor. Apt choice of words." He released his grip on her, and reached around for her hand instead. "Since you are here, well, why not?" The question was light, almost flippant, but Madelaine was not deceived; this was a cry from his heart.

With her free hand she unfastened the last buttons on his half-discarded shirt, then reached out, laying her hand on his bare chest. She felt his heartbeat quicken.

He placed his hand over hers. "If you insist on this, on going into the night of my soul, then I surrender to you for tonight." The lamplight softened his stern features, yet revealed the longing in his eyes.

She had to stand on tiptoe to kiss him. "I insist," she said before she stepped back and took off her bodice, folding it once and setting it atop his shirt. "Do you want to do the rest?"

He nodded, unable to speak aloud, and with a care that bordered on reverence, he began to untie the laces of her camisole, removing it cautiously, unsure of himself now that he had given over so much of himself to her. "And the skirt? What about your skirt?"

"It fastens in the back, with hooks," she said, never looking away from his eyes. "Shall I turn around?"

He put his hands around her waist for an answer. "If I am to be lost, I will do it with a will, and facing front. I think I can manage from here."

"I'm wearing one flounced petticoat. No hoops." There was a hand's-breadth between them, and it seemed filled with electricity, so great was the complex tension between them. She bent her head so that her forehead touched his chest, seeking the solace of touching him.

"I will manage," he promised, working on the hooks of the skirt until it slid down her legs to the floor.

"The petticoat has laces."

"If they're knotted, I swear I will break them. I won't take the time to—" He tugged the end of the lace and felt the bow-knot give; a moment later, her petticoat fell onto her skirt. Now she had only her simple gartered drawers holding her stockings, and, incongruously, her sensible laced boots. "I ... I don't—"

Madelaine reached out and unbuttoned his trousers, and his suspenders. "Now we're equal," she said as his clothes fell around his ankles. "Take off your shoes, Tecumseh, and I will remove my boots."

He hastened to obey, the pain fading from his face to be replaced with a hard sensuality; he skinned out of his drawers as he bent to unbuckle his shoes, and tossed them aside. His shoes followed the rest of his clothes. When he straightened, he was nearly erect. He flushed with embarrassment and pride as he approached her. "How do you do this to me?"

"You do it, Tecumseh," she said. She had sat down and was drawing off one boot. "That is your passion; I do nothing but suit your desires. What we have from your passion is joy."

"You've said that before, in San Francisco. I've remembered," he said, going to his cot and lying down on his back, arms extended over the sides. "There isn't much room. And it isn't very steady."

"You are a good tactician and strategist. We will find a way." She set her second boot aside and rolled down her stockings, feeling him watch her as she did.

"You are so young," he said as she came toward him; there was awe in his voice. "And so full of light."

"I am well over a century old," she reminded him gently. "One hundred forty in November."

229

"You are a glowing girl, and I am turning into an old man." He held up his hands to her as she came to the side of the cot. "You will have to get on top of me, I fear."

"Dreadful fate," she said softly, and stretched out on his thin, hard body. How she loved the sudden voluptuousness that came over him as he sought to explore their carnality in this unpromising place. He was filled with an anodyne frenzy, wanting the consolation of their fulfillment as a bastion against the horrendous weight of his grief.

"Since you will have me, have all." He held her eyes with his. "I will have you, as well, to the core." His long fingers discovered new ways to rouse her, sliding between their close-pressed flesh to the petal-folds at the apex of her thighs; all the while he watched her, searching her violet eyes for the revelation he yearned for. She shivered at the first tentative probing, moving as much as she dared to give him better access. "Deny me now at your peril," he whispered as he moved beneath her and fully into her in the same motion.

Their joining was tempestuous, ineffable, so intense that the exultant spasm they shared seemed to create its own remarkable lume. And when it was over neither was quite certain where one began and the other left off. They lay still, both rapt in evanescent unity.

"The camp will waken soon," he said, reluctantly ending the enveloping silence. "And this will be a hard day, I think."

"More fighting," Madelaine said, knowing it would be so.

"Yes." He made no excuse for what was to come as he tried to move onto his side to provide her a place next to him.

She snuggled close to him and was able to maintain a semblance of balance on the edge of the cot. "It's useless to say this, but do not be reckless, Tecumseh. I will worry for you."

"I am not a reckless man," he said, sliding his hand up her side to cup her breast. "Recklessness does not win wars."

"Of course not," she agreed, not believing a word of it.

Suddenly he gave her a businesslike kiss and pushed himself up on his elbow. "Come. You must be away from here shortly, or you will be discovered. And that would not do."

"I suppose not," Madelaine agreed, rising with him. "And I should be back at the mill."

"You have your men to tend to, and I have mine," he said companionably, reaching for his clothes. As he drew on his trousers he said, "If you would not disdain my gratitude, I would offer it wholeheartedly."

"Why should I disdain it?" she asked him, struggling to fix the buttons of her bodice.

He looked at what she was doing, and said, "I'm sorry. I should not have done that. I ought to be better self-disciplined."

She shrugged. "I will sew them properly this evening."

He was pulling on his shirt, wanting to make the most of this brief time with her. "Will you follow the army when we take Atlanta?" He held his breath waiting for her answer.

"If you need my help treating casualties, I will," she said. "I will not go if you intend to keep me isolated." Her bodice was almost closed now, and she gave up setting it completely to rights. "Tell me what you want."

"I want," he said very quietly, "this war to be over. I want the Union restored. I want the slaughter to stop. Until it is finished, I have no right to want more than that."

Madelaine sighed and sat down to pull on her boots. "When you have made up your mind in this regard, send me word." She busied herself with the laces, then stood up and walked over to him as he buttoned his tunic.

He came to her, bent and kissed her cheek. "If I did anything to offend you, I am heartily sorry. If you will attribute it to the press of circumstances—"

She interrupted him. "The only thing you did was to refuse to mourn your son and your friend; that is not for me to pardon, but for you to pardon yourself."

For a moment he said nothing. "All the good in the world is being sacrificed to this national catastrophe. I am afraid that there will be nothing worthwhile to come out of it if the cost continues to be as great as it has been."

"I have a...very remarkable friend. He has seen losses that neither you nor I can imagine." Her violet eyes were haunted as she remembered Saint-Germain, their now-inaccessible intimacy, and all he had written to her while she was at Luxor, forty years before. "He has managed to endure the losses by treasuring what he has while they are alive to be treasured, or so he has told me. He has also said it was a hard-won lesson."

Sherman caught something of her emotions, for he said, "This man, who is he?"

"His name is Saint-Germain—" she began.

"Hah! That name again! There was a charlatan by that name in Paris in the last century," he exclaimed, making no attempt to conceal his jealousy.

"Saint-Germain is no charlatan. He brought me to his life with his blood." She regarded him steadily, until he could find nothing to retort.

He conceded this to her with a gesture. "I will not dispute you; you were there to observe for yourself."

With an impulsive smile, she took his hands in hers. "How often does anyone get such accommodation from General Sherman?"

"It is Tecumseh who speaks, not General Sherman," he said, his banter gruff. "It is always Tecumseh who speaks to you, because it is Tecumseh you love."

If she had been able to weep, her eyes would have filled with tears. "There you are wrong. I love the whole of you, and wholeheartedly."

There were sounds of movement in another part of the house. He raised his head and listened. "It's time you were away." He started toward the door, drawing her after him.

"My case," she protested. "I must take it back with me." She indicated the two vials standing on his writing table. "Those are for you, to take when you need them. I will try to bring more, but..."

He grabbed the case and shoved it at her. "Hurry. I want no gossip about you."

She allowed herself to be rushed to the door, only touching her fingers to her lips and then his before she was all but shoved into the hall, to face the waiting lieutenant who had brought her to Sherman earlier that morning.

"Take care of her," Sherman ordered the young man. "See her safely back to the mill, and report to me when you return." And with that he closed the door.

"He is much better," the young lieutenant marveled. "You really helped him."

Madelaine stared at the closed door. "I hope so," she said before she turned to follow the lieutenant down the corridor and out into the waning darkness.

———————◆———————

FRENCH MILL, NEAR DALLAS, GEORGIA, 11 AUGUST, 1864

*Tecumseh's army has moved on to Atlanta, and I am faced with the deci-
sion of whether I should follow it there or remain where I am…*

TWO OF THE WOMEN WERE TRAINED NURSES; the third was a
Missus MacFarlane with the Sanitary Commission, sent to supervise the
transfer of wounded.

"We'll get them back to proper hospitals, Madame," said Lilly Mac-
Farlane, her doubts about Madelaine revealed in her severe expression.

"That will certainly please the men. Even the Confederates," said
Madelaine, looking around the old mill for what she knew would be the
last time. "They need regular care."

The older of the two nurses managed to smile at Madelaine. "I would
judge that they have had that, and better, while they were here. If only
you had a surgeon, there would be no need to move these men."

"Thank you," Madelaine said, looking to her three trunks standing
by the door, the last supply of her native earth with her. "How soon will
the carter be here?"

"Shortly," said Missus MacFarlane, her disapproval unchanged. "I
have spoken to Reverend Sparrow about your Sergeant Winfield—"

"Sergeant Wainwright," Madelaine corrected politely.

"Wainwright," she repeated with heavy emphasis. "Wainwright. Yes.
I'll make sure we have it down properly." Her attitude did not soften,
but her voice became less strident. "I don't know how you have managed here, on your own."

"I have some experience with the dying," said Madelaine quietly.

"So I have been told," Missus MacFarlane said, needing to say something. "It is a wonder you weren't driven out of this place during the
fighting in this area."

"Well, to be candid, Missus MacFarlane," said Madelaine, a sardonic tilt
to her brows, "there were times I was surprised, too. But this part of the
hill is remote, and there was no obvious strategic advantage in taking it, as
it is not close enough to Dallas to make much difference in fighting." She
indicated the trees beyond the window. "You see? Not many balls in them.
Considering what happened elsewhere, we are virtually unscathed."

"True," Missus MacFarlane said, paying little notice to this feature. "You were fortunate beyond any expectation. Praise God for sparing these wounded men. And you." The last was a reluctant afterthought.

"Certainly," said Madelaine, crossing herself to show her sincerity, and was about to leave Missus MacFarlane to her task of identifying all the men when she saw the harsh down-turn of the other woman's mouth. "Tell me what is troubling you, Missus MacFarlane."

It took some little time for her to answer. At last, as she glanced over a list Madelaine had kept of those who had come to the mill, she said, "General Sherman is a married man."

Since Madelaine was expecting worse than this, she laughed. "And well I know it. He is so proud of his family. I met two of his children many years ago, in San Francisco, where I had my first encounter with the general, though he was not at that time a military man."

Missus MacFarlane looked unconvinced. "You met his children. When you were little more than a child yourself." She folded the paper. "You would do him an ill-service if you should forget that family."

"It would hardly matter if I did: he never does, which is much to his credit," said Madelaine with deliberate lightness. "Unlike men of General Hooker's sort, General Sherman is devoted to his wife and children. They are always uppermost in his mind, even when he is caught in the frenzy." She indicated the lists of wounded men, and let Missus MacFarlane draw her own conclusions as to which frenzy she meant. "If you have any questions, in regard to the men here, I will be happy to answer them. For matters concerning General Sherman, you must address him." And with that she went out to the barn where she found Sergeant Wainwright putting her jars of tinctures into crates, as she had asked him.

"Seems strange," said Wainwright as he wrapped the jars in straw, "having you leave here. First time in more'n a year that I wanted to settle in."

"It is as pleasant a place as one can find in the middle of war," said Madelaine quietly.

"Then why not remain?" asked Wainwright plaintively. "There's wounded men a-plenty here needing our help."

"There is greater need elsewhere," said Madelaine.

"And the Union general, he won't be able to come here so smart and easy, will he, once they move on the city," said Wainwright. "Oh, I won't tell anyone. You've been too good to me; but what you see in that butcher—"

Would everyone insist on making remarks about Sherman? Madelaine held up her hand to silence him. "He is no butcher, and if you knew him, you would not think him one, either. I see in him an honorable man who is a genius at war and who hates it because he knows it for what it is, and its cost. I see in him a man who has sworn to preserve the Union he believes in. And I see in him a man who lives every day with the threat of despair over him, and grief." She said this quietly, trying to check her emotions as she stopped Wainwright's outburst; she took a deep breath. More pragmatically she added, "I also see in him a man it is not wise to speak out against where his deputies can hear you. He inspires great loyalty in his troops."

"Well enough; you're right, I don't know him, I only know his work," said Wainwright, acknowledging her demand for discretion. "But it doesn't change anything." He took more straw and wrapped another jar, taking longer than usual while he framed what he would say next. "I will not speak of him to anyone but you. I give you my word on it. So long as he doesn't hurt you. If he hurts you, Miss, I don't know what I'll do."

"He will not hurt me," said Madelaine, and hoped it would be so.

ATLANTA, GEORGIA, 2 SEPTEMBER, 1864

Word has come that General Hood is abandoning the city and setting fire to many of the warehouses as he and his troops retreat, so that the Union army will have none of their supplies. They say Hardee is gone already ...

Working here with the wounded, I have heard the men saying that this is truly Good Friday, and that the one in Spring is nothing compared to this ... Few things can so improve the spirits of these men as the knowledge that they have triumphed at last, that their sacrifices have secured something of worth for their cause.

Saint-Germain might have less charitable thoughts for this occasion, and with all his experience, his reasons are surely more cogent than mine, but I cannot help but be grateful that the worst of this fighting is over for a time. I cannot but think that it will redound to Tecumseh's

235

credit that he was not forced to level the city in order to claim it as his own ... I understand that General Thomas has been as close to gleeful as it is in his nature to be ...

I had word but two days since that Silas Wainwright has been permitted to join a group of Confederate soldiers sent west to build new roads and improve the roads that are there already ... He wanted to inform me he would be departing with another fifty or so men for St. Joseph in Missouri, and from there would start across the plains. He said he hopes the stories I told him about my travels were true, for he intends to use them as lesson books for himself. They have been informed that they are expecting to winter in Fort Sedgwick, which he has been told is on the Ogallala Trail ... He says that he is hoping to find land of his own in the West and make his home there, away from all the battlefields and cemeteries ...

Tecumseh visited the wounded men briefly, and had a few words with me in private. He was already grumbling about the politicians and what they could be expected to do now that Atlanta was won ...

"WE CANNOT STAY HERE THROUGH THE WINTER, much as you might want to; we would become too easy a target for Hood and Wheeler and that damned Forrest," Sherman declared to the wounded men lying in the nave of Saint Eustace Church. The pews had long since been broken up for firewood by the people of Atlanta, and now the vacant building provided needed shelter. "I will do what I can to get as many of you as need it transportation to hospitals in the north, and I will hope that many of you will be fit enough to return to service." He strode between the pallets, talking rapidly, his steely eyes bright. Out of courtesy to these men he had left his sidearm and sword with his aide. "I want every one of you who requires evacuation to inform my aides, or the surgeons, or the women from the Sanitary Commission, or your nurses, so that you will get the care you have so richly earned." He paused to light his cigar, then tossed the match aside. "We have work to be done yet. General Grant and President Lincoln are expecting us to do our part in ending this war, and I have told them we will." He blew out a long cloud of smoke. "It will be of no help to you or to our work if you try to remain while you are not fit. Sadly, we must anticipate other casualties in this fight, and we will have to do all we may to make it possible for the army to move as quickly as it can. We will have new casualties to contend with along the way, and cannot afford to carry any from here who need great attention. So if you will not be ready to march with us, then be prudent, and go north to the hospitals, where you may receive care without danger of new wounds, or the uncertainties of our national conflict." He stopped by one of his younger officers, a captain from a Michigan infantry regiment. "How badly are you hurt?"

"My right hand's mangled, sir," answered the young man.

"Can you pull a trigger still?" asked Sherman with a quick, encouraging look that passed for a smile.

The captain shook his head slowly. "Don't think so, sir."

Sherman regarded him a moment. "That's unfortunate for us; you will be with your family by Christmas. Your country is grateful for your sacrifice, Captain." He rocked back on his heels and resumed his pacing. "It was wise to tell me the truth, and I respect you for it. No false claims will answer now. I cannot ask men to wager their lives on comrades who are not able to support them."

One of the nurses, a pale widow from Kentucky, came forward. "General, there are one or two cases...difficult cases...it would be better...you should see them for yourself."

"Before I leave, I will," Sherman promised her, and went back to addressing his men. "They're going to try to cut us off here, the Rebel armies will. It is what they must do if they are to salvage anything from our campaign. They will want to stop our supplies getting through and seize them for themselves. And they will want to cut us off here for the winter." He bit down so hard he nearly cut his cigar with his teeth. "It's what any responsible fighter would do. And so we cannot remain here, waiting to be starved out, picked off by sharp-shooters. We must move, and move soon." He paused by a man who was half-delirious with pain. "Have you nothing to give him?" he demanded sharply.

Madelaine, who had been watching from the doorway to the choir, came forward. "I have almost none of the anodyne left, General. If I could have a day or two to search the woods, I could prepare more—"

"No." The word was absolute. "I will not risk losing any one of you who tend my soldiers. And there are bands of rebels in the woods and fields, and they would not treat you well." He indicated the nurses and the women from the Sanitary Commission. "All of you, make note of that. You must stay within our lines, or I cannot answer for your safety."

A few of the women looked frightened, but one of them, a woman of about thirty-five, raised her head. "I've lost a husband, an uncle, and three brothers to this war, General Sherman. What can a few Rebels offer me that they have not already done?"

"Rape, for one," said Sherman bluntly. "And mutilation to follow, if not death." He saw the shock this inspired. "We are at war, ladies. You are the comfort of the enemy. And in such a war as this, no one is counted indifferent to the conflict. You would be used harshly for the very goodness of your acts." He glanced toward Madelaine. "Even you, Madame, French though you may be. As you reminded me not long ago, even the Indians have taken sides." He regarded the suffering man. "If there is anything that can be done to help you, I will see it is done."

The man did not answer; his eyes were fixed on a vision only he could see. He murmured, "Harry, Harry," in a soft, languid tone.

"What chance?" Sherman asked, his voice lowered.

"No chance," said the oldest of the nurses. "It will be over in an hour or two."

Sherman nodded once, and moved on down the line of pallets, pausing to speak to many of the men as he went. He was as patient as Madelaine had ever seen him, never rushing any man to finish, never leaving a man until he had heard him out.

Forty minutes later, he joined the nurses at the back of the church, and looked at the young widow from Kentucky. "What cases did you want to bring to my attention?"

"Madame de Montalia has charge of them," said the young woman. "She has more ... tolerance than most of us."

"Well?" Sherman demanded. "What about these cases? What makes them different that these? Is it disease? Have they taken an epidemic fever?" His alarm made his inquiry sharp, and a few of the nurses looked askance at him for his manner.

"Not any epidemic, no." Madelaine sensed his concern and answered steadily. "We have put them in the building at the back, where they can be kept securely. The doors are stout and the windows small enough to prevent escape." She indicated the door that led to the path to the back of the building. "If you will come this way?"

"Will you need any assistance?" asked the oldest woman from the Sanitary Commission. "Shall we send Enoch with you?"

"No; I think the General and I can manage those two between us; Enoch has duties enough here," Madelaine answered, convinced that the dedicated former slave had more than his share of tasks to attend to. She stepped out into the heat of the afternoon, raising one hand to block the slanting rays of the sun from her eyes.

"She hasn't taken to you, has she?" Sherman inquired as he followed her out. He took quick stock of his surroundings and set the pace toward the building at the rear of the church.

"She does not approve of me," said Madelaine, disliking the need to admit it. She had to move quickly to keep up with his long-legged stride. "My methods distress her. And some of the others as well."

"Small wonder." He smoothed the front of his tunic and asked, "What is the matter with these men?"

"They are…troubled…The war has made them…" She faltered, looking for an acceptable word.

"Insane? Is that what you mean? Is that what you do not want to tell me? You saw that paper?" Sherman suggested, aware of her embarrassment. "Oh, you need not hesitate to say it. I take no offence. Insane are they? There is no terror in that word for me, not any more, given the way it was bandied about in the press." His face softened. "How good of you to care."

Madelaine stared down at the path. "They are…very bad."

"Very bad?" He touched her sleeve, the greatest contact he permitted himself with her in public. "How bad is that?"

"You will see," said Madelaine, and drew a key from her pocket to open the door. "Take care how you go in." She blocked his way. "In fact, you had best let me go first. They know me, most of the time."

He stared at her, his brows drawing down, his look now forbidding. "If they are so dangerous—"

"I can deal with them, Tecumseh," she said quietly. "I have been doing it for nine days now." With that, she opened the lock and shoved back the bolt keeping the door closed. "I will call you."

"You will not," said Sherman, and positioned himself to go through the door immediately behind her. "What sort of poltroon do you think me?"

"No sort," said Madelaine, unwilling to argue with him at this moment.

He stood very straight as she turned and closed behind them. "God. The stench!" For the little building was worse than an outhouse in high summer.

"Corporal Lucius Hayward rubs himself in excrement," said Madelaine more calmly than she felt. "He spends most of his time on his knees, praying for forgiveness." She indicated the nearer of two doors. "I've put him in this room. He will probably not notice we are here." She went to open it, calling out, "Corporal Hayward, it is Miss de Montalia," as she went through the door.

From his long hours on the hard floor, the corporal's knees were grotesquely swollen. His face and hair were matted with filth and he plucked constantly at the numerous scabs on his arms as he muttered prayers in a steady, cracked, sing-song voice. There were only scraps left of his uniform, and those were so mired that it was almost impossible to determine his rank or regiment. He paid no attention to Madelaine and Sherman, except to turn away from them to hide his determined pulling at his scabs.

Madelaine stepped up to him, and put her hand on his shoulder. "Hayward, it is Miss de Montalia. I have come to see how you are doing."

The corporal continued his prayers as if he had not heard her. His eyes remained fixed on a part of the ceiling as if watching something large and arresting there.

"You will be given your supper soon. I want you to eat it this time. You will not honor God's bounty if you don't eat the food He has made available to you." She could feel Sherman's pity and revulsion and the effort it cost him to remain still, but would not allow herself to be distracted from tending to the man on the floor. "I will have Enoch bring you water. You must promise me you will drink it. God does not wish you to die of thirst, Corporal Hayward. God does not wish you to die at all." She stepped back from him, watching him closely.

Sherman's face was stark as he looked from the corporal to Madelaine. "Good God, what happened to him?"

"I don't know," said Madelaine candidly. "By the time he was brought here, he was ... as you see him now. We could not get much useful information about him except what his comrades told us. He was in the Heavies, in some hard fighting, and seeing what his shells did and what became of his fellows ..." She swung the door open and went out into the little anteroom.

"But that is appalling!" He did not raise his voice much above a whisper, but the intensity of his emotion was like a shout. "And you've been ... Madelaine, I cannot permit this."

She looked directly into his forbidding eyes. "If it were you in there, would you say the same thing? Not that it would matter; I will do what must be done as long as I can," she went on before he could deny her question. "Who else is there to care for him? He would be abandoned and left to die if it were up to the nurses alone. They are afraid of him, and the women of the Sanitary Commission are disgusted."

"And you are not?" Sherman challenged. "Do not think to deceive me on that point, Madame."

Madelaine gave a little, shaking sigh. "Perhaps I am, but not as they are. How many more men like that do you think there are in this war?"

"Too many, far too many," he muttered, and squared his shoulders. "What about the other?"

This time Madelaine could not entirely conceal her apprehension. "He is a more ... difficult case." She nodded toward the other door. "We have to keep him locked in."

"Locked in twice?" Sherman exclaimed, his frown turning thunderous. "Why is that, pray?"

"Because he has four times tried to kill Corporal Hayward." She answered steadily and waited for him to castigate her for the risk she was taking.

Instead he wrapped his arms around her shoulders and pulled her close to him. "Oh, my sweet, good, brave, true, dearest Madelaine," he whispered, his tone amazingly gentle, as he laid his cheek against her hair. "What have I brought you to?"

For the better part of a minute she let herself take solace from him, leaning on his taut strength, and then she moved back a pace, relinquishing his comfort with resolution mixed with anguish. "I brought myself here, Tecumseh," she said. "You have offered to send me north, you have promised me protection here, you have recommended I remove myself from immediate danger, and all with the most honorable and affectionate intent, for which I thank you with all my heart. Yet I have remained. It has been my decision."

"So it has," he said, trying to match the sensible tone of her voice and failing. "Your ... devotion to me has nothing to do with it."

She was so exasperated she wanted to yell at him, but contained herself. "We must not alarm Private Rich," she cautioned him, moving toward the second door. "Be careful, Tecumseh. Keep back and keep silent. This man is unpredictable." With that warning, she unlocked the door and turned the latch.

Private Rich squatted in the far corner facing the wall, for all the world like a little boy who had been severely chastised. His hands were knotted into fists and at his sides. He turned his head to see who had come in, then let out a single, harsh cry. "Out!"

"Private Rich," said Madelaine in her most authoritarian voice, "I want you to turn around. Come to attention, Private."

Private Rich glared at her for an instant, then pushed away from the wall. He glowered down at his shoes as he straightened himself in form. He brought his right hand half-way to his brow and let it drop.

"You will be getting food in two hours. Enoch will bring it to you. You will be expected to eat it without complaint or any incident whatsoever," Madelaine said sternly. "If you do not comply, we will be forced to send for men to assist the nurses in feeding you."

"The food's bad," said the private in a strangled voice.

"The food is good; there are supervisors to be certain it is." Madelaine looked at the cot where Private Rich slept. "You will need new sheets." For he had torn those he had to scraps and tatters.

"Don't," said Private Rich, his expression darkening as he continued to stare at the floor.

"And you must change your shirt," she went on in the same firm tone. "I will not allow you to fall ill because of uncleanliness."

"Don't touch me," Private Rich whimpered. He drew his arms up to shield his face as if he expected to be struck. "Don't. Don't. Don't."

"Tecumseh," Madelaine said very quietly, without turning away from the cowering Private Rich, "be ready to get out of here quickly."

"Madelaine, surely you're not going to—" Sherman began, then was cut off as Private Rich gave a sudden bellow of rage and launched himself at the door and those who stood between him and it.

His rush struck Madelaine in the shoulder, and she staggered, turning to see Private Rich, his features distorted with wrath and madness, attempting to fix his hands around Sherman's neck; a steady, vehement stream of obscenities accompanied his actions.

Madelaine sprang to the struggling men, and although it was day, she had some of her preternatural vampire strength to aid her in battling the maniac. She took a grip on Rich's collar, tugging, only to have it rip.

Sherman regretted at once that he had left his sidearm with his aide and now inwardly cursed himself for the oversight. He managed to keep on his feet though Private Rich was nearly as tall as he, of heavier bone, and driven by the full fury of his insanity. "Get back," he hissed between clenched teeth, as much to Madelaine as to Private Rich. His breathing tightened and became strident as he fought.

Private Rich began to kick, trying to batter Sherman's legs and feet as well as striving to choke him. He used his head as a bludgeon, smashing it into Sherman's face twice, howling each time.

Then Madelaine slammed Private Rich in the back of his knees as hard as she could, and followed it up immediately with a double-handed blow to the small of his back, delivered with all the power she could summon; she slipped out of the way just in time.

Private Rich screamed as he fell backward, landing with the sound of timber falling. He lay for several seconds, then pulled onto his side as his knees drew up to his chest and he began to wail.

The flush was fading from Sherman's face, rapidly replaced by pallor. He tugged at his collar to right it, his eyes never leaving the man on the floor. "Christ Almighty!" he whispered, without a trace of profanity. He pulled Madelaine toward him. "And you actually have to come here to … treat this man?"

"At least three times each day, or he would be far worse off than he is now." She regarded Sherman with a somber gaze. "Don't forbid me to do it, Tecumseh. I cannot let these poor men be left here alone, to suffer more than they suffer already."

He considered what she said, the apprehension not gone from him. "I don't like it," he admitted after a time. "He's a madman. He might do … anything."

"Think, please think," she insisted as Private Rich's wail became a steady, pathetic keening. "Who else can have so little risk as I? Who else can deal with these men and take so little harm from them? None of the nurses are as safe as I am. And when the sun is down, I have more strength than either of them."

Sherman snorted. "In fact, the most sensible thing I could do is send all my hard cases here." He shook his head and struggled to bring his breathing back under control once again. "No, no, Madelaine, that won't wash, not with me. Men such as these two are dangerous, unpredictable. I know you can be hurt. I've seen it. And I will not permit you to make yourself a martyr to a cause that isn't yours." He laid one hand on her shoulder, his long fingers gentle and possessive at once. "No argument, young lady. I will not hear it." He managed to open the door and drag both of them through it. In the little anteroom he stopped to allow her to lock Private Rich's room, loosening his hold on her shoulder, but not releasing her. When she was done, he faced her. "I know better than to try to persuade you to keep away from these two soldiers. I will not try. I know when I am outgunned, and you outgun me, dear love. But I will insist on one thing: you are not to increase your numbers of these patients. If there is any question, say that General Sherman will not allow it."

"But the need is very great," she said, prepared to make a case for her work. "And so few are willing to do it."

"No." Only the expression in his eyes had any softness about it.

Madelaine knew that tone of voice; it was folly to object again, but it was an effort not to.

"Madelaine," he said in a far kinder tone, "you were the one who told me I must mourn my friends, and my son." He took her head in his hands. "How do you think the loss of you would affect me? You have seen what Willy's death, and McPherson's, have done to me; imagine then how much despair I would know if you were lost." Before she could answer his mouth touched hers, lightly at first, and then with more turbulent emotion.

She responded to his kiss at once, reveling in his accessibility and his sudden vulnerability. For once, he was as clear to her as still, deep water, where she could look and see only him, since she had no reflection to cloud or distort her vision. As she put her arms around his neck, she felt the surge of longing that went through him; her need matched his own.

Then he raised his head, and though he continued to look at her as if determined to fix every nuance of her features in his memory, he gave a quick, wry smile. "Much as I hate to refuse an opportunity, this is neither the place nor the time, Madelaine."

"No, it isn't," she said, and lowered herself from her toes. "Oh, Tecumseh, why are you so tall?"

He managed a chuckle. "Inconvenient, isn't it?"

"Yes," she said. "At times, very inconvenient." She fingered her hair and discovered it was in disarray. She fumbled to put it into a semblance of order.

Sherman saw what she was doing and impatiently took over the task. "You're making a mull of it." As he struggled with pins and stray tendrils he said, "You being short, I should introduce you to Phil Sheridan. He's a shade taller than you are, maybe an inch," he said, in a tone that made it clear he would do no such thing. He straightened his tunic and went to the door. "Come." Then his eyes softened again. "Tomorrow night I should be able to spend time with you."

She smiled. "Good. I have been hoping you would have a few hours that were not taken up with waiting for word from Corse or pouring over maps." She saw his scowl begin again, and went on quickly. "I know this is your work, and it is what you are here to do. I do not intend to interfere with that—"

Abruptly Sherman smiled. "Oh, yes you do. And God bless you for it."

ATLANTA, GEORGIA, 8 OCTOBER, 1864

*Most of the worst cases at Saint Eustace's have been sent north by rail.
More will be going in the next month. The plan is to have them all
moved in a month, though a few are too stricken to be moved safely and
will have to remain here until they can be moved or buried ... Corporal
Hayward is in a very bad way; for the last six days he has refused to eat,
and I fear that if he continues he will starve himself to death ... Private
Rich attacked Enoch two nights ago, broke his leg and his shoulder before I could pull him off the poor man. I dislike the notion of restraints,
but I begin to believe they must be used in Private Rich's case ...*

*Tecumseh was in a dreadful mood yesterday, as scowling and iras-
cible as I have ever seen him. He snapped at everyone without apology
and he hardly ate anything. He has also not been sleeping, insisting
that there is too much work to do to sleep. He claims that his brusque
mood was because he had to sit to have his picture made, which he
intensely dislikes, but I suspect his state of mind has more to do with
the pressures being put on him by his superiors ... He does not want to
sit here waiting for the enemy to come to him; he wishes to strike out
for one of the Gulf ports, but from what he tells me, he is encountering
opposition from the men advising President Lincoln ... Tecumseh is aggravated by what he calls their lack of foresight. He has said he may
dispatch the Fourth Corps to Tennessee for General Thomas to use
there at Nashville ...*

TWO HUGE COPPER WASHTUBS boiled on the stove, and the steam
that rose from them smelled of cotton, linen, stale sweat, urine and
blood. The make-shift laundry was dank, the walls darkening with
mildew, and the three lanterns hanging around the close room made
little headway against the gloom.

"How much longer will those be?" asked Miss Sachs of the Sanitary
Commission, a spinster from Chicago who, three years ago, had been
the organist for a Methodist church. She was looking worn to the bone,
her hatchet features now honed to a sharpness that provided her plain,
angular face an arresting quality it had never had before. Even the dark
circles that rimmed her eyes seemed instead to make their blue the more

245

startling. She no longer felt like an Angel of Mercy as she had when she first undertook her mission with the army.

"Almost done with these," said Madelaine, using a wooden paddle to swirl the washing in the boiling water. "Jeanette has the rinsing tubs waiting outside, and I'll help her hang them once I have the next load going. We should have everything hanging on the line by midnight."

"She's been a ... real help," said Miss Sachs with difficulty.

Madelaine turned and regarded Miss Sachs calmly. "Why should she not be? She had laundry, and worse, to do in that brothel; this is hardly any challenge to her, after what she has been through. A pity that her master should feel impelled to sell her because she was his daughter as well."

Miss Sachs shuddered. "And to sell her to such a place ..." She put one slim hand to her throat, and coughed delicately. "I am afraid that in another week most of our casualties will be gone."

"There will be others to take their places, as long as the skirmishing continues, and as long as the army spreads illness among its men, which, with winter coming, is bound to happen. There will be another influenza epidemic; there always is, and if not influenza, then something as bad, if not worse," said Madelaine, world-weariness coming over her with such intensity that she nearly lost her footing.

"Others cases, yes," said Miss Sachs. "But I am going with the last train. I have been instructed to return with the men, and see them established in hospitals. There are also a number of hospital ships bringing casualties to the North, and I have been assigned the task of finding quarters for the nurses."

"An advancement," said Madelaine. "I congratulate you."

"It is, I suppose," said Miss Sachs, at last getting around to the reason for her seeking out Madelaine. "One of the men I am to take with me is Private Rich. He will have to be restrained for the journey, of course, and I was hoping you would be willing to give me some of that composing draught you have made for him, to keep him calm during the long train ride. If he flew into one of his rages, I don't know how we could deal with him." She spoke very quickly, as if she was afraid she would lose her nerve before she had finished.

"If you think it will be necessary, certainly you may have a vial of it to take with you," said Madelaine without undue emotion.

"You don't think it's wise to move him, do you?" asked Miss Sachs keenly. "You are afraid it cannot be done safely."

Madelaine answered promptly and with candor, "No, I don't think it can. Not in a crowded railway car with dozens of wounded men around him, in any case, and that is all that is possible now. If he must be moved, he would do better in a compartment of his own."

"I doubt that could be possible," said Miss Sachs stiffly.

"So do I," said Madelaine, and began to lever shirts, sheets, and trousers out of the laundry tubs into waiting baskets. The paddle steamed in her hands from the heat of the water; the loads were heavy and bent the oar under their weight, but Madelaine continued with her task, undaunted. "Is there anything else, Miss Sachs?"

"No, not at present," she said, some of her habitual formality returning. "I appreciate your telling me your views."

"I will tell them to Doctor Faugh, if he will listen," said Madelaine, who had run out of patience with the surgeon assigned to Saint Eustace. "But he wants no part of those poor men who have been wounded in their minds as well as their bodies."

This embarrassed Miss Sachs, who stared off into the distance. "I have had word that Corporal Hayward has been sent to the asylum at Philadelphia."

Madelaine stifled a number of replies. "I am certain he will do as well there as anywhere."

"Yes," said Miss Sachs. "I suppose he will. So long as there is someone to watch him and keep him clean and fed..." She looked around the laundry as if she had not seen it before. "You will have less to do once the men are gone."

"For a while," said Madelaine. "And there are other hospitals here that need more hands for the work."

At last Miss Sachs burst out, "Don't you want to leave?"

"Yes," said Madelaine. "But not on troop trains going North and not while I have unfinished work here." She put the last of the laundry into the baskets and went to the door. "Jeanette, they're ready," she called, thinking as she did that the nuns would be proud of her now, after all those hours they spent trying to teach her to care properly for washing.

Jeanette, a handsome, lithe girl of eleven with caramel-colored skin and startling green eyes, and already taller than Madelaine, came in the door, faltering as she caught sight of Miss Sachs. "Yes, ma'am?"

"The baskets. You can take them out, rinse them and get them hanging," Madelaine indicated a pile of clothes in the hampers near the stove. "One more load and we're done."

"Yes, ma'am," she repeated, and went to drag the first of the baskets outside.

"She's a very hard worker, I must say," Miss Sachs approved, her long hatchet face set in rigid lines.

"Yes, she is," said Madelaine, watching through the narrow window as the girl dragged the basket across the yard toward the rinsing vats.

"I will leave a recommendation that she be given work to do, and not left behind when the army moves again." This was an astonishing offer coming from Miss Sachs, who strongly disapproved both of Jeanette's mixed race and illegitimacy. "Otherwise, who knows what will become of her?"

"You mean, you're afraid that without the labor we offer her she might turn to whoring? Or that she would give information to Hood's men, or Forrest's?" Madelaine used the bluntest language she dared. "I don't think you need ever fear that she would do either of those things."

Now Miss Sachs was flustered. "But...I mean, look at her. You can tell that her morals are...imperfect."

"How? Because her skin is darker than yours? Because her mother is a Negress? Because her father used her mother and sold the fruits of it to a brothel? Because she has seen other females of her race used for men's pleasure? Because she has no other means of earning a living? Because the people of Africa are less principled than those of Europe? Look at the work she has done so willingly for us. She is still a child, one who has worked from the time she was big enough to carry a towel, or hold a brush. She hasn't begun her courses yet, and you think of her as debauched." Madelaine saw that her challenges distressed Miss Sachs and she took some satisfaction in it.

Miss Sachs looked affronted. "Why are you talking to me in this disagreeable way? What have I done to offend you?" She was backing toward the door, not quite retreating, but not standing her ground.

"You do not offend me, you offend that unfortunate child who has done nothing to deserve your poor opinion," said Madelaine, her attitude becoming more firm. "How can you think of her so disparagingly when she has spent her every waking hour helping all of us with these wounded men? Since Enoch was injured, she has been our only real assistant, and I, for one, am grateful to her."

"And I am, as well," said Miss Sachs. "But she is so ignorant—"

"What do you expect in a place where it has been illegal to teach slaves how to read and write? Yes. She is ignorant and superstitious and all the rest of it. How else should she be? Do you think you would be different, if you were in her situation?"

Madelaine gave Miss Sachs a look of exasperation, knowing that the other woman did not understand the reason for her outburst. "You are all so shocked that these people who have been so relentlessly oppressed should show the signs of it." She stuffed the last of the laundry into the boiling tubs, saying recklessly, "When I was a girl, there were many who thought educated women were freaks, unfeminine, as if ignorance were concomitant with being female." It was true enough; she hoped that Miss Sachs had no understanding of how girls were taught in France now.

"We are not much better than you French," said Miss Sachs with a sudden sigh. "We are taught to value prettiness and compliance of manner over good minds and strength of character." She looked around the laundry. "I confess I will not miss this place."

"Neither will I," said Madelaine as the odorous steam rose afresh.

"You will go with the army, then?" Miss Sachs could not hide her disapproval of this plan.

"Yes, I will go with the army," said Madelaine, thinking that what she meant was that she would go with Sherman.

Miss Sachs concealed a sigh of resignation. "At least there will be other nurses and women from the Sanitary Commission to help be certain the proprieties are maintained."

"Gracious, yes. We must make every effort to keep the tone morally high. Heaven help us if there should be an impropriety in the midst of war," Madelaine made no apology for her sarcasm.

"Miss de Montalia," said Miss Sachs stiffly, "your free ways may be much admired in France, but we Americans are not so lax. We do not want it said that our army triumphed in the field and abandoned honor in the process."

Madelaine realized the woman was serious, and she stopped her laundry chores long enough to address Miss Sachs directly. "Have you entirely forgotten what is going on out there? Have you lost sight of the suffering those men endure? Or the excesses they need when the battles are done? Where is the honor in that? And don't tell me you believe that all these men are of blameless conduct just because they fight for a cause you endorse. Their purpose is honorable enough, I will give you that, but the men are men." She flung up her hands. "I encountered a Southern man who helped slaves to escape and thought that bought him all sorts of privileges and favors, and behaved execrably with women. You came here as an abolitionist, and yet you scorn Jeanette while you heap praise on men who may not deserve more than a passing nod, if that."

"General Sherman has ordered the troops to behave in a manner befitting—" Miss Sachs began.

"General Sherman cannot be everywhere. Nor can any of his staff. They have other things to occupy their thoughts." She felt angry now, and could not bring herself to address Miss Sachs any longer; she used the paddle to stir the boiling wash, grateful for the ordinariness of the job.

Miss Sachs hovered near the door for a short while, and then said, "Well, goodbye, Miss de Montalia."

NEAR MARIETTA, GEORGIA, 7 NOVEMBER, 1864

We, and a number of other nursing stations, have been moved outside of the city in preparation to march, so that we may see our patients put aboard trains to take the last of them north. We are expected to be here for another week at most, by which time all the wounded should be headed back to Union hospitals. It has been a difficult two days, getting these men ready for travel . . .

Tomorrow is election day for the Union, and the whole of the army is buzzing with speculation about it, though most of the men have not been able to vote. Will Mister Lincoln be reelected, or General McClellan win? I am a little surprised at the number of men in this army who do not wish to throw in with McClellan, for he once held the position General Grant now occupies. I will have to ask Tecumseh to explain it to me when the bustle around him dies down and he returns from Kingston . . .

"WE WILL BE MOVING SHORTLY, AND ABOUT TIME," Sherman said to Madelaine as he finished the last of the spit-roasted chicken, casting the bones aside onto the platter impatiently. He drank a long draught of coffee to wash it down. "There, woman. Are you satisfied? You're worse than Nichols, and he fusses like a bitch with one pup," he added, referring to his aide-de-camp.

"A midnight supper is fashionable still, in Paris," said Madelaine in

French, adding in English as she ran the tips of her fingers over the un-used crystal goblet set above his china plate, "And you cannot live on air." She blew out the last of the flames on the branch of candles before they could gutter.

"So I cannot, therefore the chicken," said Sherman, wiping his hands on the frayed linen napkin she had salvaged from the looted stores in the cellar below. "Though you seem to manage it fairly well; living on air." His steel-colored eyes glinted in the firelight and the last drops of moisture from his bath shone in his hair and beard, softening his stern features with a ruddy glow. His worn flannel robe was negligently tied, so that the curly thatch of his chest was revealed with every movement of his arms. "Both of us have bathed, I have eaten, and now I am wholly at your disposal; you may have your own buffet of me."

"It's not the same, and you know it," said Madelaine as a distant clock struck one. She hoped that Sherman would rid himself of some of his high-strung energy before he took her to bed, for that relentless urgency did not bode well for their gratification; his thoughts jumped and chirped like crickets when he was in such a state of mind, and he chafed at concern. Recognizing his need to talk, she asked, "Now that it is sure that Mister Lincoln is returned to office, there is much to do, isn't there? Have you completed your plans, at last?"

"Pretty much, or so I trust, if the politicians don't get a chance to ruin them, and the papers don't spread them all over the South." In spite of these growlings he warmed to her question at once, taking the salt cellar and pepper grinder and setting them up on the worn damask tablecloth between the remains of the chicken on the platter and his plate, where he had cleared a place for his demonstration. "We will march in two wings, Howard with the Fifteenth and Seventeenth Corps, Slocum with the Fourteenth and Twentieth. We'll have Thomas behind us to harry Hood if he comes after us. The men will be very lightly provisioned, and will forage. I have ordered that the supply wagons carry ten days' rations only. That will serve a number of purposes. We will move faster carrying less, we will encourage the men to keep up the pace in order to reach the fruits of Savannah, we will deprive the enemy of resupply by taking it for ourselves, we will have to remain vigilant against any militia parties for we will not have the means to make up for any lost supplies, and we will show the South and the world that the Union is the master in the United States of America by passing through the very heart of the Confederacy." His determination was apparent from the

251

timbre of his voice to the lines of his posture. "And we will make the South want an end to this as much as the North does."

Madelaine watched with mixed feelings as Sherman continued his enthusiastic descriptions, for she saw in his excitement and anticipation of success the ghost of his bleak despair. "Tecumseh," she said when he paused in his eager recitation, "is your intention truly to go to Savannah? Or are you telling me that so you can keep your true goal a secret?"

Sherman snorted, gave a quick shake of his head, and raised his hands in mock capitulation. "My true goal is Savannah; yes, it is." His grin was hard and flat. "Not the Gulf, not the coast south of Tallahassee, as I have let them all suppose it would be, but the Atlantic. Farragut has that part of the Gulf in the palm of his hand now, in any case. He does not need me." He rose, starting to pace, his blue plaid robe swinging around his ankles as he moved. "I would like to go directly south: it is not as far to the water, and we could at last free the prisoners at Andersonville. But it is what Hood expects me to do, and doubtless he and Forrest have plans to intercept such an effort. So we will strike out east-southeast, where we are not expected. We will cut ourselves off from everything, including Washington, so that no news of our position can find its way into enemy hands." He did not have his usual cigar to use as a pointer or visible punctuation mark, but he did his best to make up for it with his long fingers. "It is far more important that we pull up the rails between here and the Atlantic so that they cannot ship men and materiel to their own troops and confiscate all supplies we find. It is just as vital that we keep the Western and Atlantic and the Nashville lines open for our uses, which will be Thomas's work." He rounded on her. "I have sought to do this from the first, and I will do it."

"How long do you think it will take to reach Savannah?" asked Madelaine, knowing it was a long and demanding march.

"We'll be there by early January, I should think," he said with a studied laconic manner.

"Early January?" she repeated, amazed at this incredible assumption.

"If not sooner," Again he spoke with deliberate blandness. "If we can move steadily at ten miles a day—and I will ask for more, to be certain we get that—we will arrive there in early January quite handily. That is, of course, assuming our resistance is minimal, we do not have to forage too far for our food, and the weather does not turn against us."

"Ten miles a day, an army of this size, in enemy territory, and foraging at that, in winter; that vainglorious Corsican would have hesitated at such expectations," Madelaine said, wanting to be certain she had understood his incredible plan. "I don't know whether you are brilliantly audacious or stark staring—" She stopped herself from going on.

His response was very quiet, almost serene. "No, dear love, I am not mad. It can be done. You'll see. We will do it." He offered her his hands, pulling her to her feet. "Come closer." There was a somberness in his face now that troubled her as much as his hesitation and his wistful contemplation of her features. "I need you close to me now, for comfort." It was an astonishing admission, coming from him. He drew her into his arms and stared at the fire over the top of her head. There was a catch in his voice as he murmured, "The trouble is I don't know what to say to you, Madelaine." He did not go on.

"About what?" she asked, wishing she could read his silences better.

Again he did not answer her at once. "I ... When this is over, and it will be over before many more months are gone, I ... must return to my family. I should not have ... started again with you ... But with the war, and the press of fighting and death so near ... When it's finished, you and I must not ... They are my family, and as such deserve my first consideration, no matter what I ... It would not be suitable or honorable to ... cause my wife any distress when she has given up so much of me to this war. My children, as well, need to know their father again. But if I return to them, I will not have a place in my life for ... you, for us ... as much as I will long for it ... I will not be able to see you, or not very often, and then so hurriedly ..." He leaned back so he could look down into her face. "It would be intolerable, living that way, making you into a mistress, covert ..." He could not take his eyes from hers. "I don't want to lose you, Madelaine."

"You won't," she said, and to keep him from going on, she freed one arm from his embrace and laid her fingers lightly against his lips. "You could not lose me if you wished to, whether we spend only tonight together, or years and years. Oh," she went on in the same easy way, "you need not worry; I will not embarrass you. I didn't in San Francisco, did I? Why would I now? Because you are the great General Sherman, the hero of Atlanta? Because the country takes note of all you do? Because it would be a great scandal? Do not interrupt me. Why would I want scandal for either of us? What would be the use of bringing such notoriety on you or on myself? I do not like being too much noticed, Tecumseh. Notice leads to questions that are not easily answered, and those of my blood have difficulties enough without subjecting ourselves to public scrutiny."

"Are you finished?" When she nodded he turned her face up to his. "Now will you let me speak?" he demanded, his demeanor severe; his breathing was becoming labored.

"Not if you intend to threaten me, or bully me, or to talk nonsense," she responded at once. "I love you. I will love you as long as I live."

"However long that may be," he interjected with an ironic tinge to his words. "It could be centuries, from what you've told me."

"It could." She bent to kiss his fingers. "If there is a forever beyond the True Death, then I will love you that long."

"As you will love the others? You have admitted there have been others." His challenge could not entirely conceal his fear of her answer. He pulled his hand away from her.

She did not change her stance or attitude. "Of course. It is our nature for those of my blood."

He looked away, his anger revealed by the working of his jaw. "And somehow you will mark my place in line?"

"So that you will know to answer the long roll when it comes, for muster of my lovers? Is that how you think of yourself, as a man holding a place in line?" It was an effort not to answer his wrath with her own, but she contained her impulse; he was attempting to drive her away again, so that he would not have to face the pain of having her leave. "Tecumseh, love isn't something doled out, like rations, with just so much of it to go around, all parceled and labeled. You don't mete it out in portions, to starve when it is all used up. It doesn't work that way. It isn't something that comes in supplies. Love is not a quantity, it is a quality." She searched her thoughts for an analogy he would appreciate. "When a painter makes a beautiful new work, is all the art in the world slightly less beautiful because of the new painting? Does the new work leach the beauty out of the old?"

"No," he admitted grudgingly, touching her face in spite of himself, his thumb resting on her cheek. He was breathing more calmly now.

"And it is the same with love. It is not finite. It does not lessen with use, it increases. The more there is of it, the more there can be." She put her hand on his chest and felt his heart beneath her palm.

"Like Juliet? 'The more I give to thee / The more I have, for both are infinite'? For you, perhaps; I am more of 'Even till now, / When men were fond, I smiled and wonder'd how,'" he allowed after he had studied her in silence.

"You are no Angelo, Tecumseh, and I no Juliet," said Madelaine. "Their loves and their lives are plays, abstracts. We are as real as blood can make us." She endured his careful scrutiny with as much aplomb as she could summon; she said without jealousy, "And you love your wife."

"Yes, I do. But it is different than this. She is nothing like you." At last he ceased his examination of her countenance. "I can see you are telling me the truth, at least as you understand it." He laid his hand over hers. "If what you say is true, why do we fight?"

"And your children? You love them, I know you do; I can feel it in you," said Madelaine, ignoring his last question.

"They are where all my hopes are gathered: how can I not love them?" he agreed with a faint, sad smile. "Why do we fight about these things?" he persisted.

"We don't fight, you do. I have no argument with you but those you insist we have." This was not entirely accurate, and she knew it, but she would not be deterred from her purpose. "You want to wrangle and contend, you enjoy it; you are like a fencer testing his steel against any worthy opponent, for sport."

"Very likely," he said, his solemnity leaving him. "Most women know nothing of such sport, and fewer are capable of acquitting themselves well; those who try are sharp-tongued shrews, most of them."

She wanted to shake him, and realized she could, if she used her strength. But that would serve only to increase the contest he sought, so she said, "I will not be taunted into upbraiding you, so give it up now; we are not likely to have another evening like this for some time."

"And old campaigner that I am, I should make the most of any advantage I find." He smiled; again the roughness left his face. "And you are nothing more than a peacemaker caught in the toils of a battle-hardened veteran." He wrapped his arms around her, pulling her tightly against him with renewed anticipation. "Well, then, Madame, you will have to do all that you may to ... persuade me of the errors of my ways."

"I was not aware you were in error; you do not admit to making any," she said, taking the bantering tone from him, aware that he was anticipating their parting.

"Many would think I am in error now. Many have thought so before," he appended more darkly, brows drawing down into a glower. "It has been a long road to this place."

"And a long way yet to go," she said, sliding her arms around him under his robe. "Give yourself respite, Tecumseh."

"While I can?" he countered, and without intending to, relented. "How do you put up with me?"

"I don't put up with you: I love you." She spoke more briskly than he, as if she were purchasing herbs for her tinctures.

"God alone knows why. But I am thankful, whatever the reason." He slid his hands up her back and began to loosen her hair, tossing the pins aside against her protests. "There will not be many more chances for us to be together." Speaking this unwelcome truth aloud shook off his last hesitations. "I will have to rise early and I don't want to waste the night," he said as he leaned down to kiss her, his mouth open on hers, all his desire breathed into that kiss, and all his lost hopes, all his unrealized loneliness, all his sere despair. He held her, shivering with the onslaught of his need of her, his passion already combining with his dismay at their coming separation. And when he broke from her, he was seized with vertigo, and clung to her again, for fear of falling. "It is the food and the hour," he said, then added ruefully, "And you." He nodded toward his bed—one of the few left intact in the abandoned hotel—and whispered, "I'm afraid you'll have to help me get there."

If it was a ruse, Madelaine thought, it was not a typical one. She slipped under his arm so he could lean on her shoulder, as she had done so many times for wounded soldiers. "If you are ready?"

"You would do it, wouldn't you?" he marveled, his usually clipped speech turned to a slow drawl. "You would support me. I am either very flattered or you are very hungry." As soon as he said it, he regretted it, and a tic jumped in his cheek out of shame. "Pay no attention to me. I am a churl. I accept whatever reprimand you give me; I deserve it."

"No reprimand. You will do it better than I could in any case," she said. "But it stung. As you intended."

He attempted to protest, then admitted it. "I wanted to make you angry, so I would not have to be accountable for..."

Her eyes were steady, serious but without ire. "Our parting; yes, I know."

He shrugged himself free of her, determined to move on his own. "I am no invalid, Madame; the spasm is passed." As he walked, he moved with great care as if treading on a narrow beam or along a precipice.

Madelaine stayed beside him, letting him show them the way to the side of his bed. As she walked, she began to unfasten the three dozen tiny buttons down the front of her peignoir.

As he reached the side of the bed, Sherman turned and looked at her as she worked the silken loops. "I've been meaning to ask you for the last hour about that outfit of yours, if one calls such a silky, frilly thing an outfit. I like it. Where did you find it?"

"In a dressmaker's shop; I had gone to find muslin for bandages and came upon this. I ... I couldn't pass it up. But I took the muslin bolts, as well," she said, feeling that she needed to justify her actions.

"So this is loot!" he exclaimed in mock outrage. "And you dare to wear it here?"

"If it is so distressing to you, General, I will take it off," she said simply, without any display or coquetry. "I would not like to earn your disapprobation."

"You could not do that if you rode through the center of Atlanta beside that devil Forrest himself," he said, his words low and soft. He fingered the silk, saying distantly, "You know, when I was a much younger man, after West Point, before I was married, I spent some time in Savannah. I thought then that I wanted to go to France and study to be a real artist, not just a competent sketcher, but something more ... But—"

"But you didn't," said Madelaine, unfastening the last of the buttons and letting the peignoir fall from her shoulders. "There is supposed to be a nightgown beneath, but I left that in the shop."

"And damned good thing, too," said Sherman, his breathlessness for once having little to do with asthma. "You may be old as the hills, my love, but you are newer than an April morning to me." He touched her reverently, for once willing to linger over the curves and angles of her flesh. After a while, when his hands had roamed over her, he stepped back and tossed his robe aside, paying little heed to where it fell; he moved as if in a mesmeric dream, every motion slow and deliberate. "I never want to forget this, or you." He turned and tossed back the ragged covers. "The sheets are clean," he promised as he held the place for her.

Madelaine slipped into the bed, noticing that the mattress, as she had feared, was lumpy. In a while she knew it would not matter; she had been in far less comfortable places over the years. She lay back, looking up at him, seeing the excitement in every line of his lean flesh, and her compassion for this difficult, contradictory, brilliant, haunted man was as acute as her need of him.

"Do not bother with the covers," said Sherman, his voice quiet and warm. "I will warm you."

At this, Madelaine could not keep from smiling. She held out her arms to him, as he tossed the bedding back and sank down beside her, stretching his length next to her. His long hands quickly sought out the centers of her greatest pleasure, his mouth lingering to enhance what his fingers began. "You are becoming quite adept," she said as his tongue stroked her nipple.

"Shush," he replied, and resumed his determined campaign over the plains and valleys of her body, reveling in her sighs and starts of pleasure, and her soft moans of quickening need. The texture of her under his hands, against his body, was far more intoxicating than whiskey. He felt feverish and immensely well at once. He would not let her touch him, fearing that he would spend himself too quickly if she did. "Let me. This is my chance to." He did not say to what.

But Madelaine sensed that he wanted to blot all other loves from her memory, to supplant any possible rivals from the past or future, to be the only one she would think of in the empty nights ahead; under the waking passion she felt a melancholy that was as much her own as his. How strange, she thought in a distant, still part of her mind, that Tecumseh should feel their impending separation so poignantly. That anguish was familiar to her, yet she had not expected to encounter it in one who had not come to her life, and this fired her esurience as lust never could. She leaned her head back and gave herself over to him, feeling his jealousy vanish as his fervor and tenderness came over them both.

"Take. Me." He moved inside her in long, deep strokes, striving to be part of her fulfillment as she was part of his. He knew he would never have enough of her, yet he tried to sate their common appetites. And then he did not think at all, but released himself to the ecstasy of abandonment and the thrill of her lips on his neck. A joy filled him so encompassing that it welled out of them together as fathomless laughter.

Madelaine came to herself again as Sherman moved off her, but only to lie immediately beside her, prone, his arm across her just under her breasts, his face turned toward her with a look of such awe that she could find nothing to say to him as splendid as the expression in his steel-colored eyes.

ON THE DECATUR ROAD, GEORGIA,
22 NOVEMBER, 1864

Today Captain Poe said he feared that Northern and Southern deserters may well flock to Atlanta, now the city is empty, and plunder it before its people can return and rebuild. He was given the task of destroying

*the arsenal and other such military stores as could not be carried away
by the Union army ... From here it is possible to see smoke from the fires
that have been set since the army left, so it may be that Captain Poe is
right ... A great pity that such a lovely place as Atlanta must be sacrificed to war, though once it was turned from a town to a fortress, I suppose it was inevitable.*

*At present I have only three soldiers to care for: a young man from
Wisconsin with a broken wrist, a drummer boy from Vermont who is
serving with a Connecticut regiment and suffering from a putrid sore
throat, and a captain from New Jersey with a half-healed wound in his
shoulder—a far cry from those in my care a month ago ... I know there
will be more casualties ahead, and I should make the most of this time,
but I have not yet been able to bring myself to work on organizing my
notes to prepare for Amsterdam ... My monographs are still incomplete
and are likely to remain so for some time ... Try as I may, I cannot seem
to concentrate on them as I would like.*

*I have sent word to Tecumseh that I would prefer to ride a horse than
be stuck in a wagon, but he has not had the time to do more than send a
note that he will attend to it ... With his current concerns about Kilpat-
rick's cavalry, the matter of a single horse is trivial.*

*There are strict orders given that the army is not to take any refu-
gees with it during the march. Not only are supplies deliberately low,
but Tecumseh is determined to keep to his rapid march, which will not
be possible if the army is forced to take in all those fleeing war and
slavery ... In spite of this, a great many former slaves are following the
army, hailing Tecumseh as their liberator, and more exalted things than
that ... This army is now officially cut off from all communication with
the North, and will continue this way until Savannah is reached ... For
the first time in his career, Tecumseh is acting entirely as his own commander; he is the authority and no one higher than he can reach him to
countermand his decisions. He told me this morning that he had never
realized how much beholden he had felt, and for so long ...*

AT THE BACK OF THE SMOLDERING RUINS, two women were
huddled, one of them white, the other black. Both had smut on their
faces and both looked haggard. As Madelaine and her guide, Captain
Albert Foster of Minnesota, who was a distant cousin of General Foster

and was currently recovering from a dislocated shoulder and a gash in his thigh, rode up to the side of what had been a fine plantation house but was now little more than rubble and five brick chimneys, the two women leaned out of their hiding-place, an old flintlock held between them and pointing up at the new arrivals.

"Get out of here! You hear me? Get out! Now! You already took everything! We got nothing left!" shouted the white woman, her voice shrill, as ragged as her dress and faded shawl. She did her best to steady the gun. "Ain't you done enough?"

Madelaine drew her hard-mouthed horse to a stop and looked down, peering into the blackened wreckage and motioning to Captain Foster to keep his sidearm in its holster. "We are not here to forage. I'm looking for anyone who is injured, wounded, or ill," she said calmly. "Are either of you hurt? Is there anything I can do to assist you?"

"Miss, I don't think—" Captain Foster began.

"You get out of here," said the black woman, but with less determination that her companion. "We'll shoot if you get any closer."

"If you need help, I have brought a medical bag with me—" Madelaine said, unperturbed.

"You a nurse?" asked the white woman; Madelaine thought she was probably nearing forty, and not the former mistress of the house if the condition of her hands and the quality of her faded dress were any indication.

"Yes, I am a medical volunteer with the army," Madelaine began to explain. "There are quite a number of us—"

The white woman was regarding her skeptically and cut her off without apology. "You don't sound much like them other Yankees. Where you from?" she demanded.

Madelaine sighed. "I am from France. From the southern part of the country, near the Italian border," she added in the hope that this might mitigate her foreignness for the women.

The two women looked aghast at this announcement. The white woman muttered something to the black one; Madelaine heard a few scraps of it. "…sent for whores…keep American women clean…"

Captain Foster glanced at Madelaine, more shocked than she was by what the women said. "It isn't right, them talking about you this way," he said quietly to Madelaine, cocking his head in the direction of the women to indicate he would stop them if it was what Madelaine wished. "I can stop it, if you want."

"Don't be absurd. Let me deal with them," said Madelaine, and swung down from her horse. She handed the reins to Captain Foster. "Be calm, Captain; and do not draw your weapon," she said, loudly enough that she was certain she would be overheard.

"I don't think Uncle Billy would like you to do this," said Captain Foster, dreading Sherman's wrath if anything happened to Madelaine. "He doesn't want anything to hurt you, in any way. He was real sharp in his orders. He said I was to make sure you were safe—"

"Don't be missish, Captain," Madelaine said lightly, her attention on the women.

"Stay where you are!" the white woman commanded. "I'm not going to warn you again."

Madelaine continued to walk forward, her skirts looped over one arm, her case of ointments, salves, and tinctures in the other hand. "I am an unarmed woman. I have only the captain for escort. You have no reason to fear me and nothing to gain from harming me."

"You're a Yankee!" the white woman accused.

"Mais non, Madame," Madelaine said, picking her way through the ruins toward her. "I have told you I am French." She held up her case. "Are either of you in need of assistance?"

"What kind of mealy-mouthed nonsense are you talking, woman?" the black woman inquired, and pointed an arthritic finger at Madelaine. "What kind of poisons have you got in that case of yours, anyway?"

"No poison," said Madelaine, continuing her slow approach to the women. "But I do have something for the stiffness in your fingers, and I will gladly let you have it, if you will permit me to make some for you."

The black woman released her hold on the barrels of the gun and folded her arms. "Why'd you want to do a thing like that?"

"Because it is my work," said Madelaine. She was less than ten paces from the women now and she heard Captain Foster give a warning shout. "They aren't going to shoot, Captain," she called to the Captain. "Because they haven't any ammunition." She looked directly at the women. "Do you?"

The black woman clapped her hands to her face, and the white woman threw down the gun and stared haughtily at Madelaine. "The Yankees took it all."

"Of course they did," Madelaine concurred with a touch of humor. "And can you blame them? Don't tell me you wouldn't shoot one if you could."

"I'd do worse than that," said the white woman. There were tears on her face but she would not wipe them away.

"Very likely," said Madelaine, and indicated the rag tied around the woman's upper arm. "How old is that cut?"

The woman paid no attention to her. "You should've seen it," she burst out in anger and disgust. "The Negroes all running up to the road, shouting that a red-haired Moses was coming to lead them to freedom."

Madelaine privately doubted that Sherman would find the allusion flattering, but kept this observation to herself. "The army isn't supposed to take on refugees," she said, as he had encouraged her to do.

"Refugees!" The white woman flushed deeply, and looked over at her black companion. "Lillyanne here hasn't forgotten herself, the way the rest have."

"They's gone to the Yankees," the black woman confirmed, clearly shocked that this had happened.

The white woman glared at Madelaine. "And you come here to gloat!"

Madelaine's answer was light but her violet eyes shone brilliantly. "I have done no such thing. I am here to tend to any hurts or ills you have suffered. That is the whole of my mission."

Captain Foster had ridden up close to the women, and now he leaned forward in his saddle. "Miss de Montalia," he said, "if you aren't going to do anything here, we should be on our way."

Madelaine motioned him back. "Be patient, Captain Foster. Can't you see that this woman is injured?" She indicated the white woman. "Let me have a look at your arm. I will treat it, and if there is nothing else you require, we will go on."

The woman looked sullen, but she nodded once. "Since you're here."

It was not a promising beginning, thought Madelaine as she closed the gap between her and the other woman. "How long ago were you cut?" she asked as she inspected the dirty length of cloth wrapped and tied around her upper arm.

"Three days," she said reluctantly.

"Three days?" Madelaine repeated as she set her case down and began to work the knot loose. "But the army was still twenty miles away."

"The Yankees didn't do it," the white woman admitted. "There was good Southern boys through here, needing food and blankets.

We ... gave 'em all we had." She looked to the black woman for confirmation.

"They took everything," said Lillyanne with a comprehensive gesture, "and what they didn't take, the Yankees got. And burned the place down."

Madelaine sighed, recalling the harangue Sherman delivered to his officers not two days ago, warning them that while they were to leave nothing of use for the enemy, they were not to allow unprotected women and children to be without shelter. "It is one thing to make war on the South," he had said, "but is not honorable to make those who have suffered already bear more than their share of the burden. We are in the heart of enemy territory, and what we do not use, our opponents surely will, but this is not to include making those already preyed upon our victims. The women of the South hate us, yes, but see that they have as little cause to do so as you are able. Take their food and weapons and ammunition, but treat them with respect. I want to hear no complaints about your conduct." Clearly whoever had come here had not paid much attention to Uncle Billy's admonition.

"What was the name of the officer leading the men here?" Madelaine asked as she inspected the woman's wound, doing her best to conceal a frown at what she saw, for the cut was infected and inflamed.

"I don't know and I don't care. He was a Yankee devil, that's all I know," said the white woman. "Wrap it up again, and I'll take a shot at any blue coats I see coming this way."

"He was a Lieutenant Matthew Robertson. They was part of an Ohio regiment, but he spoke like a Southerner," Lillyanne said promptly. "Shameful thing, to have one of ours treat us so badly."

"You said that Southern men took your food before the Yankees came," Madelaine pointed out; there were a fair number of Southerners in the Northern armies—the reverse was also true.

"And so they did," the white woman agreed at once. "But they deserved it. The Yankees didn't. It was our food. We didn't want the Yankees to have it." She wiped her cheek with the back of her wrist. "It made the Yankees mad that we had nothing left for them to steal."

"Lieutenant Matthew Robertson will answer for what he has done here, I will see to it," Madelaine promised, thinking that Sherman would not be pleased; there had been other such instances and his response had been quick and harsh. "Did the men harm you in any other way?"

263

"If you mean did they rape us, the answer is no; they didn't have the time," said the white woman. "I thought they might, though. With men like them, you can be sure they will do whatever they think they can get away with."

Captain Foster looked dismayed. "The men have strict orders not to—"

"And you think wolves like them give a devil's hoot for orders?" the white woman demanded, her wrath increasing. "Men like that are rabid animals, and should be treated like rabid animals—shot where they stand."

Madelaine heard this out with as much sangfroid as she could summon out of her own uncertainties. "I will report this to General Sherman himself." She looked directly at the white woman. "Your arm will need treatment, and soon. The wound is deeply infected. I can leave you a medication for it that will help contain the infection, but you must have a surgeon look at it as soon as possible. Otherwise the infection will enter your blood."

"It doesn't hurt much," the woman protested. "Just kind of aches."

"Small wonder," said Madelaine, and noticed that Lillyanne was nodding in agreement.

"That's what I been telling her. She don't want to listen." Her expression had a tough, satisfied vindictiveness about it.

"What surgeon's going to make time for me?" the white woman countered.

"I will arrange it, if you like," Madelaine offered, and called over her shoulder to Captain Foster. "Make a note of this place and see that one of the surgeons is dispatched here to tend this woman."

Captain Foster drew a notebook and stubby pencil from his tunic and did as Madelaine ordered. His own, half-healed wound ached in sympathy with the woman.

"I don't want a Yankee doctor touching me, thank you," the white woman said.

"You'll take it and be thankful to the Good Lord for his help," Lillyanne informed her as if the middle-aged woman were her nursery charge. "There ain't much I can do for you without a real doctor has a look at you."

"I won't," said the white woman, and glared at Madelaine. "I'll take your medicine, and thank you for it, but if I see that surgeon coming, I swear I'll blow him to kingdom come."

"Without shells?" Madelaine asked, trying not to sound sarcastic. "Or have you other weapons your soldiers and Uncle Billy's missed?"

"I'll do it any way I have to," the woman insisted, and let Madelaine smear her arm with a viscous, clear liquid that had been obtained from moldy bread.

Lillyanne watched critically, and nodded approval as Madelaine took a length of clean lint to wrap around the woman's arm. "You're good at that."

"I've had practice," said Madelaine.

WITH TECUMSEH'S ARMY IN GEORGIA, 9 DECEMBER, 1864

I was told today that the woman I treated some days since has died. The infection was too far advanced for it to be arrested, and even had her arm been amputated, it would have been too little and too late to save her. Her servant, Lillyanne, has stayed with the surgeons to help them, and they have accepted her, for they agree she is sensible and tireless, a valuable combination on this journey...

At last I have been able to send two letters, one to Euphemia Stephens in San Francisco, and one to Saint-Germain at his house in Amsterdam, though he may have left there by now. Writing has reminded me how much I miss the sound of French being spoken. While I was with the Indians, this did not vex me, I suppose because I knew their tongues, like their ways, were foreign to me. But in the last few years, I have come to hunger for my own language...

This evening a lovely young woman of mixed race came to me, to ask me to help her. She is pregnant, either by Southern or Northern soldiers, and she cannot bear the child, for she has no means to support it and no home left to go to. She is not far along, and there are few outward signs of her condition... Against the wishes of the surgeons, I have decided to give her a tincture that will cause her to abort the fetus, for I can see no earthly reason to burden this young woman more than she has been burdened already... There will be many women with children to raise without fathers, and I do not see the need for another such unfortunate, not with Negresses attempting to hide their children in the army's supply wagons every day...

There have been few chances to see Tecumseh, let alone talk with him, and while I am pleased he is willing to be so prudent, I am less glad that I am left in so awkward a situation regarding my place in this war, for I have no stake in it, unlike everyone else… No one, not even Captain Foster, knows what to make of me… I am not an American, Northerner or Southerner. Most of the officers are troubled that I am with the army, and though they are all unfailingly polite, I have heard the whispers and I know they cause problems for Tecumseh he will not address… How like him.

The going has been hard and is getting harder. The Southerners have taken to burying bombs in the path of the army, and they are taking a toll. It is dank and chill, and the land is marshy, which causes me discomfort, but I have enough of my native earth left to insulate me from the worst… We are still making more than ten miles every day, and have been able to forage enough to keep the army well-fed… I, however, am becoming famished, for I will not visit any of the men of this army in sleep, and the one I most long to love awake is not available…

I can find it in my heart to be jealous of Hazen, Blair, and the rest of them…

"IT IS IRONIC," SHERMAN SAID to Madelaine in a brief midnight meeting at a makeshift hospital in Savannah; in another few days a new year would begin. "I have personal letters from Generals Hardee, Smith, and McLaws, now that they are run out of this city, in which they ask me to make the protection and welfare of their families my personal concern." He looked puzzled. "The women seem to trust me, or so they tell me, at any rate."

"Is there any reason they shouldn't?" Madelaine asked, trying not to make it appear that she was giving him undue attention, for though the anteroom was empty but for them it was far from private.

"Certainly not," he said stiffly, then relented. "You weren't questioning me, were you?"

"No." Madelaine left off rolling bandages and looked at him with curiosity. "Why is that ironic? That those officers should entrust their families to you?"

"Why, because they are the ones most responsible for the tales of my atrocious conduct in this war. If you were to believe the stories they spread, I ought to be hanged by my own men. They have me listed as embroiled with every sin in the catechism, and have attributed to me the most dishonorable actions any commander could commit or endorse. However," he said, straightening, some of his humor returning, "I have

266

said I will do as they ask, and I will, as I will for any officer's family here in the city. As I hope they would do for my wife and children. I will look after their families, and now, circumstances being what they are, they are willing to rely on me."

Madelaine knew this was not the reason he had sought her out. "As well they know; you are that sort of man, Tecumseh."

"I wish I knew why you, of all people, should have so much respect for me, given what you know." He glanced around.

"Why would you ask me this, when you have succeeded so well?" Now it was her turn to be perplexed.

"Yes, I have done it, now that this campaign is over I can see it is done; yet there is no decisive victory until the end, and we may still falter," he said apprehensively. "But since this success is ours, and won without discredit to me or my men, I have to contend with more notice than I have had in some time. It is not only the politicians, but the press who have taken an interest. I had not counted on that happening. I suppose I should have, knowing what ferrets reporters are but—" He cleared his throat. "There will be newspaper stories made on all I do, and there is little I can do to stop it happening; I will have little chance for privacy."

She nodded. "What you are saying is that you cannot spend time with me, any time, let alone in private." She managed a bit of a smile though her face ached with the effort.

He was more apologetic than frustrated. "No, I can't. I thought I would be able to make some arrangement for you ... for us, but—" He looked about uneasily.

"You don't need to explain. I've been expecting this," she said to forestall his long explanation.

"You have?" he asked in some surprise.

"Yes." She wanted to go into his arms but would not risk compromising him now; she sensed the same desire in him, and his careful hesitation. "Do not fear; I meant what I've told you before. I will do nothing to embarrass you, or myself, nothing."

He had the grace to be distressed by her subdued demeanor. "Just like that? No argument?"

Madelaine regarded him for a few long seconds. "Would it do any good?"

"No," he admitted, and then added ruefully, "But I wish you'd protest a little, for my pride."

She could not trust herself to laugh. "If it is solace you want, rest assured then, that I would happily defy the world with you, if that was

267

what you wanted of me; but since it is not, I will not let you goad me into anger. You are too much a part of me for that."

"I wish I could be a part of you," he said, fire shining in his steely eyes. "Right now."

"Don't," she said simply. "This is hard enough without—"

He held up his hand to silence her, and looked down at his shoes. "I don't deserve you, Madelaine. I know I don't."

It was her turn to stop him. "That is not your decision to make, it is mine." She swallowed once, finding the words as painful to speak as if they had spikes on them. "And I am more glad than I can tell you now that you and I have had so much together."

He looked hard at her. "We're parting, aren't we?"

She nodded. "Until you—"

"Until I what? Until I die?" His challenge lacked sharpness. "When I may become like you, perhaps a long time from now."

"Yes. For your sake I hope it will be a long time." She found it difficult to go on. "I am going to return to France as soon as there is a ship available to carry me there. It will not be long before such commerce resumes, and I will take advantage of it as quickly as I may. You need not bother about making arrangements for me. I can do it, and it would be wiser if you did not become part of my dealings. But to do that I will have to be put in contact with my bank, to arrange for funds, and that may not be for a few weeks yet—" He waved this away with an impatient movement of his arm she had come to recognize as his way of wanting to put irritating things behind him.

"I can vouch for your credit."

This time her smile came more easily. "So you can."

His lips twitched, his eyes going distant. "I still remember the way you looked when you came to my office on Montgomery Street, at the bank, the first time I saw you." Impulsively he touched her hand. "You took my breath away, the way you moved, the way the light made gold in your dark hair, the way you looked at me, the candor and self-possession you had. Your courage. And the way you have made me feel from the first, as if I was not alone, or strange. With you I have nothing to make up for, nothing to prove. No one ever ... I will treasure my memory of you always, as I will treasure all you have given me."

Madelaine moved her hand away. "The bond will not break, Tecumseh, no matter where you are in the world. You are part of me, and I of you."

He lowered his head. "I know."

SAVANNAH, GEORGIA, 21 FEBRUARY, 1865

*At last a letter from Saint-Germain, and copies of my first monographs
on the Choctaw, sent more than a year ago, and carried down from Baltimore. How long ago that work now seems to me. I am assured that copies
will be sent to Joseph Greentree and that initial responses to the works
are favorable. I realize I ought to feel some pride, or vindication, but I can
take little satisfaction in them, for they were done so long ago. I find I do
not want to read what I wrote, for all the memories it awakens. Worse,
reading what Saint-Germain writes is not only a great consolation, but
painful as well, for I can feel the many, many people he has lost... He tells
me that he understands too well the hurt I have felt since I bid Tecumseh
farewell; I know this is true, but it does little to assuage my pain... I told
Tecumseh he had to grieve, and ultimately I suppose I must, for the loss of
his loving, though not the loss of his love...*

*Now that money has been transferred from Brooklyn, I have been able
to lease a house for a short period; it is a small domicile, hardly more than
a cottage, built when I was truly a girl, just six rooms. I have one housekeeper to look after the place for me... It is a relief to have money in my
hands again that the local people accept without hesitation...*

*They say General Beauregard has left to meet General Hardee at
Charleston, so the fighting goes on... though I wonder how it can last
much longer, given the privations and disruption in the South...*

*Lillyanne has found herself work at a dressmaker's shop, and came to
me today to offer to make some new clothes for me. She was very kind in
pointing out that my few remaining garments are more fit for a backwoods
farmer's wife than for what she insists on calling 'a grand French lady,'
and now that a few ships are bringing goods to Savannah, there is cloth to
make the dresses with instead of using up bolts from attics and salvaged
upholstery... We spent an hour discussing what I would need for my return to France, and I have told her that I must be assured that she will
receive a commission beyond her wages for this work...*

*That I should be thinking of clothes again, and starting to miss real
theatre and good society. This is not to say that the families of Savannah have not been cordial, for they have, but I am aware that I remain a
puzzle to most of the hostesses and few of them receive me with complete
comfort...*

SAVANNAH, GEORGIA, 31 MARCH, 1865

Wonder of wonders, I have at last found a British ship willing to take me to Italy, whither it will be bound when a few necessary repairs are completed, which cannot be done at once, given the lack of supplies ... While the work is being done, I have taken advantage of this time to learn something about the captain, a man of forty years and stolid demeanor, who tells me that his brother is a don at Clair College, Cambridge, and has mentioned my work to him. Whether this is a polite fiction or the truth, I cannot guess, but at least Captain Wolverton has agreed to take me aboard when he sails, and for a price that is not so outrageous that I tremble to think of it ... The projected date of departure, given the fading state of the war, is the middle of next month, when he expects certain items to arrive from Boston ... He would rather leave before then, but as there is still fighting in the Carolinas, commercial shipping from North to South has not yet resumed with any reliability ...

Speaking of ships, Tecumseh has gone to City Point to meet with General Grant and President Lincoln. I have received one quickly written note from him telling me that the meeting has exceeded his expectations and that, upon reflection, he has come to realize that Lincoln grasps the problems of the South more comprehensively than he had first assumed, and has a deep commitment to healing the wounds the country has inflicted upon itself. This is high praise, given Tecumseh's usual opinion of politicians. He informs me that the president is eager to avoid any unnecessary bloodshed and that any reasonable terms of surrender should be considered acceptable in order to ensure the reestablishment of the Union without any more rancor than absolutely necessary ... Since Tecumseh has been afraid for so long that a punitive peace would only stir the South to greater rebellion and anarchy, he endorses this idea emphatically. But then, Tecumseh does everything emphatically, including doubt himself ... Even in this moment of triumph, he is troubled by doubt, anticipating every catastrophe he can imagine and preparing himself to face each one by turns so that he will not be caught off-guard ... General Meade is expected to join them in a day or so, according to his note, and possibly his brother John as well ...

At last today I have had word from Euphemia Stephens. She tells me she has opened a school for young women, where the study of languages is emphasized. She thanks me in the letter, for she says that the bonus I paid her financed her venture, which is doing well ... Reading her letter, I thought I was looking back on another existence, as remote to me now as my childhood is ... According to what she tells me, San Francisco is much changed in the decade since I left, and she reckons I would not recognize half the buildings in the city ... Society has changed, too, and there are many more respectable women living with their families in San Francisco. A few of the men who have made fortunes have begun to build mansions along California Street. Fanny Kent is now a widow, according to Euphemia, and the doyen of the society hostesses, something of a terror among the ambitious matrons of the city ... It is not as pleasant to remember San Francisco as I would like, for I cannot help but find Tecumseh tangled up in my memories ...

CAPTAIN WOLVERTON WATCHED as the last of Madelaine's crates were loaded aboard his *Prince of Malta*, saying as the crane swung toward the open hold, "Strange to see a lady traveling with so many books."

Madelaine was used to such observations, and only shrugged. "I think of them as my friends, and I would miss them if I left them behind."

"And books are quite an investment," added the Captain. "I know; my brother is forever in want of funds for more books."

"As are all serious scholars," said Madelaine. The morning was turning warm, but there was a sharp wind off the ocean which kept the heat at bay; standing on the deck caused her minor discomfort, but her native earth in the soles of her shoes offered some respite from the enervating effect of the water.

Captain Wolverton chuckled. "And doubtless you are one."

"Most certainly I am, and proud to be so," said Madelaine, her manner cordial but her intent plain. "If your brother has read my work, you must be aware of that."

Captain Wolverton colored to the roots of his brindled whiskers. "I meant nothing disrespectful, ma'am," he said. "But scholarly women are so often old maids, as the Americans say, crabbed and dried up. You're not like that."

"But I am," she said. "I am certainly an old maid, as you put it. I have no husband nor father living; and I never had a brother." She looked toward the end of the wharf where a number of men were gathering. There were shouts, and a few triumphant whoops. "What on earth—"

271

"You'd best stay here, ma'am," Captain Wolverton warned her, and drew his cap down over his brow as he started down the gangplank toward the excitement.

Madelaine watched him go, and noticed that the air of joyous chaos was spreading. More men came hurrying to learn what had so excited their fellows, and when they were told, more rejoicing occurred. What was the occasion for this eruption of festivities? No one had told her of any planned events. Had the last Confederate surrendered? she wondered. And would anyone here greet that intelligence with such unmixed delight? Whatever the news, it was making the men on the wharf deliriously happy. She could hear the excited hollers and shouts.

One of the sailors who had been polishing brightwork stopped to listen, watching Captain Wolverton approach the growing throng of celebrants. He cocked his head, all his attention on the rollicking, jostling crowd. "Someone's been shot," he said as much to himself as to Madelaine.

"Who? Who's been shot?" Madelaine demanded, dreading to hear that Tecumseh was hurt, though she knew through their bond he was not; she could not keep her apprehension for him at bay.

The sailor strained, cupping his ear with one hand. His eyes widened, and he shook his head. "It can't ... I don't ... "

"What is it?" she demanded urgently, her worry increasing.

The sailor looked stunned. "They say President Lincoln's dead." He did not move though he was no longer concentrating on listening. "Someone shot him."

"Shot? President Lincoln? And he's dead?" She heard her disbelief more than she felt it. For the moment she was so shocked that no feeling could make itself known. Then she looked at the sailor. "When? Do they say when?"

The sailor shook his head and moved away from her, unwilling to speak again.

The cacophony was tumultuous now, and single words were lost in the general wash of noise. The sailor tried to make something out, then pointed down to the crowd where Captain Wolverton had emerged, a newspaper clutched in his hands, his brow set into a forbidding scowl. As a dozen more men came rushing along the wharf the captain stepped carefully aside so as not to impede their progress.

"It's a bad business," said Captain Wolverton as he stepped onto his own deck, opening the paper as he did. "The president was shot night before last and died yesterday morning." He held out the paper to Madelaine. "You'll want to read this for yourself, I'd think."

Madelaine took the paper and opened it, seeing the black border around the headline: ASSASSINATION. She stared at the word as if she could not decipher its meaning, and then, slowly, she began to read the report beneath it, describing how Abraham Lincoln was shot in the back of the head while watching a play, and that the assassin, reported by some to be the actor John Wilkes Booth, had escaped with an injured ankle. The man was being hunted. There was a detailed account of the president's last hours which Madelaine did not bother to read.

"There could be the devil to pay for this," said Captain Wolverton. "It's one thing to have Lee surrendered, but there are those who will use this as a rallying cry to fight on, I'll warrant you." He narrowed his eyes and looked away from the excitement, out toward the mouth of the harbor. "We're leaving in good time."

"It's … very unfortunate, after so many terrible losses," said Madelaine, wishing she knew where Tecumseh was so that she could send him some word of condolence that could perhaps keep him from lapsing into the black despair that she had seen him fight before. It was folly to try, she knew; Tecumseh was on campaign and she would not be able to locate him without causing questions to be asked that neither of them would want to answer. "But you're right, Captain," she said, handing the paper back to Wolverton. "It is more than time to leave."

"And that we will. With the evening tide, ma'am, unless Admiral Porter's men tell us otherwise, which they may, and who should blame them? Just as well that we're ready to stand out to sea—with this news, I'll wager some ships will have to remain here for a time, and we've lost enough of that already. A pity we did not leave yesterday." He shook his head slowly. "Why kill him now, when the war is ending? Why wait so long? It's a bad business."

"Yes, it is," said Madelaine, and went to the hatch to watch her crates and trunks put in place for the long crossing ahead.

SAVANNAH, GEORGIA, 18 APRIL, 1865

The ship has been searched by Union navy men, and as no fugitives have been found tucked away with the cargo, we will be allowed to leave at tide's turn. This delay was not unexpected, given the tragic news from Washington. The country is up in arms about the murder, and even those who are pleased that Lincoln is dead are outraged that it should have been done in so cowardly a way ... The most adamant Southerner does not approve of shooting a man in the back, or the back of the head while he is sitting being entertained ...

I have my journals with me in my cabin; I intend to try to make some sense of them during the crossing ... There is so much to assess and understand, if it is possible to do either ...

Now that I am leaving I find myself wishing that Tecumseh were here so that I could see him again, and ease some of the grief that I know he feels and is hard-pressed to admit ... I wish I could take leave of him more intimately than we were able to do when he left here. But that would mean he would have to have kept from his duty, and that would have been intolerable to him, so perhaps it is just as well that we have parted ...

I know I shall be seasick ...

Europe

MONBUSSY-SUR-MARNE, 25 MARCH, 1867

*To my astonishment, I have today received, forwarded by my pub-
lisher in Amsterdam, a letter from Tecumseh. He tells me he does
not agree with my conclusions about Indians, but he cannot fault my
observations ... How like him to write so formally, in case, no doubt,
someone might happen to read the contents other than me. He does
allow one concession, saying that he misses the stimulation of my
company ...*

*What will he make of my account of the United States' Civil War as
I saw it, I wonder, when I finally finish it and deliver it for publication?
Perhaps I should ask Saint-Germain to arrange for a copy to be sent to
him for his comments ...*

*Garibaldi has continued his advance toward Rome, and the Risorgi-
mento movement appears to be growing stronger ...*

MONBUSSY-SUR-MARNE, 2 NOVEMBER, 1867

*I have again been denied permission to go to Syria in spite of Professor
del Carlos' recommendations ... How vexing it is to be refused the opportunity to explore these unknown places for no reason other than I
am female, for that is surely the reason I am denied ... It would be very
useful for me to vanish while on such an expedition, so that in ten years
or so, my niece or perhaps my cousin can take up where I left off ... It is*

275

*much more difficult to vanish here in Europe, and it did not occur to me
in America to take advantage of the opportunity...*

*So America has bought Alaska from Russia. The purchase took place
last year, or so I understand; I have just learned of it, Alaska seeming as
remote as the moon to the people of Italy... I wonder what role Baron
deStoeckl had in that affair, if any?... The news from America is tardy
here, but it is apparent that there are many changes coming in the wake
of the War... With the west opening to more settlers and more and more
states joining the Union, it may be that Tecumseh will have his way at
last and during his lifetime, with all of the United States territories becoming states at last...*

*I have been thinking it is time to travel; I may take the offer from
Milano, after all, and lecture there on what I learned about the Indians
in America. There is not much interest in the American Civil War in
Milano, but Indians are enough of a novelty that a few of the academic
masters are willing to learn firsthand about the differences and similari-
ties of these peoples... Saint-Germain has offered me the use of his villa
near Lecco on Lake Como if ever I wanted it, and I may accept his kind
invitation, although he will not be there...*

*The last volume of my Indian monographs is finally published; I will
receive copies of it in a matter of days, which pleases me profoundly, for
with the railroad crossing the American continent, as it will within a
year, the lives of the Indians will be altered forever... If the work is as
well-received as the previous volumes have been, I must hope that my
reputation is at last secure, at least as long as I dare to be myself... In
time I must adopt another identity so as not to give rise to questions
about my longevity...*

*Regarding such matters, Saint-Germain has informed me that there
have been none of his blood who have survived embalming and so there
is one other way beyond destroying the nervous system through staking
or burning or beheading to keep us from rising after death...*

RHO, LOMBARDIA, 11 JULY, 1868

*This place is near enough to Milano to permit me to travel there easily,
yet sufficiently far that I do not encourage visits from either students or
other instructors, which suits my purposes very well... I have examined*

the sanctuary here and found it of some interest, as much for the Roman
ruins I suspect are under the Renaissance buildings as for the recognized
treasure...

My villa is not large, but is pleasantly situated at the back of a grove
of cypress, with a splendid garden twice the size of the villa spread out on
three sides. The long avenue approaching the villa is shaded and easily
overlooked, which suits me very well... I have five servants, two for the
garden, one for the stable, and two for the house... Angelo and his brother
Teobaldo are both somewhat simple in mind, but they do their work well
and the plants do not mind that they cannot discuss philosophy... Marcantonio is a very capable man-of-all-work, and I may ask him to come
with me to de Montalia and fix that crumbling north wing when I leave
here; I understand he is a widower whose children are with his sister's
family in San Donato Milanese... Susanna manages the household for me
and sees to the meals of the staff... She thinks me very eccentric for insisting on taking care of my own meals, but she dismisses it as a peculiarity
of the French, which I encourage... Quinto is a man of mature years and
long experience with horses and coaches...

I am having a number of cases of books shipped to me here, as well as
a half dozen crates of good de Montalia earth, so I will be comfortable
for some time to come... I had not thought to leave France so soon after
my return from America, but there were those in the village who were
too curious about me, and I decided it was best to put distance between
their speculations and myself...

How distressing the news is from the rest of the world, with unrest
everywhere. Prussia, Spain and Serbia are all in upheavals of various
sorts... How strange to think of this part of chaotic Italy as an island of
quiet in a turbulent sea...

RHO, LOMBARDIA, 23 DECEMBER, 1868

So Tecumseh's old friend Grant is about to be the new president in
America. I wish now I had met the man, because I have been asked my
opinion on him several times and could only repeat what I had been told,
and from what source... I wonder how this sits with Tecumseh, given
his scorn of politics? His friendship with Grant has survived many difficulties; it should survive this as well. Yet if Grant has been pulled into

the fray, how will Tecumseh avoid it? Given all he has done, it would be astonishing if the politicians did not seek to recruit him for office, hero that he is ... His father-in-law would doubtless be pleased if Tecumseh were a senator or some other high official, which would dismay Tecumseh as mightily as it would gratify his wife, I suspect ... I should not dwell on him this way, as I should not long for Saint-Germain, as both are useless exercises ...

I visited Marcantonio in sleep again last night; he is a willing participant in his dreams, and there is satisfaction in this contact, but I doubt that he would welcome me awake, so I must forego the intimacy that lends savor and comfort to necessity ...

RHO, LOMBARDIA, 15 MAY, 1869

I have been reading The Moonstone *by Wilkie Collins, and have found it very evocative, though not so innovative as some think it to be ... I have been in contact with William Harris and Sons of Philadelphia, to arrange to purchase books from America, both new ones and those from my years in that country ... I left many wonderful volumes behind and now I would like to replace them ... There are a number of magazines as well as books that the bookseller carries which might provide me with information ... I am puzzled by the eagerness with which I am offered English titles, as if I could not easily procure the works of Dickens directly from London, not that I read Dickens now ...*

They are once again trying a Parliamentary government in France. May they succeed. May something succeed at last. France has shown a capacity for turning reform to disaster before, however, and I am not as sanguine as many are about this development. At the same time I do not like the notion of the state depending on a single leader as they did for so long with that opportunist Napoleon ...

There is a reception next week for a party of visiting Americans in Milano and I have been asked to attend ... There is a small chance that Saint-Germain may come, and that delights me more than I can express ... He has been traveling in Poland and Hungary, and is looking to establish himself in the west again ... He has a schloss in Bavaria, but with matters as they are, has indicated he would prefer Switzerland, where he has a pleasant holding, or perhaps Belgium, although that is so near to Amsterdam it might prove difficult, for he has colleagues there who might recognize him and ask unwelcome questions...

It will be pleasant to be among Americans again, I hope... If only I do not miss Tecumseh too much...

RHO, LOMBARDIA, 29 SEPTEMBER, 1869

If one more bewhiskered professor attempts advances to me, I shall be hard put not to break his neck... Professor Ettore Zanetto has made an annoying pest of himself for more than a month, trying to find ways to be private with me, and then putting his hands all over me and claiming to be under my spell and unable to resist me, not that there is any evidence that he has made any effort to do so; before him it was Professor Bonifaccio Adama, who was truly odious until Saint-Germain had a word with him last June... But Saint-Germain is in Stockholm for a brief stay, and I cannot be forever pestering him on this issue... If either of those men were ones I would welcome as lovers, matters would be quite pleasant, but as it is, I refuse to permit any of these salacious old goats with doctoral degrees to take advantage of me, while threatening to revoke my position as lecturer if I am not willing to accept their fumbling self-congratulatory lust...

Marcantonio is beginning to regard me with a degree of speculation that is not entirely disinterested... I will probably have to cease visiting him in dreams, so that he will not come to suspect what transpires while he sleeps... But I refuse to entertain one of those dreadful instructors as a substitute for Marcantonio; I would have to be truly desperate before I would want their blood mixed with mine. What an appalling thought...

RHO, LOMBARDIA, 19 FEBRUARY, 1870

The weather has been severe and the roads are all but impassable—there is nothing but freezing mud from here to Bologna, or so I have been told... I have not left the villa for well over a week, and I am growing bored... I look at the thousands of books on the shelves lining the walls and I cannot find anything I want to read...

My own work holds few attractions for me when I am in so sour a state of mind… Try as I will, I am not able to achieve the degree of distance from my experiences that would permit me to evaluate all that I saw and learned while I was in the Confederacy… When I try to write of these times, it all comes back so vividly that I am left thinking of the wasted lives and ruined land and the clamor of battle… and Tecumseh. That is the one, overriding memory which haunts me: my time with Tecumseh…

I have asked Saint-Germain about this, hoping he could assure me that in time it will fade. He answered from Vienna, where he is remaining for the winter, reminding me that he has lost none of his bond with me, nor I with him, and that where blood is knowingly shared, there is no lessening of that bond. He was compassionate, as I knew he would be, recalling what he called the stubborn honor of some of the women he has loved who were determined to uphold their responsibilities against all odds and his own advice… His letter mentions one woman in Toledo, one in China, and one in Germany… He also reminds me of the bond between us, which is at once his greatest joy and his greatest pain… I cannot think of this without feeling the same in myself… If only I could have the consolation of his love as I had it in life…

NEAR LECCO, LAKE COMO, 22 AUGUST, 1870

It is very beautiful here, and with the mountains to shield us from the heat of the plains below us, the nights are not stifling as they have been in Rho. I should have accepted Saint-Germain's offer of this place two years ago, but at least I have rectified my blindness now…

I have brought with me the latest shipment from William Harris and Sons, with a letter from Charles Harris, who is now running the business for his father. He has informed me that he wants to continue to serve me and has included a list of recently available titles for my perusal… I have spent three days lollygagging—that is a wonderful word, I think: lollygagging—about, reading Harte's The Outcasts of Poker Flat *and Twain's* The Innocents Abroad, *and missing America, and Americans…*

There are many foreigners here, coming to enjoy the beauty of the place, and to escape the demands of summer, whether of nature or human origin… Today I saw a group of Austrians sailing two boats in competition, yesterday three Spanish nobles arrived with their families and servants at the villa across this arm of the lake, and this evening I am asked to a reception with English and French guests at the home of a Russian aristocrat who has exiled himself to Europe, claiming he prefers European uncertainty to Russian...

Paris looks to be in trouble again, with the Germans trying to force their will on the place... I do not feel the affection to that city most French are supposed to, not after Saint Sebastien, the Terror and that dreadful incident with Fouche... So many of my experiences there have been terrible that I look upon the place as a site of misfortunes, from the death of my father to the execution of my servants... I did meet Saint-Germain there, and for that I cannot dismiss the place entirely, nor regard it as wholly without merit...

RHO, LOMBARDIA, 17 NOVEMBER, 1870

I have been reading Alice's Adventures in Wonderland and having a delightful time of it. Though I do not know the professors in question, I certainly know their counterparts; Professor Dodgson has a very sharp eye and a sharper tongue. The book has made returning to lecture less of an ordeal than it would have been, for I am able to amuse myself in casting the various professors around me as various characters in the book: Professor Roselli is very definitely a Dormouse, and Professor Stagno is certainly a Mad Hatter. I have not yet decided if Professor Senape is a Flamingo or a Hedgehog but he is undoubtedly someone's plaything... And Professor Zanetto is clearly a March Hare...

Marcantonio has given notice; he has been offered employment in San Donato Milanese, where he could be with his sister's family and his children. I will miss him, but undoubtedly it is wiser for him to go. I will see that he is provided with a generous doucement when he goes, which will be at the end of the year ... I am now faced with the prospect of replacing him, and not just as a man-of-all-work. It will not be an easy thing to do, but I must make an effort...

Professor Zanetto has at last abandoned his ludicrous pursuit of me and has, instead, developed what he calls a pure passion for the wife of Professor Aurelio Cancelli... It had best remain pure, for Professor Cancelli is a big man with a short temper...

Signora Chiodo visited me today and asked if I would be willing to speak to the girls at her school... She is mistress of a well-thought-of institution that attempts to teach her pupils more than the right way to fold napkins and the correct honorific of diplomats in French... and since I have made my way in the world as a recognized scholar, she hopes I might instill in some of the young ladies in her charge a sense of adventure and the worth of learning... How could I refuse her? I have said I will address her students early next month...

AT THE END OF HER TALK, Madelaine noticed a middle-aged man standing at the back of the little hall, hands thrust deep in his pockets, his expression one of polite interest. As the girls filed out of the hall in silent columns, the man came forward, walking up to Madelaine without haste but with definite purpose in his manner.

"Madame," he said, holding out his hand for hers and proffering a visiting card with the other. "I hope you have time for a word with me."

"Yes," she said, after an anxious glance in the direction of Signora Chiodo, who lingered in the doorway, watching her charges as they left the building.

"I am Maurizio Leonetto," he said as he lifted her hand to his lips in a formal way. He was fairly tall, though not so tall as Sherman, nor so lean. This man had a thick body, a thick, short beard, and thick, chestnut-brown hair. He was dressed in a frock coat over a long, double-breasted waistcoat, as dandified as a man in the world of academe could dare to be.

"So it says on your card," Madelaine responded, curious to know what it was the man wanted from her.

"I am an... advisor to the government, dealing with foreign affairs. I have a number of questions I hope you will be able to answer." He turned his head to the side so that she could not see him face-on; there was a speculative look in his eyes. "What do you think?"

"I suppose that it would be all right," she said carefully, noticing that Signora Chiodo was bustling up to them, her hands already fluttering with emotion.

"I told Professore Leonetto that you would be willing to answer his questions. I hope I did not tell him anything you would rather I did not?" She did not wait for an answer, but launched into another volley of observations. "You held the students quite spellbound, Madame. I was astonished to learn that you actually saw American slaves. I must tell you that I am overwhelmed by the scope of the war. To think it was fought over a thousand miles and more. What a shocking thing, to be sure." She cocked her head to the side. "They are all talking at once. You can hear them if you listen. What magpies they are at that age."

"Yes," said Leonetto with a hint of irony in his voice. "They are."

Signora Chiodo shook her head indulgently. "Most of them are not apt scholars, but there are a few, a precious few, and they need encouragement, or they will turn vapid as any. It was good of you, Madame, to come and tell them all you had encountered."

"I barely did more than sketch the events." She had made no mention, of course, of her affair with Sherman, or the appalling wounds she had helped to treat, or the men who had gone mad with war. Of the Indians, she had spoken only of the Choctaw Nation, leaving out most of her travels, as much for credibility as for her desire not to confuse the students.

"Well, it was very stimulating. I have hopes that a few will respond well to what you have said. One or two of them were frightened at first, but you were able to engage their interests without distressing too many of them. You are a very good lecturer, Madame, and my girls will not forget you."

"Thank you," said Madelaine, her face unchanged in spite of this fulsome compliment.

"I fear I have not much time," said Leonetto pointedly. "I must return to Roma tomorrow."

"Then perhaps Signora Chiodo might be good enough to lend us a place to talk?" Madelaine ventured.

"Very good," said Signora Chiodo, indicating the doorway to the hall. "The library is at the end of this hall; the carved doors. We close it at this time of day. You may use it until the bell for the evening meal sounds."

"That is most kind of you, Signora," said Leonetto, and started off toward the carved doors, not waiting to see if Madelaine was following him.

"A bit high-handed, as men in the government are apt to be," said Signora Chiodo as she watched Leonetto. She put her hand on Madelaine's arm. "But you may rest assured you will come to no harm from him."

"That relieves me," said Madelaine, thinking that Leonetto would not endanger himself by giving rise to complaints about his conduct. Any woman he used, he would arrange the whole of it in advance, and limit himself to those who knew the game.

"You'd better go along," said Signora Chiodo, as if she addressed one of her students. "I will have coffee and biscotti sent in to you."

Leonetto was waiting for her just inside the library door, where he bowed to her and indicated the settees flanking the hearth. "We should be comfortable here."

Madelaine took the settee more out of the sun, for it could be uncomfortable, though at this time of the day it was unlikely to cause her any damage, not with her native earth in her shoes. "Now, what is it you want to know, Professore?"

"You have been in America for some years," he said. "You'll pardon me if I say that you do not have the appearance of being old enough to have undertaken such an expedition."

"Thank you," said Madelaine without conviction. "Yes, I spent a number of years there."

"And you traveled widely?" He was trying to find his conversational footing.

"Yes. Have you ever been there, Professore?" she asked.

"No, but I have studied it, and I am quite familiar with its history." He beamed at her, taking pride in his accomplishments.

"That may make this more difficult," said Madelaine. "I will do my best to answer your questions."

"That is very good of you." He coughed delicately. "I have been asked to learn something of the character of President Grant, and, since it appears you met him—"

"I beg your pardon," Madelaine interrupted. "I never met him. The only figure of any consequence I had dealings with is William T. Sherman, and my opinion of Grant has been formed from Sherman's report of him. I spent most of the war in the states of Alabama and Georgia, and those were not theaters of operations for General Grant." She smiled a bit to reassure him.

"I see," said Leonetto, thrown off his pace by this information.

"I will tell you what Sherman said of Grant, if that would help you, though I had better warn you that the two men are friends, and Sherman is very loyal to his friends." She watched the man attempt to decide what to do.

Leonetto took the other settee. "I had assumed you had traveled in American centers and cities."

"Oh, I have, and widely. But I did not visit the capital, nor many of the metropolises. I spent most of my time in the West. I went as far as California." She recalled her days there with Sherman, now well over a decade ago. His absence struck her poignantly, as it did when she was unprepared for it; discussing him only made it worse.

"I see," Leonetto said again. "I didn't understand that. I supposed you must have been traveling more..." He gestured with his hands to finish his thoughts.

"Circumspectly? Safely? With more protection?" She laughed. "No, Professore, I did not do those things. I traveled to learn. I did see Saint Louis, of course, and San Francisco, and Atlanta, but not under the best circumstances."

"Yes." He adjusted the pull of the fabric of his trousers over his knee. "I thought that perhaps you might have encountered some of these men in your travels."

"Just General Sherman; and a few of his staff, as well." She added this last so that it would not appear she was holding anything back. "None of them were doing much socializing at the time."

"Of course, of course," said Leonetto, his faint smile showing her answer puzzled more than amused him. "But what can you tell me in regard to Grant? I must present a report to the government and the information you provide will be much appreciated. I understand that anything you say is colored by General Sherman's representations of the man."

Madelaine sighed. "Well, he came from a simple background, went to West Point because the family feared he had no head for business, which Te—General Sherman thought was probably the case. He was posted to the Far West and did not like it. He had successes early in the Civil War, principally in Tennessee, but after the battle of Shiloh, he became less active. Surely you know these things."

"Yes, we do," Leonetto admitted. "What we are not so sure of is the matter of drink."

"Oh, that," said Madelaine. "It is General Sherman's opinion that Grant only drinks when he is bored. When he is with his wife, or on active campaign, he rarely touches alcohol of any kind." She smiled a little. "He does not like to be idle; it weighs upon him, and he escapes it."

"According to General Sherman, who is his friend," Leonetto amended.

"Yes, according to General Sherman." She looked toward the westering sun and felt the first solace of the coming night.

Leonetto considered this a short while. "If you know General Sherman well enough, can you tell me if he is likely to run for high office?"

At this Madelaine laughed aloud. "If there is one thing in this world Sherman despises, it is politics. He has contempt for the profession, and a dislike for the men who make up the trade." She tossed her head. "I pity anyone who attempts to dragoon him into a candidacy."

"You are sure of that? It is several years since you've seen him, and it might be that he has changed his mind." Leonetto allowed his skepticism to show.

"Professore, if you think Sherman would change his mind on this matter, you have no conception of the man. He would rather be flayed alive than sacrifice his principles." She paused, fearing she might say something that was too revealing. "I have known him to speak highly of one politician only, and that was Abraham Lincoln, though it took him most of the war to come to approve of him."

"Then he did change his mind," Leonetto said sharply.

"Because he could not deny Lincoln's character, in spite of his profession. The terms upon which Lincoln ended the war earned him Sherman's admiration for the reasonable demands made regarding the Confederacy. Sherman is a fair man, Professore, and he came to like Lincoln as a human being, not simply as the president of his country. Or a politician." She looked up as one of the school servants arrived with a tray which she put down on the end-table by Madelaine's settee. "Thank you, Signorina," Madelaine said, and motioned the young woman away.

When she was gone, Madelaine poured out two cups of coffee, and handed one to Leonetto, setting hers aside.

Leonetto took the cup and tasted the coffee, making sure it was hot, and then accepted one of the biscotti on the plate Madelaine passed to him. "In spite of what he saw in Lincoln, you do not think Sherman will run for office?" He ran his eyes over the front of Madelaine's dress with the easy confidence of a man who is certain he is attractive to women.

"No, I do not," said Madelaine, wishing she could turn away from this inspection without being so obvious she gave offence. "His brother has been in Congress—he may still be there, for all I know. And his stepfather has been a major political figure for many years. If Sherman were going to change his mind about a political career, he would have done it long ago." She regarded Leonetto closely. "Why do you want to know these things?"

He shrugged, attempting to pass over her question. "Any new government needs to gather as much information as possible about the rest of the world."

"There are many others who could provide you a more accurate account of these things than I can. Why come to me?" Her manner was pleasant but it was clear to them both that she would not accept another such facile response.

"There is some fear that the American war may flare up again. If that happens, we must be prepared to make the most of it." He put the coffee aside to let it cool. "Should that occur, what do you think General Sherman would do?"

"Go back to the front, I suppose," Madelaine answered, trying to keep the edge from her voice. "He is determined to preserve the Union at all costs."

"And you think he would rather do that than be president." He was very much on the alert now, poised for her answer.

"Yes, I do," she answered quietly. "As much as he hates war, he would fight again to keep the country intact." She looked at Leonetto somberly. "I am utterly sure of it, Professore."

"And would Grant back him in this?" asked Leonetto.

Madelaine was more careful with her answer. "I would expect him to, yes."

"If he had to fight again, would he win?" The question came quickly; it was another he had been prepared to ask.

"I think it would be easier to stand against a tidal wave than against Sherman," said Madelaine, remembering the march from Atlanta to Savannah. "And the North has more men and guns than the South."

"But if that changed?" asked Leonetto. "If the South had more men and guns at their disposal?"

Now that Madelaine sensed his intention, she took a sterner tone with him. "I think that the United States were ... was damaged very badly by that war, North as well as South. I think it is like a family that has come through a tragic quarrel, and has at last reached a point where it can begin to mend. If it is disrupted again, with all the wounds still apt to bleed, I doubt if either North or South could survive it intact, and that would be the ruin of the place. As it is, it will take generations for the damage to be forgotten." She also suspected it would be the ruin of Sherman, who might well kill himself in despair at such a calamity.

"Clearly you trust General Sherman," said Leonetto. "Can you tell me why that is?"

"I have seen him at his best, and at his worst," she answered, presenting her argument carefully. "I know he has never deserted his men or his friends when the situation was desperate."

"How do you account for that?" Leonetto inquired.

"It is his character. He walks a path he chose for himself; he will not leave it. He has a few strongly held beliefs and they shape him and his life. He is not so much a proud man, but a … faithful one." She was aware of a slight wistfulness in her voice, so she added, "It has cost him a great deal to do this."

"You count him your friend?" This question surprised her, coming as it did as a casual afterthought.

She thought about it, wanting to give an answer that could be corroborated if such became necessary. "He was my banker, in San Francisco. In that capacity he was a great help to me as a visitor to a city I did not know. And I aided him: he had a severe attack of asthma; I was able to help him, and so I would suspect he feels some obligation to me." She consoled herself with the inward reminder that this was the truth; she paused. "During the war he stood by his men, even when they were suffering. Even when he was suffering. So it follows he might have a similar attitude toward me."

"Well enough. I will remember that." He reached for his coffee, tasted it and drank it. "Whom else can you tell us of?"

"No one who would help you," she said, gently enough for him not to be offended. "I spent most of my time with ordinary people. And Indians."

"Oh, yes, the Choctaw." He reached into his coat and pulled out a slim volume. "I had this from a … colleague in America. I was hoping you might know who a few of these men are." He handed the little book to her. "We have no one to tell us anything more than what is in the book. Perhaps you can help us?"

It was no more than fifty bound pages of photographs, taken mainly from newspapers, a few with short articles appended, but many pages held simple portraits.

"A few are marked. They are the ones we do not recognize." He leaned back and watched as Madelaine studied the faces.

"I do not know this man, but his garments are Sioux. I know very little about the Sioux as I was not able to go among them. This man is

Arapaho. The people are traders. This man is Cheyenne. The Arapaho and the Cheyenne are traditional allies against the Sioux." She turned the page and saw a photograph, declaring the subject to be Cochise, of the Apache, the fierce raider sought by the U.S. Cavalry for massacres of whites. She stared at the face. "I have met this man," she said quietly.

"Cochise?" asked Leonetto, when Madelaine held out the book to him.

"Yes; several years ago. He did not tell me his name, only that he was the son-in-law of Mangas Coloradas. Many Indians will not tell outsiders their names." She recalled the evening they had talked, the man's many precautions against exposing himself to attack or capture. "He speaks good English and excellent Spanish," she said inconsequentially.

"That's remarkable," said Leonetto, his attention caught.

"Not as remarkable as you might think: were you going to learn Apache?" she asked. "This man on the next page is Tavibo, the spiritual leader of the Paiute."

"How likely is it that the Indians will unite against the whites?" Leonetto put the question to her as if he expected a particular answer.

"Not likely at all, I should think," said Madelaine. "It is more likely that all of eastern Europe should unite against western Europe if western Europe was sending settlers into Bohemia and Poland."

"I see," said Leonetto. "A difficult matter."

"An impossible one, I should think," said Madelaine, returning to the book. "This man is Shoshone, but I do not know his name. This is Satank of the Kiowa Nation; his name means Sitting Bear. This man is Coweta-stick Creek. These two men are Navajo." She closed the book and handed it back to him. "I am sorry I can tell you nothing more."

"Yes; well, you have been most helpful, Madame," he said with a show of sincerity. He rose. "I thank you for the time you've given me, and I'll keep your remarks in mind when I make my report." He bowed slightly and started to the door.

"You will forgive me for saying it, Professore, but I doubt you have any comprehension of the state of affairs in America." She did her best not to make this a challenge. "I have been there, I have seen the peoples of that country, and I do not have audacity enough to suppose I understand America. It is a fascinating place, but that makes it difficult to appreciate."

"I'll keep that in mind," said Leonetto in a tone that promised the opposite.

"If I can be of any more help, do not hesitate to contact me," said Madelaine, a trace of mischief in her voice now.

"Yes; of course," said Professor Leonetto, and let himself out.

* * *

RHO, LOMBARDIA, 2 APRIL, 1871

It is quite a splendid day. No rain, and no clouds. It is warm but not uncomfortably so, and the breeze is pleasant and filled with the scent of growing things. This is the sort of spring day the poets write about and painters wait whole years for. I have been out twice this morning, once to ride, and once to walk in the garden. It will not be easy to leave this place, but in another year or so, two at the most, I fear I must. Not only will it be wise for my own protection, but it is getting to be time that I undertake another expedition so that I can disappear and my "cousin" or "niece" can take up my work on my behalf. But on a day like today, those demands seem so remote that I suppose I can postpone those events for a while; in the meantime, I will see what I can find about recent antiquarian discoveries around the world and begin inquiries about an expedition ...

Saint-Germain has promised to come to Montalia before the end of summer. He and I have not spent more than a few days together in the last thirty years. It is always awkward to be with him, knowing that we can offer each other nothing of what we need. I always try to persuade myself that I will not be daunted by this desire that goes through me like a strong current, and become as philosophical as he appears to be. If I did not continue to love him as I do, it would be easier, I suspect, though he claims I will grow more accustomed with age, as he says he has done. Still, our conversaton is happy. But I can see the longing in his eyes when he is not on guard ...

In the wake of the letter from Saint-Germain, I find I am missing many of the men I have loved: Saint-Germain himself most of all, but also Falke and dear Trowbridge, who never touched me, and Alexander, and Tecumseh. How Tecumseh refuses to leave my reverie. He wanted so much to banish any other love from my memory, and occasionally he succeeds but for Saint-Germain, especially on a languorous day like this one when studying has no charm for me, and the lure of the countryside reminds me of all those days in the endless countryside of America ...

RHO, LOMBARDIA, 19 JUNE, 1871

Thunderstorms again today ... I have been filling the time with work on my Civil War experiences. I think that perhaps now I can begin to assess what happened to me in those dreadful years ... But I am shocked at the pain reading my journal pages brings to mind. It was not my country, nor my cause, and yet it holds me, for Tecumseh's sake, if no other ...
In today's post came word that Joseph Greentree died last winter of fever. I was saddened to learn of it, for he was a good friend to me, and did not think me strange or unwelcome simply because I was an outsider ... He was kind to me, more than I had any reason or right to expect, and for that alone I will miss him ...

If the thunderstorms abate, I will venture out tonight, to visit Marcello Capinello in his sleep. When there are thunderstorms, the risks are too great. One good clap overhead and I would be discovered ... Marcello has proved a useful partner in his sleep, and I suspect that many of those who praise him as an advocate would be amazed to learn what a yearning he has for grand romance. In the midst of all those deeds and trusts and wills, he longs for a chance to rescue fair maidens from outlaws, or to capture a citadel and be recognized as a wise and magnanimous ruler ... So handsome a man, and with such fire in his soul, it is a pity that he masks his desires so thoroughly. Still, he has drawn up my will to my satisfaction, so that my "descendants" will be able to claim this place should anything happen to me. I think he will be satisfied with the explanation my "niece" will provide him ...

Is it just the thunderstorms making me restless, or something more? I cannot help but wonder if this signals a change, for good or bad? ...

RHO, LOMBARDIA, 11 OCTOBER, 1871

To my amazement, I have received a telegram from Professor Leonetto telling me that Tecumseh is coming to Europe. I never thought he would actually do it, yet it would seem he will be here shortly. The Professore has asked if I would be willing to meet with Tecumseh, to ask him a few questions on behalf of the government. I am preparing a telegram to

*send an answer to this request, with the suggestion that we arrange a
meeting at the Lake Como villa, where I will not have to be beholden to
Professore Leonetto for the opportunity to see my old friend. If Leonetto
wants to use me to gain information from Tecumseh, he will have to be
content to meet at Lake Como ... Saint-Germain will surely let me have
it for such an occasion, and as Tecumseh is arriving first in Spain, it will
be a convenient place to stop on his way to Roma. Even if it isn't convenient, I would suppose that he might be willing to detour a few miles for
me, after coming so far ... A day or two at Lake Como would certainly
be a pleasant respite from travel, even in winter, and would give us privacy which would otherwise be impossible ... I will tell Leonetto how it
can be arranged, and then I wonder what will happen ...*

IT WAS NEARLY DUSK WHEN THE CARRIAGE ARRIVED, and the
steely light of winter nearly matched Sherman's eyes as he climbed out
behind Professor Leonetto. Both men wore greatcoats against the chill,
with their tall hats pulled down to shelter their eyes.

From her place at the window near the loggia, Madelaine watched,
doing what she could to contain her excitement. Could he sense it as
well, she asked herself as she watched the two men come across the loggia toward the main door. Or had Professor Leonetto revealed who the
"expert on America" was? She saw Sherman look around as if checking
for observers. Then he gave a little shrug and stepped up to the door
just behind Leonetto, already loosening his muffler.

Anamaria, the housekeeper, appeared in the doorway of the withdrawing room, saying, "The guests are here. Should I bring the hot
brandy now?"

"They probably need it," said Madelaine, hoping her composure
would not desert her in front of Professor Leonetto. "Has Andrea let
them in yet?"

"The door has just opened," said Anamaria, as if they could not hear
it in the withdrawing room, or feel the cold air that came as its vanguard.
"They will be with you in a moment, Madama. Be patient." She glanced
along the corridor and said over her shoulder as she went to get the
drinks for the newcomers, "The American is very tall. Tall and thin."

"Yes, he is," said Madelaine, and rose to her feet, adjusting the fall of
the lace over her burgundy velvet bodice. All at once she worried that the
neck was too low, and that her ruby-and-pearl necklace was too grand.

Professor Leonetto had rid himself of his greatcoat, muffler, gloves and hat as he came into the room, moving as if certain of his welcome. He spoke in Italian-cadenced English out of courtesy to his guest, though his cordiality was marred by his officious manner and his appearance of a hunting dog in pursuit of prey. "I am sorry we are arriving so late in the day. I am afraid there was quite a crowd to see General Sherman at the train station, and it took over an hour, getting away, what with one thing and another."

Sherman was still pulling the gloves from his hands for Andrea to put into the closet with his coat, muffler and hat as he came into the room, and so his attention was not on his hostess. "It's my fault. I do apologize for the inconvenience; it couldn't be—"

Madelaine filled the silence of his stare, saying, "It is no inconvenience."

"I understand you have met before," said Professor Leonetto, letting his own doubt of it color his words. He assumed that Sherman's hesitance to speak was the result of his attempt to place Madelaine in his recollection. "This is Madame Madelaine de—"

"Montalia," Sherman finished for him, having recovered himself somewhat. He continued to stare at her, taking in the whole of her with his searching eyes. "I should have guessed. I should have known." He was as straight as ever, but his hair was paler now, a curious coral-pink shade that was faded all the way to white at his temples and in the center of his beard. He was perhaps fifteen pounds heavier than the last time she had seen him, which softened some of the harsh lines of his face and smoothed out his wrinkles, though he had none of the look of a man run to fat about him; he had lost the gauntness Madelaine recalled from Atlanta, but he was still markedly more slender than Leonetto.

"How have you been, General Sherman?" she asked, thinking the question was inane, but needing to say something to put the professor's qualms at rest.

"Harried almost to death, if you must know," he answered, with a quick look of gratitude to her. "Ever since Thomas Ewing took ill, I have been pestered and prodded by politicians and my own family, trying to convince me to take his place. Once he died, the importunities grew more frequent, and from my own family as well as others, so I came to Europe. I reckon with the Atlantic between us, they will not bother me as much."

She wanted to touch him, to feel the life in him, to be wrapped in his arms. But with Professor Leonetto there she could only play the proper hostess, so she said, "It is a pleasure to have you here." These banalities gave her a chance to recover herself. "My housekeeper is getting hot brandy to help warm you. My staff will see to your coach, horses and coachman, and take your bags to your rooms. And there will be supper at eight."

"A good thing you were not an officer for the South, Madame, if you are so prepared for our three-day stay," Sherman said to her archly. "It would have been a more difficult fight had there been a greater attention to supply."

"Hence the Georgia campaign, as I recall," she said to him. "To cut off supplies."

"Precisely. An army without supplies cannot fight. If the spring before had not been cold, we would not have been able to do as much as we did, but the South was already low on supplies, thanks to fighting and poor crops." His voice was a little huskier than it had been six years ago, a sign that the asthma was still with him; he sounded impatient, as if he was tired of answering Leonetto's questions. He looked around the room, as if sizing up its defensive possibilities. "Only an incompetent leader would fight once supplies are lost."

"Hood, Johnston, and Forrest were not incompetent; you said so yourself," said Madelaine, trying to keep a tone that would satisfy Leonetto. This was more difficult than she had anticipated; she knew Sherman had missed her, had sensed it through their bond over the years, but she wanted him to tell her so, to admit it. It was suddenly very important to her that he speak the words aloud.

"No, they were not, and they surrendered, as any leader worthy of his men must do, to protect them. To fight on would have been profligate with lives and have gained nothing but more complete ruin." Sherman agreed at once, adding, "Joe Johnston is my good friend now." At last he gathered enough of his courage to take her hand. He did not shake it, as she anticipated, but raised it to his lips, his eyes locked on hers. "I should not be surprised, Madame, but I am." Then his eyes crinkled appreciatively, and he murmured, "Burgundy velvet and with a train; very elegant."

His approval was disconcerting, as she knew he intended it to be. "What can I be but flattered? And I must thank Professor Leonetto for keeping my confidence."

She turned to Leonetto and smiled, all the while wishing he would vanish. "I was not certain you would be willing to do it."

The professor bowed and offered a self-satisfied smirk. "It was my little experiment. I was curious to see how General Sherman would respond to a former acquaintance after the passage of years."

"No," said Sherman at once, his voice sharp and determined, cutting at the words. "That was not your purpose, sir. You were not completely satisfied that Madame de Montalia actually knew me, as she claimed she did. You did not mention her to me to test her, not to test me. Because you were not wholly convinced that she and I are truly friends." He directed his piercing steel-colored eyes at the man. "I trust you are satisfied now?"

Leonetto had nothing to say in his own defense. "I did not mean to offend you, General."

"You don't offend me, you offend Madame de Montalia," said Sherman with an impatient gesture with his left hand; Madelaine recognized it as his sign of wanting to be finished with the matter. "Offer your apology to her, not to me. I am not due one; she is."

"I ... I am sorry to have doubted you. But such a tale, and from a woman of your ... quality," said Leonetto with a slight shrug. "You would have doubted such an assertion yourself, I daresay."

"Your apology is accepted," said Madelaine, grateful to Anamaria for arriving with the hot brandy.

"Good; very good," said the professor, noting that there were only two steaming cups on the tray she offered.

"And when you are done serving the gentlemen, please light the lamps, Anamaria, and send Giorgio to light the fire; it is getting chilly in here," said Madelaine in Italian.

"Certainly, Madame. It is growing dark so early." She presented the tray to the tall American first, looking at him speculatively, trying to discern what it was about the man that so intrigued Madelaine de Montalia, for she and Giorgio had never seen her this animated except when Saint-Germain was also here.

Professor Leonetto took the second cup and then glanced at Madelaine. "You are having none, Madame?" He faltered, uncertain how to proceed if his hostess did not also have something in her hand.

"No. I have a tiresome condition that limits my diet severely. But do not let that take away from your pleasure. Pray, enjoy them," Madelaine responded.

"And she won't eat supper with us, either, Professor; several times I've tried to convince her to join me and she never has," said Sherman dryly. "Though, if she's up to her usual standard, she will have a good meal to offer us." He sipped at the hot brandy. "What else is in this?"

"Other than brandy? A little honey and nutmeg and lemon peel," said Madelaine at once. "It is a more pleasant drink that way."

"You know that from experience, do you?" Sherman asked her with a sudden grin. He looked about the room again, with less determination. "Is that a Botticelli?"

"I believe so," said Madelaine, looking at the painting over the mantle. "I will find out if you are curious."

He was about to say no, and then he looked at her closely. "Yes, I would like to know." He had more of the brandy and said, "There was a time I did some sketching, you know."

Anamaria left the withdrawing room, taking her tray with her.

"Yes," Madelaine said, hoping that the emotion would not be too obvious in her voice. "I remember." She thought of his sketch of her, sitting in a frame on her writing table. Later, she promised herself, she would show him.

"Do you? From so long ago?" he said lightly enough, but with a suggestion of knowledge beyond the ordinary. "I haven't done much since the war."

"It was not so long as you might think. You forget that I am older than I appear," Madelaine said pointedly.

"True. You do not change," said Sherman, the statement almost an accusation.

Anamaria returned with a taper to light the lamps; soon the room was ruddy with the soft light from them. For the next few hours, as they sat first in the withdrawing room and then in the dining room, Sherman held forth, for Professor Leonetto's benefit, on the subject of American politics, American expansion, American scenery, and American cooking. "No criticism intended, Madame," he interjected to Madelaine. "That is not to say that this fare is not delicious," he added quickly to Madelaine, "but for me, the savor is lacking. It is more sophisticated, no doubt, and the result of long traditions of cooking, but I am a plain man, and I prefer simple, American fare. This stuffed veal breast is wonderful, but my tongue is more set for a stew than this. I'm afraid that most of this is wasted on me. Not that this isn't superb, but my wants are far simpler. Plain food for a plain man. My wife, now, she might be more appreciative than I am."

Madelaine wondered what sort of fool would think Sherman a plain man; he was easily one of the most complex men she had ever met. She did not challenge this assertion, but said, "The foods of home have one advantage that no other can best, as I am sure your wife would agree. When it comes to nourishment, there is no spice so savory as love."

Sherman gave her a sharp look, the first indication of hope in his eyes. "Very true, Madame. Very true."

At ten, Professor Leonetto and Sherman broke out their cigars, and Madelaine ordered that port be served to them. She did not leave the dining room, though custom required she leave the men to themselves, so that they would be at liberty discussing matters of interest to men. Considering the variety of subjects Sherman had already addressed, Madelaine could not imagine what else might be said that would be unfit for her ears.

"Supper in the English fashion," approved the professor as he lit his cigar. "With port at the finish."

Madelaine said nothing to him. She was growing weary of his constant attempts to wring more information from Sherman, and his obvious self-serving intentions. She should have warned him Sherman would not dance to that tune. She wished the evening were over and these two retired to their rooms so that she might send the servants to bed and then be free to visit Tecumseh before he began to dream.

"But the food here is better than the English, or so I am told," Sherman said, trying to make amends for his earlier pronouncements. "I certainly have dined well since I came to Europe. Not that I am one to dwell over my dinner."

"The English are the worst cooks in the world," Professor Leonetto declared roundly. "But they are very capable sailors and fine weavers and they make excellent sweets. It is the cold that makes them like sweets."

Sherman nodded. "I'll remember that, for when I am there," he said, and blew out a long stream of smoke. "Though I haven't much of a taste for sweets. I prefer a richer savor to my foods; sweetness must have taste, or one might as well eat sugar." He looked directly at Madelaine.

Another hour passed in a discussion of the importance of railroads in warfare, and the improvement in rifles and heavier guns, Sherman doing most of the talking, making rapid gestures with his cigar to emphasize a point or to draw a map in the air. His speech was fast and crackling with ideas; he avoided mentioning politics as much as possible, claiming that since his father-in-law's death, he had not kept up with "the shenanigans in Washington at all. Though with my wife writing a book about her father, it's probably just as well I'm away at present."

Professor Leonetto tried in vain to get Sherman to criticize Grant's presidency, or to indicate his own plans in regard to high office, but could not shake him from his support of his friend, and his assertion that he had no such ambitions. "John and Philemon are enough politicians for one family. They enjoy it; I do not. I want no part of that life." And then, at last, Sherman stubbed out his third cigar and rose. "Well, it has been a delightful evening, and I must thank you before I retire. You are a young fellow, Leonetto, but I am coming on fifty-two, and after a day of traveling, I need my rest. These bones are getting old. You will have to excuse me or prepare to listen to my snores." Nothing about him suggested fatigue; he looked prepared to continue holding forth for hours.

But Leonetto did not question this. "Of course, General. I should have realized. But the time got away from me; this has been so fascinating I was not paying attention to the hour," he said promptly as he, too, got to his feet and shook hands with Sherman. "It has been a very pleasant evening. And most enlightening. Most enlightening."

"Do you think so?" said Sherman, his tone implying that he thought otherwise. "Well, you will have tomorrow and the day after to learn more, if you like. Though I can't imagine what you haven't asked me already, or what other answers I could give you than what I have done." He stretched, his back arching with the effort. "Which room did you say was mine?" he asked, looking at Madelaine.

"I have given you the one with the view of the lake, over the withdrawing room. Andrea will lead you up," she said, and rang for her butler, noticing that he concealed a yawn as he came through the door.

"That's good of you, Madelaine," said Sherman, apparently unaware of the sudden scrutiny of Professor Leonetto. "I will wish you goodnight."

"And I will do the same," said the professor, a speculative glimmer in his eyes at this unexpected familiarity.

Madelaine waited until Anamaria had cleared the table, and then went up to her own room, which was located in the same wing as Sherman's. She knew she was delaying the privacy with Sherman she so desired, but she did not challenge her own reserve. She felt apprehension as well as excitement as she climbed the stairs, for she was aware of Sherman's ambivalence, the same undercurrent of conflict that he had experienced from the start of their affair. As she changed out of her burgundy velvet dinner dress and into a silken, ruffled peignoir, she wished she could see herself in the mirror, to take stock of her appearance before venturing down the corridor to the large room that overlooked the lake. She let down the elaborate chignon and her coffee-colored hair tumbled. Taking her brush she worked at it impatiently, not willing to take the time for her usual one hundred strokes, fearing now that if she waited much longer she would lose her nerve. "Ridiculous," she said aloud as she put her brush down, made a loose knot of her tresses at the back of her neck, retrieved a vial from her jewel case, got to her feet and stepped out into the deserted hallway, confident that her servants were abed and Professor Leonetto was in a room at the far end of the villa. When she reached the door, she tapped lightly, then, without waiting for an invitation, she opened the door and stepped into the room.

The fire in the grate crackled merrily, the lamps were lit and turned down to a soft glow, the bed was turned back and the curtains tied back with satin sashes, but of Sherman there was no sign.

Madelaine stood still for an instant, trying to think what had happened to him—was he bathing in the adjoining room, or had he taken a turn about the villa?—when the door-latch was swung roughly out of her hand as Sherman pushed it closed.

"Walked right into my ambush," he declared triumphantly as he pulled her into his arms and kissed her enthusiastically, straining her close to him for some little time as his arms reacquainted themselves with the shape and weight of her. Then his hold eased and he straightened up so that he could look down into her face, and said the one thing she wanted most to hear: "God Almighty, I have missed you, Madelaine." His voice was a caress. "There have been nights when I have lain awake and tried to recall everything between us. When it seemed my veins would boil for want of you. When I have thought that my heart would break free of my body and fly off in search of you." He released her and tugged at the tie of his dark-blue velvet robe.

"I have missed you too, Tecumseh." She reached out to touch his chest; the crisp hair there was now almost totally white.

"And look at you," he went on, taking her face in his hands and staring down at her as if to photograph her. "The same radiant girl I met, all those years ago, in San Francisco. These days, I remember your house on Franklin Street better than my own on Rincon Hill."

"I am not quite the same," she protested, seeing the frown line between his brows deepen.

"Perhaps not," he conceded. "But it hasn't touched your face."

"It touches my soul," she said seriously.

He nodded, his eyes never leaving hers. "I know. I can see it. I can feel it, as well."

"Does that trouble you?" she asked, watching his belt drop to the floor. "Tell me: does it?"

"It shouldn't," he admitted. "And your youth should not bother me, but it does. And I am a fool for it."

At last he had said it. She cocked her head to the side and looked at him. "Why? Why does it bother you?"

He shrugged and drew her close against him. "It's nothing. Megrims, or nerves, probably." His smile was sudden and fierce. "Nothing to concern us now."

She let herself warm to him, but a reservation niggled at the back of her mind, and she could not wholly silence it as she opened his lips with her own, and felt his probing tongue on hers. It was the same quest he had pursued with her from the first, and for once she was truly glad of it.

When he drew back, he was breathless. "I haven't much nitre paper with me," he said, making an effort to fill his lungs with new air. His features showed more embarrassment than fear. "I didn't want this to happen, not now."

"I have something for that," she said, and drew a vial from the pocket of her peignoir. "I assumed you might want this, whether you needed it or not." She handed it to him, a tentative gesture that showed her doubts as much as her angled brows.

"Yes." He took it, scowling at it. "I don't know. I have thought all my life that there should be a way not to endure this... intrusion." He moved back with an apologetic hitch to his shoulders. "It will go better for us if I have a little of this first." He reached for the ewer on his night stand and filled the glass set beside it. "Five drops, do I remember correctly?"

"Five or six," she said. "When you have an attack, then take half the vial, directly." She studied him as he drank the water. "I have a full supply for you, for when you leave. You may take it with you."

"What admirable foresight." He set the glass aside. "No doubt I should be grateful and thank you for this, but right now, all I want to do is—"

"Curse?" she suggested. "Declaim? Protest?"

This time his smile was rueful. "Something like that. How can you endure such a surly fellow as I am? But thank God fasting you do." He opened his arms to her, his robe falling open. "Come here, girl."

She went into his arms, and this time it felt that she was at last home after a long voyage. His flesh, until then oddly unfamiliar, warmed to her, and she found the places where they balanced against one another—he, tall and lean and angular, more elbows and shoulders than deep chest—she, small and voluptuous, all curves and rounded muscles—their separate textures of clothes and skin and senses and soul complimenting one another.

"What is this spell you have over me?" he asked her, his long fingers busy with loosening her hair from its casual knot.

"No spell. It is the bond between us. I wish you would believe it exists. It works as much on me as on you. For as long as I am alive, I will have the bond with you." She smiled up at him and waited to see what he would do. There were many desires within him, all in conflict, and she did not want to trigger any more disputes between them.

He was combing her hair with his hand, letting the dark strands slide along his palm. "I always forget how the light plays yellow on your hair."

She did not know why she shivered when he said that, but covered it by saying, "You may be comfortable here, but the bed is warmer."

He stared down at her. "You're never cold." He looked truly shocked. "In the worst San Francisco fog, you did not get cold."

"Perhaps, but now I would like to be comfortable." She slid her arms around him under his robe. "We would both enjoy it more."

"So we might," he said in sudden compliance. "Though I'd like to leave the lamps burning. I want to see you."

"Do you?" This surprised her; she found it disquieting. "Why?"

"Humor me, my love. Unless the light will bother you?" He saw her shake her head; satisfied, he went to the side of the bed, flung back the covers and sat down, watching her as she came to stand in front of him. "I have all my memories. How am I going to know if they are right if I don't see you?" He looked at her peignoir, and asked in sudden wistfulness, "Will you let me take that infernal thing off you?" His face softened again, and there was something very like grief in his steel-colored eyes. "I don't mean it isn't lovely, all soft and promising to the touch"—his hands trailed down the elaborate ruffles—"and enough to drive any sane man mad, but what I long for is you."

The passion in his voice was more determined than she had anticipated, and she was reassured by it. "If it would please you," she said quietly.

He had undone the first six buttons when he stopped and looked around as if he feared interruption. "Leonetto isn't going to know about this, is he? Won't there be talk?"

"Not if we both say nothing, and I was not planning on boasting," she answered. "And before you ask, the servants are gone to bed. They would not gossip in any case." Saint-Germain, she knew, would not tolerate it. She put her hand on his shoulder. "I am not a novice at this, Tecumseh. And I learned from a master."

"So you keep telling me," he said, resuming his efforts with the buttons. "Why, in the name of all that's holy, does this have so many of these damned things?"

"Fashion," she answered at once. "And to prolong the suspense."

"Fine state of affairs," he muttered as he at last got the final button free. He tugged at the sleeves of the peignoir and tossed it aside as he pulled her into his arms. "This is better."

"What about your robe?" she asked, half teasing as she lay across his chest. It was now her turn to feel breathless.

He half-rose and wrestled his way out of the thing, wadding it hastily into a ball and flinging it across the room. "There. Gone." He stretched out on his back, dragging her with him, atop him. His mouth was unexpectedly gentle on hers, but persistent, and his hands began to make unhurried sallies over her back, down her flanks. He was willing to take his time. "It has been so long, I want to know all of you. I don't..." his words were lost in another long, searching kiss.

Some time later she broke away from his kisses, but only to excite him more fully, her lips and tongue drawing more pleasure from him than he had ever permitted before. As she widened her explorations, he propped himself against the pillows and reveled in all she did, half-watching her, half-lost in the flood of voluptuousness, his lower lip caught between his teeth so that he would not cry out. When she slowly straddled him, he uttered a long, shivering sigh, then drew her down far enough to nuzzle and caress her breasts with his hands and lips as he let her set the pace for them both, to be transfixed with ecstatic spasms, head flung back, as her mouth brushed his throat.

When he came to himself again, she was lying beside him, her leg over his, her head on his shoulder, her eyes half-closed. "I can never remember how... enormous the feelings are." He spoke softly, more to himself than to her, and more in wonder than disappointment.

"They are what you are capable of—" she whispered. "I cannot summon what is not within you."

302

"What I don't understand is how you find it," he confessed, more affection in his demeanor than she could recall encountering. "What made you look in the first place?"

"You did," she said seriously, her eyes fully open now, and set on his. "When we first met, you reached out to me, for me. I don't know any other way to explain it to you."

He rolled onto his side, toward her, then stared over her shoulder toward the dying fire; when he spoke his voice was soft and abstracted. "I'll believe you, for your sake, but..." He ran his hand along her side, then drew the covers up higher. "I feel the chill these days. I didn't used to, that I can remember."

"It's cozy, all wrapped up together," she said, snuggling nearer to him.

"And not a cannon or rifle being fired," he marveled. "For two years after the end of the war, I'd wake up in the middle of the night, thinking I had heard guns somewhere. It doesn't happen very often any more. I won't disturb you, I promise." He kissed her brow. "It's hard to imagine you went through all that. You look too young to have been there."

She felt a pang of loneliness somewhere deep within. "And I was like this in San Francisco, and in Egypt, when you were a child in Ohio, learning to read. And I was as I am now when your parents were children." She touched his face, letting her hand rest against his short beard. "And I will be like this a century from now, if I escape the True Death."

"Breaking the spine or burning or destroying the nervous system. That's how it happens, isn't that what you told me?" he said lightly.

"Embalming will probably do it as well, or so Saint-Germain thinks," she replied.

He was silent for a short while. "I'm going to Egypt, you know."

"It is a fascinating place," she said neutrally.

"So you have told me. I will see for myself now." He rolled onto his back once more, and made sure she was lying as near to him as possible. "What are you doing with that bore, Leonetto?" He directed his distracted gaze up at the ceiling.

"He came to me, with questions about you and Grant, among others. He knew of my books." His crisp chest hair pressed into her cheek, oddly reassuring. She moved to kiss the place on his neck where a little blood still remained. "At least he brought you to me."

"Fellow's impossible—worse than a reporter. All the way here: General Sherman this and General Sherman that." He made his voice a reasonable imitation of Leonetto's, accent and all. "Tell me, General Sherman, do you think you'll have any influence over foreign affairs if President Grant asks you to be his vice-president?" He laughed once, harshly. "I told him Sam Grant has better sense than that."

Madelaine shifted her weight so that they were both more comfortable. "He is dreadful."

"King Victor Emmanuel had better think twice if he intends to rely on Leonetto and his ilk for intelligence." He turned his head toward her and the brusqueness left his voice. "I never thought I would see you again."

"Don't tell me you are surprised? I hoped we had settled that." She could feel him begin to settle toward sleep, and she wondered if this badinage were a ploy he wanted to use to keep awake.

"If I could find you in the middle of war's hell, I shouldn't wonder at finding you in Italy." He kissed her just above the bridge of her nose. "Though you are not Italian."

"But my name: think of that, Tecumseh," she protested, squirming upward so she could see his eyes more readily. "You know enough about French to cypher it out."

"Madelaine?" he teased affectionately.

"De Montalia," she corrected him.

"Means something like 'of the Italian mountain', as I recall. And if it were more French, it would end in an 'e' not an 'a'. Are we going to sleep the whole night together?"

"If you like. Anamaria will say nothing." She felt the tension in his shoulders ease. "We have tomorrow night, as well," she reminded him.

He studied her face in silence. "How is it you do not age?" And before she could answer, he said, "I know what you have told me about those of your blood. Does that mean when I die, I will be restored to youth as well as life?"

She shook her head. "No. You will keep the appearance you have at the end of your life. And we do age, but very slowly. In another century, I will probably look all of twenty-five."

"Then I had better hurry up and 'shuffle off this mortal coil' before I get any grayer." He chuckled, but there was sadness and apprehension mixed with his amusement. "Won't do to be an old man addling about, looking for inviting necks."

"How can you say that?" she demanded of him. "When you have told me you have no wish to be a vampire."

"Unless someone cuts off my head, burns my corpse, or drives a stake through my spine, I will be, for I cannot see any of my family doing those things, no matter how I ask. They think me odd enough as it is. And those who would like to do such things to me living will not be allowed to do it in death. So I had best resign myself to my fate." He chuckled once. "Of course, they will embalm me, and if your information is right, that will be the end of that. No more avoiding death."

"You speak as if death is the enemy," said Madelaine with some apprehension.

"Well, isn't it? How can it not be?" he asked, startled into greater wakefulness.

"Suffering is the enemy, not death," she said quietly, and with such seriousness that he stared at her intently. "Death comes to all of us in time, even those of my blood. It is no more an enemy than birth is. But suffering, that is another matter." She tried to subdue the memories which came over her, knowing that in this instance his were far worse; she clung to him.

"That's how you do it," he said to her, his voice filled with amazement. "You are not frightened out of love by death." He pressed her head onto his shoulder, his long fingers in her hair, his other big hand spread over her shoulder. "Where do you get the courage? To love in the face of death?"

She considered her answer, listening to his heart beat. "Because if there were no love, the suffering would be unendurable."

His arms tightened around her and held her as he faded into sleep.

RHO, LOMBARDIA, 15 MARCH, 1872

I will present my last lecture in five weeks, and then I will turn my attention to leaving Lombardia ... At least the roads between here and France are said to be in good repair, and the railroad can carry most of my things the greater part of the way, saving time and money.

I have another telegram from Professor Leonetto, once again proclaiming Tecumseh's travels a great triumph for him. He has informed me that he is planning to meet with "The Great General" in Switzerland, and has asked if I will accompany him ... I have not yet made up my mind, for by the summer I will return to Montalia for a short while

as I conclude plans for travel into Syria. I will have to learn when Te-
cumseh plans to be at Bern, and then decide.

And I am not sure it would be wise to see Tecumseh just now. Our
time together at Lake Como was more fulfilling than anything I might
have hoped for. Should I be satisfied with that, and not attempt to attain
the same intimacy with him again? Or is it possible I might have more
with him than we have had until now? ... And how do I decide? ...

MADELAINE SIGHED AS SHE LOOKED AROUND the morning parlor
of the villa, now seeming strange to her, with her belongings packed
away in chests and trunks and crates. She had come to like the place and
wondered again if she had been mistaken in not purchasing it, for a later
time. She chided herself for her hesitation, recalling that she had once
longed for a villa somewhere along the Strada in Chianti in Tuscany,
and had not yet acquired one. She sighed again as she touched the four
remaining chests of her native earth.

"The wagons are coming, Madama," said Eugenio, who had seen to
most of the packing. He was proud of this accomplishment and preened
as he looked at the crates. "All is in readiness."

"Fine," she said distantly. "Your organization has been excellent.
With nine workmen on the job, they will be loaded quickly, thanks to
you. I will be away from here by mid-afternoon, I trust."

"I should think so, and at the train station by evening, to catch the
west-bound to Torino," said Eugenio. He was about to leave when he
reached into his coat and held out an envelope. "Oh, here is a letter for
you brought from town." He handed it to her. "If you want to stop to
send an answer when we leave?" He looked around the room again,
taking stock of what was there. "Have you checked all the rooms thoroughly?"

"And the attic, and the cellar," said Madelaine, nodding to show her
appreciation for his concern. "Everything has been packed. If anything
is left behind, it will not be important."

"A diamond is a small thing, and easily left behind," said Eugenio.

"Not by me," Madelaine countered, though she was not confident it
was so; she had left so many things behind over the last hundred forty-
odd years.

"Very well, Madama," said Eugenio, and left her alone with the letter.

It was from Tecumseh, and the tone was tersely affectionate, asking if she would meet him in Bern, but privately, without "that fool Leonetto around." He warned her he would not have long, and would be permitted little privacy, but that he wanted to see her again, before both he and she left Europe.

She held the note for some time, her eyes fixed on a distant place, her mind feeling supremely blank. At last she came back to herself and called for Eugenio once more.

'What is it, Madama?" he asked, out of breath from his efforts.

"I have a request. It is a major one, but I will have to depend on your help here." She looked around the room. "Would you be willing to accompany these crates and cases to Montalia?"

"You mean, to ride the train with them and see them carried to your estate in France?" He looked shocked, which did not surprise her.

"I would pay you well for it," she said, anxious to have her plans in motion now that her mind was made up. "And I could arrange for someone to accompany you as well." She tried to smile at him. "I realize it is an imposition, and the notice is much too short, but if you cannot do this, I will not be able to go into Switzerland on my way home, and that would be a great disappointment to me." She lowered her head, not quite looking at Sherman's letter.

"All right," said Eugenio, his eyes lighting with sudden determination. "I will notify my family at once." He was curious enough about this request to look directly at Madelaine for a short while. "Nothing bad in the letter?" Then he shrugged and started away from her. He was almost to the door when he added, "My family will need money while I am gone. You will take care of that?"

"At once," said Madelaine, her lethargy completely gone. "I will issue a draught on my bank to be paid to your father."

Eugenio grinned merrily, warming to the spirit of the occasion. "Excellent. He will take my family into his house while I am gone, and my brother will care for my house." He gave a quick grin. "I do not know why you have done this, Madama, but I am grateful that you have asked this of me. I have not been to France before."

"You will go there now," said Madelaine, her face serious. "And if you wish a companion, he will go there, as well."

"My cousin Mercurio would enjoy the adventure, and he is unmarried, so he can leave without much trouble. I will fetch him directly." He bowed slightly and hurried from the room.

Madelaine watched him go, trying to convince herself to call him back, to change her mind again and stay with her plans as she had arranged them already. She heard a door slam closed. As if that were a signal, she set about preparing her new plans. There were a number of arrangements she would have to change in order to do as Sherman asked. These changes would delay her departure by one day, she realized, but that could not be helped. She hoped that she would have no difficulty in reaching Bern in the next two weeks. Passage was usually reserved well in advance, and she would be getting it on short notice. But it was not in her to refuse the invitation, she realized; Sherman only sent for her when he was in need of her.

By the time Eugenio returned with his cousin and two hastily packed bags, most of the crates and trunks and cases were loaded on wagons for transport to the train station. He rushed into the dining room where Madelaine was finishing up her new arrangements. "Here is Mercurio," said Eugenio, bowing to present the newcomer. "This is Madama de Montalia."

Mercurio colored to his scalp, giving him the look of a sulky boy instead of a strikingly beautiful young man. He stared at her. "Good day, Madama," was all he was able to say.

"To you as well, Mercurio." She wondered if his shyness was so deeply established that he would not be able to speak with her. "I am grateful you are willing to do this for me, and with so little notice."

"It is a pleasure," he said with greater certainty.

"I hope so," Madelaine said.

BETWEEN CHAMBERY AND GENEVA, 3 MAY, 1872

We are now going different ways, my belongings and I. Save for a single chest of my native earth, everything but clothing is now on another train, bound for Grenoble and then down to the Rhone. Eugenio and Mercurio are with the cases and crates and will supervise their transportation the rest of the way to Montalia. I, on the other hand, will continue on to Bern to meet Tecumseh. I will take a suite and wait for him to come ... Have I been wise or foolish to agree to this?

"I'M GOING TO HAVE TO LEAVE SHORTLY. Byers is expecting me for some grand flummery or other," Sherman said as he strode into Madelaine's suite at the small but splendid Imperial Hotel. He stopped, straight and arresting, his duster concealing his formal wear beneath. His beard was freshly trimmed and his grooming was immaculate. He held out his hands for hers, and carried them to his lips, looking down into her eyes as if he wanted to lose himself in them. "Madelaine."

"Good evening to you, as well, Tecumseh," she said quietly. She moved back from the door, drawing him with her, as much to give herself the illusion that this meeting was not hurried as to get him away from any potential eavesdroppers. The room was suffused with the pale glow of afternoon, long purple shadows interspersed with glowing light from the tall windows. In another hour it would be dusk.

"I apologize for arriving so late. I spent the afternoon with some cadets. They offered me very flattering attention." He released her hands but only to remove his hat and shrug out of his duster, both of which he dropped on a chair without ceremony. "I had no idea they would take up so much time." He came back to her side. "But I am sorry I have been delayed. I wanted more time with you."

She waved his remarks aside, and said nothing about the worry that had seized her while the three hours dragged on. At least her afternoon dress of silk and lace was still appropriate to the hour. She indicated the chaise near the window. "Would you like to sit down?"

"I would like to lie down, with you in my arms, for the rest of the evening and all through the night," he said as he sank onto the chaise, his hand out to her in wistful supplication. "But, I fear—" He indicated his boiled shirt and brocade waistcoat.

"Yes. Ambassador Byers has claim on you. No royalty tonight, though, judging by your white tie. You must be the guest of honor. So there are those who will notice if you do not appear promptly." She could not bring herself to ask how long he could stay. Instead she sat on the opposite side of the chaise so she could more easily face him. "Has it been a good trip, Tecumseh? Has Europe been what you hoped for?"

"It has been fascinating," he admitted at once, grateful that she did not upbraid him for the brevity of his stay. "And most everywhere the people have been enthusiastic and friendly, though Americans abroad have been an embarrassment to me. So many of them observe nothing. They are here to have things pointed out to them and discover nothing on their own. They have no sense of the history around them, and no desire to know of it. I find out all I can about a place." Then he stopped abruptly. "You do not want to hear this."

She took his hand in hers. "I want to know what has happened to you. Truly."

He sighed, and managed a slight smile. "The Sultan charged me six hundred dollars for the banquet and cruise on his yacht on the Black Sea. I have had a chance to use those scythes I have seen in the fields." Again he stopped abruptly. "And I have longed to have you with me every mile of the way. From the Pyramids to Russia to Berlin, I thought of you."

"And I of you," she said, knowing this was the truth.

He touched her face with his free hand. "When I saw the Pyramids, it was as if you spoke to me again. When I saw the treasures of the Turks, I thought of all you seek to discover about vanished peoples. When I saw the magnificence of Russia, I wanted you to help me encompass it. You have haunted all my travels." He bent forward and kissed her, a long, lingering kiss that seemed to hold them suspended in time; it gathered intensity as he wrapped her in his embrace and felt her hands on the back of his neck. "If only there were some way you could be with me." He drew back. "Not just here, not as a hidden lover, but at my side." Before she had a chance to answer, he put his fingers to her lips. "Oh, I know. It would be imprudent, even in Europe, where such things are less remarkable. But I cannot, for it would shame my wife and distress my family. It would be difficult for me and dangerous for you. But I wish it were possible. That's all."

She moved his hand aside. "And I," she agreed softly.

"Do you?" There was urgency in his question now, and an innocent desire that made her heart ache. "I have thought from time to time that I sensed something of it, but always—"

"Always you dared not trust the feeling," she finished for him. She rested her forehead on his shoulder so she would not have to see the longing in his eyes. "You may trust it, Tecumseh. My word on it."

"As in your bond?" he asked, using his hand to turn her face up to him again. "I will try. I promise I will try." His kiss this time was deep and desperate, and he held her as if she were a floating spar and he a shipwrecked sailor. When he drew back, he was as shaken as she. "Oh, God, Madelaine. If I could draw all your sweetness into me..."

"It is yours, if you want it," she said, holding very still in the circle of his arms.

"How?" he demanded, his voice low but his eyes bright as sabers. His hands tightened on her back. "Don't toy with me, Madelaine. I cannot bear it, not from you."

"I am not toying with you. If you are certain you want to fulfill the bond with me, there is a way. You may do it without risk, for you are already changed enough to be one of my blood when you die." She saw the doubt in his face and she went on quickly, hoping he would finally believe her. "If you taste my blood, as I have tasted yours, then my bond will become wholly yours as well."

"Taste your blood?" he repeated. "You mean bite you?"

"You have not objected when you have been ... bitten," she countered. "You have felt joy in it."

He shook his head. "That was different. You are—"

"A foreign woman, allowed to have her whims? A vampire?" she challenged, all the while wanting to hold him.

"No. Or yes. Yet you are more than that, so much more. You are a woman who makes music when she moves, who gives me exultation with a look. You are the woman who has brought me beauty when there was nothing but hideousness and barbarity. You are the woman who has taken my blackest despair and restored me to hope. You are the woman who makes my sleep tolerable when I dream of war's cruelty. You are my haven in a mad world. And you are a temptation that archangels could not deny." He shook his head. "But I am married and the public watches everything I do. I will not disgrace my family's trust in me."

"Then take my blood. At least you will have the consolation of our bond, as I have." She reached out to him. "I welcome it, Tecumseh. You would honor me to taste my blood."

He mumbled his answer. "It is not fitting for an officer of the United States Army to ... bite women."

"Then I will cut myself," she offered at once. "You need only taste what I provide." As she said this, she had a sudden, poignant memory of the night in the coach when Saint-Germain had at last capitulated to her desire for his blood. How ecstatic she had been.

"Lord, woman, that's worse," he burst out and tried to rise, his face flushing to match his beard. "I don't want you to bleed for me. There's been more than enough of that already."

She held onto his hands, realizing that the amount of effort she used would not hold him if he wanted to be free of her. "That is how it is done; it is not painful or unpleasant." she said firmly.

He sat back down, looking somewhat awkward from his own protestation. "Then I will have to forego it, my love." He looked squarely at her, his eyes haunted with the past. "I've seen too much blood to want to see more, for any reason. Especially yours."

"But this is not hurtful, or harmful. It will not give me any pain, only joy. You will know the rapture I know when we lie together," she said, her attention wholly on him. Her next words were gentle. "Let it be my farewell gift to you, so that we will never be wholly parted."

"Farewell?" he asked blankly.

She shook her head once. "Don't do this, please."

It took him a short while to answer. "I ... Madelaine ..."

Had she been able to weep she would have done it now; as it was, her throat tightened, making it difficult for her to speak. "That is why we are here, isn't it? You asked me to meet you one last time. So that we can say good-bye?" She had felt this since she had read his letter, but speaking it gave her a sense of finality that was new to her, and hurtful. "Tecumseh?"

His breathing was becoming labored; he reached into his pocket and took out the vial she had given him at Lake Como. "I'm sorry to ask, but may I have some water?"

She rose at once and went to her bedroom to fetch the ewer and glass. "Here," she said, putting them on a side-table. "Take what you need."

Without saying anything he put several drops of the liquid in the glass, then filled it with water and drank it down. As he set the glass aside, he remarked, "I cannot tell you how grateful I am for that tincture of yours. It has saved me as many times as my infantry has." He tried to make light of this, but he could not conceal the pain in his eyes as he turned to her.

Madelaine rose and went into his arms, treasuring the strength in him, and the yearning; they clung together in silence for more than three minutes, each second passing too quickly, the whole seeming more than a day. With an effort of will she released him at last. "Ambassador Byers will wonder what has become of you," she said.

"So he will." He nodded, and tried again to make it right between them before he left. "If I could endure the blood, if I were certain it would not give you any hurt to take it, I would like to have the bond completed, but—" As he moved back from her, to make their separating bearable, he said, "So. More than twenty years of love wasted."

She watched him pick up his hat and duster. "Was it wasted, Tecumseh?" she asked.

"Well, it is surely incomplete, according to you. What else can you call it?" There was a shine in his steel-colored eyes that he strove to hide.

"But do you think it was wasted?" she persisted, the hurt of his leaving holding her to the spot.

He paused in the door, one hand on the latch, and he met her eyes, knowing she would see the tears, and the love. "No, Madelaine. It wasn't."

MONTALIA, 29 SEPTEMBER, 1872

Word has come at last in regard to the Syrian ruins, a two-day journey from Aleppo. I will be given permission to excavate them beginning in March. After that unpromising beginning we have been given all the access I requested at the first... I must make my preparations at once so that as soon as the worst of winter is over, I and those in my party can begin our work, before the Syrians can change their minds. I will send out inquiries first thing tomorrow, to see who among the antiquarians wishes to join me... If we arrive in Athens in December we will be able to have our supplies ready for our trek to the site... And regarding preparations, I must also begin preparations for creating another identity for myself since, when I return, I must be my own cousin or niece or some such relation...

Tecumseh should have arrived home by now, back in Saint Louis, I must assume. In spite of the distance, I can still sense his anguish from time to time, as I will do no matter where he goes, and I wish I had some means to solace him... but he refused the bond, and so there is nothing I can do that will end the recriminations he visits upon himself. If he had taken the bond for his own, he would not have to castigate himself for leaving me, because he would know in his blood that he has not left me, nor ever could...

Mercurio has agreed to remain at Montalia, in charge of the household until I return. I have provided a generous payment for this service... If I must return to my native earth, as surely I must, it will be the more enjoyable for having a beautiful young man here, who is willing to banish the world in his dreams, although, sadly, only in his dreams...

Why is it that knowing love is so terrifying to so many? I have asked Saint-Germain and he has little to tell me beyond what I know—that it is. And those who can accept it may not accept it for long...

313

ATHENS, 14 JANUARY, 1873

I have six antiquarians who have agreed to join me on this expedition. Two are German, one is a Scot, two are Dutch, and one is Belgian. Three of them are already experienced in such explorations; the other three are novices, and that will mean taking time to be certain they are properly instructed in cataloguing ... I have also hired a guide named Mustapha, who has done such work before, and seems to have some understanding of its importance. He has offered to supply me with the necessary crews I will need for the work. We will depart in a month, if all goes well.

ALEPPO, SYRIA, 18 JUNE, 1873

We have come to this city for more supplies, and to send back our findings. I think Professor van der Groot will be returning to Holland shortly; the heat of this place has proven to be more than he can endure, and so he has, quite sensibly, elected to leave while he has a semblance of health left. It will be a loss to the expedition, for he has proven to be the most apt and careful member of the expedition, meticulous to a fault and determined to preserve the integrity of the work we do ... He has agreed to carry some papers to Amsterdam for me: more of my recollections of the American Civil War, at least part of them. They will be published to accompany my volumes on the Indians, and will, I hope, impart some understanding of the American character in all its forms ...

Why this desolate place should cause me to recall those terrible years, I cannot say, but since I have been on this expedition, I have found my thoughts casting back to the Choctaw Nation, and my trek through the Confederate states. And of course, I have been filled with memories of Tecumseh. I cannot think of any part of my journey there that he does not intrude. For me, he and America are completely interwoven. I cannot banish him from my thoughts; I do not wish to ...

If only I could discover someone who would receive me knowingly, as he did, and not be limited by dreams ...

CAIRO, EGYPT, 28 OCTOBER, 1873

A new antiquarian has approached me to join our expedition. The fellow is called Paul Danner, and is one of those endlessly curious Englishmen, hardly more than twenty-two or -three. He has some education, at Exeter College at Oxford, and has done a little work in Egypt. His enthusiasm is tempered with a kind of prudence that makes for good work ... As we need someone to take the place of Professor van der Groot, I have given my provisional approval ...

It is alarming to hear the news from France. I fear for my poor country.

DAMASCUS, SYRIA, 4 JULY, 1874

Today I have sent off another packet of manuscript pages on the American War to Amsterdam. The date of this may be fortuitous ... I think these will be the last of what I write on the subject, at least as myself. I may research my "ancestress" at some later time for more work on the subject, when I have gained more perspective on it ...

The expedition is going fairly well, and our work should conclude in another eighteen months. I have insisted on an accurate catalogue of everything we discover at the site, from bits of pots to the metal of spear-tips ... Of our discoveries thus far, the most interesting is a small statue of a goddess dedicated, it would appear, to horses, for she has a foal at each of her breasts. The piece is about ten inches high and of silver. At first it was so tarnished that it seemed little more than a lump of blackened metal ... I wish Saint-Germain were here, to give me some notion of its age and origin, for it is clearly not like the rest of the pieces we have found so far ...

I have made the attempt of visiting Paul Danner in his sleep and found him most receptive to the delights provided. I am pleased that one of these men on the expedition is willing to have such dreams. Only Bethune, the Scot, has shown any interest in his nighttime fancies until now, and he is worried about his soul if he has such nocturnal visions, certain that he is being tempted as the desert fathers were tempted, fifteen centuries ago ... If only Paul were willing to know

315

me and my love for what it is ... That may be too much to wish for, and certainly the joy he takes in his sleep is better than no contact at all ... And more than we have could prove dangerous, for the Syrians have strong views on vampires ...

I will return to the site next week, Mustapha acting as my guide again. He has proven quite reliable, and in spite of the fact that I am a foreigner, which is bad, and a woman, which is much worse, he has developed a grudging respect for me. He admitted not long ago that he did not suppose I was a serious scholar, but he is beginning to think that I might actually have some—albeit limited—capacity for learning.

EXPEDITION SITE, TWO DAYS FROM ALEPPO, SYRIA, 30 NOVEMBER, 1874

It seems we will not be allowed to remain here much longer. There have been objections raised by local officials, and I cannot find a way to persuade them that we do no harm ... I have no wish to put any of us in danger ...

It is unfortunate that I will have to give up Paul Danner along with this site. I was beginning to hope that he might come to a point where he could know my secret and not despise me for it. He has warmed to me in ways that were beginning to give me hope ... But I doubt I will have the opportunity for that now ... He is bound for studies in Spain, or so he says ...

In an ironic way, this will prove useful in my establishing my new identity back in France ... As I must leave Syria before I planned, I will be able to "disappear" and reemerge later, in my new identity. I have decided I will use one of my second names for this identity, as I have done before ... Much as I dislike the name Bertrande, I had better use it, as I used Roxanne the last time, and a few may remain who recall me from then ... So Bertrande it is, and I will make my way to Tunis slowly, so that I may emerge as my own cousin. I think cousin will do this time ...

ALEXANDRIA, EGYPT, 11 AUGUST, 1875

*... For the first time I have seen a copy of my work on the American
Civil War just arrived from Amsterdam. I am a bit apprehensive about
reading it, for fear of what it may stir in my memories... In time, I suppose I must, but for now, I will carry it with me, and look at it when my
circumstances are more certain than they are now. I doubt I could read
Tecumseh's name, even made distant by calling him General Sherman,
without feeling his absence as keenly as a thrust from a knife.*

*... I have had word from Montalia that Mercurio has married and is
willing to remain as caretaker of the estate... I wonder if he is still the
handsome young man I remember? And being a married man, what use
would he have for the dreams I can give? Tecumseh, knowing my love
for what it is, never stopped loving his wife...*

TUNIS, TUNISIA, 9 APRIL, 1876

*Bertrande is becoming established here, as the orphaned niece of Robert
de Montalia, and daughter of Etienne—I might as well use another family name—who has been left a large estate by her cousin, Madelaine.
Like her "late" cousin, Bertrande has a bent for antiquarian scholarship,
which is regarded as an odd turn for a wealthy young woman...*

*Luckily, there are Roman ruins I can explore in this area, and though
I am thought eccentric, no one has forbade me to do the work. Assuming
I encounter no opposition, I can fill my time quite pleasantly while I es-
tablish my new identity, as well as a few academic credentials... I begin
to hope that this transition will go well, and I will be able to return to
Montalia before too many years go by...*

MALTA, 24 DECEMBER, 1881

*A year-old letter has caught up with me, sent to "Madelaine's" publisher
in Amsterdam, from Tecumseh. It was sent on to me as her heir... He*

has read my war monographs, and wanted me to know how he views my account ... I saw his name and it was a jolt to me. I suppose some of the trouble is that I have not yet found a lover willing to have me as anything more than dreams ... Or do I miss him for more than that? There are times I miss the talk we shared as much as I miss the weight of his body and the life of his blood. I can feel his presence through my bond with him, and that may account for it, though I doubt it. He has a niche in my soul, and will always have it, no matter what the True Death may do. Or perhaps Saint-Germain is right in telling me again that I have a weakness for Americans?

He informs me, with a tone of tremendous disappointment, that his son Thomas is training to be a Jesuit. Given his intense dislike of religion, and all the hopes he had pinned on his son, this blow must strike him deeply. He mentions only that is wife is very pleased, and hopes that he—Tecumseh—will convert at last ... Tecumseh did his best to joke that he is going to be sixty-two in February, and I, he is certain, still look like a girl just out of school. That he should be troubled by this appearance with me, of all women ...

I have decided that this time next year I will return to Monbussy-sur-Marne, and make Bertrande mistress there. I am beginning to miss France once more ...

MONBUSSY-SUR-MARNE, 6 AUGUST, 1883

This place is in excellent repair, and the fields are doing well. I have every hope that I can remain here for a decade or so, and catch up on my reading, if nothing else: Maupassant and France and Flaubert to start, then Henry James, and a few of the other Americans, such as Mark Twain and Ambrose Bierce. And the new discoveries in science, especially this light bulb ...

MONBUSSY-SUR-MARNE, 19 NOVEMBER, 1886

It was a great shock seeing Paul Danner again. He is looking quite distinguished now, at the middle of his thirties, his hair turning silver at the

*temples and the lines of his face settling in, giving him the air of a man
who has gained some understanding and possibly some insight as well.
Had I thought he would attend the salon, I would not have gone to Paris
for it. Occasions of this kind are often awkward or worse… He told me I
am prettier than my cousin was, and said he was sad to learn of her death
while she was still so young… I felt my interest awaken in him again…*

PAUL DANNER DREW IN HIS CARRIAGE, letting Madelaine alight
at the entrance gates to her own courtyard at Monbussy-sur-Marne. "It
was a pleasure to have your company today, Mademoiselle Bertrande."

Madelaine looked up at him. "Are you not going to come inside?"

He looked around, his expression awkward. "I would not like to
cause you any embarrassment."

"Are you worried that my reputation in the neighborhood would be
damaged for my entertaining you?" Madelaine asked, her violet eyes
lighting with amusement. "There is a butler, a housekeeper, two cooks,
and three chambermaids to chaperon us. And I think that most of the
staff would be heartily relieved if I had a man visit me. I fear they think
me past praying for." She pulled her fur coat more closely around her,
glad that she no longer had to maneuver the tremendous bell skirts of
twenty years ago. The bustle occasionally made sitting uncomfortable,
but was nowhere near as difficult an encumbrance as the multi-tiered
hoops had been. She smiled at Paul, enjoying their flirtation.

"It is a very tempting offer," he said, with a glance at the lowering sky.
There had been a sprinkle of rain earlier but now the clouds had massed
and darkened and their threat was more troubling.

"And consider the hour, and the weather." Madelaine regarded him
with amusement. "You will not get very far before either nightfall or a
downpour. If you come in you will have a good meal, a bottle of wine,
a comfortable bed for the night, and your horses rested and fed for your
journey tomorrow. Or you can hope to reach an inn before you are
soaked." She started through the open gates, letting him make up his
mind to follow her.

"I would not want to take advantage of your youthful generosity,"
said Paul, his expression showing clearly that he wanted very much to
accept her offer.

"It is merely the hospitality I would expect were I in England," said
Madelaine over her shoulder.

Paul faltered. "I suppose, with your staff on hand, it would not be too improper," he said at last.

"Bring your carriage around to the side. My coachman will take your team in hand and see they are watered and fed and bedded down for the night in box stalls." She knew this was a handsomer gesture than any he could expect at an inn on his way back to Paris. "And you could use the evening to examine my ... cousin's library."

This last temptation was more than Paul could resist. He tipped his hat, saying, "If you are certain that I will not betray your kindness with compromise, I will do it." With that he whipped up his team and went around the curve of the stone walls.

Madelaine went into her hall, calling out to her butler as she did, "Pierre, Monsieur Danner will be my guest this evening. See that he has a room prepared, and tell the cooks to start a supper for him." She stripped off her gloves and cast them aside, then draped her coat over the back of a sixteenth-century chair as she went on into the main withdrawing room, which was furnished in more modern style, with overstuffed chairs in dark brown plush and a Turkish carpet.

"Mademoiselle Bertrande?" said Pierre, coming into the withdrawing room from the morning salon beyond.

"Good evening, Pierre," said Madelaine, giving her butler a quick glance. "I trust there will be no gossip about this visitor. Given the hour and the weather, I thought it would be best to make sure he did not get caught on the road, in the rain."

"Very wise of you, Mademoiselle," said Pierre, his manner correct to a fault. "I will give the cooks their instructions at once. Doubtless you will want your 'tire woman to meet you in your chamber when you change for supper?" This last suggestion was made in such a controlled way that Madelaine knew Pierre was all but bursting with curiosity.

"I suppose I should change to a more suitable ensemble," said Madelaine, enjoying the suspense of her butler. "Very well, inform Lucette that I will want her help shortly, and I will need her to sleep in the sewing room tonight."

The butler bowed slightly. "Very good, Mademoiselle. There can be no gossip if you take such precautions."

"No, indeed," said Madelaine, and indicated her coat and gloves. "See to those, won't you? And take Monsieur Danner to the Yellow Suite as soon as he comes in from the stable."

"The Yellow Suite. Very suitable," approved Pierre, since the Yellow

320

Suite was at the far end of the fortified chateau from Madelaine's own rooms.

"So I thought," said Madelaine, and waved Pierre away before going herself to climb the stairs to her rooms.

Lucette arrived a short time later, looking slightly flustered, her cap askew on her neat, rolled braids. A thirty-four-year-old widow, she had been in Madelaine's employ for almost two years. "I was told I am to sleep in the adjacent chamber tonight, Mademoiselle Bertrande."

"If it is not inconvenient, please," said Madelaine as she opened her larger armoire and inspected the various dinner dresses there. "I think the violet silk, don't you?"

"It is very suitable," said Lucette with ill-disguised excitement. "Here. I will help you out of your driving frock and into the dress." She smiled her encouragement. "And there will be time, won't there, for me to do something with your hair?"

"It's probably necessary," Madelaine admitted, not bothering to do more than finger her hair.

"If Mademoiselle had a mirror, I could show her a number of fetching modes with her hair," Lucette ventured.

"We're not going to have this argument again, are we?" said Madelaine impatiently. "Help me out of this dress and bring me the silk one. I haven't time to cover old ground again." She knew that this was only a delaying tactic, and that Lucette was determined to have a mirror installed in Madelaine's suite.

"Of course, Mademoiselle," said Lucette, all good behavior now.

"And as a reward for this extra service," said Madelaine as Lucette finished unfastening the back of her dress, "you may have a ration of brandy when you are through with your supper in the servant's hall." It would serve the dual purpose of ensuring that Lucette would sleep thoroughly through the entire night, and that she would attend to her duties without feeling ill-used.

"Thank you, Mademoiselle Bertrande." The punctilious behavior faded into a mildly conspiratorial display. "This Monsieur Danner, is there any chance? ..."

"I don't know," said Madelaine honestly. "He knew my cousin, years ago, and I was hoping he would tell me something about her." That much was truthful, though it was only a portion of what she sought.

"Ah, of course, you hardly knew your cousin," said Lucette in that knowing French way. "Everyone must begin somewhere." She gave

Madelaine's petticoats a critical inspection, decided that they must be changed as well, and went to get the proper undergarments for the violet silk dress.

Madelaine occupied this short time pulling the pins out of her chignon and brushing her hair, so that by the time Lucette returned with the appropriate petticoats, Madelaine was ready for her to finish her ministrations.

"Put this on, Mademoiselle," said Lucette, her mind now wholly full of making the most of the evening for her employer.

"All right," said Madelaine, and bent over so that Lucette could slip the petticoat over her head. "Not so bad as twenty years ago, when it took three maids with rods to raise the dress over the wearer's head."

Lucette chuckled. "I remember watching my older sister being taught to use rods, to aid Madame des Pauclin dress for her wedding."

"Was it amusing?" Madelaine inquired as she stood upright, adjusting the buckles at the waist and preparing for the skirt of the violet silk to be eased over once the petticoat was in place.

"It was difficult, and ridiculous, to dress that way." She sighed as she gathered the skirt, preparing to lift it over Madelaine's head. "If you will kneel, Mademoiselle Bertrande?"

Madelaine did as she was asked, and rose into the opening for her waist. "I would like the violet scent, as well," she said as Lucette fastened the skirt into place.

"An excellent idea," Lucette approved, and held out the bodice to Madelaine, preparing to fasten the hooks down the back as she tugged it into place. "This man, this Monsieur Danner, he is pleasing to you, yes?"

"He is interesting," said Madelaine carefully. "It remains to be seen if he is pleasing."

"Ah. Tres bien. It is always best to begin this way." She completed her task on the bodice and moved Madelaine to the vanity stool where she set about dressing her hair. "Neat, then, and not too coquettish."

"Yes, I think that would be wisest." Madelaine lowered her eyes to her hands, trying to decide which of a dozen rings to wear. She decided on a simple amethyst-and-pearl band set in gold. "I should go down soon."

"Yes, you should," said Lucette with that faint scolding tone Madelaine had long associated with French servants. "If you will hold still, I will finish your hair, get your perfume, and then you will be ready."

"Fine," said Madelaine, growing restive. Already she was wondering how to talk with Paul Danner now. It had been one thing, riding about in his open carriage, discussing the expeditions they had been on. But the privacy of dining would be another matter entirely.

"You are ready, Mademoiselle Bertrande," said Lucette with a slight sigh. "Here is the scent." The crystal bottle was fitted with a jeweled stopper. "Not too much; he will want to be able to smell his food." She said this last with a trace of amusement. "It is a mistake so many women make, putting on too much scent before a meal."

"Thank you," said Madelaine in a neutral voice as she applied the perfume to her wrists and the base of her throat. This done, she handed the bottle back to Lucette and rose from the stool. "Is he in ..."

"The Red Salon," said Lucette. "Pierre thought it would be nicer than the dining hall. All those books ..."

"Excellent," said Madelaine, and started to the door.

"Mademoiselle Bertrande?" ventured Lucette.

"What is it?" Madelaine was poised, her hand on the latch, to leave.

"If there is any trouble, you have only to call out, and we will know what to do." Her smile was more of a simper, but Madelaine accepted it for the gesture it was.

"Thank you," she said quietly, and went out of her rooms, down the fine staircase to the main hall. She could sense her servants watching her as she made her way to the Red Salon, a small parlor adjoining the large chamber which served as her library. As she entered the Red Salon, she noted with satisfaction that a single place had been laid for supper on the table in the window embrasure. A fire was burning on the hearth and a branch of candles had been set out but not yet lit.

Paul Danner was already in the room, a glass of sherry held in his hand. He rose from the plush settee as Madelaine came into the room. "Mademoiselle Bertrande," he said graciously. "You look quite lovely in that dress."

"Thank you," said Madelaine, unaccountably disliking his smooth address. "Please be seated again. I am sure your supper will be served shortly."

"No hurry is necessary, I assure you," he said, indicating beside him on the settee. "I am enthralled by what you have here."

"It is an enviable collection, isn't it?" she said with innocent pride. "I understand the library was begun well over a hundred years ago. I realize that many collections are older, but few, I suspect, are more diverse than this one." She thought briefly of the library at Montalia with its hundreds of ancient volumes, and found herself missing her native earth with a fierce longing.

"I can see your cousin's hand in much of it," said Paul, holding up the book he had selected. "This monograph about the Indians of the Far West. It is fascinating."

"Oh?" said Madelaine, doing her best to conceal her curiosity. "Why do you think so?"

"For a very young Frenchwoman to assume that she can know the ways of these savages," said Paul with a shake of his head. "Your cousin was quite young when I knew her, and I cannot think that she was more than a child when she made these observations."

"She was like most of the women of my blood—she did not show her years," said Madelaine a little stiffly.

"Well, even if she were in her thirties—which, incidentally, I doubt— while we were in Syria, she would not have been more than a youngster twenty years before that, wouldn't she? And what can a schoolgirl know of such barbarians as these Paiute? I think you can dismiss most of what she says regarding their society; she was not capable of making a sensible judgment."

"I am certain she was…older than you assumed," said Madelaine, trying to maintain the right tone with him. "That was my understand-ing, in any case."

"It is possible," said Paul, in a tone that suggested it was not. "You look a great deal like her, though you are prettier."

"You mean," said Madelaine sharply, "that I am better dressed."

"No," Paul responded seriously. "There was a hardness about your cousin Madelaine that is lacking in you. She had spent too much time with savages, I would suppose. You have not made that error to the de-gree that she did."

"I did some exploring in Tunis," Madelaine reminded him. "Before coming to France for my inheritance."

"That is another matter entirely. You were part of a French com-munity, and the Roman ruins there have no sinister associations, not as the American War has, or the expedition in Syria; you did little more than what inquisitive youth must do, just as I did when I went to Egypt," said Paul, lifting his glass in a toast. "You did not put your-self beyond good society, as your cousin was wont to do. And you now live an ordered and appropriate life, which was not the case with your cousin Madelaine. Think of all those years spent in the American War?"

It took all of Madelaine's will to keep from challenging the condescending attitude Paul Danner showed. "I think they were terrible years, judging from what she wrote in her journal."

"Yes, and such things coarsen a woman more than they do men," said Paul with a look of vindication. "Fortunately Ingrid, my affianced wife, has not been touched by any of the upheavals and disasters your cousin appears to have sought out deliberately." He put the book aside and looked directly at Madelaine. "I hope you will not make your cousin's error, and allow yourself to be tainted by cruelty."

"Tainted by cruelty," Madelaine repeated, and was shocked by how vividly she recalled Sherman's condemnation of war.

"It could happen easily to one as young and delicate as you are," said Paul. "I have no wish to see you lose the sweet candor you possess. You need only look at the women who have chosen the cloister to know how precious that candor is." He smiled at her. "It would probably be best if you did not read your cousin's journals. They will give you absurd notions about going into the world, which would spoil you."

Pierre arrived then, bearing a covered platter which he put on the octagonal table near the window; he lit the branch of twelve candles before he drew the heavy red curtains—which gave the salon its name—closed against the night. "Your supper, Monsieur Danner."

"Very good," said Paul, taking it upon himself to instruct the butler. "I think it would be best if you provide a place for your mistress, as well. Who knows, I may be able to persuade her to join me, no matter how incorrect it may be." He took the bottle of wine Pierre had brought and inspected the label. "Quite a respectable vintage."

"Do you wish a plate, Mademoiselle Bertrande?" Pierre inquired with interest. "Or a glass?"

"No; it would not be suitable, since there are only the two of us." This was correct as far as it went, and Madelaine was glad that society provided her so convenient an excuse to avoid the meal.

"Shall I decant the wine, Mademoiselle?" Pierre asked Madelaine, making it clear he took his orders from her.

"That would be best, I think," said Madelaine, already regretting that she had ordered a bottle of wine from Saint-Germain's vineyards.

"There is lamb in a sauce of rosemary, pepper, juniper berries, wine and onions. And a soufflé of cheese and spinach, in the Italian style," Pierre said as he uncovered the platter. "For a side dish, peas in butter." He bowed slightly as he set these out, then gave his attention to decanting the wine.

Paul approached the table with real hunger in his expression. "Let me congratulate you on your chef, Mademoiselle. This is truly impressive."

"I am so pleased it meets your approval," said Madelaine, hoping he could not hear the sarcasm in her words.

"I would be a useless fool if I could not be satisfied with this," he said, and held a chair for her. "It is a pity that you will not join me, but I bow to your sense of propriety."

"How good of you," said Madelaine as she took her place at the table and watched while Pierre served supper to Paul.

"It has started to rain," Pierre announced as he poured the decanted wine for Paul. "The groom says that the road will be impassable in another hour."

Paul cocked his head. "Then, Mademoiselle Bertrande, I am doubly in your debt, for your hospitality and for saving me from the storm." He tasted the wine and announced, "This is superior."

"So I have been told," said Madelaine, and gestured dismissal to Pierre.

"I hope you are not offended by my remarks about your cousin?" said Paul as he cut himself a first slice of lamb. "I would be a poor guest, Mademoiselle Bertrande, if I caused you any distress on your cousin's account."

"Not offended so much as instructed," said Madelaine, making no attempt to keep the irony from her remarks.

Paul was wholly unaware of it. "Very good; then I have done you a service."

"You certainly have," said Madelaine, wondering what it was that had originally drawn her to him, back in Egypt. A certain mischievous impulse seized her and she said, "Suppose I were my cousin. Suppose I was the one who had lived those years with Indians and during the American War. What would you say to me then?"

"But that's ridiculous," protested Paul through the lamb.

"Perhaps it is, but indulge me, if you will," said Madelaine. "Think of it as a supper time amusement."

"Oh, very well," said Paul, giving in to her request.

"Suppose that I was the one who had gone all across America—" she began.

"Thirty years ago?" said Paul, trying to get the spirit of the game.

"Yes, in the fifties," she said firmly. "Suppose that I had known the Kiowa and Cheyenne, and the rest of them?" She paused. "Suppose I had lived in San Francisco in 1855? What would you say to me then?"

He chuckled. "That you are a very youthful old woman," he answered at once, and sipped his wine.

"And if I were a youthful old woman, what would you think?" Madelaine persisted. "Suppose I had lived for, oh, years and years without aging, that I had traveled to America and Egypt and many other places. Suppose I was the woman who had come through the terrible American war? Suppose—"

"This is too fanciful for me," he objected. "And why would someone like you want to be old?" His gallantry was sounding a bit forced. "I will admit when I met your cousin I found her captivating. But I was a much younger man, and in Egypt I saw few women of quality. I do not find it astonishing that she would catch my fancy then. But now? I would hope I know better than to let an aged hoyden engage my interests." He gave her a long, thoughtful look. "I think you wish to emulate her. That would be a grave mistake. For she died without husband or child to remember her. Surely you do not want that to happen to you?" He put his wine glass down and leaned toward her. "Mademoiselle Bertrande, do not let yourself be seduced by what you see as adventure."

"Hardly adventure," said Madelaine quietly.

"That is a good sign," said Paul, resuming his eating. "For men do not want women who are forever traipsing about the world, uncaring of the good opinion of others. My fiancée is more the model you would do well to choose for yourself. She has the good sense and reserve that has made Swedish women prized throughout Europe."

Madelaine sighed inwardly, and said, "Tell me about her," resigning herself to a paean of the ordinary.

* * *

MONBUSSY-SUR-MARNE, 10 FEBRUARY, 1888

I have rarely been so glad to see a guest depart than when Paul Danner left this morning, full of effusive thanks and warnings about taking after my lamentable cousin. What in the world made me think he might be able to know my secret, would consider sharing it with me? Or am I so lonely to be loved with knowing that I am willing to consider someone of Paul Danner's bent?

Again I miss Tecumseh, and the bond that holds me to him is cold comfort when what I want most is his body and the love in his eyes. And

327

who dare blame me, for he was willing to know me for what I am, and to accept it as much as he was able. He has just turned sixty-seven, and I know I would love him today as when I was in San Francisco... But unless he has changed beyond all recognition, he would not be able to see past my appearance, so it is probably just as well that an ocean lies between us...

I miss Saint-Germain more keenly, and more poignantly. And more futilely; for while Tecumseh lives I have the chance to love him, but once come into this life, Saint-Germain tells me that we no longer can give each other what we seek... This day, more than most, I wish it were not so...

MONBUSSY-SUR-MARNE, 13 DECEMBER, 1888

Something dreadful has happened to Tecumseh. I have felt the blackness around him for more than two weeks. Whatever the catastrophe is, I know it has struck him to the heart; I can only feel his anguish with no chance to succor him... If I thought I would be welcome, I would go to him, never mind the unpleasantness of an ocean crossing, let alone in winter... But he would not want me near him while he is in such torment, and for once I am certain that I could do nothing that would not distress him more deeply than he is distressed already...

Since that fiasco with Paul Danner, I have been disinclined to venture into society again. I suppose I am being a coward, to restrict myself to the dreams of servants... It would be best to go back to Montalia, not only for the solace of my native earth, but to avoid questions and suppositions that can only serve to make my stay here increasingly hazardous.

I have at last prepared a monograph on Tunis, and this will go to Amsterdam in a matter of days, as soon as the weather improves. With the Boulanger matter finally at an end, France is once again ready to become the heart of Europe. The Germans have already lost two rulers this year, and who can say if this young Wilhelm II will prove capable...

LYONS, 22 MARCH, 1889

*I have come upon newspapers for New York for last autumn and winter,
and I have discovered what has driven Tecumseh into such despair: his
wife died late last November. I think it is past time that I ventured into
the world. Little news of anything but France has reached me while I
was at Monbussy. Now that I am bound for Montalia, I must not make
the same mistake again, not with the Boulanger matter in upheaval once
again, and rumors of an epidemic of influenza beginning. I fear it is necessary to keep up with events...*

*I have taken advantage of my travels to send Tecumseh another three
bottles of the tincture for asthma. That should last him another year at
least, and by that time I will have prepared more for him...*

*There seems to be some question about the death of Archduke Ru-
dolph and his mistress, Baroness Marie Vetser. Some are saying it was a
suicide pact, others are claiming it is a double murder...*

MERCURIO WAS THICKER ABOUT THE WAIST then the last time
Madelaine had seen him, though he was still a handsome fellow, proud
of his wife and two young children, and the state of Montalia.

"As you can see, I followed the instructions your cousin ... she was
your cousin, wasn't she? The instructions she gave me." He indicated
the orchards angling down the hill, and the formal rose garden at the
end of the salon des fenetres in the new wing at the north end of the
chateau. "You can see the full glory of spring for a few weeks more. The
farm is producing well. We have surplus produce which is sold in Saint-
Jacques-sur-Crete on market day, and my wife can show you the records
of those transactions." His French was spoken in Italian cadences, but
correctly and with ease.

"I will look at them later," said Madelaine. "Who is in charge of the
household as butler? My cousin's records said it was a man named
Yves."

Mercurio colored. "I suppose, since Yves took ill, I have been doing the work, with the help of Ignace, who is Yves' half-brother, many
years younger, of course." He was flustered. "Madame Bertrande, I must
apologize. Your letter announcing your arrival came only three days

ago; hardly enough time for us to prepare a proper welcome for you." He bowed respectfully. "I knew your cousin only slightly, but permit me to say that you have a resemblance to her. Though she was taller and had an air about her."

"Thank you," said Madelaine, trying not to be too amused.

Mercurio smiled distantly. "I should not say it, but I had the most amazing penchant for her, when she first engaged me to come here from Rho, in Italy." He looked directly at Madelaine. "She was a woman to dream about, your cousin Madelaine."

"How very kind of you to tell me," said Madelaine, with genuine feeling.

Mercurio opened her main doors for her. "Please. Your staff is in the old hall, at the south end of the chateau." He gave her a look to encourage her. "I don't know if you can find your way around. It took me two weeks before I was certain of the arrangement of halls and rooms."

Madelaine made a gesture of appreciation. "I have been here as a child. I am certain to orient myself quickly."

"Certainly," said Mercurio without any hesitation. "But if I may be of any assistance, you have only to inform me."

The annealing presence of her native earth began to ease the ache deep in Madelaine's soul. She was able to show Mercurio a genuine look of approval. "You have done well. My ... cousin would be grateful, and so I will see you are rewarded for your work on her behalf."

They were almost to the hall where the rest of the staff was waiting. "I must ask: do you plan to remain here long, Madame Bertrande?"

"Why do you wish to know?" Madelaine inquired, pausing to wait for his answer.

"Well, if you are planning to open the chateau for entertaining and grand occasions, you will need a larger staff. Those we have now can manage with half the rooms closed, but if you open them, we will need to engage more maids and cooks and grooms and all the rest of it."

Madelaine shook her head. "Have no fear, Mercurio. I have no plans to turn this into a fine country seat. It is too much of a refuge for me to want to do that."

She stepped into the hall, and looked at the eleven servants gathered there. She recognized three of them only: her old coachman Gerard; her housekeeper, Madame Nicole, who had been a new maid the last time she was home; and the gardener Jean-Gaston.

"Madame Bertrande de Montalia," said Mercurio, presenting Madelaine to those who, all unknowing, watched over her native earth.

MONTALIA, 14 SEPTEMBER, 1889

The repairs I have ordered on the old windows are almost complete, and I am satisfied that we have no reason to fear leaks this winter...

Today a box of magazines and books was brought up from Saint-Jacques-sur-Crete, sent by Harris and Taylor in Philadelphia. I can hardly wait for evening to catch up on all that has been going on in America. A superficial review of the contents shows me that John Taylor has made a good effort to procure some of the papers I asked him to get, including issues of The New York Tribune *and* The San Francisco Examiner, *which I look forward to reading.*

The library here is much in need of cataloguing I find, and I suppose I will have to hire someone to tend to the work, though not just at present. By next year; there are too many other demands on me regarding needed repairs and improvements...

I have not yet found anyone to share my secret, and so continue to content myself as best as I can with the dreams of those in Saint-Jacques and the posting inn on the Provence road... It is hardly satisfactory, but Saint-Germain has survived in this manner for many decades, and so I suppose I will learn...

MONTALIA, 10 MAY, 1890

If I have to read one more tirade against M. Eiffel's tower, I think I will be ill. Fashion changes, and if it can welcome bustles and hoop skirts, it surely can accommodate the tower. It has stood for a year now, and there are still those who insist it is an insult to France to permit such a monstrosity to stand...

I am finally about to read my published accounts of the American Civil War. I think I can look at my own work with some perspective now that a quarter of a century has passed since I left Savannah... I know it will trouble me, but I can endure that if I can resolve my sense of turmoil about that time that continues to linger with me...

The worst thing will be reading about Tecumseh, for it will waken my need for him once again, at a time when all hope is past. I will have to steel myself against the bond, which is a strange experience for me to seek ... He is like the whisper of the wind in this chateau—always present, but hardly noticeable except when storms come ... The worst of his despair seems to have faded, which reassures me. His desolation takes a great toll upon him ... As much as I long for his company, I know it would be foolhardy to seek it. He is seventy now, and he would not want to deal with me. There are many men who in age want the company of young women, and while I am not a young woman, I have that appearance. But Tecumseh would not be comfortable with it. So I will not set out for America except in the pages of my own books ...

MONTALIA, 9 DECEMBER, 1890

There has been a discovery in Java, one which has caught my interest: a Dutch surgeon has found the bones of a prehistoric human. I have read all I can find on this fascinating discovery, and perhaps next summer I will leave from here and travel across the ocean—which would be an ordeal, but necessary—to help continue the explorations with those who have begun them ... I am no Nelly Bly, to try to race around the earth in less than eighty days, but I would welcome anything that would lessen the days I must spend on water ...

I have received the first volume of what promises to be a protracted work by a Scottish anthropologist—to give the study its preferred name—James George Frazier. He calls his work The Golden Bough ...

Two of the new windows are leaking, in spite of all the work done ... I will have to arrange for replacement in the spring ... At least the slates on the roof have not broken or cracked, and once the flues are all repaired we will be as snug here as anyone can be in a centuries-old stone house ...

MONTALIA, 14 FEBRUARY, 1891

Tecumseh is dead.

MADELAINE RAN ACROSS THE STEPS and into his arms as he descended from the coach; she did not care who saw.

He held her silently a short while, a neat figure of less than average height in black with a flash of immaculate white at his neck, ignoring the impatience of his coachman, the presence of his manservant, and a faint, misty rain. At last he said quietly, "Come, my heart. We should go inside."

She released him, stepping back. "Yes. You're right." Taking his small hand in hers, she led up the steps and across the threshold, finding a comfort in the familiar ritual of greeting this newcomer. "Welcome to Montalia."

"I have been here once before, though you may not recall, some years before," he said, by which he meant a century. "You have improved it."

She remembered the dangerous times at the height of the Terror, but said only, "Thank you," and stood in front of him to look deep into his dark, compassionate eyes. "I knew you were coming. Knowing it has sustained me."

He nodded. "It is always difficult when there is a loss like yours. We would have been here sooner, but your roads are morasses." He paused, watching her. "How long ago was it?"

"Not quite two weeks. Tomorrow is two weeks. Just six days after his birthday." She shook her head, her throat tight with emotion. "I knew he was ill, but he had had asthma for so long, and I had sent him more tincture just eight months before—" She put her hands to her face. "He was embalmed. If only I could weep."

"I know," he said with such empathy that she had to force herself not to cast herself into his embrace again.

"I didn't think it would be so hard...The others have not affected me so...so much. Not Piers, not Falke, not Alexander, none of them." She took a step back from him as she saw Mercurio approaching. She smoothed the front of her simple dark-grey half-mourning dress, and turned to address her Italian butler.

333

"Madame Bertrande?" said Mercurio, looking at the stranger with curiosity.

She indicated the man beside her. "This is the guest I told you to expect: Ragoczy, comte de Saint-Germain."

Mercurio bowed.

"His manservant will be in with his luggage. He is Roger." Madelaine belatedly dropped Saint-Germain a curtsy, then said to Mercurio. "Put my guest in the southern suite."

Now Mercurio looked puzzled; the choice seemed an arbitrary one, and not worthy of a man of rank. "Surely the Rose Suite would be better," he suggested; the Rose Suite was newer and had a better view.

Saint-Germain intervened with practiced diplomacy. "Do not fault Madame...Bertrande. I have stayed in the southern suite before and found it to my satisfaction. I prefer it to the newer rooms." His native earth was under the floor, to restore and protect him.

"If that is what you wish," said Mercurio, puzzled by Saint-Germain's preference in accommodations. "I will have the staff see to it at once." He raised his hand to signal his assistant when a lean, middle-aged man with sandy hair and faded-blue eyes came to the door.

"If you will tell me where I may put my master's things?" said Roger with a nod to Mercurio.

"You know which suite," said Saint-Germain, and then gave his attention to Madelaine once more. "Where do you want to talk?"

"My library?" she said, and added to Mercurio, to offset the shock in his face. "We are of the same blood. There is no impropriety in this."

Mercurio's bow was so perfect that it made the point that he was reserving judgment in the matter.

"The library is down the second corridor, isn't it? Near the tower? Do I recall correctly?" Saint-Germain said, certain that he did. He glanced at Madelaine as he started in that direction, leaving Roger and Mercurio to tend to his belongings.

"I have missed you," Madelaine whispered as they made their way down the corridor. "Though we are never truly separated, I have missed you."

He motioned her to silence. "We are not yet private, my heart." As they reached the door to the library, he turned casually to look back down the corridor. "A woman, about thirty, is listening to everything we say," he told her in an undervoice.

"Mercurio's wife," said Madelaine, and added in a tone intended to carry. "I hope you will tell me what I am to do, since I cannot attend the funeral."

As Saint-Germain closed the library doors behind her, he caught her by the wrist. "Now you can tell me what is locked in your soul."

She hesitated now that the opportunity was hers. "I do not want to cause you pain, Saint-Germain."

"Seeing you in such agony causes me pain, my heart; I am not jealous," he said quietly, his voice low and oddly penetrating.

"I know it; as you know I am not," she said. "It is what we are."

"It will only please me that he loved you." He saw something change in her face, and added, "Do not think he did not love you."

The words struck to the heart of her grief. "But he chose the True Death. How can I think otherwise?"

"You may think he could not live as those of our blood must live. Surely you told him how it would be?" He released her, but continued to hold her with his compelling eyes.

She nodded once. "The second day at Lake Como. I know I should have told him the whole earlier, but it was during the war, and ... He admitted he had not realized what it would mean. He listened and asked me many questions. But he ... he would have learned to live as we must," she defended him, going to light the lamp beside the largest of the bookshelves. "I learned, for all that I have adored you from the hour we met, and have your blood in my veins."

Saint-Germain let out his breath very slowly. "My heart, you and I are not the trouble here. Your General Sherman is."

"Tecumseh," she corrected in a whisper, her voice unsteady. "Did you know that Tecumseh means Shooting Star?"

"How could I?" Saint-Germain asked, so gently, with no trace of accusation, that Madelaine could hardly hear him.

She held her lucifer until it almost burned her fingers; she waved it out and struck another, this time succeeding in lighting the lamp before blowing the little flame out. "You might have learned, once."

He shook his head, letting her choose the course of their conversation for the moment. "I went no farther north than Mexico; I would not have learned any of the Shawnee words in Mexico."

Madelaine sat down on the long Empire couch at one end of the library, remarking as she did, "This piece is wasted in here. I should move it to a more spacious room."

Saint-Germain went to stand behind her, his small hands resting on her shoulders. "Tell me how you remember him."

She did not answer at once. "Tall. Red-haired," she said at last.

"Impatient. Active. Complex. Brilliant. Easily wounded, though rarely willing to admit injury. Steadfast. Eyes like steel, blue-grey. Principled. Given to despair. Energetic. Uncommonly clear-minded. Tender. Rarely playful, except with his children."

Saint-Germain kissed the top of her head. "What else?"

"He was tactless. Arbitrary. Demanding. Relentless. Loyal. Nervous. Abrasive." She was shaking now as she spoke, and each word shuddered through her with increasing strength. "Occasionally infuriating. Purposeful."

"An admirable man, though not quite likeable," Saint-Germain observed.

"Most men were afraid of him. Most women liked him. Trusted him. I did, from the first." Madelaine lowered her head. "I suppose, until the end, I hoped he would change his mind, and taste my blood."

Saint-Germain came around the end of the couch and lifted her chin with his hand. "You have no reason to blame yourself for his refusal."

"Are you convinced of that?" she asked, speaking too quickly.

"That is not important: you are not convinced," he pointed out, and touched her lips with the tips of his fingers before turning away and crossing the room.

"What else can I think?" Her question pursued him. "He would not accept either my bond or my life."

For a short while Saint-Germain said nothing. "Tell me how he was as your lover."

Madelaine looked up sharply. "Are you certain you want to hear?"

He regarded her steadily, his dark eyes enigmatic. "I am used to being impotent, after four thousand years, my heart. That he was not will not distress me."

Her unexpected laugh shocked Madelaine. "That is what I think troubled him the most, when we talked at Lake Como—the impotence."

"I found it difficult at first," Saint-Germain confessed with a wry smile. "When I supposed that all there was to achieve was penetration."

She turned away from him. "The first time we were alone together, in a private room in a casino in San Francisco, he spent too quickly to do anything but apologize for an hour. And the second time we were together, at my house on Franklin Street, he was too nervous at first to stiffen. We had time enough that night to enjoy each other once he grew more at ease. He was ... adventurous with me. He always seemed to be on a quest when we were intimate." She folded her hands in her lap. "He never fully got over a sense of betrayal of his wife when he was with me."

"Does that surprise you? With how you have described him, if he truly cared for you, he would do it with reservations." Saint-Germain came back across the room and stood before her. "Madelaine, you loved his depth of loyalty. Why does it worry you that he gave it to others? Surely you did not want it all for yourself?"

She shook her head in dismissal. "You know I did not."

"Yes," he said, and dropped to his knee, taking her hands in his own. "If he had shown disregard for his wife, would you have loved him as much? Would you have trusted him?"

"Of course not," she said testily.

"And you did not expect him to abandon his family on your behalf, did you?" he prodded. "Would you have held him in high regard if he had?"

"No. Nor would he have done it." She caught her lower lip in her teeth, unwilling to meet Saint-Germain's calm, loving gaze.

"And you admire him for that," Saint-Germain added.

"Yes." She freed one of her hands, but only to touch the neat, dark waves of his hair. "The worst thing was the bond, losing it so completely. It has been there, as constant as a note from a string. Only now the string has snapped, and the note is silenced."

"I know," he said, and slipped his arms around her waist.

"At least, if he had come to our life, the bond would remain." She felt his arms tighten. "As it is—"

"I know," he repeated, with such sorrow that it caught her attention. "The loss is devastating, for the bond can never be forgotten once it is created."

"As long as I am ... alive, I will have to endure this loss?" she asked, shocked. "I felt no such anguish when Falke died, or when Alexander was killed. Why should losing Tecumseh be so painful?"

Saint-Germain released her, but only to sit beside her, his arm low across her back. "He accepted you more wholly than Falke or Alexander did. Or Piers. He was willing to take you as you are, not as his idea of you." He let her think about what he had said. "And you saw him over a period of almost twenty years and were able to sustain your passion. That, my heart, is a rare gift. In time you will come to appreciate it."

"When the ache is less, perhaps I will," she said.

"It will pass, in time. And fortunately," he added in a deeper tone, "you will have time."

"And I may need it. The last time he and I were together was nearly twenty years ago, and his loss is as fresh as if I had slept at his side a month ago." She leaned her head on his shoulder.

"Yes," said Saint-Germain, not wanting to tell her how many times he had felt the keen misery she was experiencing now.

She took his free hand in hers. "It is impossible, I know, but I wish we could have the consolation of—"

He broke away from her. "Do not torment yourself, my heart. You have my love until the True Death, and beyond. Let that be enough."

"How long are you going to stay?" she asked him in a quiet voice.

This time he had trouble answering her. "Not very long. It isn't wise." For a short while Madelaine sat and did not try to think. Then she rose and went to stand behind him. "Saint-Germain, you are my dear, treasured love, and will be all my life long. But Tecumseh was—"

"More mortal?" said Saint-Germain, staring remotely down at the laid but unlit fire. "Yes, that is the poignance of it, that fragile brevity."

Madelaine sighed. "Yes. And because I had more years to love him, I began to think I would always have the chance to persuade him..." A little of the tight, hot coil of grief that had lodged in the middle of her chest began to loosen.

He swung around and drew her into his arms. "Good, my heart."

She stood with him that way for some time, as the worst heartache started to release its ferocious hooks from her soul.

MONTALIA, 19 MAY, 1891

In a month, I will be gone from here, and when I return again, I will be Madelaine again, this time my own grand-niece. I have already put these changes in motion.

Turkey has promising sites, more unusual than the Greek ones...

The papers in my latest shipment from America are full of accounts of Tecumseh's death and funeral. I have read them and put them away. When I come back from Turkey, I will read them again, and by then they will, I hope, bring little more than a pang to me.

BURSA, TURKEY, 2 NOVEMBER, 1891

I am told antiquarians are now being called archaeologists—those who make a study of ancient things. I cannot see that this is a great improvement on antiquarians, but that it makes us sound less like furniture dealers than we did before...

Two Germans are joining this expedition. They are eager and scholarly and methodical, both Wilhelm and Bruno. To me, they sound too much like names given to large dogs...

INONU, TURKEY, 31 MARCH, 1892

I am as much inclined to study the people here as the ruins at the edge of the city. My experiences with the Indians in America have given me a taste for working with living people, and not only with ruins. The observations I have been compiling over the last three weeks have at last drawn some notice, not the sort I would welcome. There were complaints about me, it appears, and today I have been ordered to stop talking with the peasants. My protestations that I wish only to record the nature of their lives was not accepted. The people are surely the more intriguing. But ruins are safer, and so I will not go against the strictures of the local authorities...

"I HEAR THEY'RE KICKING YOU OUT OF TURKEY?" The young man had a marked American accent which caught Madelaine's attention amid the noise and scramble of the European Hotel in Izmir. He came up to her, open-faced and straightforward, his suit with a short jacket that marked him an American as much as his accent. "Jacob Wills, Boston and Cambridge," he said, offering his hand to her. "You're Madelaine de Montalia, aren't you?"

She adjusted her posture at the small table where she had been watching the clutter of the lobby for some sign of the British official who was supposed to be bringing her the final decision on her departure. "Yes. I am Madelaine de Montalia, Mister Wills."

"That monograph that just came out from Amsterdam caused quite a stir," he said as he drew up a chair to join her.

"So I have discovered," she said with a sardonic smile.

"It should light a fire under some of those government toadies." He chuckled at the thought.

"Not in Turkey, I fear," said Madelaine, more somberly. "They are more apt to exact a price from the villagers. They were told not to talk to me. The embarrassment of the officials is therefore my fault."

"Surely they will listen to appeal," said Wills, smiling at her.

She regarded him carefully. "What is your interest in this, Mister Wills?"

He coughed once. "I am preparing my doctoral thesis on the history of the Crusades, which of necessity brought me to this part of the world." His expression took on a determined quality she remembered all too well from her years in America. "When I heard about your trouble, I thought I would talk to you, as a means of securing a footnote to my thesis. I could show some of the continuing difficulties between Europeans and the Mohammedan peoples. Demonstrate, you know, how the Crusades was only part of a long history of misunderstanding and cross-purposes which plague this part of the world."

"I see," she said.

"Sort of like the comments your … grandmother? made about the Indians and the whites in America." He said this last as if to catch her off-guard.

"My great-aunt," Madelaine corrected without any show of upset. "So you have read her work?"

"Yes," said Wills. "You might say it started me thinking along the lines that led me here." He leaned forward, his face flushed with excitement that went beyond the heat of the afternoon. "I wanted to meet you, and would have tried even if you had had no trouble with the Turkish government."

"You are very … flattering. I'll thank you on behalf of my great-aunt." She did her best to return his smile, but could not quite make it.

"I didn't mean that quite the way it seemed," amended Wills.

"And how did it seem?" she asked, beginning to feel awkward. It would be easy to make a mistake, to let something slip and then have to recover herself. She had rarely done that in the past, but she had not had to be as careful as she sensed she would have to be with Jacob Wills.

"That I had only an interest in your great-aunt, that I am ignorant of your work. She must have inspired you more than she did me, if you are doing this kind of work here." He paused to give her a chance to answer.

Her answer was polite but discouraging, or so she hoped. "I would feel better about it, Mister Wills, if I were not being compelled to leave the country."

If he had been aware of her intention, he gave no sign of it. "Well, then, would you be willing to share your last evening with an American? As a token to your great-aunt?"

"I . . ." She looked to see if anyone in the crowd appeared to be looking for her. "I doubt that will be possible, Mister Wills." She started to rise when he stopped her with a single request.

"I want to know how your great-aunt got on with General Sherman." He saw her hesitate and took full advantage of it. "I have read her books, and everything she writes is all propriety, but there are all these stories that he had a mistress on the Georgia campaign. I thought you could shed some light on it."

Madelaine stared at him, answering with care. "All I can tell you, Mister Wills, is that all her journals speak of a high regard and affection for him. I hardly knew her and she never mentioned him to me."

Wills sighed. "Too bad. I had hoped to . . . But no such luck," he said, speaking more to himself than her. "All right." He got to his feet. "I won't impose on you any longer, Miss de Montalia. Sorry to have intruded this way."

"Good luck with your thesis research, Mister Wills," she said by way of dismissal as the young American turned and walked away.

IZMIR, TURKEY, 10 JUNE, 1892

How like Tecumseh to disturb my last night in Turkey. Now that I have heard his name again, my memories come back and I miss him afresh . . . No matter how history judges him, now, and decades from now, he will always be to me the American who loved me as I am, in the face of battle, in the face of death.

No wonder he haunts me.